THE
Werewolf
Count AND THE
Trickster
Tailor

by Yuruka Morisaki
illustrated by Tsukito

Cross
World

The Werewolf Count and the Trickster Tailor, Volume 1
Yuruka Morisaki

Translation by Charis Messier

Illustration by Tsukito
Title Design by KC Fabellon
Editing by Nicole Brugger-Dethmers
Proofreading by A.M. Perrone
Book Design by A.M. Perrone

The Werewolf Count and the Trickster Tailor
© 2017 by Yuruka Morisaki
English translation rights reserved by
Cross Infinite World.

English translation ©2019 Cross Infinite World

Cross Infinite World
contact@crossinfworld.com
www.crossinfworld.com

Published in the United States of America
Visit us at www.crossinfworld.com

Facebook.com/crossinfworld
Twitter.com/crossinfworld
crossinfiniteworld.tumblr.com

First Digital Edition: August 2019
First Print Edition: July 2020

ISBN-13: 978-1-945341-35-9

🐺TABLE OF CONTENTS🐺

👑 Chapter 1: The Werewolf Count and the Trickster Tailor

THE bell hanging over the shop door rang, drawing tailor Rock's attention. Someone's shadow loomed in the dark doorway. The enormous figure nearly touched the ceiling and pressed against the doorframe.

Rock had become so engrossed in joining garment parts with basting stitches that closing up shop for the night had completely slipped the tailor's mind. Floria Clothes Shop was almost always closed by this time, and the shop assistant had already gone home for the day.

Rock stood and called out to the late-night visitor over the counter. "Welcome. I don't usually receive customers at this hour."

The towering figure hidden in the shadows ponderously swung its head, its gleaming eyes—a brighter shade of golden yellow than the swaying candle flames—locked on Rock.

Tailor Rock was a trickster who lived a double life.

Roxy "Rock" Floria was a full-fledged twenty-year-old woman who assumed a male identity while operating her tailor shop. Disguising herself was the only way to survive and run a successful business in the slums where crooks, thieves, ruffians, and other riffraff called home.

As luck would have it, her God-given trim figure and catlike, sharp facial features proved useful in assuming a male guise. Cutting her wine-colored hair to fall evenly beneath her ears and donning men's shirts and slacks made her look just like a poor and unambitious young man. In spite of being mocked for her fragile appearance by those who thought she was a man, she had in turn gained a peaceful life in the Empire's imperial capital.

But on this night, Rock met a trickster who lived a double life on par with her own.

"May I have a full set of clothes?"

The owner of that low, rumbling voice was a werewolf.

Pointed upright ears twitched on top of the werewolf's head, his sinewy body bristled with fur blacker than night, his arms—thick as logs—hung at his side, and a bushy tail swayed behind his long, powerful legs. Rock had heard the rumors—that a werewolf was living hidden somewhere within the imperial capital. Word had it that the werewolf normally disguised itself as a human, living among the people as if it were one of them, only to show its true colors with night's arrival when it fed upon the unsuspecting citizens like cattle.

"Eek…" A small cry spilled passed Rock's lips.

The werewolf raised his clawed hands in a submissive gesture as if to set the tailor's mind at ease. "Don't be scared, lad. I only came for clothes."

Razor-sharp fangs flashed from his big mouth with every word he spoke, his visage exactly like that of a wolf's. Asking Rock not to be scared was an unreasonable request, but she answered him through her violent trembling.

"*You* came…for clothes?"

"Indeed. As you can see, all my clothing has ripped." The werewolf spread his forearms, showing off his entire wolfish frame.

Fur blacker than the night sky was all that covered his body, the faint outline of tempered pectoral muscles peeking through the tufts. By every definition, he was stark naked, but the customer was a ginormous werewolf whose head grazed the shop ceiling and whose arms barely fit through the door. It begged the question: Does a werewolf need to wear clothing as men do?

"You aren't looking to purchase ready-made items, are you?" Rock asked apprehensively. Seeing the werewolf bob his head, she continued in a hoarse voice, "As you can see for yourself, this is a clothing shop for ordinary humans. It is questionable whether such clothing will fit you, sir."

Among the selection of ready-made clothing were tunics and other stretchable garments, but this werewolf was several times bigger than even her largest customer. Watching her precious wares ripping one after the other was unthinkable.

The werewolf met Rock's doubts with a refined bow. "That's just it, lad. I'm seeking clothes meant for an ordinary human." Sweeping his eyes about the shop with his perked ears twitching, he asked, "Is it all right for me to take a full set of clothes off your hands? You are...the shopboy, I presume?"

His bizarrely gentle-mannered question only amplified Rock's distress. "I am the shopkeeper here."

The werewolf appeared startled by her honest answer. His wolfish visage did nothing to hide his dilated golden pupils. "You are? You look surprisingly young to be one."

"I may not look it, but I am twenty."

"Heh...you are a *man*, correct?"

"Yes, I am." After lying, Rock mustered her courage to step out from behind the counter. She set about coordinating a full gentleman's outfit from the ready-made pieces in the shop per the werewolf's request, then placed the clothing in his fur-covered hand.

"Where might I find the fitting room, shopkeeper?"

"Um, you can change in the back."

"Thank you." The werewolf vanished into the back of the shop as directed, his fluffy tail swishing behind him.

After seeing him off, Rock sunk to the floor.

To think the rumored werewolf would visit her shop.

Rock had never met anyone who'd actually seen one in person either. But whispers of people who'd glimpsed a werewolf or had been devoured by one in the imperial capital spread from person to person as if they were true. She thought the stories of a monster that prowled the streets in the dead of night, sinking its fangs into human prey moments after ensnaring them, was nothing more than an old wives' tale—until she saw one with her own eyes

The werewolf was real.

He had appeared in her shop and was currently changing in the back.

For all the stories of werewolves attacking and feeding on people, this one acted like a courteous gentleman. All the same, he had a monstrous appearance. Rock had best gather her wits about her and come up with a plan in case he decided to snack on her after he finished changing.

"But how do you defend against a werewolf...?" Rock muttered in despair.

Currently the only person in the shop, she had no one to seek help from. Screaming wasn't going to spur the lazy city constables into taking on a werewolf or rushing to the aid of a resident of the slums. The impulse to turn tail and dash out of the shop coursed through Rock, but she couldn't abandon the business that meant more to her than her own life.

In the end, she gripped one of the canes for sale and waited for the werewolf's return.

What stepped out of the fitting room after a short wait was—

"This is some fine tailoring. You're skilled, shopkeeper."

—a handsome young man with hair the color of burnt sienna.

He appeared to be in his midtwenties with a symmetrical physique and taller than average height. Rock's tailored shirt and pants fit well against his toned arms and legs, which had no trace of werewolf fur. His chiseled Adonis face didn't bear the slightest resemblance to that wolfish visage, except for the golden gleam of his almond-shaped eyes.

"What I normally wear doesn't fit my werewolf body." The young man spoke to the frozen Rock with the same gentleness as earlier. "But you saved me from a great embarrassment. I came very close to not being able to return home. You have my thanks, lad."

Rock slowly lowered the cane and stuttered in a quivering voice, "I-I am glad to have been of service."

The young man chuckled lightly. "I seem to have given you quite the scare. A natural reaction, but please forgive me."

His apology only served to further Rock's confusion.

Werewolves were said to transform into humans during the day, but this was the middle of the night. And he was boldly revealing his true form to Rock. Just who was this young man?

"Incidentally, shopkeeper, I feel bad about doing this after you assisted me, but—"

When the young man suddenly spoke in an overly polite manner, Rock braced herself for the worst. He wasn't going to attack her now, was he? "Wh-What...is it?"

"I currently don't have any money on hand. My wallet exploded somewhere with my clothing when I transformed."

"...Pardon?"

This...shouldn't have been completely unexpected. The werewolf had been naked. He had nothing on him that could've held money, so not having his wallet wasn't a convenient lie. But that was problematic for a tailor.

"I will pay you back with interest in the near future. Could you add it to my tab until then?" the young man requested without batting an eye.

Rock hurried to object. "I can't do that. My shop's policy is not to let customers pay at a later date."

Letting people pay later in the slums would put her out of business faster than the pickpockets nicked watches. This was a policy Rock had sternly adhered to for the three years she'd run her shop. Even a werewolf became subject to store policies the moment he took clothing from her.

"But I don't have my wallet. A tab is the only option," the young man brazenly insisted, showing little remorse despite being in the wrong. "I promise to pay you back. I can make an oath before God if you like."

Swearing to God had less value than trash in this godforsaken district, but since he was willing to say that much, Rock compromised.

"Please tell me your name and address, then. If you don't come back to pay me, I will go to you to collect the debt."

The young man held his chin in his hand contemplatively before answering. "I'm Ebel Mateus. My home is located in the aristocrat district."

Mateus was the same last name as the count's. Rock knew the name even though she wasn't raised in the imperial capital. She could hardly believe a werewolf was a member of the famous Mateus family.

"You jest. A werewolf in the count's family wouldn't end at just being a big scandal." Rock glowered in reproach of his lie.

Ebel shook his head, his expression unchanged. "I'm not lying. I won't deny there would be a massive uproar should the people discover the count's a werewolf, but if no one ever finds out, there's no uproar to be had." The brazen young man was even claiming he was His Excellency the Count. Adding to Rock's feeling of light-headedness, Ebel lowered his voice and stressed, "And, shopkeeper, I presume you can keep your customers' secrets confidential?"

Having her pride as a businesswoman called into question, Rock spontaneously agreed. "O-Of course, Your Excellency."

"Then please do. I will return on the morrow with your money." Ebel graced her with a classy smile before vanishing into the sleepless slums.

He just deftly escaped with my clothes, Rock thought with regret once she pulled herself together. But not even the droves of scammers and crooks nesting in the slums would turn into a werewolf to pull off such petty thievery. He absconded with only a shirt, pants, and shoes. Valuable wares that they were to Rock, they weren't expensive goods worth stealing at the risk of exposing his identity.

What just happened? She pressed a hand against her forehead.

PHOEBE scrunched up her nose when she came to work the next morning. "Blimey! What is with this smell? It reeks in here!" Phoebe's throaty complaint echoed painfully through Rock's sleep-deprived brain. She looked up from the newspaper to see Phoebe's beautiful feminine face glaring at her. "Don't tell me you picked up a stray dog off the streets?! You can't do stuff like that when you run a business!"

"I didn't take in a stray," Rock demurred.

Suspicion creased Phoebe's brow. "Then why the smell? I sure hope you didn't bring home a vagrant."

"I didn't do that either. Maybe you smell last night's customer," Rock speculated, even though she didn't remember smelling the werewolf after fear had numbed her senses. She did, however, catch a whiff of an unfamiliar beast when she opened the door in the morning.

Last night hadn't been just a dream.

"Turn away smelly customers. They're bad for business, Rock." Phoebe brushed her bony right hand through her thick chestnut hair.

She—*he*—was someone living a double life just like Rock.

At first glance, she looked like a tall, big-boned, glamorous beauty, but a gruff male voice came out whenever she opened her rouged lips. She insisted she wanted to live as a woman and had no desire to return to being a man.

Apparently, Phoebe was Rock's long-lost father's lover.

Rock's mother, the woman who raised her single-handedly, revealed the whereabouts of her father on her deathbed. Following her mother's final request to rely on her father living in the imperial capital, Rock departed the rural village she was raised in to visit him. Three years had already passed since then.

Sadly, Phoebe was the only person present at the address her mother gave her, and she informed Rock that her father had already departed this world too.

"I'm Phoebe. I was very intimate with your father."

At first, Rock had mixed feelings about Phoebe, who introduced herself that way in a husky voice.

But Phoebe had fastidiously held on to the inheritance left by Rock's father without taking a single coin. She even encouraged Rock, who had no other relatives, and suggested she live in the imperial capital. Before she knew it, Rock was drawn to Phoebe's outgoing and affectionate personality.

Phoebe stayed by Rock's side, supporting her business venture in the slums. It was at Phoebe's suggestion no less that Rock dressed as a man to protect herself, and that smart plan paid off in Floria Clothes Shop's success.

But her male disguise did nothing to ward off last night's customer. Rock's weak arms wouldn't stand a chance against the werewolf if he bared his fangs at her. Though she doubted being a strong man would've made a difference.

"Phoebe, do you know of Count Mateus?" Rock questioned Phoebe indirectly about her surprise customer.

"Mateus? Members of that family have been counts for ages. Hard not to know of them." Phoebe shrugged her broad shoulders. "The previous count died several years ago, leaving his young son to inherit the title. His name is… What was it again…"

"Ebel Mateus?" Rock supplied.

"Yes, that's him. He's a fine young man, you know?" Phoebe related with delight, then suddenly became suspicious. "Why the sudden interest in Count Mateus?"

"I-I wouldn't say I'm interested in him. I was just curious because I overheard the customers gossiping." Rock told no one, not even Phoebe, about last night.

She wanted to talk about the fear she felt with someone else, but speaking of it would drag Phoebe into trouble with her. Phoebe was a sympathetic listener who worried about Rock more than anyone else, but there was no telling what the werewolf would do if he found out.

And above all else, as tailor, she needed to keep her customers confidential.

"I'd say the previous count is more well-known in these parts." Unaware of Rock's inner turmoil, Phoebe giddily reminisced about the noble. "The late Count Mateus was known for his incessant passion for all things antique. He was renowned for buying even the most worthless old jars and sculptures for a good chunk of coin if the seller made up a good story about it." Phoebe chuckled and delightfully added, "But then the conmen were left holding the bag when young master Ebel took over and stopped buying from them."

From Phoebe's explanation, it seemed the previous count had a reason to wander around the slums, but Rock heard no rationale for why Ebel Mateus should be doing so. Then it was questionable whether the man last night was really His Excellency the Count. Chances were increasing that neither her clothes nor the payment for them were coming.

"I wonder if I was tricked…"

Enduring a traumatizing experience was one thing, but Rock was more frustrated by the werewolf making off with her wares.

EBEL visited the shop again that day, disproving Rock's doubts.

He arrived at the same late hour as the prior night and in the same werewolf form.

"Shopkeeper, forgive me for not keeping my promise." The werewolf's pointed ears folded flat against his furry head as he stood in front of Rock while she closed up shop after sending Phoebe home for the day. How scary he came across to her yesterday felt like a lie when she saw him submissively hunched over like a badly scolded dog.

"You didn't keep your promise? I didn't think you would actually come back at all," Rock told him frankly, her fear left in the dust after waiting a whole day for him in vain.

"I don't steal," Ebel burst out, offended. "My appearance runs counter to what I'm about to say, but I endeavor to act in a manner that doesn't disgrace my title."

Certainly, if theft were his goal, he could've threatened her and gotten away with anything in his werewolf form. His gentlemanly behavior devoid of aggression proved he at least had no intention of harming Rock.

Ebel spoke apologetically over Rock's reluctant acceptance of his excuse. "On that note…this is incredibly difficult for me to say, but I lost my wallet again."

"How did that happen?"

"Drunkards often pick on me when I'm walking in the slums. Things were going well when I took on this form to casually sidestep them, but then the soldiers were called for along the way."

Some people definitely had a way of always finding trouble with others, but in Rock's opinion, he only made things worse by transforming into a werewolf every time that happened. Nothing was reported in the morning paper, but "Werewolf Disturbance" seemed like a likely headline for tomorrow's edition.

"I was so preoccupied with throwing them off my trail that I failed to retrieve my wallet." Ebel scratched the area between his fluffy ears with his sharp black claws. "And I find myself without clothing yet again this evening. I am fully aware I'm asking for a lot, but…"

Exasperated to the core by the way he broached the subject, Rock sighed. "Do you waste good clothing every time you become a werewolf, Your Excellency?"

"I do not waste clothing…because I want to—"

"No, you do waste clothing. As a tailor, it is difficult for me to forgive anyone who doesn't respect the clothes on their back, even if that person is His Excellency the Count himself."

Rock had put her heart into each stitch that went into every piece of clothing she gave him yesterday night. The material may have been too inferior for the count's wardrobe, but that didn't make it any less valuable to her. Picturing the results of her labor in shreds aggravated her more than not being paid.

"I am sorry. But I made every attempt to care for the clothing I bought at your shop," Ebel beseeched in a thin voice, his head drooping along with his ears. His stunning bushy tail tucked between his legs.

At a glance, he looked like a supernatural werewolf, but he showed his depression like a big dog. He was becoming more difficult to understand by the minute.

Losing most of her anger to exasperation, Rock let out another sigh. "Your Excellency, am I correct to understand it is not your desire to waste clothing?"

"Absolutely! You could say what happened last night and tonight were entirely out of my control. So-called acts of God." Ebel nodded his head vigorously. "I would jump at any solution that wouldn't destroy my clothes in the transformation process. If this keeps up, one of these days I'm going to return to my mansion naked as a newborn babe."

"I might be of service in that case." Fortunately for Ebel, Rock had both the skill and knowledge of an expert tailor. "If you will pay me for last night and tonight, plus add extra for the custom-made tailoring fees, I will tailor an outfit to fit your needs. Naturally, these will be no ordinary clothes. It will be clothing that doesn't rip apart when you transform. How about it, Your Excellency?" Affected by Ebel's depression over ripping his clothes every day, Rock made this offer.

Ebel's drooping head jerked up, his golden eyes sparkling in the candlelight. "What a brilliant plan!" With his ears perked and tail wagging, he leaned forward and gazed into Rock's eyes. "You have my thanks, shopkeeper! I most assuredly want you to do that for me!"

"P-Please wait. Money comes first, Your Excellency." Panicked by his wet black nose rubbing against her cheek, Rock quickly pushed the werewolf away.

He answered her with a roaring laugh. "You have a point there. Then I vow to have the money to you on the morrow."

It was a verbal promise, but Rock had little choice but to believe he'd keep to it.

Rock handed Ebel a full set of gentlemen's clothes as she had the prior night, and he returned from the fitting room dressed as a dashing young man.

"Shopkeeper, may I ask your name?" Ebel inquired on his way out the door, burnt sienna hair on his head in place of furry black ears.

Rock found his unexpected question suspicious, but she had already learned his name. It wouldn't be fair if she was the only anonymous one. As it stood, Phoebe was the only person in all of the imperial capital who knew her real name.

"I go by Rock Floria," she said, introducing herself with her alias.

Ebel repeated it with a refined smile. "Rock… It seems a little too lackadaisical to be your name."

"I'm fond of it, thank you."

"Then I shall do my best to grow fond of it too," Ebel conceded. His eyes, gazing straight into hers, gleamed the same striking shade of gold in human form too.

He must grab the attention of everyone in the slums with his attractive looks, Rock mused, then added for good measure, "Do whatever it takes not to quarrel with drunks again tomorrow."

She warned him with a hint of cynicism, yet Ebel's eyes widened into golden saucers, his face lighting up. "Thank you, Rock. I will keep my promise this time."

ROCK closed up shop earlier than usual the next day. Naturally, she sent Phoebe home early too.

"What's the big idea trying to get me out of the building at this time? You really are bringing home a man, aren't you?" Phoebe was deeply suspicious of her, but Rock brushed off the question with a vague answer.

"A well-paying customer is coming. They reserved the place for the evening is all."

"A trustworthy customer, I hope?"

"Obviously. Phoebe, I'm not a child anymore."

After managing to send Phoebe home at the end of their heated dispute, Rock hung the "Closed for a Private Fitting" sign on the shop door.

Ebel arrived in the evening as a young man with burnt sienna hair. "Forgive me for being late. Before we start, take the money owed to you."

He paid her with interest as he had promised. Rock accepted the leather pouch stuffed with gold coins, counted each coin within, and gleefully thanked him. "Thank you very much, Your Excellency!"

"...This is the first time I have seen you smile, Rock," Ebel noted with an enigmatic grin, but to Rock, money was the only thing you could really trust in this world. Receiving payment, not just promises, finally made her willing to trust him. "Should I pay for my tailor-made order today as well?"

Apparently, His Excellency was a generous spender as long as he had his wallet. Thrilled to get her hands on a good customer, Rock ecstatically informed him, "I will give you the estimate once I measure you. Follow me, Your Excellency." She showed him into the fitting room in the back and began taking some basic measurements. "Let's design it so it readily comes off when your body grows bigger."

Ebel looked doubtful as Rock held the measuring tape up to his body. "Is that possible?"

"Using hooks instead of buttons will make it easier to slip on and off."

She planned to alter the shirt and vest to close with hooks. Trousers posed the biggest challenge, but tailoring them to the bigger size of his werewolf body and making the waistline adjustable with a sash belt should make it easy for him to strip off when the time came.

"You have a knack for finding yourself in brawls with drunks, after all," Rock said with a laugh, amused. Ebel smiled along with her, although his smile came across as tentative and lonely.

"That was a lie, Rock."

"The part about drunkards picking on you was a lie?"

"Yes. I was actually patrolling this area."

Rock lowered her hand with the cloth measuring tape and blinked at the word *patrolling*.

Ebel softly recounted the past. "My father—he's no longer with us, but he used to speak of his love for this neighborhood."

That had to be the previous Count Mateus—Ebel's father, who was renowned for his love of antiques.

"He used to look forward to slipping out of the house during his breaks from work to shop in this district. He told me how he even enjoyed the disorder here, despite the ill-bred scoundrels inhabiting it." Ebel lowered his golden eyes. "The werewolf power is the greatest fortune Father left me. I am making use of it to patrol this area. I plan to forever protect this part of the city Father so dearly loved." The corners of his lips lifted into a bashful smile. "With a great shop like this around, I think I'll come to love it here too."

Curiously enough, Rock sympathized with him at that moment. Perhaps because neither of them had fathers. Or perhaps it was because they both actively made use of the inheritance left to them by their fathers. Ebel didn't seem ashamed or disgusted by his werewolf side.

That, too, mirrored Rock's own feelings about pretending to be a man.

This was the third year since she set up shop in the slums. She always thought she was proud of her work, but this was the first time anyone called her business "a great shop."

The warmth spreading through her chest might've been caused by those three words. Before she knew it, Rock found herself captivated by the handsome man standing before her. And Ebel, with butterflies in his stomach from her strong gaze, bashfully brought her attention back to the task at hand.

"Are you done taking measurements, Rock?"

"Ah! …I am done measuring your human form, Your Excellency. Your werewolf form is all that's left."

"All right. Wait just a moment, then," Ebel said as he pulled off his shirt, exposing his muscular upper body in a matter of seconds. His hand went to his trouser buckle next—

"P-Please stop right there, Your Excellency!" Rock rushed to stop him. "Why are you undressing?!"

"Why? Naturally, because my clothes will rip if I become a werewolf while dressed."

"Th-Then give me a chance to leave first!" Rock bolted from the fitting room like a panicked deer from a wolf, and she shut the curtain with her hand behind her back.

"Why are you flustered? Are we not both men?"

Rock was about to argue with the dubious voice coming from inside the fitting room, but the uncanny sound of bone crackling and flesh tearing grew louder behind the curtain, cutting off her response. Large, triangle-shaped ears cast a shadow on the curtain, and then came the sound of the stealthy shuffle of a large beast's feet.

"…I'm finished, Rock. Please continue with this form." Ebel's deeper voice beckoned Rock back into the fitting room.

What in the world was the story with his body? A young man with an average physique had transformed into a werewolf in less than a minute.

In all her years making a living as a tailor, this was Rock's first time measuring a customer more urban legend than human.

"You are truly giving me an experience few people will ever come by, Your Excellency." Rock held each end of the measuring tape with her fingers and took down werewolf Ebel's measurements.

Thicker fur covered the scruff of his neck, his chest and shoulders curved with strong muscles, and his long legs and arms were thick and solid like logs. Ebel silently looked down and watched as Rock's slender fingertips slowly followed the outline of his form. His golden eyes flashed meaningfully every time the measuring tape pressed against his body and whenever her fingers brushed along his fur.

"There's one thing that has been on my mind," Ebel brought up once Rock finished measuring his werewolf form.

"What is that?" Rock asked, the measuring tape hanging around her neck. Suddenly, the werewolf's ponderous hand seized Rock's wrist. He held on tight enough that she couldn't shake him off, while being careful not to let his black claws touch her delicate skin.

"What is the meaning of this, Your Excellency?" Rock raised her voice in protest.

The penetrating gaze of the werewolf's golden eyes probed her. "You smell like a woman." As his big mouth moved, it revealed all of his sharp fangs.

Rock freaked out internally. Driven by the uneasiness of her slender wrist—unhidden by her male disguise—being on display, she countered him in the calmest voice she could muster. "Isn't that a…misconception on your part, Your Excellency? I'm a man, I'm afraid."

"I'm confident in my nose. I know this is a woman's scent." Ebel twitched his wetly shimmering black nose.

Did he figure it out because of his sharper senses as a supernatural being?

Rock picked her words carefully as she tried to mislead him. "Female customers often frequent my shop, and one of my shop assistants is a woman. Is it not them you smell?"

"Are you in an intimate relationship with that woman?" A hint of jealousy flared in the wolf's eyes. "The smell is ingrained in your very body. I take it you are physically involved with a woman, then?"

He has a keen eye—or rather, a keen nose.

Ebel was in the midst of seeing right through to Rock's true identity. His fixation was obvious from the way he didn't let go of her wrist during the whole conversation, and Rock sensed she was in danger. It was exactly because customers like this were a dime a dozen in the slums that she had donned a male guise until now. Learning that Count

Mateus, who seemed like a gentleman at first, was the same breed of man as the rest was positively disappointing.

"Your Excellency, do you make a habit of hitting on men?" Rock asked in a blunt refusal of his advances.

Ebel gasped as if snapped out of a dream. The ardent flame ablaze in his eyes sputtered, and he slowly let go of Rock's wrist. "…I'm sorry. That was rude of me." He slumped with his triangular ears pressed flat back against his head and his tail curled between his legs. "I know it sounds strange, but I just had to know— Nay, whatever my reasoning, it was still impolite. I sincerely feel sorry for my actions."

If Ebel was telling the truth, then what just happened was nothing more than a temporary lapse in judgment.

It'd be unfortunate if he, of all people, desired a poor young woman who disguised herself as a man. Rock tried to laugh it off, but her nerves stiffened her face, hindering any attempts at a smile. She would've had an easier time rejecting him if he were vulgar like the rest of her customers from the slums.

"Don't beat yourself up about it, Your Excellency. I'm not bothered by it." Rock schooled her features and managed to shake her head.

Thoroughly crestfallen like a puppy in the rain, Ebel let out a short sigh. "Thank you for saying so."

After that, Rock calculated the invoice as if nothing had happened, and Ebel paid a sum several times larger than her asking price.

However, nothing could be done about the uncomfortable mood between them, and the wrist that Ebel had grabbed burned with an indescribable heat for a long time afterward.

IN any event, Rock tailored the werewolf count's clothing in five days. Then she sent a messenger to Ebel's manor to inform him that his order was ready, to which he replied he'd immediately come to retrieve them.

Rock sent Phoebe home early again on the day Ebel was scheduled to arrive.

"Is it just me or are you hiding a lot from me lately? Introduce me if you've got yourself a man." Phoebe tried to pry more information out of Rock, but she left the store without much fuss this time.

The dapper gent with burnt sienna hair appeared right after her departure.

"Sorry about the other day, Rock." The moment Ebel saw Rock, he apologized for his rude behavior. However, unlike when he was a werewolf, his expression this time was awfully bright and cheery.

"Don't be... I stopped minding already," Rock answered with a superficial smile, hiding the fact that she hadn't slept well the past few days because of him. Even if he saw through her exhaustion, she could just chalk it up to being busy with work.

In any case, they moved on to talking about the job instead.

She handed Ebel the shirt, vest, and trousers she had finished sewing. He gingerly spread out each piece of clothing and meticulously examined every inch. After confirming the finishing details on every stitch, hook, and the sash belt, he exhaled deeply.

"Your masterful skill impresses me every time. You're impressive for one so young, Rock."

"You honor me with your compliments, Your Excellency."

"Do you have any interest in becoming my exclusive tailor outright?" Ebel placed his hands on the counter and leaned toward Rock, who was standing on the opposite side. "I want to hire you to live and work in my manor. Naturally, I will pay you wages corresponding to your excellent skills. I will also prepare a room for you to live in and assign you a maid."

If she considered only the money and nothing else, that was an extremely attractive offer. But Rock laughed off the count's invitation.

"I am afraid your offer is wasted on me. I have this shop to tend to, after all."

Rock cared more for this clothing shop, established with the money her father left for her, than her own life. She didn't want to walk away from it—no matter the opportunities elsewhere.

And aside from that, she had a hunch that getting further involved with the young count would not be good for her. She couldn't shake the feeling he'd easily unravel all the things she had obstinately held to until now.

"...That's most unfortunate." Ebel stared regretfully at Rock's imperturbable smile. But he quickly recovered and took the chance to hold her hand. "Allow me to alter my invitation, then." The young man's large hand wrapped around Rock's dainty one calloused from working with needles all day. "The other day you asked me if I make a habit of hitting on men, yes?" Ebel asked the frozen Rock with a dashing smile.

"Y-Yes...I guess I did."

"I thought it over and came to the conclusion that I've always been different. It's foolish for me to get hung up over my partner's gender."

"...Pardon me?" Rock's voice cracked.

Ebel paid it no heed, continuing his wooing with his golden eyes glittering. "Rock, I fell for you. I don't care if you are a man—let me court you."

"Y-You jest!" The color drained from Rock's face at this unexpected love confession.

She had gone to great lengths to disguise herself precisely to avoid these situations, but he just obliterated the whole point of pretending to be a man. He eliminated the ability to use her gender as a reason to turn him down.

Meanwhile, Ebel's heart-stopping golden eyes were watching her. Between the twinkle in his eyes and the smile dimpling his handsome face, his high spirits made it easy to imagine his werewolf tail wagging— Rock carelessly found herself captivated by his face too.

"I KNEW IT! Rock, you brought a man home with you!" Phoebe, who Rock thought had gone home, barged into the shop as if she were waiting for this moment. She scowled at the man holding Rock's hand until she saw his face, and her eyes bulged. "Count Mateus!"

"Indeed, I am Ebel Mateus," the count said, introducing himself while still firmly holding Rock's hand. Then he asked, "Who is this lady—nay, gentleman? They appear to be a lady at least— Anyway, who is this?"

"M-My shop assistant, Phoebe," Rock answered politely. And then she candidly turned to Phoebe for help. "Phoebe! What should I do?! His Excellency is trying to woo me!"

"Woo you? ...Your Excellency, you are aware this child is a young man, despite his looks, I hope?"

"Of course. I am wooing him with that knowledge," Ebel affirmed unwaveringly. "I care not whether Rock is a man or a woman."

"...Uh-huh. Well, if you think you can win him over, why don't you just go ahead and try?" Phoebe drawled, sounding exasperated, and headed for the door.

"Hello?! Phoebe?! Aren't you going to save me?" Rock cried out, earning a shrug from Phoebe.

"Do something about it yourself. He's not the first customer to put the moves on you."

"What…?" Ebel gawked at Rock. Phoebe's comment apparently had the unintended consequence of lighting a fire inside him. Flames of jealousy blazing in his golden eyes, he importuned Rock. "The possibility of others trying to seduce you hadn't even crossed my mind… Please, Rock, choose me!"

"Uh, simmer down, Your Excellency! You're putting me on the spot!"

♛ ♛ ♛

BY all appearances, His Excellency the Count was serious about Rock. Phoebe could tell by the look in his eyes. Now how was the trickster tailor going to respond to his feelings?

"…A count, eh? If things go well, she'll marry into the purple," Phoebe muttered to herself after retreating outside the shop alone. She spied on the couple inside.

Ebel was insistently closing the distance between himself and Rock, while she turned bright red at his pursuit. She was an innocent girl, completely ignorant of all things related to love.

"That's why I told her to disguise herself as a man."

Phoebe was worried sick about Rock's defenselessness. She had offered on multiple occasions to teach Rock how to handle men but was always gently turned down.

"In any case, I have to help that child find happiness," Phoebe quietly muttered, taking advantage of the deserted street to voice aloud her thoughts.

The count appeared to have fallen for Rock regardless of her gender. That would be splendid if it was the truth, but Phoebe couldn't shake the possibility this was just a temporary fancy for the toff.

Making sure of his feelings might be a part of my job too, Phoebe thought with a sigh.

"Count Mateus, I'm going to see just how good of a match you are for our daughter."

That whisper reached no one's ears but the street cats'.

Phoebe returned to the shop wearing the usual expression of a beautiful woman.

The werewolf count and tailor Rock weren't the only ones living double lives in the imperial capital.

👑Chapter 2: How to Take a Stroll in the Shantytown of Junk

ROCK stood rooted to the spot inside the clothes shop after Phoebe had left in a swish of skirts.

The reason being Ebel's chiseled face inches from her own. Earnestness brimming brightly in his golden eyes, he appealed to Rock again while holding her hand. "Rock, I want you."

She couldn't run away with her hand caught in his, and something kept her from averting her eyes. In an embarrassed quandary, she found herself returning his gaze as if held captive by him.

"U-Um, just because you say that doesn't mean I can respond in kind…"

"Even if others are trying to court you, I swear on my name that I will love and cherish you more than anyone. I want to obtain you no matter the cost."

Dizziness washed over Rock at his passionate words. Ebel's affections had exploded to new heights thanks to Phoebe's unnecessary meddling.

Some customers did indeed hit on Rock while she was dressed as a man. Her far-too-dainty-for-a-man frame temporarily aroused the interest of the riffraff living in the slums, resulting in their tossing vulgar invitations her way more than once in the past. But those were nothing more than demands for her to act as a substitute to satiate their desires, so she never took any of them seriously. She shot them down as quickly as they came.

Today was the first time anyone said they wanted her for her, not as some sort of stand-in because of the lack of women in the slums.

"P-Please stop this, Your Excellency." Inordinately flustered, Rock tried to shake off his hand. But her strength was paltry compared with his, leaving her to make her counterargument while still in his grip. "It will become a big scandal if someone of your standing makes a move on someone from the slums, and man at that."

"I don't care about those things." Ebel punted away Rock's concerns without a second thought.

"Y-You don't care...?" she stammered.

"Only fools give up on love because they fear scandals. Besides, as long as I have you at my side, I can lose myself in the sound of your sweet voice. I won't have time to be bothered by the whispers of idle people." Ebel pressed on with his seduction.

Rattled, Rock played her next big card. "Moreover, it will be a great disaster if the Mateus family line ended with you. That is to say...two men can't leave behind an heir..."

"That's nothing to worry about. We can just adopt."

Rock could guess from his instantaneous responses that this idea had taken root in him and he wouldn't be dissuaded so easily. The way things were going, it seemed Ebel had already thought through all the excuses Rock would come up with and had a counter for everything.

"I'm grateful you are worried about me, but I'm more interested in hearing your thoughts on the matter." Ebel gazed into Rock's eyes and continued, "Rock, will you allow me to court you?"

"Huh? Um..."

"What do you think of love between men? I would love to hear your opinion."

"Wh-What do I think? I-I'm..." Rock sank further into confusion at his straightforward question.

She started dressing as a man to ward off the indiscriminate, promiscuous creeps haunting the slums. Phoebe recommended she do so as soon as she started living in the imperial capital. She had looked after Rock, who was her lover's hidden child, more than anyone else and taught her how to survive here. It was thanks to her that Rock's days had until now been peaceful, if not somewhat turbulent.

But Ebel was upending that peace with his actions. What in the world was she supposed to do if dressing as a man did nothing to scare off men?

Stuck for an answer, she could only look up at Ebel nervously. He was serious through and through. Fire flared in his eyes, and she felt her skin tingle under his passionate stare. Did he swallow loudly because he was anxious while waiting for her reply? If so, she should say something.

But what should she say? Rock was a woman in mind and body—she couldn't experience a relationship between men even if she tried. That would be her honest reply, but no way would Ebel back down once he knew the truth. Since he claimed "I care not whether Rock is a man or a woman," he'd doubtless rejoice at the news she was a woman, rather than be discouraged.

Then there was but one answer.

She needed to persuade him that she had no interest in romantic relationships period.

"I—" Rock was about to tell him when the doorbell abruptly rang, and Phoebe appeared in the doorway, after having disappeared once already.

"I seriously can't stand to watch you, Rock!" she huffed.

"Phoebe!" Rock half shouted the name of the person she thought had abandoned her to fend for herself. "Where the heck did you go?! You abandoned me!"

"Oh? I did, did I? Weren't you the one who said 'I'm not a child anymore'?" Phoebe teased. Rock swallowed her words. Phoebe took advantage of the pause to cast a sidelong glance at Ebel and confidently proclaim, "As you can see, Your Excellency, this young man here is still but a kid. I don't think you will get an immediate response to your entreaties, so please don't corner the poor child like this."

Evidently, Phoebe was trying to give Rock a hand now.

Rock didn't know why she had come back after leaving her high and dry, but her presence was comforting nonetheless.

Ebel, on the other hand, was perplexed by the sudden intruder. His well-groomed eyebrows knit together as he answered with an air of keeping his cool. "A child...you say? I greatly disagree, but if you are suggesting I shouldn't push things along so impatiently, I'll do as much as that." He finally let go of Rock's hand. "But there is one thing I would like to know first," he stated, his eyes still locked with hers. "Is it all right for me to continue having feelings for you?"

His words made Rock take another look at him. She had been disoriented by his passionate advances, but he'd remained serious throughout. There was no mistaking that he meant it when he said her gender didn't matter and when he shared his ardor for her.

Rock was the one lying. Of course, she knew nothing good would come of telling him the truth, but then why did she feel oddly guilty about it? Since she felt bad, she wanted to at least convey the one truth she could.

"Your Excellency, I have no intention of ever being in love." Rock's declaration earned a wide-eyed look from more than just Ebel.

"What do you mean…you have no intention of being in love?"

"You wanting to become a monk is news to me," Phoebe cut in, her objection spoken in a skeptical tone.

This wasn't easy to say in front of her, but Rock couldn't get around it in this situation. Rock opened her heavy mouth and confided the truth. "My mother, who died three years ago, was a woman who went through much to raise me alone."

Rock's mother, Vale Floria, raised her daughter in poverty while making ends meet as a tailor in a rural farm village. The gossipers traduced her for giving birth to a fatherless child, but Vale never once complained in front of Rock. Nor did she ever speak grudgingly about Rock's father.

It was exactly because she watched the hardship her mother went through up close that Rock harbored complicated feelings about the father she'd never met.

"If only Father had hung around, he could have married Mother and lived with her, easing the stress she had to endure. Then she wouldn't have died so early—" Rock paused. "But Father left my hardworking mother and me to go off to God knows where."

"COUGH! COUGH!" Phoebe began loudly hacking.

"What's wrong, Phoebe?"

"…Nothing. Please go on."

Encouraged, Rock continued, though she found Phoebe's coughing fit to be oddly timed. "I don't resent my father. But when I think his presence could have made a difference for Mother… I haven't the least desire to live like she did."

"Is that the reason why you don't want to be in love?"

Rock gave a great big nod to Ebel's question. "Yes."

"I see... It appears you have many dimensions to your life as well," Ebel responded, his voice curiously colored with an intimate understanding. "And what about your father?"

"He is no longer with us," Rock answered honestly.

Ebel exhaled a lamenting sigh. "I see... You and I are very similar." He gave a lonely smile. "I won't force you into something you have no interest in."

"I am sorry, Your Excellency." Rock had been able to make her intentions clear. Relief washed over her as she apologized to him.

"No desire to be in love, huh...?" Phoebe somberly brushed her hair back and sunk into contemplative silence.

As for Ebel, he recovered from his gloom and cheerfully played his next card. "You don't mind if I retain your services as a customer, though, do you?"

"You are of course welcome to shop here. I warmly welcome your business."

Between his not rushing the order and splurging on payment, the count was the best possible customer a tailor could have. A smile slipped past Rock's guard, and Ebel beamed beautifully when he caught sight of it.

"In that case, I want to put in a clothing request right now."

"All right. What would you like to have made?" Rock immediately slipped into business mode.

"Good question. I would like to speak about it at length with you, so let's change venues."

"...Come again?" Rock's voice cracked at his unexpected proposal.

Undeterred, Ebel doubled down by further proposing, "How about dinner together? My treat, of course."

"Um... You mean to discuss...business, right?" Rock had an inkling that that wasn't his intention, which was why she asked.

But Ebel grinned, insisting, "That is what I said. I can't talk on an empty stomach."

Ebel was the very same man who'd been seducing Rock with sweet nothings and trying to make a pass at her merely moments ago. Common sense dictated that it wasn't smart to share a meal with him. He seemed earnest, but that didn't change his infatuation with her. Remembering their flirtatious exchange superheated Rock's cheeks and caused her heart to hammer so hard it hurt. If possible, she'd rather never think of it again.

On the other hand, she'd forever regret letting such an excellent customer off the leash after catching him. She even closed shop early just for him. While he'd already paid her for that work, she couldn't resist another opportunity to earn even more money when it was dangled in front of her.

Besides, she'd already turned him down loud and clear. *I'm sure he understands,* Rock, inexperienced with relationships, obliviously concluded.

In the end, she jumped at the attractive deal that seemed, at that moment, the right one.

"I will join you at your table if you are going to place an order."

"Of course. I'll place an order that will please you." Excitement filled Ebel's voice.

Rock's heart did flips at this unique opportunity to make a huge profit, but—

"…Oh dear. I wonder who has the upper hand here."

Something stirred restlessly inside her at Phoebe's muttered remark.

DO you mind waiting while I lock up?"

Ebel happily agreed to Rock's request. "I'll change into the garments you tailored for me while I'm waiting." He picked up what she'd given him when he'd arrived. "It's only fitting for me to wear new clothing on an excursion with you."

She had forgotten, in all the hullabaloo triggered by Ebel's abrupt love confession, that he hadn't tried the clothes on yet. Thinking it'd be smart for him to do so before leaving, Rock showed him to the fitting room.

"Please call for me if anything doesn't fit right. I will fix it," she told him once he stepped inside.

The area around his eyes softened as if he was remembering a fond memory. "I will. Though I must be careful not to call for you while I'm in the midst of changing."

"I only panicked the last time because it was so sudden! I am quite fine, thank you!" Rock yanked the fitting room curtain shut in a tizzy.

Losing her presence of mind when he stripped in front of her that last time had been a huge failure on her part. This was her third year since donning a male guise. She'd believed she had grown fully accustomed to living as a man, but perhaps she had made this blunder because she'd become less cautious after growing used to it.

She couldn't slip up in front of Ebel either. His nose was too good as it was—she mustn't give him grounds to further suspect her. Rock reassessed the situation and put up her mental guard.

She returned to the front of the shop where Phoebe was lowering slatted shutters over the windows.

"Are you seriously going out to eat with His Excellency?" Phoebe probed, looking over her shoulder at Rock.

"Of course I am. Opportunities like this don't fall into my lap every day."

Phoebe shrugged her broad shoulders at Rock's instant reply. "If it were me, I wouldn't raise the hopes of someone I have no interest in."

Rock understood what Phoebe was getting at. But she also couldn't bear to look the other way when a big account was dangling just out of reach.

"His Excellency is an outstanding customer, Phoebe," Rock said in a whisper so he couldn't hear her in the fitting room. "I'll be able to increase your wages if he places another order."

A tailor in the slums couldn't expect to make much on any single order, and Floria Clothes Shop's profits were just barely enough for Rock to live off of. She paid Phoebe a pittance, but she worked for it without complaining.

"No point in changing things now. Don't do it for me," Phoebe huffed, tossing a curl behind her shoulder.

But Rock felt a debt of gratitude and deep affection toward her. On a daily basis, she wished she could afford to pay her according to the work she did.

"Then how about I make you a new dress?"

Phoebe's dresses were tailored by Rock to make up the difference in her lacking wages.

While her looks left no room for doubt that she was a beautiful woman, Phoebe's figure was still that of a man's. So Rock accordingly reduced the amount of skin showing and ingeniously sewed the dresses to hide the body's curves. The dress collar she designed to hide Phoebe's protruding Adam's apple, the puff sleeves were to distract from her muscled arms, and the skirt was draped in layers to obscure the shape of Phoebe's legs. The first time Rock tailored a dress for her, Phoebe pulled her into a thrilled hug and even rubbed her cheek against Rock's.

"I'll make this one with even better materials. It'll be a dress you can wear to a banquet."

Rock's dress details finally drew a smile out of Phoebe. "You're a genius at getting someone's hopes up as high as they can go, dear."

"Look forward to it, Phoebe!"

"I will. But watch yourself. Men are wolves."

Phoebe's warning was a common expression, but what gave Rock the chills was the reminder of a completely different meaning.

Men are wolves.

In a sense, no man suited that saying more than Ebel Mateus.

"I'll be okay. Worse comes to worst, I'll run for it," Rock asserted, more for herself than Phoebe. "This is my garden. It'll be a piece of cake to lose him."

Ebel mentioned he patrolled this area, but he shouldn't have a more intimate knowledge of it than Rock, who'd lived there for three years. Left out of the various land readjustment projects to hit the capital, the slums were an easy place to escape from those who weren't familiar with its layout.

"I sure hope that's true." Phoebe recommended lowering the shutters despite looking as though she had more to say.

Rock balanced the shop ledgers at the counter to do her part in closing for the day too. After she put the day's proceeds into the safe, she noticed Phoebe looking pensively in her direction.

"Are you that worried about me?" Rock asked with a laugh.

Phoebe smiled weakly in return. "Not in that sense… Say, about your mother—"

"Aah, sorry about that." Rock quickly apologized when Phoebe broached the subject.

Rock may have brought up her mother to reject Ebel's advances, but she had still spoken of her in front of her father's lover. It couldn't have been a pleasant story for Phoebe to hear.

"Don't let it bother you, Phoebe. I believe my father had his own reasons for what he did."

Phoebe nodded as if to say Rock's apprehensions reached her loud and clear. "...I see. All right." But she seemed gloomy and deep in thought afterward.

Rock wanted to talk more, but Ebel had just called for her from the fitting room, so the conversation ended there.

AFTER locking up the shop, Rock descended into the slums with Ebel.

"As I'd expect, the clothes tailored by you feel remarkably comfortable." Having finished changing, Ebel was in the best of moods and showered the ultimate praise on Rock's handiwork.

Rock was satisfied with her work too. Ebel pulled off the new look with ease. The white hemp shirt covered by the black hook vest paired perfectly with the leather trousers held up by the sash belt. Every piece stunningly fit his sleek frame and surprisingly suited him to a T. The style might not be up to the standard that social etiquette and the rank of count required, but it worked perfectly for a dandy going about town.

"I am honored you like it, Your Excellency," Rock responded.

A disapproving smile strained Ebel's face. "Stop that. I wish you would call me Ebel instead."

"Isn't that...rude?" Rock cautiously asked, looking for clarification and hesitating over his unexpected request. She had never possessed even an inkling of respect for the aristocrats, but she wanted to avoid anything that might negatively affect business.

"I don't enjoy needless controversy either," Ebel explained clearly. "Precautions should be taken when walking in this area."

If word got out that a count was aimlessly wandering the slums, money-grubbers would flock to him to extort money. Rock had heard Ebel's stories of running into situations during his patrols where transforming into a werewolf was his only option, so there probably already outlaws who'd carelessly jumped him and had the tables turned on them.

Wanting to safely wrap up their business discussions, Rock also didn't want to cause pointless commotion. "I will consent if that's the reason, Ebel." She awkwardly fumbled over the name she wasn't used to saying.

An ecstatic smile burst onto Ebel's face. "Thank you, Rock." He said her name in the softest, most caring voice.

Taken aback by his tone, Rock forcefully moved the conversation along. "By the way, Your E—Ebel, are you acquainted with the eateries in the area?"

"My knowledge surely pales in comparison to yours." Ebel shook his head. "I thought we could just walk around for a bit and enter a good restaurant when we came by it."

"Allow me to lead the way, then. There is a cheap and delicious hash house near here."

"Lead the way," Ebel said in agreement, and he fell in step beside her.

The complex layout of the slums turned it into a maze for people unfamiliar with it. Unlike the urban areas managed by the imperial capital's government, hovels were built on whatever leftover parcel each person wrested for themselves. To make the most effective use of the limited terrain, people recklessly constructed extensions from the roofs of already unstable buildings and arbitrarily laid ladders across to the surrounding buildings, and some even took over bridges and built makeshift houses on top of them. Oftentimes the street one passed through yesterday would be gone today, for the shantytown constructed from a mishmash of junk expanded and changed on a daily basis.

But even the shantytown could be dyed in beautiful evening colors.

Rock loved strolling through these streets at this hour. Because it was in these fleeting moments that the filthy slums took on a brilliant light like a candle's flame. Whenever she slipped out of the shop for dinner, she always walked while watching, with fascination, the sunset glow.

Not that she had the time or leisure to be taken by the sunset today. She needed to show Ebel the way. He seemed unfamiliar with the area, as she'd expected, because he followed her as if he were glued to her side.

"It's this way, Ebel," Rock said, courteously explaining the directions for his benefit. It was a kindness meant for a customer who didn't know much about where he was, and Ebel relied entirely on her, gazing her way every time they came to a fork in the road.

"Which way do we turn on this street?"

"Left. We will travel straight for a few minutes before taking a right turn."

"All right."

Rock couldn't walk too far away from him while leading the way. They advanced down the dusk-colored streets at the same pace.

"A fine sunset," Ebel commented, satisfaction in his voice, as he walked shoulder to shoulder with her.

Just like the shantytown, his handsome profile was gorgeously dyed by the changing colors. Rock felt the urgent need to not look at him or be fascinated by him.

At last, the hash house came into view across the street.

"Ebel, that's the place."

A two-story stone building, rare for the slums, housed their destination. The second floor had been turned into a bathhouse, while a bakery took up the first floor. Boiling the bathhouse water with the heat of the bread ovens was fairly commonplace in the capital.

The first-floor bakery doubled as a hash house and was Rock's favorite place to eat. A wide variety of pubs, from respectable to reprehensible, littered the slums, but this spot was the easiest for Rock to relax in because she wasn't a drinker.

"Their potato bread is famous. It's delicious," Rock explained.

Ebel blinked once. "Oh, you mean that shop?" he confirmed with a knowing tone, taking Rock by surprise instead.

"You know of it?"

"I've dropped by on multiple occasions during my patrol. A young married couple runs it, right?"

"Th-That's right…"

By the sound of it, Ebel knew this area somewhat. He stepped ahead of Rock toward the bakery storefront, leaving her to muddle through her bewilderment.

The proprietress, Justia, happened to be out front, and her face lit up when she noticed Ebel. "Oh, why, if it isn't His Excellency! Are you dropping by to honor us with a visit again today?"

"I wanted to get a bite to eat. Is the back table free? I have someone with me."

"Yes, go right ahead and take it. I will bring your food right out!"

Justia hospitably received Ebel, who acted like a regular. The moment Justia recognized Rock as his companion, she gave them a curious look. "When Your Excellency said you had someone with you, I assumed it was a lady, but it was you, Rock? I didn't know you were acquainted with the count."

"I'm not really... He's a customer..." Rock fumbled over her words, still trying to get a grasp on the situation.

Ebel smoothed things over for her. "He's tailoring clothes at my request. We're having dinner together today to discuss business too."

"Oh my. I didn't know. Please do come inside, then."

His Excellency the Count had to be a golden customer to the bakery as well. Justia gave a winning smile Rock had never seen in her three years of being a regular there, and the proprietress showed the pair to the best table in the house.

At the back of the store illuminated by lanterns, Rock sat across from Ebel. And then she aired her grievances to the count, who watched her with great amusement. "I wish you had told me that you're familiar with the area."

"Didn't I say I've dropped by on multiple occasions? Why are you upset?" Mirth danced in his golden eyes.

True enough, he never lied to her, so why was she holding a grudge?

"There was no need for me to show you around, was there?"

"I wouldn't say that. I had great fun on my short guided tour by you."

From the sound of it, he had a real blast getting here.

Rock sighed and addressed her other point of dissatisfaction. "Justia—the proprietress—called you 'Your Excellency' and 'Count.'"

"She did. What about it?"

"Then what need is there for me to call you by name?"

Taking precautions was meaningless since his face and identity were already known at Rock's favorite hash house.

Ebel laughed off Rock's complaints. "I asked you to because I want you to. Isn't that enough of a reason?"

Men are wolves. The aphorism Phoebe used suddenly came to Rock's mind.

Setting aside his being an authentic werewolf, it appeared the count truly was a crafty man.

JUSTIA came back a short while later carrying a small mountain of food. "Thank you for waiting!"

Finely chopped potatoes were sprinkled over the dough before putting the bakery's special potato bread into the oven to bake until browned. It was one of Rock's favorite foods, but it lost some of its appeal when brought out in stacks of five to six slices.

"H-Hold on, Justia. Why did you bring so many?!"

"Because His Excellency's a special patron, of course!"

Corn soup, pickled red radishes and cabbage, and honey and baked cheese were brought to their table next, topped off by a high-quality cut of cured pork. As the dishes piled up, Rock's anxiety went through the roof because of her scarce wallet contents. Ebel said he'd cover the bill, but on the off-chance he ate and ran, she'd be stuck paying for the whole feast.

That'd be a big problem. Or more like impossible for me.

"Ebel, are you comfortable with all this?" Rock asked him in a quiet voice once Justia returned to the kitchen. "If you don't stop her, Justia will continue bringing out food until the table is covered."

"It's not an entertaining meal if the table is bare. I'm fine with this," Ebel calmly reassured her, smiling in welcome as Justia returned with another plate of food.

"His Excellency eats a lot." Justia, in the best mood Rock had ever seen her in, placed a bowl of grapes on the table. "Rock, why don't you learn from him and start eating more? You're nothing but skin and bones. Otherwise, you'll remain weak and frail forever," she nagged, then turned to seek affirmation from her husband in the kitchen. "Isn't that right, Cargus?"

Taciturn where his wife was talkative, Cargus's voice couldn't be heard in the dining area, but Justia apparently saw him nod, since she spoke confidently of his agreement. "See, even Cargus thinks so."

"I eat my fair share!"

Justia snorted at Rock's protest and firmly pinched her upper arms. Rock was always mocked by others for her arms, which were far too slender for someone claiming to be a twenty-year-old man.

"Hey, that hurts, Justia!"

"Don't cry over a little roughhousing! This is why you're weak!" Justia laughed like a horse, then dropped into a proper curtsy in front of Ebel before departing.

A new patron had just entered the hash house. Rock caught a brief look at the large figure hidden under a deep hood being greeted by Justia at the entrance.

Rubbing her pinched arm, Rock told the count, who'd watched the whole scene, "She's always like that. She loves to pick on me…"

The good-natured yet foulmouthed Justia worried about how little Rock ate whenever she came in for a meal. Occasionally, she added an extra plate of food for free, calling it a "bonus." By no means was Rock a light eater, but she gave that impression when Phoebe, another regular, ate three times as much as she did. The care and concern showed to her by the proprietress was one reason why Rock was a repeat customer.

She couldn't do squat about her frailty, so she wished Justia would lay off it.

"You certainly are slender." Ebel glanced at Rock's arms, then smiled with just his lips. "But you're more attractive than you are slender."

"…Pardon me?"

"You have looks that no one can ignore. They treat you kindly because of that too." The smile didn't reach Ebel's eyes, which gleamed more golden than the swaying lantern flames.

Ebel perplexed Rock. He seemed to be complimenting her looks, when her deceased mother and Phoebe were the only two people in the world to ever do so. Not to mention, Ebel, the one complimenting her now, seemed displeased about it.

Before she could figure out why, he pulled himself together. "All right, shall we eat?" he asked, changing the topic.

Rock agreed for now. "I will eat the food you pay for, Ebel." She had to stress that point. The money she had on hand wouldn't come close to covering this evening's check.

"Good. Eat as much as you like." Ebel's smile reflected true mirth this time as he picked up his fork.

This was Rock's first time dining with someone of noble status. *Maybe that's why?* Without even realizing she was doing it, she watched Ebel's every move with fascination.

For example, he gracefully scooped up the corn soup with his spoon and brought it to his mouth. He smoothly cut through the bread and cheese with his knife. Rock thought he was the attractive one when even his expression possessed an air of refinement as he enjoyed food with his eyes cast down.

"…Is something the matter, Rock?" Noticing Rock's eyes glued to him, he flashed an astute smile. "You seem awfully interested in my table manners. Did I do something to pique your curiosity?" Ebel acted amused by her scrutiny.

"You really are a count."

He burst into laughter, perhaps because she showed she was impressed. "You could tell by my table manners?"

"Yes. Slum dwellers don't eat like you do."

The handsome young count was refined down to his etiquette at the table. No one would ever believe his true identity was the rumored werewolf.

According to the city gossipers, werewolves attacked people and dined upon their flesh and bones. But if those rumors were true, Rock should've been devoured long ago. Besides, it was strange to believe in rumors spread from people who would sooner scam you then tell the truth.

"So what kind of clothes do you think would fit me the way you see me?"

"The way I…see you?"

"Yes. I want you to choose my next order." Ebel gazed at Rock as if he had total faith in her. "I absolutely want to know what you conceptualize when you look at me."

A fairly difficult request, but her pride as a tailor wouldn't allow her to say she couldn't do it. Rock took a moment to carefully ponder his question.

To start with, was there actually any clothing Ebel couldn't pull off?

From traditional court clothing to the latest fashion trends, he'd look like a model in whatever he wore. His chiseled face, tempered body, and graceful bearing made him the perfect customer for Rock to flex the tailoring skills she took pride in.

Trousers with suspenders were the most popular item with the men who frequented her shop in the slums. Suspenders used to be a fashion accessory for the upper classes, but their popularity had spread to the commoners in recent years. Meanwhile, snug-fitting jackets called doublets were all the rage at top-tier tailor shops in the commercial district because of the fashionable shape and padding it added to the male body. The best shops tailored clothing with velvet, silk, and satin, but customers with that kind of money rarely visited Rock's shop. She often used the cheapest textiles such as quilt fabric and wool to make affordable clothing for her clientele.

But she needn't be frugal with materials for Ebel.

This might just be the optimum opportunity for Rock to create the kind of clothing she had always envisioned.

"I want to tailor a doublet with the finest materials for you," Rock informed Ebel with enthusiasm. "I would like to try my hand at tailoring a jacket at the forefront of the current trends."

"I see. I guess it's only natural for a tailor to be knowledgeable about the latest fashions." Ebel sounded surprised by this, but he immediately consented. "Sounds good to me. I'll have many occasions to wear a doublet, and I'd like to be able to walk around wearing what you made for me." He paused, then added for emphasis, "I'd be very happy if you would tailor the clothes with love."

"Of course I will. I always put my heart into what I create." Rock never cut corners when it came to work. She sewed each piece together with her whole heart.

This order was a rare chance to create high-end clothing for a particularly well-paying customer. Better yet, it was for the good-looking count, who was worthy of wearing the finest clothing. Jobs that stirred up this much enthusiasm in a tailor didn't come often.

"Please leave everything to me, Ebel. I will tailor a doublet that suits you better than any other in the world," Rock grandly promised as she stuffed her cheeks with potato bread.

Ebel's eyes softened as he watched her. "I leave it in your capable hands, Rock." He gently laid his hand on the shirt covering his chest. "I have to treasure these clothes even more now that I know your love has been included in every stitch," he said in a whisper.

Joy radiated from his face, which looked divinely beautiful to Rock's eyes. His smile, like a ray of light bursting forth through a gap in the clouds, sent her heart fluttering.

"Um... Treasuring the clothes you wear brings great joy—to the clothes." Forgetting to chew the bread in her mouth, Rock barely managed to choke out those words.

Ebel watched Rock's reaction with heavenly satisfaction.

THE sun had sunk below the horizon long before they finished eating and set out from the bakery. A starry sky loomed above, and a chilly breeze blew through the alley. Light spilled from the windows of the public bathhouse on the second floor, illuminating the surrounding alleyways in a soft light.

"Thank you for treating me to dinner, Ebel," Rock said as soon as they left the hash house.

Ebel paid for the entire food bill as he had promised. His voracious appetite was eye-catching, just as Justia had said. He polished off every single plate of food by the end of dinner, prompting Justia to nag Rock again about learning a thing or two about a hearty appetite from him.

The big eater shook his head with a tender smile. "I'm the one who's grateful. I had fun, Rock."

"Nonsense. I'm grateful to have received another order from you."

Now that it was over, she realized she was saved from having to pay for dinner that night and had received a new, expensive job order. It had been a really good night indeed.

Phoebe was likely fretting with worry over Rock's safety, but she could go home with her head held high as she announced the good news to her. Rock planned to let her know about how things went when she saw her at work tomorrow morning.

"Then if you will excuse me for the night—"

Ebel swiftly stopped Rock from bidding him good night. "I'll escort you home, Rock."

"You jest!" Rock naturally laughed off his offer. "It's unnatural for two men to go out to eat and then have one escort the other home."

Even without that aspect to consider, the slums were Rock's playground; she had nothing to worry about here. The room she rented was within a stone's throw of the hash house, and Phoebe lived in the neighborhood. Ebel didn't have to be concerned for her safety.

"And besides, your residence is far from here, Ebel. You can arrive home without being late if you leave me to look after myself."

There was a significant walking distance from the shantytown that took rise as a home for drifters on the outskirts of the imperial capital to the center where the aristocrat district was located. A partial smile appeared on Ebel's face from Rock's show of concern.

"I'm confident in my legs to get me there fast. You needn't worry about me."

"Hah," she openly sighed. "But—"

"Something else concerns me right now." Ebel suddenly frowned, cutting Rock's argument short. His golden eyes whipped around the alleyways.

"What is it?"

He grabbed Rock's arm and walked in a random direction down the street in front of the hash house. The memory of his furry werewolf hand clutching her wrist was still fresh in her mind. Uneasy with his hold on her, Rock called out to Ebel, though she did not stop him from dragging her along.

"Hello? Ebel?"

He dropped his voice and whispered in her ear. "…It appears we're being followed."

"We are?!" She instinctively went to look over her shoulder, but a tug on her arm stopped her.

"You mustn't look. Let's lose them before they suspect we notice."

His advice rendered Rock incapable of knowing who pursued them or what they wanted. She simply let Ebel lead her away.

Leaving the street in front of the hash house, the pair slipped ever deeper into the maze of the slums.

Very few people were out and about at this hour, and their two sets of feet echoed loudly on the night street. Yet the footsteps of their pursuer never reached Rock's ears. Should she truly believe what Ebel told her? Could he have just imagined it? Such thoughts crossed her mind.

Losing confidence in him, she questioned, "Who exactly are you claiming is following us?"

"Your guess is as good as mine. More than one person for sure." Ebel gradually increased walking speed, grimly shaking his neatly groomed sienna hair. "Four—no, make that three and one. The three are hired thugs at best, but the separate one is no amateur."

"You can tell all that?"

"My ears are as sharp as my nose, Rock." Unwavering confidence filled his voice, quadrupling Rock's already hyped-up tension.

If what Ebel said was true, what in the world were these skilled pursuers after?

Without any proof, Rock was guided by the arm deeper into the back alleys where the streetlights scarcely reached.

AFTER Ebel and Rock had turned down several different roads, a wall blocked their path. Jury-rigged by randomly nailing dilapidated plywood together, the flimsy wall looked as if a sudden gust of wind could knock it over. But it stood tall enough to cast a shadow on Rock and block her view beyond.

"Huh. Now that's odd. This wall wasn't here yesterday," Ebel groaned, his frustration understandable. This was just the kind of place the slums were.

But before Rock could explain that to him, she heard the incoming footsteps of the people trailing them. Just as Ebel had said, there were several pairs of feet. She couldn't tell who they were by the sound of their steps, but she acutely sensed they meant trouble.

"Ebel, let's turn back for now. We don't want to get stuck with our backs literally up against the wall," Rock advised.

"We don't have to turn back." Ebel shook his head. "Come here, Rock." He wrapped his arm around Rock's waist, taking her by complete surprise.

"Hyaah!"

Ignoring her screams, Ebel crouched down and then sprang into the air.

He easily leaped over the quickly-slapped-together wall with Rock in his grip and landed on top of a private house's rooftop on the other side. Then he whirled around to ascertain the identities of the stalkers rushing into the dead-end alleyway.

Still held in his arm, Rock looked down at them from the rooftop as well.

Three burly men wearing patchwork clothing searched the alley. Their hardened, scarred faces looked villainous at a glance, and disturbingly, they each carried a dangerous weapon.

After doing a sweep of the dead end, they looked up and spotted Ebel on top of the roof. "Yer runnin'?! And ya call yerself a count! Ya wuss!" one of the thugs cursed at him.

"Now that's a rude way of speaking when you're the ones who started tailing me for no reason," Ebel fearlessly countered as he hid Rock behind his back.

Rock hadn't grasped the situation yet, but she knew having her face exposed to nasty thugs would be bad for business. She clung to Ebel's back for the time being.

"What business do you have with me?"

Each of the three men smirked vaguely at Ebel's question.

"Some people are sick of ya gallivantin' 'round these parts."

They were presumably hired by someone, then.

Many people in the slums accepted dirty jobs for quick and easy money. Most of them were vagabonds who lived day to day scraping out a meager existence, so hiring them didn't pay off much. But with nothing to lose, their rashness occasionally made them excellent hunting dogs.

"Get yer arse down 'ere! Ya bluebloods can't stand to run from a fight with a lass watchin'!" one of the crooks provoked, peeved his target was out of reach.

Apparently, they hadn't realized that Ebel's companion was the slums' tailor. Being mistaken for a woman, though she was one, upset her, but she sucked it up for the sake of her business.

Another one of the scoundrels strained his eyes to see behind Ebel's back. "Oi, take 'nother look. That's the Market Street tailor," he blurted, causing the other two to recognize Rock.

"Bloody 'ell. He's so slender I mistook 'im for a woman."

"Hidin' behind 'nother man's back makes 'im even more of a woman."

"Sh-Shut up!" Rock lashed out without meaning to.

Ebel held out his hand. "Don't let them provoke you, Rock. They can't do anything to you up here."

"...I'm sorry. Shall we just shake them off our trail now?"

Fortunately, Rock and Ebel were standing on top of a roof two stories high. Escaping over the rooftops posed some risk of falling, but it was a convenient way to get rid of the thugs.

Ebel answered her without a moment's delay. "Of course. But I'll take care of them first."

"You will? There are three of them—"

"Less than usual," Ebel asserted flatly, looking over his shoulder at Rock. A roguish smile unsuited for the situation played across his face. "Plus, this is a great chance to try out your clothes."

Put another way, he planned to use his werewolf powers.

"You needn't worry." Ebel knelt before Rock and, without any sign of embarrassment, swore, "I'll protect you to the end no matter what comes." He leaped from the roof and smoothly landed in front of the thugs.

"Ebel!" Rock shouted, but she knew not to follow him. It was painfully obvious to her that she wouldn't be much help in a fight.

She watched from the safety of the roof while Ebel boldly squared off with the men closing in around him with their knives and cudgels. It was starting to look as though she was finally going to witness his transformation into a werewolf with her own eyes tonight. But should that happen, the clothing Rock tailored to easily slide off would do just that, and she would have to find somewhere else to look.

Ebel reached for the sash belt around his waist.

"Ugh…," Rock groaned, red in the face, and averted her eyes.

"Hold it right there!" A familiar gruff voice shook the tense backstreet. Rock immediately looked to where a tall figure had rushed into the alleyway. "URAAAH!"

A big-boned "beautiful woman" with curly chestnut hair kicked one of the thugs gunning for Ebel in the back.

"BLERGH!" The thug pitched forward, smashing face-first into the dirty ground, startling his friends.

"What the 'ell's the big idea, ya molly?!"

"I hope ya interfered prepared for an ass whooping!"

Not even batting an eye at their insults, Phoebe tightened her fists. "Rock's in danger. Of course I'd interfere!" She made it sound as if she had come to save Rock. It was a mystery how she knew where Rock was, but Phoebe's words and actions moved her.

"Phoebe!" Rock called out encouragingly. Phoebe grinned and raised her right hand in greeting.

Meanwhile, Ebel shot a grudging look back at Rock. "Rock, cheer me on too," he pouted.

"S-Sure! Please be careful as well, Ebel!"

"Thank you!" he exclaimed with newfound enthusiasm. Still in his handsome young man form, he charged at one of the thugs.

Phoebe likewise pounded her fists into the last remaining scoundrel. The fight was finished faster than Rock could blink.

The thugs were laid out on the ground after taking an intense beating and never getting a counterpunch in, while Ebel and Phoebe towered over them, not even having broken a sweat.

"Thanks for having my back, Phoebe," Ebel said.

Phoebe snorted. "I simply happened to be passing by the area, Your Excellency. Anyway, please take Rock away from here."

"Why?" Rock asked from the rooftop.

"We can't just leave these Neanderthals lying around. The rats will eat out their eyes. I'll take care of the cleanup, so please vacate the area." Phoebe gave her shoulders a tired shrug. Ebel seemed to suddenly understand everything.

"Then I leave this to you. I promise to safely escort Rock home."

"You'd better! Let me be clear: if you bring that child home with a single scratch, I will make it so you can never enter our neck of the woods again!"

"I wouldn't want that." Ebel cracked a smile and leaped back onto the roof. "You heard Phoebe, Rock. Let's make haste from this place."

"A-All right. We had better get down from here first—"

"No. We would be in a tight spot if more come. Let's travel over the rooftops." Before he finished talking, Ebel lifted Rock onto his shoulder with one hand.

"Whoa?! Hey! Um…I can walk by myself!"

"I can't put you in possible danger. Hang on tight." Ebel sprung off the rooftop. Just when Rock was reeling from the incredible power and height of his jump, he broke into a run, traveling faster than a whirlwind.

"Aaaah!" The wind whooshed away Rock's screams as Ebel dashed across the buildings. Nimbly transferring from roof to roof, he carried her while easily jumping across the spaces between the hovels.

Slung over his shoulder, she could only see the cityscape and sky as it whisked by with dizzying speed. The force of the wind pressure dried out her eyes, and Rock's hair whipped her cheeks. Consumed by fear of the extreme speed, she couldn't think about anything else.

"WAAAAAAAAAAAH!" Her reflexive screams were absorbed by the starry sky.

HOW long had Ebel been running before he finally decelerated, leaped across another roof, and lowered Rock from his shoulder?

"We should be fine at this distance. How are you feeling, Rock?"

"Urgh…I-I'm all right…" Her legs trembled on the solid rooftop. Unable to stand on her own, she remained seated and glanced up at Ebel standing beside her.

Ebel offered a faint smile when their eyes met. "I'll bring you home once you recover. You should rest a bit first."

She wholly agreed with him. Her head still spun, and her pulse and breathing came fast and uneven. Hired thugs might still be prowling the area too.

"I'm sorry for putting you through that." Ebel sat next to her and brushed down her windswept hair.

Startled by his gentle touch, Rock cleared her throat, feeling the need to keep up appearances. "…I apologize for the unsightly display earlier."

"Unsightly? At what point did you put on such a display?" Ebel sounded doubtful, but as far as Rock was concerned, what had happened was pure humiliation.

"I screamed…while you were carrying me…," she admitted weakly.

Ebel eased the moment with a light chuckle. "Almost anyone would have done the same in your position."

"They would?"

"They would. I wish I could've carried you more gently," he admitted, his voice soft as he stroked her hair some more.

Hair didn't have any feeling, and yet Rock's heart drummed away. "I-I can fix it myself, thank you." Flustered, Rock gently batted away his hand.

Blinking his golden eyes, Ebel didn't look particularly put off. Rock, on the other hand, squirmed under awkward guilt as she raked her fingers through her messy hair and finally had enough mind to look around her.

They were sitting on top of a building that was especially tall for the slums. Except for the part directly under the narrow rectangular rooftop, the unattended lookout platform was in plain view. Ignored by the constables who viewed patrolling the area as a waste of time, the slums' lookout tower never had visitors. Because of that, their negligence had created a space where Rock could relax right now.

She could see a panoramic view of the whole district from this roof. What looked like a disorganized shantytown of junk during the day became beautiful when seen lit up at night. Just like the star-studded sky sprawling overhead, the town was speckled with warm points of light too.

"That light over there belongs to the bathhouse," Ebel observed, pointing toward the dimly glowing circular building in the distance.

"Yes, it does." Rock nodded. "We came a long way."

Ebel let out an amused laugh. "Our stroll turned into quite the extreme after-dinner exercise. Though we finally get to be alone thanks to it."

Deserted at night for the safety of the indoors, the roads below were clear of their pursuers and any sign of Phoebe catching up to them. And they were on top of a lookout tower even the soldiers didn't visit.

Realizing they were truly alone together, Rock struggled to calm herself. She went out to dinner only to receive his clothing order, yet she unknowingly ended up coming to a place like this with him. She timidly stole a peek at the man beside her.

Ebel was staring at the night scenery with an unexpectedly serious visage. "I have a question for you." He suddenly lowered his voice to a barely audible whisper.

"Y-Yes? What is it?" Rock nearly jumped to her feet.

"Phoebe—who is she?" Ebel calmly inquired. "The way she handles herself in a fight makes me doubt she's an amateur."

"Oh, I can answer that." Unusually relieved by his topic choice, Rock happily explained, "She used to be a mercenary."

"A mercenary? She doesn't look the type."

"Yes, I often think the same thing. But she's actually an incredibly strong fighter."

Rock had never witnessed Phoebe lose a fight. Every time drunks challenged her, shady conmen stalked her, and brainless jerks tormented her for her looks, Phoebe used her physical strength to knock them down a few notches. She'd said herself that she was a famous mercenary in the past.

"Apparently she met my father through their mercenary work." Rock stopped talking when she noticed the dubious expression on Ebel's face. She rushed a mumbled explanation: "Er...it's hard for me to say this, but Phoebe was my father's lover."

"...Is that the story?" Even Ebel sounded astonished.

"After my mother passed, I came in search of my father when I learned he lived in the imperial capital. But I only found Phoebe and the news that my father was gone..."

And to this day, Phoebe was the sole person Rock considered family.

She harbored mixed feelings about the father who had abandoned her and her mother. At first, aggravated, jumbled emotions swirled in her toward the person her father had chosen to love. But after all this time, she had come to understand the reasons why the father she never met fell in love with Phoebe.

"But she surprised me earlier. I never thought she would come to our rescue... I'm glad she happened to be passing by the area when we needed her," Rock innocently shared.

Ebel, however, was pressing his fingers against his temple. "I don't know how to tell you this, Rock..."

"What is it?"

"She was following us the whole time. Since we entered the bakery."

"No way!" Rock demurred with a half smile.

Already positive it was true, Ebel wryly smiled back at her. "Remember the customer who entered soon after us? The tall customer concealed under a deep hood? That was her."

"...Ah." Rock remembered.

Now that he mentioned it, Rock never did spot that customer again after they entered the building. Perhaps the proprietress, Justia, knowingly sat her somewhere out of sight.

"I think she probably tailed us out of concern for me...," Rock speculated, attempting to vindicate Phoebe while wrestling with her embarrassment.

"I'm sure she did. It's a good thing because she assisted in repelling the other pursuers as a result..." So Ebel said, sounding vaguely discontent about it.

It was then that Rock suddenly noticed a tiny snag in his shirt collar. "Ebel, your shirt ripped," she told him, pointing to the spot.

He looked down at his collar. The color instantly drained from his face upon spotting the tear. "When in the world did that happen?!"

"Perhaps it snagged on something earlier."

"I can't believe it..." Ebel lamented, his face pensive, crestfallen over the discovery. "Forgive me, Rock. I had decided to wear the clothes from your shop with great care...yet I ripped the clothing you sewed with love!"

"P-Please don't apologize." His grief threw her for a loop. "Clothes will naturally tear when you fight and run over rooftops in them."

"I ruined your hard work because of that..."

"But you saved me too."

"Even so, what I've done to you is inexcusable." Depression had completely overtaken Ebel. If his werewolf ears had been visible, they would've surely been sagging against his head.

As a tailor, she couldn't let things stand. "I can make it so the rip doesn't stand out, if you don't mind me using a temporary patch," she offered in a placating tone.

"You can?!" Ebel jerked his head up as if brought back from the edge of despair. His honest joy was so funny it drew a small laugh from her.

"It won't be as good as new, but I can mend it."

"With your skills, anything is possible. Please do fix it."

"I accept your order. In that case..." Rock procured the sewing kit from the tool bag hanging from her belt. Being a tailor, she always walked around with needle, thread, and fabric on hand. After all, being prepared tended to earn her some extra coin.

Next she leaned toward Ebel and inspected the tear. A small hole the size of a fingertip had appeared in the cloth, requiring a patch. Fortunately, she had some spare fabric left over in her tool bag from tailoring his clothes. But with the tear located where it was, she couldn't do a thing about it while he was wearing the shirt.

"I'm sorry, but could you lend me your shirt?" Rock requested.

Ebel's eyes narrowed suggestively. "You want me to remove my shirt and hand it over to you?"

"Yes. I can't sew unless you do."

"Got it." Giving his consent, Ebel started by removing his vest, then set about pulling off his shirt. It slipped off in no time, just as she had designed it to.

Thanks to that, Rock got to see with her own eyes that Ebel wasn't wearing anything else under his shirt. "Wow! U-Um, I'm sorry!"

"Why do you apologize? And avert your eyes?"

"I-I'm not. Y-You just surprised me is all…"

She should've been used to seeing naked chests in her line of work, but when it came to Ebel, she never reacted normally. With her eyes still averted, she accepted the shirt and hastily mended it.

Rock began by inserting the needle into the fold of the hem, in between the two layers of fabric, and pulling the thread through until it was taut. She continued carefully sewing through the fabric one stitch at a time. There weren't any lights on top of the lookout tower, but the starlight shining down on them illuminated the area enough to see her hands.

"Interesting. So that's how you mend it?" Ebel hummed, impressed as he moved closer to observe Rock pull off a slip stitch.

Rock was frazzled by having a half-naked man right next to her, closing the last few inches of space between them. Her concentration was shattered by the glimpses of bare chest she caught out of the corner of her eye.

"Anyway, you sure do find yourself the center of trouble often, don't you?" Rock said in a bid to change the subject. Someone had to have hired them with money, but who? "Did you incur someone's wrath? Be careful. The slums are crawling with brutes."

"Yeah." Ebel's response to her warning was perfunctory. Her eyes were focused on the needle at the time, so she didn't catch the look on his face. After pausing a moment, he softly divulged, "It appears one of the people I confronted during my patrols is a tad ornery. He occasionally sics his hired dogs on me."

"You have my condolences. Why don't you cut back on your patrols some?"

"Hearing you worry for me makes me one happy man," Ebel purred, as if his happiness came from the heart, but it didn't seem as though he intended to listen to her advice. "You live here. I want to make this district safe and peaceful for your sake as well." His tone gave away his unwavering will of steel.

"I can't even picture safe and peaceful slums," Rock remarked without sarcasm.

The majority of the residents weren't bad people, but it was a chaotic town where the meaning of freedom was often misunderstood. That was exactly why a country girl like Rock could run a business within the imperial capital. It wasn't the best place in the world to live, but it was considered the last place where people who had no alternative could go to eke out a living.

A titled member of nobility like the count shouldn't have any reason to loiter around the area to the point of exposing his identity.

"...Oh, that gives me an idea on what to do about your next clothing order." Suddenly striking upon a golden idea, Rock suggested it to Ebel. "A cloak with a cowl to cover your face might be better than a doublet. If you insist on continuing your patrols, that is."

"Good idea. I'm growing weary of running into trouble every time I go for a walk in these parts." Ebel instantly approved of the idea. "Please take the appropriate measurements in the near future."

"Sure. I will be waiting for you at my shop." The conversation they held during their last measurement session vividly replayed in the back of her mind. Ebel seemed to have learned his lesson, so it shouldn't happen again...

"After all, I need concealing clothes so I can invite you out to eat again," he exclaimed, his voice filled with enthusiasm that didn't help his case.

"Please don't get the wrong idea... I only joined you for dinner to discuss work," Rock stressed, but Ebel neither agreed nor disagreed with her.

After that exchange, he studiously watched Rock work in silence.

Before long, Rock finished the nearly invisible slip stitch and passed the shirt back to Ebel. "The hole shouldn't stand out now. Please check for yourself."

Ebel accepted the shirt and looked over where the tear had formed in the collar. The hole had been neatly mended to the point where it was invisible even when he brought it up to his eyes.

"Your skill impresses me every time, Rock. Commendable work."

"Any tailor can pull off a slip stich," Rock said humbly as she put away her sewing kit.

Deeply impressed by her abilities, Ebel scrutinized the shirt. "You know that isn't true. With your skills, you could become His Imperial Majesty the Emperor's personal tailor."

"Th-There you go joking around again..."

To Rock, the emperor who resided in his castle within the imperial capital was a godlike existence. She highly doubted she'd ever have the opportunity to even lay her eyes upon His Imperial Majesty in her lifetime.

"Of course, then you would be out of reach for me," Ebel said, discouraged, his tone lacking any hint of a joke. "I don't want to hand you over to anyone, even His Imperial Majesty the Emperor." Before Rock could object, he smoothly flowed into the next topic: "By the way, what do I owe you for the mend?"

"You don't owe me anything for it." She shook her head, still hung up on what they'd been discussing.

Ebel scrunched up his face. "We can't have that. You shouldn't sell your work short."

"But the tear happened the same day you received it. I can't accept extra money for it," she said, rejecting him again.

She had already taken in more than enough money from his earlier payment. Mending fell under the realm of customer service. Doing this much for her best customer was more of a gain than a loss.

"It would make me happier if you wear it with care instead."

"Of course. I'll treasure these clothes," he promptly agreed.

This was the same man who turned blue in the face just by getting a small tear in his shirt—she believed him when he said that.

"Also…," Rock started, keeping her customer service charm turned on, "I am glad you are unharmed. You would have been cut if you weren't wearing the clothes I made."

Clothing was originally created to protect the human body. The garments Rock tailored served their rightful purpose that night.

Her remark was meant to be a calculating one. One said to prevent Ebel from growing upset over a tear forming in his shirt after having it for less than half a day, and to lure him into happily returning to shop with her again. Yet once the words left her tongue, she felt oddly embarrassed and lowered her head.

That was why she didn't see Ebel's reaction.

A second later, she couldn't lift her head—Ebel had tightly wrapped his arms around her.

"Wah! Wh-What are—"

He tightened his grip so much it cut off Rock's raised voice and locked her in his embrace. Ebel hadn't put his shirt back on yet. She was pressed up against his bare chest, where she heard his soaring heartbeat directly through his warm skin.

There was nowhere to run on top of the lookout tower. Captured where she sat beside him, Rock froze in place from the fright.

"As I thought, I want you," Ebel whispered sweetly in Rock's ear as he clasped her to his chest. "I don't mind if you are a man. What you are has no bearing on my feelings. Please be mine."

Rock's earlobes were tickled by his warm breath as he beseeched her to accept him. Instantly rendered motionless, she leaned against his chest, dazed.

"U-Um, er… We already covered that…earlier today." She struggled to move her twisted tongue to form an answer for him. "I don't intend to be in love. I cannot return your feelings."

"In that case, I shall continue to inquire until you can respond to them," Ebel firmly replied. "I'll give up if you have someone else in your life. But if you don't, then who's to say what the future holds? If you ever decide you want to be in a relationship, I hope I am who you choose to be your partner."

His ardent love confession confused and intoxicated Rock.

Plus, this was her first time being in contact with a man's bare skin for this long. With no memories of being hugged by her father, the male body was an unknown realm for her. His muscled chest firmly held her, and the heat radiating from his skin felt as if it were going to melt her where they touched.

"I don't want to let any other woman—or man—touch you." Ebel's hand brushed Rock's waist and followed her hip bone. Gooseflesh sprung up on her skin from more than just the unfamiliar sensation.

"U-Um, ummm, even if you say that…" She was going to lose her head if she stayed with him any longer.

Sensing the danger, Rock abruptly shoved away from Ebel's chest. It had seemed as though he'd been tightly embracing her, but his arms easily slipped away, freeing her. When she spotted the fervent yearning in his face, she impulsively shouted, "This is a first for me! I don't understand how it works! Sorry!"

It took everything she had left to say that.

Rock moved on impulse then. She slid her way down the roof to the inside of the outlook tower and descended the ladder to the ground with trembling legs. Wanting nothing more than to race into the safety of her room, she bolted into the dark, tripping and stumbling.

"Rock!"

She pretended not to hear Ebel calling for her to stop.

Rock just ran. Back to her sanctuary she scurried.

CALLING the slums her playground wasn't empty boasting—Rock arrived at her building despite running senselessly.

She lived in a tiny room she rented on the second floor of a shady antique store. The building was located one backstreet away from Market Street, where Floria Clothes Shop was. It didn't get great sun exposure, but the rent was cheap. Phoebe lived in the neighborhood and frequently dropped by.

Did Phoebe already go home? The thought crossed Rock's mind, but she didn't particularly want to see her right now. She didn't want even Phoebe to see her face right now.

"Of course I'd be startled by his actions..." Something inside her snapped when she made it to her room, and she collapsed to her knees in front of the door. Her hammering heart and flushed cheeks were the result of running all this way. "How do I handle this...?"

Not even Rock understood why she muttered those words to herself.

For a while after that, she stayed crouched on the floor with her head between her knees without entering her room.

So she didn't notice the figure watching over her from a different rooftop.

Till the very end, she never became aware of the figure in the properly worn white shirt who'd chased her all the way here from the lookout tower and who was wholly relieved when he saw her finally rise and enter her room.

Then he, too, turned on his heel and, surprisingly happy, made his long trek home.

♛ Chapter 3: Sweet Memories at Werewolf Mansion

WITH a yawn, Rock opened her shop.

The sun rising into the blue sky lavished its morning light upon the imperial capital, granting its blessing to even the shantytown slums pieced together with random junk. But the bright morning sunlight was too much for the sleepless Rock, its rays tormenting her eyes as she swept the storefront. She quit sweeping to retreat within the dark confines of Floria Clothes Shop, where she rested her chin in her hands with her elbows propped up on the counter.

The previous evening filled her every waking thought. Everything that had happened with Ebel luridly replayed in her mind even after a whole night had passed.

"…S-Stop thinking about it!"

Rock shook her head, trying to chase away the persistent memories brought about by the sleepless night. Yet the warmth of human skin was curiously hard to forget and obstinately stuck with her.

The very antithesis of Rock, Phoebe arrived at work in her usual splendor. "You're here early. I was debating what to do if you hadn't opened yet," she casually said in greeting before doing a double take and frowning at Rock's drawn face. "You look horrible. Don't tell me he kept you out till morning?"

"No way!" Rock's unintentionally loud shout rang painfully through her sleep-deprived brain. Moaning as she clasped her head in her hands, she felt Phoebe patting her a few times on the back of the head.

"Not even I would think you'd do something like that, dear."

The comforting gentleness of Phoebe's hand on her hair helped cheer her up. She looked up at Phoebe's perfectly made-up face and voiced her biggest worry. "Did you get by all right last night too, Phoebe? What happened to those thugs?"

After their run-in with trouble in the alleyway, Phoebe had let Ebel and Rock run away while promising to handle the rest. Rock had been waiting to see Phoebe again to ask what had happened after they left.

Phoebe shrugged her broad shoulders, sending her curls bouncing. "I smacked them awake and put the squeeze on them to see who they were hired by."

"Did they say who?"

"They said they don't know. Sounds like whoever it was sent a middleman over with money and the job request to run the count out of the slums."

Just as Rock had assumed last night, the thugs were nothing more than hired hands.

Naturally, the shady types living in the slums took affront with His Excellency the Count's patrols through the shantytown streets for the sake of peace. Finding the person behind it without any clues would be about as difficult as finding a needle in a haystack.

Rock had no desire to flush out the vipers by poking the thorn bushes either. So she decided not to think too deeply about the crooks from last night.

"Okay, my turn to ask the questions." Phoebe turned probing eyes on Rock. "What did you two do after that? His Excellency didn't try any funny business with you, did he?"

"H-He did not! ...I think." The events of the previous evening were too stimulating to assert his innocence unequivocally. Phoebe's sky-blue eyes peeled open at Rock's hesitant addition.

"Did he do something to you?" she ground out between her teeth.
"No. Just a little…"
"What is it, child? Spit it out already!"
"H-He hugged me tight…," Rock nervously confided.
"Hmph. So what did you do?" Phoebe's voice instantly sharpened.
"I ran away in confusion." Rock's childlike faltering reply earned her the greatest sigh.

"Rock, aren't you twenty? Responding to a hug by turning your back and running away is bordering on shameful. If you don't like it, be sure to properly say so."

Phoebe made a sound argument.

But Rock had her own objections. How could she do anything but run when it wasn't only being hugged that had stunned her last night?

"B-But I was in shock...because His Excellency was naked—"

Phoebe's whole demeanor changed before Rock could finish explaining. "What the—?!" Astonished, she pounced on Rock. "Why was he naked?! Don't tell me he stripped in front of you?!"

"H-He did. Because he had to."

"Why did he HAVE to strip?! WHY?!"

"AH! N-No, Phoebe. I don't mean it that way!"

"Then what way do you mean?! Wait, you didn't undress too, did you?!"

"No, no! Not me! Just him!"

"What kind of situation calls for just him to undress and hug you?!"

"Uh, like I was saying..."

Phoebe was terribly distressed, which forced Rock into disclosing the events of last night in order. She told Phoebe about how she had discovered a tear in Ebel's shirt after escaping to the lookout tower and how she'd offered to mend it. Then how he had embraced her after she'd finished her work—without his shirt on. Rock abridged the conversation they'd had during that moment. It was too embarrassing to repeat.

"...That's it? You scared me, child!" Phoebe finally regained her calm after hearing Rock out. She combed the curls off her face and caught her breath. "Even so, what I said before is still valid. You have to flat-out tell someone **NO** when they do things you don't like or are uncomfortable with."

"I know," Rock agreed, but oddly enough, she wasn't uncomfortable with Ebel's actions. She had defended against plenty of men before him. She knew how to hold her ground against someone she *disliked*.

The issue here wasn't a matter of like or dislike. She couldn't even wrap her head around what was happening. And that was why she couldn't turn him down in any way other than escaping the situation.

If he had continued to hug her like that—

"Your face is red, Rock."

"It is not!" Rock frantically shook her head at Phoebe's acute observation.

After observing the girl with concern, Phoebe lazily advised, "You'd better watch out. If you don't do anything about it, he'll get close and have his way with you before you know it."

"O-Okay. I'll be careful."

"And then once you fall for him, he'll be the one to run for it. That's the kind of game this is." Phoebe made it sound as if she had personal experience with affairs of this sort as she stared into space.

Curious, and wanting to take the conversation in another direction, Rock tried to feel her out. "Sounds like this is familiar ground to you, Phoebe."

"Who knows? Perhaps that's how it was."

"With my father?" Rock pressed on doggedly when it seemed as if Phoebe was trying to avoid the subject. Phoebe quietly lowered her eyes to the ground.

"No. It happened much longer ago than that," she replied and said nothing more, as if to imply the rest was her personal secret.

And so, Rock couldn't find out more about her father as she had wanted to.

♕ ♕ ♕

FLORIA Clothes Shop was the epitome of peacefulness during the day, so much so that the prior night's commotion felt like a tall tale. Barely any customers dropped by, giving leeway for Rock and Phoebe to enjoy their lunches at a leisurely pace.

"Blimey, the day is dragging on with nothing to do," Phoebe remarked between bites.

"Days like this are nice every once and a while with how busy things have been lately."

"Business owners shouldn't say such ambitionless things."

"Only occasionally. I'd be in trouble if it was this way every day."

They cracked jokes to overcome the sunny early afternoon that threatened to lull them to sleep.

Once evening rolled around, Rock performed routine maintenance on her work tools behind the counter while Phoebe arranged the clothes on display.

The bell over the door jangled.

"Welcome!" Rock lifted her face from her work and froze when she saw her customer's face.

Peace and tranquility didn't last long. Through the door entered a handsome young man with burnt sienna hair swept to the side over his golden eyes—it was Ebel.

"Hi there, Rock. How are you doing this fine evening?"

Like a coward, Rock averted her eyes from his generous first-rate smile. "Wh-What brings you here, Your Excellency?"

"Your invitation. You told me to come for new measurements," Ebel explained with a joyous lilt. "And have you already forgotten my request from last night? I wish you would call me by name."

"D-Didn't that just apply to yesterday...?"

"I humbly request you call me by name from now on. I don't want any kind of walls to form between us," his rich bass voice asserted.

Embarrassed, Rock found herself looking down at her twiddling thumbs. She never thought he would show up less than a day later. She needed time to get over the excitement from yesterday. What all those feelings culminated in was her complete and utter inability to look him directly in the face.

"Your Excellency must not have much work to do since you come here every day," Phoebe remarked with a thorny tone. "Are you one of those nobles disposed to excessive idleness? From what I know, the late Count Mateus was a terribly busy man."

"You knew my father?" Ebel calmly asked, not letting her goad him.

"He was a famous man. Rumors abound about him."

"I'm curious in what ways his name was renown." Ebel let Phoebe's provocation roll right off him and faced Rock behind the counter. "Now then, Rock, I would like you to tailor the clothing per the order I put in last night."

"A-All right." Rock consented after finally slowing her breathing and getting her racing heart in check. She hung the measuring tape around her neck and stepped out from the counter, only to stop when she noticed Phoebe closely watching her.

She needed to send Phoebe home before taking measurements. Ebel required two different body measurements, one of which would end poorly if someone else witnessed it. Being alone with him weighed a tad—no, it weighed EXTREMELY heavy on her mind, but the situation required it.

"Phoebe, I'll handle the—"

"I'll take his measurements, Rock." Phoebe slid the measuring tape off Rock's neck before she could finish.

"Phoebe?"

"His Excellency seems like the handsy type. Don't you think I'm more suited to this job?"

Evidently, Phoebe was offering to help for Rock's benefit. She had experience assisting another tailor in the past, so even if tailoring wasn't in her skillset, she knew her way around a cloth measuring tape.

But her kind offer was more trouble than help this time around.

"Thanks for the offer, but I want Rock to do it," Ebel responded with a smile that didn't leave room for objection. "I returned to this shop because I fell in love with his skills."

"Rock's skills aren't the only thing you fell in love with."

"Obviously. That's even more reason for me to want Rock to do it, no?" Ebel nonchalantly sent a flirtatious sidelong glance Rock's way.

"Very well…," Rock consented, restless. "Phoebe, I'll be okay. You can go home."

"Not happening." Phoebe bristled. "Rock, speak what's on your mind. Don't you feel uncomfortable being alone with him?"

"Huh? Uh, um, er, well…" She wanted to deny it, but as the events of last night crossed her mind, the words died on her tongue.

"I'm not leaving, then. I'll stay here and look after you while you take his measurements," Phoebe declared without hesitation upon seeing Rock's reaction.

Ebel smiled dryly. "It appears your assistant doesn't trust me."

"I-I'm sorry. Give me time to properly explain it to her." Panicking, Rock tried to badger her sluggish brain into coming up with a way to persuade Phoebe.

Ebel peered into Rock's spinning eyes as if to stop her from burning out the gears in her mind. "How about I suggest a plan we can all agree to?"

His face is close! His handsome face spread into a suggestive smile right in front of her eyes.

"I'm sorry, but this fitting room is a bit too cramped. If your assistant is going to join us, let's change locations."

"Change locations? What do you have in mind, Ebel?" Rock asked as she struggled with where to look.

The count smoothly replied, "I would like to invite you both to my manor."

Phoebe audibly gasped at his unexpected suggestion. Rock, too, was so taken by surprise that it took a significant amount of time before she could speak again. "Your manor, Ebel? Wouldn't that be in the aristocrat district?"

"Indeed. You can take your time measuring me there without feeling constrained." Ebel's golden eyes were riveted on only Rock. "How about it, Rock? I'd be ecstatic if you accepted my invitation."

👑 👑 👑

SEVERAL days later, Rock and Phoebe boarded a carriage just outside the slums first thing in the morning.

Of all possible conveyances, the carriage Ebel sent to pick them up was the latest luxury berline, fully equipped with steel spring suspension and drawn by two gorgeous white Clydesdales. The young coachman didn't make a single disgruntled face despite waiting outside the gate that led into the slums. He even opened the carriage door for them.

"I have come to escort you to the manor today. Please get in, Master Rock, Mistress Phoebe."

The coachman with finely groomed hazel hair was courteous on all levels. He shut the door only after confirming that Rock and Phoebe were safely seated on the cushion, and then he opened the window from the coachman's seat to politely inform them that the carriage was about to depart.

"If you are all set, we shall be departing now. His Excellency is eagerly awaiting your arrival." The coachman's respect and affection for his employer could be gleaned from the joy coloring his tone.

"…Did you hear that? He called me Master Rock," Rock muttered restlessly to Phoebe once the carriage rolled forward.

The carriage rode smoothly, and the plush velvet seats comfortably embraced them with their softness. The steel spring suspension system reduced the shaking to barely noticeable. Rock gazed out at the cityscape through the high-quality, clear glass windows separating her from the outside.

"I've only ever ridden a wagon. This is incredible!" The extravagant luxury carriage overwhelmed Rock just for the first few minutes. Excitement surged through her, and before long, she was excitedly taking everything in with a twinkle in her eye. "Phoebe, look! It's the castle! I didn't know you can see it from this far away!"

She saw the emperor's castle looming in the distance. The white stone building that towered so high it seemed to pierce the heavens was too far away from the outskirts of the imperial capital to be visible from the slums.

The imperial capital was erected in a circle around the emperor's castle, and the aristocrat district where Ebel's manor was located was constructed just outside the castle grounds. In other words, the higher the noble's status and value, the closer they were allowed to live near the emperor.

"I never dreamed I'd someday set foot in the aristocrat district," she mused.

Phoebe raised a cynical eyebrow at the overly excited Rock from the seat across from her. "You are a child through and through." She coquettishly crossed her legs and admonished, "Don't lose your head over fancy frivolities. Aren't you going there for work?"

"I know. I am," Rock agreed unenthusiastically, earning a scrutinizing look from Phoebe.

"As long as you *actually* understand."

"We're going there today to take his measurements," Rock repeated for Phoebe's benefit. "We aren't his guests."

"That's right. You will be eating out of his hand before you know it if you let yourself be distracted by the foofaraw." Phoebe was the definition of calm. In Rock's eyes, she looked dependable as she sat on the cushion like a queen surveying her domain. "Be prepared, because we are heading straight into the wolf's den."

Her addendum jolted Rock. "Wolf... You mean how all men are wolves, right?"

"You remembered. Good. Take precautions at all times, unless you want to be eaten."

Rock hadn't been able to give an immediate answer when Ebel invited her and Phoebe to his manor. His ulterior motives were as clear as day for all to see—not that he ever tried to hide them. He planned to lure Rock into his territory and win her over with increased efforts of wooing. She was fully aware that taking his measurements in the comfort of his home was nothing more than a pretext to get her there.

She was torn over the blindingly large sum of money that had been offered to her on a platter for this job order. She just wanted to quickly wrap up his measuring session and skedaddle out of there. But her intuition honed by recent experiences told her loud and clear that that was not going to happen.

What eventually helped Rock make up her mind wasn't the money.

"Responding to a hug by turning your back and running away is bordering on shameful."

Phoebe's candid advice, lingering in her ears, swept away her hesitation.

I need to sit down and have a proper talk with Ebel. He's probably still trying to court me because he thinks there's room to win me over. Rock felt she was equally responsible for the situation. She needed to clearly lay out for him that she had absolutely no interest whatsoever.

Rock didn't share her decision with Phoebe. She didn't want to cause any more problems for the person who enjoyed treating Rock as if she were Phoebe's own child. While Rock loved her like family, that became the biggest reason why she felt it wasn't right to cause further mental anguish on her behalf in someone who wasn't blood related.

Phoebe surprisingly didn't object when she told her she was going to accept the invitation, conveniently omitting her true intentions. She actually encouraged her to go and make a huge profit off it, but she never stopped advising her to tread carefully.

Before long, the berline passed through a stunning gate and reached a strikingly beautiful block.

Maturing pin oaks and red maples flush with verdant leaves lined the stone-paved street. Colorful imported potted flowers decorated key locations along the tree-shaded street, and a fountain shaped like a goddess holding a water jug sprayed tiny rainbows into the air in the center of the lawn-covered square.

"I take it this is the aristocrat district?"

"Yes, it is. The nobles' estates are located a short distance ahead," Phoebe explained as she smiled at Rock, who clung to the window and was gazing outside with fascination.

"You sound like you know your way around. Have you been here before, Phoebe?"

"A bit for my old job."

"Heh. You've done a lot of different jobs in your day, huh?"

The carriage rolled into the residential block where the estates were located, leaving Rock's suspicions behind.

Palatial residences designed with architectural excellence stood on breathtaking sprawling grounds, and a number of the meticulously landscaped gardens were visible from the carriage windows. Flowering shrubs that essentially screened some of the grounds from street traffic decorated the wide borders paralleling the wrought-iron fences.

Rock tried to burn into her memory the splendorous scenery she'd likely never see again, but two eyes weren't nearly enough to capture every gorgeous garden that whisked by.

The berline carriage eventually arrived at one of the sculpted iron gates providing an elegant and theatrical entry to the grand manor beyond. It rode through the gates and passed the stunning front garden, which contained purplish-red plume thistle, bright-blue dyer's alkanet, and white roses blooming in their full glory, before stopping right beside another luxury carriage. The coachman came around and opened the door.

"Wow...," Rock breathlessly exclaimed upon stepping out of the carriage.

Nestled beyond the vast garden was a stately three-story limestone mansion. Bay windows adorned with traditional decorative ornamentations elaborately lined the third floor, a generous balcony with ivy crawling up it wrapped around the second floor, and central loggias welcomed visitors on the first floor. Sunlight pouring down from the sun at its zenith directly above the mansion made the outer limestone walls appear as white as snow.

The sculpted entryway made use of six arched wrought-iron doors, all of which were presently wide open, and a white-haired man dressed in livery stood in waiting before them.

He bowed in welcome to Rock and Phoebe. "Welcome, Master Rock." He seemed to have been informed of what they looked like in advance. Greeting Rock first after seeing her face, he then shifted his eyes to Phoebe at her side. "Welcome as well, Mistress Phoebe. Thank you for taking the long journey to grace us with your presence."

"Th-Thank you very much for honoring us with your invitation." Rock fumbled over her words, earning a good-natured smile from the man's deeply wrinkled face.

"His Excellency informed me of your visit. I am the head butler at this estate. You may call me Ludovicus." Though slightly too old to be called a quadragenarian, Ludovicus wasn't quite a septuagenarian either. He showed Rock and Phoebe inside with the utmost hospitality, then calmly informed them, "I apologize for having to ask this of you when we invited you over, but His Excellency is currently preoccupied with an unexpected guest. I am under orders to have you wait for him in the reception room, so please follow me this way."

Another carriage had indeed been parked in front of the mansion instead of in the carriage house. Rock didn't get a good look at it, but it likely belonged to Ebel's unexpected guest.

Ludovicus led Rock and Phoebe past the grand staircase to the first-floor reception room. "Please wait briefly while the maid fetches you tea," he said in parting, leaving the room without them.

The reception room where he left his two guests was decorated with the highest quality furnishings and fixtures money alone couldn't buy. The magnificent crystal chandelier hanging from a stylized gold-leaf sunburst on the ceiling was too dazzling for the eyes, and its light played off the heavily engraved silverware housed within the curved silver-mounted ebony glass display cabinet. Rock and Phoebe sat on an intricately carved leather-upholstered sofa that felt like sitting on clouds, with a round polished marble slab table situated directly in front of them. On top of the table, unblemished white roses from the garden adorned a porcelain vase hand-painted with flowers and birds.

Not used to such extravagance, Rock's eyes were beginning to hurt from taking in her surroundings.

"I'm shocked they left us alone in here... Do you think they trust us?"

"Isn't it more that they know we can't escape from here?" In direct contrast to Rock naturally dropping her voice to a whisper, Phoebe was just as loud and unreserved as usual. She rose from the sofa and walked over to the window-sized portrait on the wall. "This is the previous Count Mateus."

Rock left her spot on the sofa and approached the painting.

Two people were drawn on the impasto texturized canvas that smelled of linseed oil. One appeared to be a man in the meridian of life, sitting on a gilded chair in the finest morning dress, a quiet smile on his lips. Standing beside his chair was a boy no more than fifteen, and from his burnt sienna hair and handsome face, Rock assumed he was Ebel.

Which would make the seated man the late Count Mateus.

"It's a fabulous portrait. It's scary how much it looks just like the man." Phoebe let out a deep sigh.

Meanwhile, Rock was unconsciously tilting her head to the side, her full attention captured by the oil painting.

The boy in the portrait unquestionably looked like Ebel, but something about him was different—and it wasn't just his age. Something else was at play. After studying the details for a few long minutes, the words slipped right off her tongue.

"The eye color...isn't the same as His Excellency's."

The boy's eyes were the tender green of fresh verdure in early spring. Ebel's eyes were like golden orbs plucked from the sun. His eyes were the only thing that stayed the same between his human and magical werewolf form.

"Oh, you're right." Phoebe noticed it, too, and voiced her confusion. "But that's strange. Ebel Mateus is Count Mateus's only child. This boy has to be His Excellency."

Rock wouldn't have doubted it, either, if not for his eye color. The boy undeniably shared features with the Ebel she knew today. From his chiseled chin to his kindly smiling lips, almond-shaped eyes, finely shaped eyebrows, and handsome hairline, the boy was a picture of Ebel's youth.

"Maybe the painter mistook his eye color?" Rock ventured.

"Even if he did, it's weird to leave a public room meant for receiving guests decorated with an incorrect portrait."

Both Phoebe and Rock were perplexed, but making assumptions wouldn't lead them to an answer.

Not fully satisfied with their conclusions, they returned the sofa.

"Forgive me for making you wait!"

The reception room door opened with the sound of a woman's melodious voice. In stepped a woman a little younger than Rock with wavy blond hair tied in pigtails. She wore a plain black twill dress with a crisp white apron pinned to her bodice and a neat white cap of the same material on her head. By the look of it, she was the maid Ludovicus had said would be coming with their tea.

"It's a pleasure to meet you. I am His Excellency's maid, Johanna." Johanna knelt at Rock's feet where she sat on the sofa and beamed up at her with a radiant smile. "I have been longing to lay my eyes upon you, Master Rock!"

"Y-You have? Th-Thank you...?" Rock played along, not quite sure where that reaction had come from. Johanna looked up at her with stars in her eyes.

"From what His Excellency tells me, you are his destined partner in life! Your romance will surely be filled with obstacles, but I shall be supporting your noble love with all my heart!"

"Wh-Whaaaaaaat?!" Rock was thrown off guard by this sudden declaration.

How exactly did Ebel speak of her to others? If the maid's choice of words was anything to go by, he'd already announced they were a couple.

As if she had intuited Rock's discomfiture, an I-know-how-it-is look crossed Johanna's pretty face. "You needn't speak of it! I am sure it isn't easy to talk about. I just wanted you to know that I am your ally and that I wish to be a pillar of support for your love from the shadows, no matter what anyone else has to say about it!"

Did she misunderstand their relationship? Or did Ebel, accidentally or intentionally, tell a story different from the truth?

Either way, Rock needed to set things straight with the maid.

"Pardon me. Nothing is between His Excellency and I—"

"Like I said, you needn't explain yourself. I won't be so impolite as to ask for the nitty-gritty details," Johanna interrupted, shaking her head. "Just a little...if the opportunity for you to speak of it presents itself, I would love to hear just a little...a tiny bit about your relationship!" Forgetting to pour the tea, she dreamily breathed, with a euphoric look,

"Oh my heavens… You are the ideal lover I always pictured for His Excellency, Master Rock…!"

"…What's going on here?" Rock whispered to Phoebe on the sofa, having given up on explaining.

Phoebe shrugged, as if throwing in the towel before even trying. "I haven't the faintest idea, but I know exactly how His Excellency has been talking about you now."

Rock didn't know "exactly how" Ebel spoke of her, but she was starting to get a pretty good idea of it herself. It turned out she really did need to have a firm talk with him after all.

Thoroughly satisfied after her moment of excitement, Johanna finally poured their tea. "His Excellency said to wait on you hand and foot as two of his most important guests."

As if to prove the count's hospitality, the deeply aromatic, unique scent of the tea leaves smelled better than anything that had graced Rock's nose before. The tea was so excellent she was overwhelmed by the rich depths of flavor from her first sip.

"Phoebe, this is incredibly delicious," Rock whispered offhandedly. Phoebe shot her an exasperated glance.

"You're drinking it like normal."

"Should I not?"

"…It's not a big deal."

On second look, Phoebe hadn't touched her tea or cookies. Rock found that strange, but Phoebe spoke to Johanna as if to escape any probing into the matter.

"His Excellency isn't coming yet?"

"I am very sorry. He has an unexpected guest taking up his time, and I cannot say how long he will be away for," Johanna answered, sounding at her wit's end. "But His Excellency is a man who keeps his word. I believe he will send his guest packing as soon as possible. Please enjoy the tea cookies in the meantime."

Johanna offered her the freshly baked treats, so Rock reached for them without reservation, but Phoebe still didn't touch anything served to her.

The way Johanna described it, their "unexpected guest" was more of an uninvited and unwelcome guest. *Just what kind of person can barge into a count's home uninvited?* Rock wondered.

Her thoughts were interrupted by the sound of quickly approaching, stomping footsteps. Some man's voice boomed outside the closed reception room door.

"All right, which reception room is he in? I'll go home once I get a look at the chap."

"I'll introduce you formally if things go that direction. But not today."

The second voice trying to stop the first belonged to Ebel. Rock didn't recognize the first, but she saw Johanna stiffen beside her.

It didn't take long before the reception room door was thrown open without so much as a knock.

"Is this the one? ...Yeah, this is it." The young man who barged into the room sneered confidently when he spotted Rock perched on the sofa. "This is your urchin? He's more fragile than I expected."

Icy contempt filled the emerald eyes looking both literally and figuratively down on Rock. Unforgiving sternness exuded from his hard facial features, not a single raven-black strand was out of place in his slicked-back hair, and his arrogant pose left no room for backtalk. Rock's first impression of him, informed by the man's noticeably high-handed and haughty aura, was not good.

"I told you no. Go home for today." Entering the room after the man, Ebel moved between him and Rock, blocking his view. But the man shoved Ebel's shoulder aside and rudely stared at her.

"I was wondering what kind of bloke you'd fall for, and this is it? You're beyond help, mate."

"I never asked for your help, Guido." Ebel sidestepped him with an annoyed sigh and glanced anxiously over his shoulder at Rock.

Rock was offended by Guido's crass remarks, but she was discerning enough not to let anything show on her face around a nobleman. She silently communicated with Ebel through her eyes.

Picking up on her feelings, he took charge of the conversation. "You've finished your business here. I'll ask you to go home now."

"You aren't going to introduce us, Ebel?"

"I only just told you I would if things go in that direction."

"You shouldn't treat your childhood friend so callously." Guido gave a smile that didn't quite reach his eyes, then drew Rock into the conversation. "You there. What do they call you?"

Unable to ignore a nobleman's request, Rock unwillingly answered him just as Ebel and Phoebe turned to look at her at the same time. "My name is Rock Floria."

"Your name's the only thing that's manly about you. You're the kind of man that gets passed around when there aren't any women." Guido ridiculed her after hearing her name, finally pushing Ebel over the edge of his patience.

"Guido! Take back your insult!"

"Fine, fine. That was rude of me, Rock."

"...Don't trouble yourself to apologize to me." Rock coolly shook her head in response to his empty apology.

"Johanna, Guido is going home. Inform his coachman to prepare his ride," Ebel ordered, unable to put up with Guido's antics any further.

"At once, Your Excellency!" Johanna energetically replied and flew out of the reception room as if she'd been waiting for that order.

Once the maid departed, Ebel grabbed Guido's shoulder and tried to drive him from the room. "Off with you. You'll put our friendship at risk if you utter another reckless remark."

"Come to my house next time, Ebel," Guido coaxed, unaffected by Ebel's threats. "My younger sister is longing to see you."

"Sorry, but that's not happening."

"She was once your fiancée. It wouldn't hurt for you to show her a little love and affection—"

Ebel succeeded in propelling Guido out of the room at that point. He pushed him into the corridor, then deeply inhaled with his back against the door he'd forcibly slammed shut. Then he ran his hands through his disheveled hair to put the loose strands back in place.

"I'm sorry about all that, Rock. I put you in an uncomfortable spot."

"It's not the first time. I'm fine."

The whole ordeal was definitely unpleasant, but people mocked her all the time for not being manly enough. She knew when she should swallow her pride and let it slide off her.

Something else was bothering her more than that, but—

"Was that possibly Guido Linus just now?" Phoebe asked, joining the conversation.

Ebel's golden eyes rounded. "You know him? His name is indeed Guido Linus."

"Isn't he Duke Linus's son? The Linuses are a distinguished family of dukes. Who doesn't know of them?"

Rock knew of the family name too. But she couldn't help being impressed with Phoebe for knowing the duke's son by name. "You're amazing, Phoebe. You know everything."

"It's a coincidence. I just happened to remember the name." Phoebe shrugged, then suddenly directed a diabolical grin at Ebel. "Oh, and if memory serves me well, the Linus daughter and Mateus son were once engaged to be wed. I didn't know the engagement had been annulled, though."

"Your knowledge knows no bounds, Phoebe," Ebel responded, sounding more suspicious than impressed. "The engagement was real, but we broke it off over eight years ago. Both Michaela—Guido's younger sister—and I are perfectly happy with the arrangement now. He's the only one who won't move on." During this attempt at clearing his name, he glanced at and away from Rock. "So please don't let it bother you. I no longer have a fiancée."

"Is that so? It doesn't bother me either," she remarked, a tad baffled by the way he put her on the spot.

"Not even a little?"

"Yes, not in the least," she answered honestly.

Disappointment flashed across his features. "…I see. I was hoping you would be just a little bothered."

Something else troubled Rock more than this talk of Ebel being engaged. The teenage boy with burnt sienna hair portrayed in the oil painting shared distinct similarities with Ebel, especially when she compared the real man with the portrait. There was no question about it—the portrait captured Ebel as a teenager.

Eight years ago, he broke off his engagement to a duke's daughter, and he used to have verdure green eyes as a boy. Were these two seemingly unrelated matters connected somehow?

Now that their conversation about Guido had run its course, Ebel proposed they leave the reception room for his private study. "We had a measuring appointment, yes? My study is spacious, and few things can interrupt us there."

Rock and Phoebe left the reception room and followed Ebel through the winding corridors.

From its enormous exterior, Rock assumed the Mateus mansion would be large, but the interior boasted of sprawling spaces she couldn't even imagine. The first floor alone could fit more than ten of her apartments with room to spare, and it took ample time to navigate the complex passageways. They ascended the crimson carpeted grand staircase and walked until they arrived at mahogany double-leaf doors down one of the second-floor corridors.

"This is my study." As he opened the doors, Ebel addressed both Rock and Phoebe: "Please come in, you two."

"Both of us?" Only Rock raised her voice in surprise. Phoebe's presence would just make taking his measurements difficult—they couldn't let her see him turn into a werewolf.

So why did he openly invite Phoebe into the study despite that?

"I'll be joining you for this session. It'll be too late to do anything once something happens to you." Phoebe's grave tone made it sound as if Rock's very life was in danger.

"I-I'll be fine. You don't need to worry about me that much." Rock quickly tried to diffuse the situation, turning to Ebel for confirmation. "Right, Ebel? You prefer me to take your measurements alone, correct?"

"Absolutely—if that is what you want." For some reason, Ebel chose to frame his answer in a way that made it seem as though this was Rock's preference, not his.

Isn't he the one who will be in trouble if Phoebe sticks around? Rock was trying to figure him out when Phoebe furrowed her pretty brow and sought confirmation.

"Are you sure, Rock? Don't you feel it's dangerous to be alone with him?"

"N-No, well, yes...I do, but I thought it might be okay?" Rock found herself stuck, trying to justify the situation to Phoebe without Ebel's assistance. "Why don't you wait outside the room, Phoebe? Isn't it boring to quietly keep watch over me while I take his measurements?"

"Well, I can easily run to your assistance from out here, too, if that's what you want." Phoebe reluctantly backed down, throwing a loose curl over her shoulder. She shot a sharp look Ebel's way and made double sure this was what Rock wanted. "But are you positive it's all right to put this much trust in the count? He's already got a track record with you."

"He does, but..." Stuck for words, Rock looked to Ebel for help.

He joyfully came to her rescue. "Phoebe, Rock has said it himself that he wishes to spend time alone with me. Won't you adhere to his wishes?"

No one said they wanted to spend time alone with him. She didn't say that, but they wouldn't get anywhere if she pointed it out, so she silently nodded.

"...Since when did you get so hunky-dory with each other?" Phoebe didn't hide her suspicion, but she relented.

"In that case, come this way, Rock."

Ebel entered his study first, with Rock about to follow him, when Phoebe grabbed her arm and whispered, "I need to ask you this to be sure: are you actually into him?"

"ME?! Wh-Why would you think that?"

"You wanting to be alone with him makes me interpret it that way. Duh."

"...It's not how it sounds. This is all for work! FOR WORK!"

It finally dawned on Rock what Ebel was after. He'd deliberately set the stage to force her into saying she wanted to be alone with him!

The count's study enjoyed a spacious layout on par with the downstairs reception room, if not slightly bigger. Stunning geometric patterns and graceful scrolls combining shades of soft gold, ivory, and aqua green were hand embroidered into the wool area rug. The doors were painted and surmounted by panels with bas-reliefs in colored stucco; the fireplace had a painted wooden frame and, on top of it, a stucco work with rosettes and lozenges that framed antique mirrors; and the walls were decorated with elaborate embossed carvings that painted an image that continued up to the tall ceiling.

The doors closed behind Rock as she entered the room, her eyes taking everything in until they landed on Ebel leaning with his back against the magnificent rosewood desk, a suggestive smile on his lips. "We're alone at last, Rock."

She let out an exasperated sigh. "Phoebe can hear you. She has good ears."

"Not as good as mine, I'm sure. Let her overhear. It does us no harm."

"...I came to take your measurements. That's all."

Ebel had succeeded in making her dance to his tune. Frustrated that she fell for his trap, she pulled out the measuring tape with her guard up.

Ebel closed the space between them with two strides and gently grabbed the hand not holding the measuring tape. Big, strong hands with visible veins, clearly not those of a werewolf, lifted up Rock's dainty hand and playfully flipped it over. He studied the details of her palm with the zeal of an antique dealer assessing a precious curio.

"Wh-What is it?" Rock asked, flustered.

Ebel shook his head and gave a mysterious smile. "I was simply admiring your hand. So this is what a tailor's hand looks like."

"I can't relax with you staring that much."

Ebel's hand felt like a warm summer day, and that warmth felt as if it was going to slowly permeate through her body if he continued to touch her. His appraising gaze sent shockwaves of fear through her that he would see through to her true identity.

Rock tried to shake off his hand, but he thwarted her attempts with a debonair smile. He tightened his hold on her hand just enough to prevent her from getting free, but not enough to cause any pain. The measuring tape floundered, and still her hand couldn't break away.

"Ebel…you are disquieting me."

"You're cute when you're disquieted," he merrily replied, as if that'd been his goal. He suddenly brought her hand up and planted his lips on her slender wrist.

"Ah," Rock squeaked, responding to the sensation of unfamiliar, soft lips brushing along her skin.

He didn't miss the instant reddening of her cheeks. "You're a mystery to me," he said, his voice rumbling in the back of his throat. "I couldn't ask for a better, more experienced tailor, and yet you surprise me with your innocent inexperience at my touch."

"I already told you I have no experience with these things…!"

"So you did. I adore that part of you as well." Ebel encompassed her hand in both of his and sweetly whispered, "Not because I want you as a substitute for something else. I love you for who you are, Rock."

Rock gasped.

"Now then, I hate to make you let go, but we should get started soon. Otherwise you will be late getting home," he said slyly.

"…You're the one who wouldn't let go of me, Ebel!"

Just how did Phoebe interpret Rock's shout echoing into the corridor?

There was no way to tell from the stationary double-leaf doors.

"All right, enough dawdling. I'm going to start measuring you," Rock informed Ebel once she collected herself. She glanced at the curvaceous study chair with dark finishes and embellishments. "Do you mind sitting in that chair, Ebel?"

"Your wish is my command." Ebel complied on the spot. He went out of his way to carry the heavy chair from behind the desk to in front of Rock, then gracefully sat down on it with a pleased smile. "Does this work, Rock?"

"Yes. I am going to measure your head and around your neck." Rock stepped up to him with the measuring tape in hand as his golden eyes followed her every move. She couldn't relax with him studying her so intently. "Don't move your head."

"I can't help but move it—I want to watch you." Ebel blew off her instructions and took it even further by pointing to his lap and suggesting, "How about you sit on my lap to get a better measuring angle?"

"I don't foresee that ending well, so no." He exasperated Rock with his ceaseless advances.

"That's just your imagination. I promise you something wonderful will happen."

"I highly doubt that," she sighed, moving around to stand behind him so she could measure the back of his head.

She wrapped the cloth measuring tape around his head covered in burnt sienna hair. His hair was stiff and glossy, reminding her of the werewolf fur it shouldn't hold any similarities to.

"The plan was for you to make a cloak with a cowl, right?" Ebel asked, feeling ticklish from her touching his hair.

"Yes. You tend to be blithe and careless, so you should conceal your face when you walk around the slums."

Rock wrote down his head size in her notebook, then removed the tape measure from him. She touched his neck next. The nape of his neck peeking out from his shirt collar was smooth and barely touched by the sun. When she placed the measuring tape underneath his prominent Adam's apple, Ebel moved his head again to look back at her.

"I'm weak when it comes to the neck. Please be gentle with me, Rock."

"Thank you for letting me know. I promise it won't hurt."

She wrapped the measuring tape around his neck front to the back and held it in place with her fingers. The hair falling on the nape of his neck hid the numbers, so she gently brushed the soft strands away with her free hand. The feel of her fingers grazing his neck drew a small exhale from him.

"Mn…"

"Does it hurt? Should I loosen the tape some?"

"No, it just tickles."

"I'm sorry. I will be done shortly." Rock quickly added up the numbers and hastily took them down before removing the measuring tape.

Ebel looked over his shoulder at her once more. "I can't get enough of you taking my measurements. It might become a habit."

The light gleaming in his golden eyes swayed like scorching flames. Rock was momentarily frozen by those eyes that shone in a different color from the portrait. His eyes said more with one look than a thousand words could, which was why she found his gaze more difficult to deal with than his words.

"Not many customers say they enjoy having their measurements taken. You have peculiar tastes." She shrugged, trying to dodge his implications.

He smiled wickedly and took her to task for glossing over the subject. "They just don't voice their opinions. I highly doubt anyone could make it through such a sensual moment without losing their presence of mind." When she didn't answer him, he regretfully went on. "I asked you once before, but do you have any interest in working exclusively for me?"

"You did offer me the same position before, which I refused."

"I can't stand the thought of you touching anyone else this way. I want to form an exclusive contract with you," Ebel said beseechingly, catching hold of the wrist Rock held the measuring tape with.

His hand, so quick to display his possessiveness, held her tight and was hot enough to melt her on the spot. The heat emanating from his palm added to Rock's dismay, and in vain she quickly tried to shake it off.

At the end of her rope, she pleaded with him instead. "P-Please stop."

But seeing her troubled expression only made him increase his grip. "It makes me want to let go of you even less when you beg like that."

"Can you be any more of a nuisance?!"

"You are making me one. You drive me crazy and pretend not to realize it." Ebel's lips were curved into a smile that didn't reach his eyes.

He was a pain to deal with once he got like this. He toyed with Rock, using any means at his disposal. She could seek help from Phoebe in the corridor, but calling her now would impede taking the rest of his measurements. Rock swung her eyes to the unmoving door and shook her head, deciding it was best to save that option for last. She needed to find a way to continue giving him the slip.

His golden eyes directed an unwavering gaze at her. A light bulb went off in her head as she looked down into those eyes.

"I saw the portrait in the reception room," Rock blurted under his fiery gaze, her wrist still in his hand.

Ebel's eyebrows shot up. "What is this about, Rock?"

"According to Phoebe, that's a painting of you and your father, Ebel."

"Indeed, that is a painting of Father and me." Realizing she was trying to redirect the conversation dissatisfied him. But she spotted a hint of a completely different emotion flicker in that expression. Almost as if he was deeply intrigued—as if he was even enjoying their game of cat and mouse.

Rock wasn't enjoying herself in the least, but she carefully proceeded anyway. "Then why do you have different colored eyes in that portrait?"

She couldn't help being curious. The supernatural werewolf form looked nothing like the handsome young man. Only the eyes didn't change color. She couldn't get it out of her mind, the way these golden eyes differed from the boy in the portrait.

"I would love to ask you why that interests you so much," Ebel started, smiling from the heart this time. "You've already guessed it, haven't you? My eye color is the wolf's."

"Then—"

"That's right. Eight years ago, when I was sixteen, I became a werewolf." Under normal circumstances, that should've been a horrifying revelation. But his tone remained lighthearted, with even a hint of pride. "It's been publicly explained away as the aftereffects of an illness. I was afflicted by an infectious disease when I was sixteen. My eyes changed color after being anguished by a high fever for days on end. Or so the story goes."

That story was nothing more than a lie of convenience. Rock swallowed the lump in her throat as Ebel continued his tale.

"But the truth is different. What anguished me wasn't a disease, but a curse."

"Did you just say...a curse?"

"I did. One day, my antique collector father unleashed the power of a cursed statue and turned me into a werewolf." Ebel released Rock's wrist. Freed from the warmth that could melt the thickest ice, Rock's body instantly became chilled. He saw through to that and let the seriousness show on his face. "Father blamed himself until the day he died.

"I can understand why. I can't believe it's a curse..."

"Here's the thing, Rock. I don't bear a grudge against Father. I'm actually grateful to him."

His words weren't an empty sentiment for show—his deep trust and love for his father bled through his tone and expression. Of course, Rock had a hard time believing that was all he felt about being cursed.

"That's why I want to use this werewolf power to protect the things Father loved." Ebel gazed searchingly into Rock's eyes. "And...those I care for too."

Ultimately, the golden eyes that ardently watched her were the mark of a cursed man. It was a wonder how he showed no signs of being anguished by that fact. Even on closer inspection, not a single shadow darkened his expression.

"Isn't it...painful for you?" Rock couldn't resist asking.

Ebel's throat rumbled with laughter. "You're kind. Are you concerned for me?"

"No, I'm not— Yes, I am."

His story was so outlandish Rock couldn't take it all in at once. A curse that turned people into werewolves, the late Count Mateus's costly mistake, Ebel's loss—she needed time to understand Ebel and how he could come to grips with everything.

The one thing she knew for sure was that Ebel had overcome it all on his own and that he didn't need her to worry after him.

"It doesn't pain me. I've long since grown used to it," Ebel answered glibly, but Rock wasn't going to let him off the hook that easy.

"But if the curse happened eight years ago, was it the reason why you broke off your engagement?" The two unrelated matters were connected after all.

Ebel confirmed it with a slow smile. "Yes. Michaela was understanding when I told her why." After a slight pause, he sadly added, "You saw Guido's reaction for yourself. He didn't used to be that obstinate in the past…" His expression fell when he spoke of the duke's son, but he quickly replaced his frown with a practiced smile. "I'm fine. Nothing is tormenting or hurting me."

"Is that so…?" It took all Rock had to give that tepid response.

She felt that she should've said more, but words escaped her. Extremely mixed emotions whirled through her. She understood neither the reason nor the nature behind those complex feelings.

"Also, you can rest easy. This curse isn't transferable." Ebel was casual about the whole thing from beginning to end. "We can touch as much as we want without fear of you turning into a werewolf as well. So it's all right if I touch you, right?"

"Of course it's not all right!" Ebel's familiar banter helped Rock recover from the shock.

The Mateus family once experienced a major tragedy that exceeded Rock's imagination. But now that the past was behind them, was Ebel's werewolf powers the only remnant of that incident? Or was there more to it?

"By the way, have you finished measuring my neck? What's next, Rock?" he redirected the conversation.

"Oh, right. I need to take measurements for the cloak's length. Would you mind standing?" Rock requested, returning to her work.

Ebel rose from his chair, reversing their positions to have him looking down into her eyes now. A mischievous expression flashed across his face as he bent down slightly and blew on her neck.

"Eep!" Rock jumped at the hot breath brushing over her skin. She shot him a killer glare and received a triumphant grin in return.

"Revenge for you changing the subject. We'll be revisiting that conversation later."

It appeared the winner of this game of chase was still in the air.

Rock shrunk back and furtively glanced over her shoulder at the study doors. Even after she screamed, they didn't burst open.

After finishing up Ebel's human measurements, it was finally time to bring the werewolf out.

"If you will, Ebel…"

"Certainly. Wait a moment." He began pulling his shirt off. Flustered, Rock whirled around until her back was to him.

"Why are you stripping right here?!"

"It's too much trouble to go into my dressing room. We're both men here. You don't mind. Do you?"

"W-We are, but still!"

Rock minded a great deal. Given her occupation, she should've been used to seeing the naked male body, but Ebel was the one person she couldn't look at directly. Even more so with the memory of being held to his bare chest still fresh in her mind.

"I have to wonder why you get embarrassed over every little thing. I'd be fine with it if it means you're conscious of me as a man."

Ebel's baritone voice accompanied by the sound of rustling clothes filled the still room. Rock wrapped her arms around herself and simply waited for him to finish getting ready.

Before long, the crunching of bone and ripping of flesh replaced the other sounds.

"I'm ready, Rock."

She turned toward the rumbling voice and found a towering furry werewolf with gleaming golden eyes standing there.

"Your transformation always astonishes me," she admitted.

The werewolf scratched the black fur–covered spot between his ears. "I'm more astonished by how calm you are. I'm amazed you've grown used to it in this short amount of time."

"I was frightened at first, but not in the least now."

Strangely enough, her fears had been replaced by a fondness for the werewolf form. From his twitching, pointed ears to his wagging, bushy tail, he was a million times cuter than the wild dogs prowling the mountains.

Rock instructed the werewolf count to crouch down, and she set about measuring his head much the same way as she did for the human count.

Someone suddenly knocked on the door.

"Rock? Are you there?" Phoebe asked from the other side.

Rock never left the room, so of course she'd be there, but that didn't matter at this point—they were in deep. Things wouldn't end pretty if Phoebe saw werewolf Ebel. Rock swallowed her response and silently looked to Ebel first.

"…What should we do? Hide?" she asked in a hushed voice.

Should she have him hide? Or make it so Phoebe couldn't come into the study? Which would be more successful?

"Let's hide," Ebel decided and swept Rock into his arms.

"Whoa…!"

"Quiet."

A furry hand covered Rock's mouth, and Ebel carried her toward the door deeper within the study. On the other side of the door, soundlessly opened by Ebel, was a dressing room. Dinner jackets, frock coats, topcoats, and hats hung inside the small room that acted as a walk-in closet. He brought her inside and noiselessly closed the door.

The tight space had no lights or windows. With all the clothing inside, it was too cramped for a hulking werewolf and another adult to fit comfortably. Ebel settled into the closet with Rock pressed right up against his chest. She struggled to breathe with his soft fur covering her like a heavy blanket.

"Ebel, I can't breathe…"

"I'm sorry. Please bear with it."

Squished painfully together, they peeked into the study through the crack in the door.

The study doors eventually opened, and in stepped Phoebe and Johanna.

"Rock? You aren't here?" Phoebe raked her eyes over every nook and cranny in the room. Rock watched her beautiful face rapidly grow grim when she realized the study was empty. "What's the meaning of this? His Excellency isn't here either!" Her voice sharpened with suspicion, and she shot a needling glare at Johanna.

The young maid smiled to smooth over the situation. "Oh! They might have changed locations!"

"Why would they do that?" Phoebe arched a skeptical eyebrow.

"Because…um, our mansion has many different rooms, including a billiards room!" Johanna's reply wasn't much of an answer. Rock was sweating bullets in the closet.

She could've just stepped out and explained the situation, if Ebel weren't a werewolf. No way could she expose the werewolf rumored to devour the townsfolk to Phoebe. Not to mention that would go against Ebel's wishes to keep his secret safe. Frustration at being trapped in the closet gnawed away at her.

Most of all, she was in the painful position of having to cling to a werewolf inside a stuffy closet. They were both remaining perfectly still, but Ebel was starting to breathe heavily.

Rock also felt weird being hugged by his werewolf form, and it was hot being surrounded by thick fur. An indescribable animal smell filled her nostrils with every breath, and she was growing dizzy. Leaning against the thick, fur-covered chest, she prayed Phoebe would leave without a fuss.

Meanwhile, Phoebe completely distrusted Johanna. "Where did you put that child?" she asked in a murderous tone, sending Johanna jumping a good few feet off the ground.

"Where? I don't know!"

"Rock disappeared in the short time I was called away. Was this your plan all along?"

Phoebe was called away? Rock latched on to that remark. *I thought she was outside the doors this whole time. She wasn't?* Now that she thought about it, Phoebe should've reacted when she'd screamed, but she hadn't.

"I swear to God I don't know!" Johanna was shaking her head so hard her pigtails were flying horizontally. "Surely Master Rock finished his work and they went for a stroll together."

"A stroooll?" Phoebe drawled, disbelief coating her every syllable.

"Yes! Um, if you like, shall I escort you to where they might be, Mistress Phoebe?" Johanna seized Phoebe's right arm with both hands and began dragging her away before she could answer. "Right this way, please!"

"Hold on! I never said I'd go!"

"But don't you have to search for His Excellency and Master Rock?" she wheedled.

"I do, but… Aah, geez. Don't pull on me, girl! I can walk with my own two feet!" Phoebe shook off Johanna's hands and irritably departed the study. She ran her eyes over the room one last time before the doors shut, but she never noticed Rock and Ebel hiding in the closet.

Once the pair's footsteps were out of earshot, Ebel and Rock took a breath at the same time.

"Looks like we got through it."

"So it seems. I feel bad about Phoebe, though…" Rock felt guilty for deceiving her.

Something else was eating away at her, too. What had happened that made Phoebe leave her station? Who had called her away?

Rock's pondering was cut short by Ebel heavily panting above her head. "Ebel, are you all right? You sound like you're having a hard time breathing."

"Yeah… I'm not in pain, but it's just one of those things…"

"You must be hot with all this thick fur."

"I'm definitely getting *hot*. I wouldn't have been able to stay in control if not for being in this predicament."

Rock was starting to get the idea they weren't talking about the same thing.

"As much as I hate to end this moment, let's leave this room," Ebel recommended before she could think too much about it. "Johanna is quick-witted, but not a very good actress."

"Let's do that," Rock agreed immediately. She pushed her arm through the space around his fur and reached for the closet door.

"Wait. We'll be taking this exit instead." Ebel stopped her and pressed the back closet wall with his rock-solid arm.

The light spilling through the closet door crack let Rock see the wall slide down with the sound of rolling chains, unveiling a pitch-black stone passage in its place. She would have to crouch down to pass through the crawl space, though whether the width was enough for two adults to squish past each other was debatable.

"Wh-What is this?" Rock's question echoed down the stone passage. It seemed to go on forever.

"A secret passage. For use at times like this," werewolf Ebel answered, his white fangs sharply glistening. "We wouldn't want to accidently bump into Phoebe like this. Let's return to the study from another location."

"From another location? Where does this lead?"

"Everywhere." Ebel gave a concise answer and stole into the passage with Rock held in his right arm. He advanced surprisingly quick through the tight confines.

He had taken Rock by such great surprise, she went along with it without a fight.

The closet door and sliver of light vanished behind her in the blink of an eye as the furry werewolf carried her deeper into the darker-than-black passage. Wind seemed to be blowing from somewhere, swaying Ebel's fur into her face and tickling her cheeks.

The wind current told her there were forking passages here and there in the dark. Did werewolves have good night vision? Ebel took all the right turns, advancing through the mansion until he finally stopped at a dead end.

"This is the spot. I'm going to dive inside once the trapdoor opens, so hold on tight."

"O-Okay." With little choice, Rock wrapped her arms tightly around the werewolf's sinewy neck.

Ebel pressed against the stone wall, and the floor beneath them snapped open. They plummeted through as if being sucked down a drain and dropped into a small bright room. He shifted Rock, who was clinging to his neck, into both arms and stuck the landing with the grace of his feline counterpart.

"We're there. Let's prepare ourselves here first," said the very face of a wolf as it peered down at her.

Rock swept her gaze over the room while still in his arms. Only a lantern with a swaying flame, a large wooden chest, and a door leading out marked the drab stone room barely large enough to fit three people.

Why was the lantern lit in a place that clearly didn't see many people?

"What is this place?"

"An evacuation room, should the worst come to pass. A network of secret passages and small rooms like this were built throughout the house to hide my werewolf form from prying eyes." After answering her question, Ebel quietly placed Rock on the floor. Tail wagging, he ambled over to the chest and flipped open the lid with his clawed hands. Stored inside was a full set of gentlemen's clothes.

"You're well prepared," she marveled.

The werewolf looked over his shoulder at her compliment, his triangular ears twitching. "Thank you. My father had it all constructed for me." Whenever he spoke of the late Count Mateus, Ebel's voice took on a gentle yet lonely tone. "Father wrestled with a guilty conscience over the curse that befell me... He did anything he possibly could in order to atone. He reconstructed this historic manor for me and only hired servants he trusted with his life."

Unknown to him, Ebel's words froze Rock to the floor. Just as he had once said to her, she sensed the similarities in their backgrounds that spanned beyond class differences.

"He built all this for you..."

"Indeed. Father may have made a grave mistake. But I don't bear a grudge against him for it. Because I received his love."

Ebel's candid declaration brought a swell of emotions surging through Rock that she didn't quite comprehend.

Not bearing a grudge against a father. Rock felt the exact same way. She didn't resent the man who had abandoned her and her mother. But she was beginning to detect something akin to envy within Ebel when he spoke of his father.

"You had a wonderful father." What Rock intended as a casual comment contained traces of sadness.

The werewolf blinked his golden glowing eyes. "What's the matter, Rock?"

"N-Nothing. Why?"

"You look deeply hurt. Did I say something that caused you pain?" He leaned over to gaze into Rock's eyes, but unlike his human form, the werewolf was too large to comfortably angle himself to be level with her face.

His awkward bent position pulled a small smile from her. "You needn't worry about me. I was just thinking of my own father."

"The one you said was a mercenary?"

"Yes. As I told you before, Father abandoned Mother and me." Rock shook her head. "Or rather, that's how it should have been, but he left me everything he had. It was more than enough money for me to open my shop."

Rock didn't know how much money a mercenary made with a single job, but the sum her father left her would take her five years of saving up every coin she made to attain. When Phoebe first told her about it, it shook Rock to her very core.

"That's why I can't bring myself to hold a grudge against him... Or more like it would be strange to have hard feelings. I understood just how much he cared after I saw how much he left for me."

The confusion she felt at the time stirred back to life within her, and she unconsciously held her hand over her face. The werewolf gently rested his paw-like hand on her back. His was clearly different from a human's, but it was warm all the same.

"But I never met my father," Rock continued, pouring out her feelings while receiving support from his warmth. "What kind of person was Father? What was he thinking as he saved up all that money for me? What did he think of Mother and me? I wanted to know those things... I still can't get over wanting to know them even now that he's gone."

But she would never have the opportunity to meet her father again. Not the man who'd already departed this world by the time Rock had arrived in the imperial capital.

"What about Phoebe? Wasn't she your father's lover?" Ebel asked kindly. "Can't you ask her about your father?"

"Phoebe doesn't like to talk about him much."

Letting her curiosity get the better of her, Rock had both directly confronted Phoebe about it and tried sounding her out on the subject. Yet every time, Phoebe clearly didn't want to speak about it.

"I think she's probably being considerate of me. So it's hard for me to ask her about it these days."

As far as Phoebe was concerned, Rock was her lover's secret child. Most people normally wouldn't want to accept the existence of such a child. Yet Phoebe was nice to Rock and always looked after her. Truth was, Rock was comfortable with their relationship the way it was and didn't want to shatter it.

"…I'm sorry for suddenly bringing this up." Rock quickly tried to put an end to the conversation so she could shove the sadness under the rug from whence it came.

The werewolf took a short breath. "Nothing for you to apologize for. You and I truly are similar."

"Yes…you might be right," Rock agreed.

Ebel scratched the area between his ears as if lost in thought. Then, suddenly striking upon an idea, he asked, "Rock, what's your father's name?"

"…Why?" Rock replied.

Fangs gleamed from Ebel's open mouth in a wolfish grin. "Like I told you before, my father loved to collect antiques. He used to hire mercenaries to scavenge through ruins for items to add to his collection."

Mercenaries. That word was enough to catch Rock up to speed. "Are you suggesting you might know of my father?"

"Obviously I can't ask my father about him, but I have an old-timer butler who has been around since then." Ebel gave a big nod. He lightly patted Rock on the back as if to set her mind at ease. "Plus, I might arrive at the pertinent information if I go through the intermediary my father used at the time. I can be of service to you if you tell me his name."

The possibility to learn more about her father—that was the most irresistible offer anyone had ever made to Rock. Ebel might be able to tell her more about the father she thought she'd never have a chance to know, about the father Phoebe refused to speak of. If there was even a chance at learning something, she wanted it more than anything.

But—

"I can't. I can't tell you." Rock took a small step to the side, indirectly rejecting Ebel's gentle hand. The werewolf's claws hovered in midair as he cocked his head in confusion.

"Why not?"

"Because…I know your feelings. Asking something of you like this would be taking advantage of you," she answered shamefully.

Put another way, relying on Ebel here might lead to a situation where she would be forced to accept his courting.

Rock wanted to avoid getting involved with him outside of work at all costs. Being rattled by his past had the unintentional effect of making her share the feelings she kept bottled up. Allowing him to do this for her posed a serious risk of his stripping off each layer of her shell until everything was laid bare.

"If you don't want to take advantage, just accept being courted by me." Golden eyes glittering in the lantern light, Ebel placed his large hand on her cheek. He lifted her chin up to face him and brought his wet nose tip to hers. Flashing his sharp fangs at the stiffening Rock, he asked, "You don't hate me, do you?"

"Wha—? Well, no, but…"

She didn't hate him. She simply had a hard time with him constantly leading her around by the nose, taking her by surprise, and sweeping her off her feet.

"Then you should just love me." His sweet, inviting whisper came from a mouth filled with sharp teeth. "All you have to do is entrust your heart and body to me and desire my love for you. That's it."

She glimpsed his wet tongue, redder than fresh blood, past his fangs. His warm breath caressed her lips. It tickled so much she wanted to laugh aloud. In a daze, Rock listened to the love proposal from the werewolf who once stood as a symbol of fear. She wasn't afraid.

Nevertheless, when he pushed her onto the floor, her slender body shivered.

Before her back touched the stone floor, his hand softly cushioned her, preventing her from feeling any pain from her soft fall.

Of course, that didn't make her happy. The werewolf's enormous body hovered over her, his broad shadow swallowing her whole. She nervously looked up at the werewolf's slowly narrowing golden eyes.

"Now then…shall we begin?"

"B-Begin what?" Rock's voice cracked.

Sensing the danger, she struggled against him, but Ebel's hands gently pinned her arms to the floor. Restrained, she couldn't writhe around without hurting herself, so she was stuck glaring up at the muzzle directly above her.

"Please release me!"

"No one can beat me physically. You, especially, can't shake me off."

Feeling as if he was shoving her weakness in her face again, Rock forgot her fear and let anger take over. "Do you also think I'm like a woman?" she snapped at him.

He appeared to be smiling a little, if a wolf could smile. A long sigh escaped his open mouth. "I don't think you are 'like a woman.'"

"Come again?"

"I have confidence in my nose." His calm voice was in direct contrast to the restless gleam in his eyes. "Since becoming a werewolf, my senses have become far more acute than a human's. My nose tells me you are a woman."

Ebel had pointed that out before too. Paralyzed with shock, Rock felt her strength drain from her pinned but struggling arms. Taking advantage of that momentary lapse in her guard, the werewolf licked her cheek. She shuddered from the rough, lukewarm tongue that was clearly not human.

"S-Stop this nonsense!" she yelled at him.

"I can't give you a gentle kiss in this form." He removed one of his hands from her wrist and slowly brought it to her cheek. The palm of his werewolf hand had tough pads like a wolf's paw, but the coarse fur covering the back of his hand and fingers tickled her. Careful not to cut her with his bladelike claws, he poked her cheek, making her increasingly more confused by the situation.

"Are you doing this because you think I'm a woman?" she accused. "I already told you before that I'm—"

"And I also told you that I don't mind whether you are a man or a woman." The werewolf hand pulled away from Rock's cheek and slowly descended. He ran his palm over her slender, round shoulders, down the weak arm he had previously pinned, and over her soft sides with little fat, and finally his clawed hand stopped at her toned waist, which he deliberately stroked to confirm the feeling and shape.

"Hyaah…" In the heat of the moment, Rock moaned, and she felt disgusted by the pathetic sound that escaped her. Pushed passed her tolerance level, she slammed her free hand into the werewolf's stone-hard chin. "Please stop this right now! I'll punch you!"

"You're too cute." Even with his chin being forced to the side, Ebel was full of composure, adding even more to Rock's agitation.

"I'm not cute. Don't treat me like a woman!"

"I won't if that is what you want. But…" The werewolf hand hadn't left her waistline yet. He ran his palm over the outline of her hips as he noted, "It's not just your smell. Your body shape is just like a woman's too."

Rock finally realized he wasn't trying to tickle her or feel her up; he was ascertaining the difference in bone structure between a man and a woman.

"Please tell me. Are you really a man?" he queried. Desire burned in his golden lantern-like eyes, but he kept his tone cool and calm as he sought the truth above all else.

Alas, she suspected words alone wouldn't get her out of this.

Rock dressed as a man to protect herself and survive in the world alone. Even Roxy Floria, a single young woman with charming looks and no family, could obtain a peaceful existence in the slums filled with riffraff by transforming herself into the delicate wisp of a young man known as tailor Rock.

When Phoebe had suggested she disguise herself that way, Rock had leaped at the idea. It didn't matter that the crazy suggestion had come from her father's "lover," who she barely knew at that point. The thought excited her.

The reason was extremely simple: Rock had always wanted to become a man to take the place of her absent father and protect her fragile mother.

The mother she should've protected was no longer with her, but she was happy that her secret desire was granted. But she never imagined someone would show up in her life and try to expose her.

"Why are you...trying so hard to dig into my life?" she asked the werewolf above her, heaving a heavy sigh.

Depending on his answer, she might have to divulge the truth. As it was, dressing as a man did nothing to keep him at bay. It wasn't as if telling him the truth would stop his advances either.

"That's a silly question." His eyes glittered. "People aren't satisfied unless they monopolize everything about the person they have fallen for. I want to know everything about you."

Is that how it worked? That state of mind was foreign to her.

"I'm dying to lay bare the secrets you harbor and the heart you keep locked away." His hand returned to stroke her cheek. He brushed so gently along her jawline that thoughts of coarse fur and unbending claws didn't enter her mind. "Won't you tell me about you, Rock?" Ebel's whispers were sweet, and it was that honeyed tone that made up her mind.

If it was love that made him want to know more about her and expose her secrets—Rock couldn't answer him.

So she sliced into him with her implacable glare. "I am a man, Ebel."

The werewolf gasped, something impossible for wolves, and inquired, "Does that mean you…don't want to answer me?"

"I am telling you that I am a man. That is my answer."

Only Phoebe and I need to know my secrets. I don't plan to confide in anyone else, Rock thought, staunchly holding on to that belief.

"You won't tell me?" Ebel's voice sank with disappointment. Still he refused to give up and pushed again: "Please. I swear I won't tell a soul."

"You heard my answer. I have no secrets to tell."

"I can't help wondering. You are so very much like a woman—"

His entreaty finally managed to enrage Rock. "I am a man! I'll come to hate you if you continue prying into me!"

The werewolf's ginormous body trembled as if struck by lightning. "You will…hate me?" His pointed ears fell flat against his head, his broad shoulders drooped, and his tail tucked under him as he asked that lonely question.

He naturally loosened his grip on Rock's arm. Taking advantage of the freedom, she sat up and thrust her finger at his nose. "I will!" she admonished. "Neither a man nor a woman would be happy to have someone making uninvited inquiries into their life!"

"Is that so? When you put it that way, I have to agree…"

"Also, people who suddenly push down others are the worst! Don't do that unless you want to be hated!"

"…I'm sorry."

Was His Excellency the Count unused to being scolded? He became despondent and docile just by Rock raising her voice with him. Phoebe was right about when to say no if she didn't like something.

She was confounded by his sudden obedience. "I'll forgive you this once as long as you understand."

The werewolf gave a big nod. "Yes, I understand. There is one thing I would like to ask of you while we're at it."

"What is it?"

"What should I do to make it so you won't hate me? I desperately want to know how to get you to like me," he implored.

Rock sighed at him. "You want my approval that badly? Why?"

"Because I fell in love with you."

"I don't understand how."

"You lent me a hand several times when I was in trouble. You helped me when I couldn't prove my identity as a count and had no money to pay you with. Do I need any more of a reason to have fallen for you?"

Rock still didn't get it after his explanation. She cocked her head.

Ebel jerked his head up and begged, "Will you at least not hate me if I look into your father?"

"What? No. That's a different matter altogether." Bringing up Rock's father was clearly the way to sway her feelings. Obviously Ebel wouldn't back down after he saw her reaction.

"Please allow me to investigate. I want a chance to make up for what I've done."

"Y-You don't have to. I feel bad having you go that far for me."

"You are simply giving me an opportunity to apologize. Don't think of it as using me."

Sincerity filled the words that pressed her for an answer, and they were tempting words at that. They penetrated right through the defenses guarding her heart, which had been shaken by the dizzying events of the day.

"I swear I will find information on him. Please tell me your father's name," Ebel repeated one final time.

This last time was the charm for Rock, who'd made the long trek to the imperial capital seeking her father and who'd dressed as a man in pursuit of his shadow. "My father's name is Fredericks Berwick."

When had she last uttered that name aloud? It meant the world to her. It was the name of the man her mother loved until the end, the name she cried out over and over again on her sickbed.

Ebel gave a deep nod, as if accepting the feelings that came with the name. "Got it."

"Um…please don't go overboard trying too hard. It's all right if you find nothing."

"Don't fret. I'll definitely pass along any plausible leads to you," Ebel cheerfully told her. She was still hesitating even after divulging the information.

"Thank you very much. But I mean it when I say it can just be something you look into on the side."

The werewolf's golden eyes locked on her stiff smile. He leaned toward her on the floor and opened his fang-filled mouth. No sooner did Rock think *He's going to bite me* than he suddenly snapped his mouth shut on her neck.

"Ahh?!" The yelp died in her mouth at the painless werewolf bite. "Uh, um, er, excuse me…?"

The puppylike love bite left the feeling of his fangs on her neck without nicking the skin. She got the chills from his hot breath caressing her skin and the smooth tip of his tongue briefly touching her.

"Wh-What are you doing this time?" Rock asked, her voice shaking.

"Giving you an oath kiss and expressing my affections. This is a symbol of my vow to grant your wish," Ebel answered.

"That was a kiss?" she asked skeptically.

"I can't kiss gently in this form. So that's my replacement for one."

"Was it even necessary to do such a thing?" Rock questioned with her hand on the spot where he'd nibbled on her neck.

"Don't family members share kisses of this level?" Ebel retorted, seemingly forgetting his earlier bout of depression.

Family members kissed each other only on the cheek or head. At least, that was what Rock did with her mother. She had no experience with her father, so she couldn't be sure. Was that why she felt terribly flustered after Ebel's kiss? Heat rushed to the spot where he'd pressed his fangs.

Ebel helped Rock to her feet, and she finished taking measurements of his werewolf form. Once that was done, he returned to human, put on clothes, and left the evacuation room with Rock.

They exited into the Mateus mansion's first-floor corridor and returned to the reception room as if they'd come back from a stroll. Inside, an exhausted Phoebe languished on the sofa looking as if she had been dragged all around the mansion and grounds by Johanna.

"**WHERE** did you get off to? You made me search all over because you weren't in the study." Phoebe waited to grill Rock until they left the Mateus estate and boarded the same carriage they had arrived in.

"We had time to spare after I measured him, so I had His Excellency show me around his manor."

Phoebe's keen blue eyes narrowed at Rock's lie. "Hmm… You guys sure are peachy together."

"No, we aren't." Rock decided to keep it a secret from Phoebe that she'd told Ebel her father's name and asked him to look into him. "And you're one to talk. I thought you had my back outside the study the whole time, but you weren't there. Where did you go?" She threw the question back at Phoebe.

"I was summoned by that butler, Ludovicus." Phoebe sounded miffed.

"Why?"

"He invited me out to dinner alone with him. I shot him down, though." She shrugged. "Then I was captured by that annoying maid and dragged all around… She was one loud, grating woman. Didn't give me a chance to rest."

"Sounds rough." Although Rock felt bad for Phoebe, she sensed something off in her explanation.

Why did she think Phoebe was lying? Was it because she was lying too?

"Were you okay while I was away?" Phoebe asked, concerned about Rock as well. "His Excellency didn't try anything funny with you, did he?"

"I-I'm okay." Rock's response classified as yet another lie.

Inside the swaying carriage, she rubbed her fingers along her neck where the feeling of fangs still lingered. Far from capable of saying she had been bitten by a werewolf, Rock mulled over those events alone.

It remained as a strangely sweet memory within Rock long into the future.

👑 Chapter 4: The Cross-Dressing Lady's Love and Aspirations

GETTING ready in the morning took extra effort when Roxy dressed as Rock. After slipping off her pajamas, she had to strap on her handmade corset before wearing her work clothes. The corset hid her breasts.

When she first started dressing as a man, she had wrapped a cotton roll 'round and 'round her chest. But hiding her body shape with a roll of cloth wasn't easy. Failing to wrap it well created bumps and gave her a disproportional thickness. Ugly marks left by how tight she had to wrap it depressed and hurt her, so she chose to make a corset to solve the problem.

She tied the corset around her chest, wore her shirt over it, and then pulled on her tailor vest. After all of that, a flat-chested, skinny, fragile-looking young man was meant to appear in her mirror.

"I should look like a man at every angle...," Rock muttered to her reflection in her bedroom's full-length mirror.

Maybe the image was ruined by her wine-colored hair growing just to her chin.

Maybe it was because she no longer had to worry about food since coming to the imperial capital and that made her cheeks plumper.

Or maybe Ebel was telling the truth when he said he could tell by her smell. Rock had no way of knowing how keen a werewolf's nose was. Did men and women really have distinct smells discernible by a superior nose?

Rock took a whiff of her hair and underarms. "Is it really that different?"

She couldn't tell the difference. Having never used perfume, makeup, or feminine hair products, she was unaware of anything artificially giving her a womanly scent. The only thing she could think of was the fragrant bar of soap Phoebe shared with her. Perhaps that left some sort of feminine smell?

At any rate, Ebel saw right through Rock's disguise.

The "how" was now a secondary concern. Rock's primary concern was how she should come to grips with being seen through.

Barely three days had passed since Ebel correctly guessed that she was a woman in that secret room inside his manor. To be precise, that was his second time getting it right. His werewolf form pointed it out for the first time inside Floria Clothes Shop's fitting room.

"You smell like a woman."

Both then and the other day, Rock sidestepped his probing with empty talk. But that amounted to little more than obstinate insistence to tide over the moment. Even if Ebel took her request to heart and stopped making inquiries, his suspicions, which had probably been confirmed within him already, wouldn't just go away.

In which case, she might be better off confronting him with the truth and getting it over with. Ebel was quick to initiate physical contact with her, but he was also the man who protected Rock at risk to his own life even though he was a count and she was a girl from the slums. They knew each other's darkest secrets as it was, and he wasn't the type to spread sensitive information.

Most of all, the man who didn't hesitate to declare that her gender was irrelevant wouldn't suddenly change his attitude upon learning the truth.

"...Actually, I wish he'd change," Rock sighed, responding to her thoughts aloud. She unconsciously massaged her neck, her cheeks flushing.

It didn't matter that three days had passed—she remembered that moment as if it'd just happened. The feeling of his dreadfully gentle love bite lingered.

Ebel had called his love bite a kiss replacement. Surely, it was because she had zero experience when it came to romantic relationships that she couldn't forget it after three days.

"I'm being strange…," she whispered, running her fingers along her nape. A young woman with cheeks dyed rosy red reflected back at her in the mirror. Disgust filled her when she realized it and she purposely scrunched up her face. "If I make this face, I'll get called the kind of man that gets passed around when there aren't any women."

Guido, the nobleman Rock met at Ebel's manor on the same day as her sweet memories with him, had cut her deeply with his mockery of her and the persona she had achieved.

People made fun of her on a daily basis for being a weak and delicate man, but Guido's malicious words packed a different punch. They oozed with his contempt for what and who she was. Of course, he ridiculed her with every intention of striking a painful blow. He openly shunned Rock. His contempt seemed to stem from more than just disgust at Ebel's partner being a man and that person coming from a lowly status.

Guido may very well become an even bigger nuisance if Rock confided in Ebel. If that was a possibility, then it'd be better to say nothing at all. No one in their right mind would willingly make an enemy of a duke's son.

"I should just work out until I pack on muscle." Rock flexed her shirt-covered arms in front of the mirror and pinched the toneless flab there.

Rock had always dreamed of becoming a man. She'd wanted to start working early in life in order to make her single mother's life a little easier. Boys could find all sorts of work, but there weren't many respectable jobs hiring a girl in her early teens. Knowing what the future held for her daughter, Rock's mother taught her everything she knew about tailoring, but by the time Rock became accomplished at it, her mother had fallen ill, never giving her a chance to thread a needle for her sake.

Dressing as a man was more than just a disguise for Rock—it embodied her unfulfilled dreams.

So she was happy as long as she could remain a man. She just had to become the kind no one could mock as being a woman's substitute.

"Yeah, that's what I'll do." Rock hurried away from the mirror as if running from those sweet, lingering memories.

THE sun had begun to rise by the time she left her room. From there she headed out to open her shop for morning customers. People rarely showed up at daybreak, but she opened the doors and cleaned up the shelves so she could welcome them whenever they chose to arrive. Putting in extra effort that way had a habit of turning into opportunities to earn money, so she never overlooked the small things.

Someone was standing outside her shop before she arrived today. A young man with burnt sienna hair leaned against the locked door waiting for Rock.

"Good morning, Rock. You come to work awfully early, huh?" A slight smile graced his handsome face, which didn't look the least bit tired despite the early hour. He wore the shirt, vest, and sash belt trousers Rock had previously tailored for him.

"G-Good morning, Ebel," Rock spluttered.

At what insane hour did he arrive to be waiting in front of her shop before even the birds woke up? Ebel had dropped by on countless occasions as a customer, but never before opening hours. The unexpected visit completely flustered her.

And it didn't help that she was already unhinged by the vivid memory of his *kiss*.

"A-And what b-brings you here at this hour?"

Ebel answered Rock's shaky question with unusual seriousness. "I need to speak with you. I chose this time explicitly for that purpose." He paused to scan the morning-mist-covered market streets, then lowered his voice. "...Where's Phoebe?"

"She isn't here yet. She usually comes later."

Phoebe arrived around the time Rock put out the "Open" sign. She often offered to be there from opening until closing, but Rock had her pride as shop owner. She didn't want to overburden Phoebe with how little she paid her.

Ebel appeared relieved she wasn't around. "I see. Let's wrap things up before she arrives then."

"What is it you want to discuss?"

"What I discovered in regards to the matter you entrusted me with."

The only thing she had entrusted him with was her father's name. Could it be?

"Did you learn about my father?" she asked, jumping right to the point.

Ebel nodded, his gaze focused on her. "Yes. There are several things I want to make you aware of."

Not even three days had passed since she told him, yet Ebel had uncovered information on her father. Though baffled by how fast he moved, Rock was genuinely excited.

"Thank you so much! Let's talk in my shop. Please come inside."

"Pardon the intrusion." In direct contrast to Rock's billowing excitement, Ebel was mellower than usual this morning. He watched her unlock the door with a pensive expression.

She saved preparations to open the shop for later. Cleaning was the last thing on her mind.

Rock invited Ebel to sit on one of the chairs meant for customers and she sat on the stool behind the counter. "So? What is it you have to tell me?" she asked, restlessly playing with her hands on her lap.

Her impatience softened Ebel's frown into a partial smile. "I obtained information on the mercenary known as Fredericks Berwick."

Fredericks Berwick was undeniably the name of her father and also the name of the man her mother, Vale Floria, loved up until her final breath.

"I think this is what they call an odd twist of fate..." Ebel started, his golden eyes intently watching her. "You see, Ludovicus—my butler— knew your father's name."

"Ludovicus does?"

Rock thought back to the white-haired butler she met at Mateus Manor. Ebel had introduced him as a butler who'd been with the family for generations. She had only exchanged greetings with him, but he left a kind impression.

"It seems my father used to hire his services. He had him partake in his antique-collecting hobby by sending him to explore ruins."

"Father did stuff like that...?"

Rock didn't know much about mercenary work. Judging by what Phoebe told her, mercenaries accepted any job to keep from missing their next meal. Mercenaries did everything from going to battlefields as just another soldier, to serving as an individual's bodyguard, and even partaking in dirty work such as extortion.

Among the various types of jobs, exploring the ancient ruins scattered around the imperial capital was said to be a great endeavor for mercenaries who needed quick cash. Money could be made by selling to dilettantes like Ebel's father who paid top coin for antiques or to scholars who spared no expense to obtain historically valuable artifacts. As good as that sounded on paper, the architects had designed the ruins with ingenious, deadly traps that spelled death to anyone who challenged them with half-baked skills. Phoebe had once told Rock stories of those ruins.

"According to Ludovicus, your father was extremely talented." Ebel softened his tone. "He was a genius ruin explorer who succeeded at every job he accepted. And he returned from the majority of his adventures unscathed. Father put his full trust in him and apparently invited him into our home on many occasions."

Rock leaned across the counter to hear every word he said. She felt as if she were catching glimpses into her father's life. He was just the kind of man she had hoped.

"What's more is that it sounds like he was an incredibly good-looking man." Ebel glanced at Rock's face when he said that part.

She didn't know her father's face, but she remembered the way her mother spoke of him. "Mother said the same thing. She always said my father was a gorgeous, wonderful man."

Whenever she talked about him, she sounded happy for a woman who had been abandoned. No matter how much Rock pestered her, she absolutely never spoke of his hair or eye color, or about the details of how they met and fell in love. Sometimes she wondered if that was her mother's way of monopolizing her memories with him. They were surely precious reminders that she treasured. Perhaps speaking of them would taint her image of him somehow.

"Did you learn anything about my father's hair or eye color?" Rock asked, wanting to know the details her mother never told her.

Ebel paused before shaking his head. "...No, Ludovicus didn't mention it. I can ask him next time for you if you like."

"Thank you very much! You have made my day, Ebel," Rock exclaimed in sincere thanks.

She wanted to know anything and everything about her father. She could count on one hand the number of things she knew about the man whose blood ran through her. For whatever inexplicable reason, both her mother and Phoebe were tight-lipped when it came to him. That was why every bit of information Ebel shared with her brought Rock untold joy.

"I barely know a thing about my father... So I want to learn anything I can about him."

Ebel squinted at Rock's face, as though her passionate pursuit of information made her shine brightly in his eyes. "I will do everything in my power to assist you."

"Ebel... Thank you. I truly mean it."

"But allow me to ask this of you first." A grave expression overtook his usually smiling face and he continued in a cautionary tone: "Should the information I obtain not be...favorable to you, would you still wish to hear it?"

"Um..." Naturally, Rock didn't know how to respond.

It was a fact that she'd had mixed feelings when she learned of her father's lover. She likely would have sustained a greater blow if Phoebe hadn't been the amazing person she was. Digging into her father's life would probably dredge up painful stories. They might even stumble upon the reason why he left Rock and her mother.

However, longing to know her father was strong enough to push back the fear of what she might find.

"...I would still want to know," she answered, letting her desire win.

Ebel's eyes widened ever so slightly. Those golden eyes burrowed into Rock without blinking. "Is that so? In that case, Rock..."

"Yes?"

"There's something I was hesitating whether I should tell you or not." His unusually heavy tone made it sound as if he'd already obtained information that wasn't favorable to her. He falteringly informed the astonished Rock, "It's about her—about Phoebe."

Rock was baffled by his bringing up her name. "Uh...what about Phoebe?"

They were supposed to be talking about her father, Fredericks. While Phoebe wasn't completely unrelated, the mention of her felt like an abrupt change in subject.

But Ebel proceeded carefully as he slowly elaborated, "You told me she used to be a mercenary and that's how she met your father, yes?"

"Yes, that's what I heard."

"As far as I can tell from looking into it, I can't find anyone who knows of a mercenary named Phoebe."

"You can't find anyone at all…?" Rock blinked.

Ebel carefully picked his words. "Up until today I had the opportunity to meet and speak with several dozen retired and currently active mercenaries. Many among them knew of your father, Fredericks Berwick, while none knew of Phoebe."

That Ebel spoke with so many mercenaries in such a short period of time surprised Rock.

"You asked that many people for me? I'm sorry for putting you through so much trouble."

"I had other things to discuss with them. I just asked about your father along the way." Ebel smiled for a moment before his face hardened. "But I didn't expect to learn nothing about Phoebe. Few everyday mercenaries move and fight like she did. I thought for sure she'd have made a name for herself far and wide, but I have yet to meet someone who knows a mercenary going by the name Phoebe."

He stopped there but looked as if he had more to say. Something was making him hesitate, though. The golden eyes that reflected Rock wavered with an unexplained emotion.

She stared back into those eyes, doubts beginning to fill her thoughts. Why was he so concerned with Phoebe?

The imperial capital was teeming with mercenaries; add in those who claimed to be one without doing much work, and there were more mercenaries than stars in the sky. Not finding information on her after asking a few dozen people didn't prove Phoebe wasn't a mercenary.

"Are you sure it isn't just because you didn't happen to meet anyone who knows her?" Rock asked.

"Perhaps," Ebel conceded, though he still couldn't shake his suspicions. "But I can't get over the fact that so many people knew your father, yet none of them know Phoebe who was supposedly so close to him."

It was certainly strange when he put it like that.

According to Phoebe, she had taken on some jobs alongside Fredericks. Rock didn't know how often they had joined up, but she always imagined Phoebe and her father working together as close partners. Of course, even if the truth was different from her image, that didn't make Phoebe a liar.

It'd be a different story if she was never a mercenary, but then why would she lie about that?

"Do you think Phoebe wasn't a mercenary, Ebel?" she pressed.

His expression became unreadable. "No…that's not what I think."

"You aren't being very clear. Do you think she was lying about how she met my father then?"

Ebel didn't answer her second question. He pressed his lips together and searched Rock's face for something.

Apparently, this question hit closer to the truth. In which case, she could see why Ebel was slow getting to the point. Perhaps his earlier warning about unfavorable information had more to do with Phoebe than her father.

"You believe I will be hurt if I learn that Phoebe lied to me?" Rock asked as a follow-up question.

Ebel's eyes widened partially before he confirmed it. "I…don't want to hurt you, Rock."

He came across as very sincere, but Rock thought of it as an overblown reaction. "I'll be fine. I have long since been scarred and wounded by things to do with my father."

Deep wounds had been carved into her heart ever since the day she found out he had abandoned her. Another wound bled when she found out about his secret lover. But that lover had held on to her father's inheritance and had given her the full amount. And she cared for Rock daily. Rock's wounds didn't vanish, but they no longer bled.

"Besides, I won't be put out even if Phoebe wasn't telling the truth. She has been caring for me all this time. That's enough for me."

What's the big deal if Phoebe lied about being a mercenary or how she met Father? Rock thought.

"…I see." Hearing Rock's answer softened Ebel's expression. He squinted his eyes as if she were the radiant sun, and he said, voice heavy with envy, "You trust him."

"Him? It's rude to refer to Phoebe that way," she chided with a smile.

He didn't return her smile at first. But then he rushed to agree. "True. *Her*, then."

"Yes, her. Please refer to Phoebe that way."

Phoebe didn't like to talk about it much, but as a cross-dresser, Rock understood how difficult it must be for her to live as a woman with a man's body. She'd witnessed countless occasions where vulgar punks in the slums verbally abused Phoebe with crass remarks. Of course, she beat them to a pulp every time, but just because she was physically strong didn't mean her heart came away unscathed.

Rock knew that hurt well when others made a fool of her for being a weak man.

"If that is how you wish it to be," Ebel consented, but his expression turned grave again. "But, Rock, you told me you wanted any information I can find on your father, no?"

"Yes, if it's about my father, I want to know everything."

"In that case, there is one bit of information that I want to impart to you not as a joke or with the intention to confuse you. I just want you to consider the possibility." Ebel started with that warning, then suddenly brought his face close to hers.

Clothing rustled as their bangs brushed and overlapped. His handsome face and beautiful eyes like amber gems being within an inch of her face froze Rock in place.

Ebel had no ulterior motives. He spoke seriously as he carefully chose his words. "There is a chance your father is—"

There is a chance Father is?

Rock couldn't guess what came next. She earnestly returned his gaze, prepared to accept whatever followed.

Floria Clothes Shop's bell rang with impeccable timing.

"Hey, Rock, you haven't tidied the place up for— Oh?" The moment Phoebe became aware of Rock and Ebel staring passionately into each other's eyes across the counter, her voice dropped several decibels. She shot them both a sharp look. "You're heating the place up first thing in the morning, eh, you two?" she said, ice dripping from her usually friendly words.

"Th-This isn't what you think, Phoebe!" Rock panicked for two completely different reasons, but Ebel was unfazed.

He faced Phoebe and greeted her with a composed smile. "I woke up early this morning and felt the need to start off my day with Rock's face."

"How quaint. I hate to burst your bubble, Your Excellency, but it's almost time for us to open our doors."

"I guess I will make myself scarce, then." Completely undisturbed by Phoebe's piercing glare, Ebel took Rock's hand into his. "Before I go, how would you like to have dinner with me again tonight? I still have much to discuss with you."

"You do? All right. I would love to…"

They weren't finished discussing her father yet. She had to hear the rest. She warmly agreed with that in mind, bringing to Ebel's face a profoundly suggestive smile that replaced his earlier seriousness.

"I'll pick you up tonight, then. I'm looking forward to our tryst, Rock." He planted a kiss on the back of her hand, winked, and then turned to leave.

Rock stayed rooted to the ground all the way until Ebel went out the door and disappeared down the dirty streets.

"…What kind of relationship do you two have right now?" Phoebe's deep sigh was warranted.

Rock finally pulled herself together and weakly murmured, "N-None. His Excellency is our very important customer—"

"So you allow all your well-paying customers to kiss you?"

"I never allowed it!"

He caught her off guard, was all. She never once openly agreed to it. She was more concerned with whether it was another oath kiss. It was a gentle gesture that let her briefly feel the softness of his lips brush across her skin.

Ebel was making another oath to her before he left.

Under Phoebe's melancholy watch, Rock gave serious thought to what he might have left to say. She absentmindedly contemplated what came after "There is a chance your father is—," even though thinking about it would never lead her to the answer.

FLORIA Clothes Shop had a very busy morning. On top of trying to catch up to her morning store-opening routine, Rock had to contend with Phoebe's incessant attempts at sounding out her relationship with Ebel.

Time nipped at her heels as she raced against the clock while juggling the insanity of prepping the shop and evading Phoebe's inquisition.

Fortunately, few customers arrived in the morning, and peace and quiet returned to the shop just past noon—or that was how it appeared at first.

Dragging the morning's craziness into the afternoon, a fancy carriage suddenly pulled up in front of the shop.

"Oh? Carriages are rare in these parts."

Just as Phoebe said, such conveyances rarely traveled these streets. Running a horse-drawn carriage through these squalid, narrow, and intricate parts was a daunting task for even the best coachmen. Hearing hooves and wheels happened about as often as the constables actually doing their job in the slums.

"It's a luxury carriage to boot. Doesn't look like His Excellency's."

Rock followed Phoebe's lead and peered at the street outside the window. The carriage blocking the tight road by parking in front of the tailor shop wasn't the same one Ebel had sent for her last time.

"His Excellency usually runs here anyway," she laughed.

Ebel had once raced through the streets carrying Rock in his human form. She'd never seen him riding a carriage and couldn't imagine him arriving at her shop in one.

The coachman opened the carriage door, and an imposing man with black hair stepped out. Rock recognized that smug face.

"Guido Linus…"

"Duke Linus's spawn? What'd he come for?"

While Rock and Phoebe grimaced in unison, out on the street, Guido was offering his hand to someone inside the carriage. A slender white hand took hold of his, and out stepped a woman. The young lady shared Guido's raven-black hair.

"…Who's that?"

"From the look of things, I'd say that's the duke's daughter. In other words, she's Lady Michaela Linus," Phoebe said in answer to Rock's whispered question. She glanced at Rock's face before unhelpfully adding, "His Excellency the Count's former fiancée."

Before long the bell over Floria Clothes Shop's entrance loudly chimed, and in stepped the two nobles.

"Say, do you truly plan to place a clothing order at this store…?" The young lady hesitantly glancing around the interior appeared around the same age as Rock. She was a beautiful lady with traces of her cherubic youth still lingering in her soft cheeks, plump lips, and big eyes. Her wavy hair cascaded to the middle of her back and shimmered like polished obsidian. Aside from her hair, she had nothing in common with Guido, especially when it came to his domineering, cruel aura.

"This is the right place. Ebel's a regular here," Guido whispered.

The fair young lady instantly lit up. "My, Ebel is? Then we know it's good, Brother."

That proved it—she was Michaela Linus, Ebel's former fiancée and Guido's younger sister. In any case, she wasn't an appropriate customer for a tailor shop located in the slums. Preventing Phoebe from saying what was on her mind, Rock approached the nobles herself.

"Welcome, Lord Guido. What business brings you here today?"

The Linus siblings directed their attention to Rock at once. Michaela's gaze brimmed with curiosity above all else as she appeared to be studying every detail about Rock.

On the other hand, frosty contempt burned in Guido's eyes and he even seemed annoyed at having to look at her.

"I want you to tailor a dress for my little sister," he requested of Rock in spite of the hatred pouring off him. "A dress to make my beautiful sister the most gorgeous woman in the world."

"Oh, Brother, you tease…"

Guido smiled softly at his blushing sister before haughtily demanding, "If you have the skill to pull it off, I want a dress that can enchant even the most thickheaded of men and win them over. Can you take this order, tailor?"

Rock wasn't simply imagining the dive her heart just took. "…I can take your order, my lord." She lifted her head after respectfully bowing to him and saw Phoebe grimacing out of the corner of her eye.

She was signaling her to not do business with a customer like him. But it was plain to see he'd become an even bigger nuisance if she turned him down. If he was going to be a pain either way, she might as well accept the job and charge him an enormous sum for the temporary displeasure.

Guido demanded a very specific tailor-made dress for his sister.

"Make an evening gown out of the finest silks. I expect you to make the most bewitchingly beautiful gown in all the realm."

Currently trendy evening gowns exposed the shoulders and were tied in a ribbon at the back of the neck. Young nobles were drawn to this latest dress style that revealed the ladies' beautiful collarbones and drove the fastidious generation before them crazy with disapproval. Another popular design choice was to sew the dress tight to the body from the waist down, so the ladies could show off their trim waistlines and elegantly slender legs.

Guido seemed to be placing an order for that exact seductive dress style.

"The finest silk in the realm is a must for the material used. The color should be..." Guido shifted his eyes to Michaela's black hair. "Purple. A mystical color to make you stand supreme in a room."

Michaela strained a troubled smile. "Do you believe I can pull off such a dress, Brother?" She currently wore a conservative dress that exposed very little skin.

"How could you not? You have become a fine woman of late," Guido said, casually dismissing his sister's concerns. Thorns bristled in his glare meant for Rock, but his expression was softer than butter in the brief moments he looked at his sister. "It's a waste to conceal your beautiful skin. It's about time for you to try alluring clothing."

"I am only nineteen, though." She smiled sheepishly. Guido gently stroked her luscious black hair.

"You will be twenty next month. You're no longer a child, Michaela."

Apparently, Michaela Linus was almost Rock's age, though her manner of speaking was immature, and she behaved like a spoiled child with her older brother. "I wish to remain a child for much, much longer... Can't I?"

"You can't. Ebel won't come to his senses if you stay a child," he chided and flicked her porcelain chin. "You're the only one suitable to be his fiancée. Don't you agree?"

"I..." Michaela's long eyelashes fluttered shut as she struggled with what she wanted to say. Between her embarrassed fidgeting and sad profile, it was too soon to read how she truly felt.

Rock watched their exchange in silence until Guido shot her another antagonistic glare.

"You heard it with your own ears, tailor," he spat, insinuating something with his provocative tone. "My sister has her heart set on a lord. Tailor a dress that will attract, tempt, and seduce him into the realization that she is his destined woman."

"I accept your order," Rock answered as calmly as possible, uninterested in taking his bait.

Phoebe warily watched them from the back corner. She had wisely kept quiet ever since the Linus siblings had entered the shop, though Rock was encouraged by her occasional eye signals.

Rock knew Guido's intentions. He wanted to stress that his sister, Michaela, was the one for Ebel, not her. Of course, emphasizing it with words wasn't enough for him—he wanted to prove it in a visible form too. Ordering a dress that brought out Michaela's feminine beauty was a part of that ploy, and if things played out well, he planned to tell Ebel to "stop dabbling in loving men."

As for Rock, it didn't bother her if that made Ebel change his mind and choose Michaela instead—she shouldn't have minded, so surely that growing gloomy feeling stemmed from her being agitated by Guido's low jabs.

Guido aside, she felt strangely uncomfortable around Ebel's former fiancée. Her discomfort was likely born out of guilt.

"I will take your measurements now. Please come this way," Rock said, addressing Michaela, and she began to show her to the fitting room in the back.

Guido stalked behind them as if it were only natural. He threw open the curtain and inspected the small fitting room. "You plan to stuff my sister into these cramped quarters?" he complained, earning a scolding from that very sister.

"Good grief, Brother… You are too much! Wait out there!"

"Michaela, call for me immediately if this grungy tailor offends you in any way," he said on his way out.

Michaela lowered her voice and apologized. "I'm sorry. My brother is always like this."

"It doesn't bother me," Rock lied with a professional smile.

A sunflower-like smile bloomed on the face of the duke's daughter. "Thank you. Now then, shall we wrap this up quick so as not to make my worrywart of a brother wait?"

Internally, Rock was shocked by the complete disparity between these siblings, for the sister spoke sweetly without a barb in her voice, while the brother was all thorns.

Michaela removed her dress down to her undergarments and allowed Rock to solemnly measure her. Though she was a decorous unwed young lady, Michaela's status as a duke's daughter gave her no qualms about stripping down to her undergarments before a male tailor. Not even her brother questioned it. She stood tall and unabashed even as Rock's fingers pressed the measuring tape against her body.

Then again, she seemed to be experiencing a different sense of security around Rock.

"Say, tailor, are you a man?"

Rock hid her bitter smile at her casual question. "Yes, I am."

"How strange. You don't really give off that feeling… Is it rude if I say that?"

"No." Rock shook her head, which encouraged Michaela to innocently rattle on.

"I have always had a hard time with male tailors. I wonder why that isn't the case with you. I can relax with you looking at my body."

Was that her intuition speaking? Or did she possess some extra knowledge she wasn't sharing? Either way, her remarks were enough to give Rock a fright.

"I believe it is surely because I take pride in my work," Rock responded, keeping her voice level. "Scoundrels who forget their work before a beautiful lady are not fit to be tailors."

"I wholeheartedly agree. No wonder Ebel is a regular at this shop." Michaela complimented her while bringing up the name of her former fiancée.

Rock's pen tip shook a little as she wrote down the measurement numbers.

Not noticing Rock keeping her head down, Michaela cheerily asked, "Do you tailor Ebel's clothing as well?"

"…Yes."

"Isn't he a wonderful man? He is very good friends with my older brother." Her voice lilted as brightly as the sun unobstructed by a single cloud of gloom.

But a very different impression of their relationship had been engraved in Rock. When she had seen them together at Ebel's manor, bad air seemed to fill the space between the two. Ebel's expression had been far from cheerful when he'd introduced Guido as his childhood friend.

Meanwhile, Guido treated Rock like trash. She didn't have to hear what his motives were to draw her conclusions.

"Brother adores Ebel. I just know he would have married him if he had been born a woman." Michaela giggled behind her hand. "And that is why he is desperate to marry me to Ebel no matter the cost. We broke off our engagement once already eight years ago, but Brother still won't give up. He always talks about how we can make Ebel reconsider."

Rock didn't know how to react to what Michaela was telling her. Quietly returning the girl's gaze resulted in her cutely tilting her head.

"Please make me the most fabulous dress in the realm."

"A-All right. Y-You can trust me with your order."

"Make it a dress capable of changing Ebel's mind." She didn't speak with urgency or personal desire. Her request betrayed her childlike, innocent desire to make her brother happy.

Rock struggled to find the right words to say regardless. Giving a deep nod was about all she could manage. "It will be as you request, my lady."

♚ ♚ ♚

ONCE Michaela had her measurements taken, Guido paid for the dress upfront and happily went home with his sister. Phoebe didn't speak a word until the carriage that had stuck out like a sore thumb was out of earshot.

"Was it really smart for you to accept that job?" Though Phoebe's voice sounded calm, Rock heard the warning in it.

"…Yes. A well-paying customer is a well-paying customer," Rock said, giving her official stance on the matter.

Phoebe scoffed, "I'm not talking about financially. I'm talking about how he makes you feel."

"I don't feel anything really. Work is work. I'll do what he paid me to."

"I'm willing to bet good money that rich boy is plotting something."

Rock agreed completely with Phoebe. But Michaela had put in the same request. She wanted a beautiful dress to catch Ebel's eye. Rock had no right to intervene.

"All I can do is make the dress according to their order." She sighed to release the tension in her body.

I'll procure the glossiest violet silks and make the ultimate dress. I'm going to imitate the latest fashions and tailor the finest evening gown my skills can pull off.

A dress that showed off the wearer's figure without losing class would draw out Michaela's dainty beauty and give her the seductive allure Guido desired.

How would Ebel view Michaela wearing the dress Rock made?

"Tell His Excellency," Phoebe advised, as if she were privy to Rock's inner thoughts.

"T-Tell him what?" Rock jerked her head up from her hands. Phoebe was watching her with an exasperated smile.

"About that spoiled toff. Let him know he came to your shop."

"Aah. Yeah. I'll be sure to tell him that."

Michaela aside, Ebel needed to know that Guido had shown up at her shop. As it was, their visit didn't come across as being an introduction from Ebel. Guido clearly wasn't a normal customer if he deliberately searched her out to spite his friend.

Michaela's childish innocence was the only thing stopping Rock. Guilt lurked in the back of her mind over tattling on the girl.

"But you've got to wonder why they ever broke off their engagement." Phoebe's concerns lingered on another matter. "As far as we've seen and heard, the duke's side didn't want the annulment. Was it the count's arbitrary decision?"

Rock knew the answer to that. The werewolf's curse had torn Ebel and Michaela apart and changed Guido for the worst.

But there appeared to be a huge disparity between how Ebel and the Linus siblings perceived the situation. The siblings didn't forsake Ebel after he became a werewolf and were even trying to restore the annulled engagement. It sounded like a beautiful story if she looked at it only on the surface, but Rock couldn't get past Guido's behavior.

Just as Michaela had pointed out, Guido was the one obsessed with Ebel.

EBEL arrived that night per their arrangement.

Rock decided to go out to eat with him after she closed up shop. Their destination was the same hash house on the first floor of the public bathhouse.

Proprietress Justia merrily welcomed them and showed them to their special table in the back.

"Duke Linus's son showed up today," Rock said before they toasted.

Ebel had been restless up until that moment. He seemed as if he wanted to talk about something, likely the remainder of what he was going to say that morning, and his fidgetiness also arose from pure excitement at having dinner alone with Rock. He sat there brimming with energy, so much so that she could just imagine his werewolf tail wagging behind him. But that nervous energy dissipated the instant she brought up his angry friend.

"Guido came to your shop?"

"Yes. Together with his sister."

"Michaela too? What brought this on?" Ebel groaned, suspicions mounting. "This may come across as rude to you, but they aren't the kind of people to shop in the slums. I highly doubt it, but was it a social visit?"

Michaela's wariness when she set foot in the shop certainly proved they didn't patronize businesses in the slums.

Rock firmly shook her head. "No, they came as customers. They requested I make a dress for Lady Michaela."

"That makes even less sense. That pigheaded Guido is making you tailor clothes for the sister he dotes on beyond healthy limits...?" Bumping into an unsolvable mystery, Ebel pressed his fingers against his temples.

Rock practically held the answer to that question in her hands. Guilt for tattling still prickled at her, but it had to be said. After all, it had more to do with Ebel than her.

Making excuses to appease her conscience, Rock exhaled before announcing, "According to the duke's son, there a lord whose attentions he wishes to gain."

"For Michaela? I have a hard time believing that..."

"He wants to make you reconsider, Ebel," Rock spelled it out for him, but rushed to amend her statement because she heard the cynicism in her voice. "The only reason I divulged a customer's information is because I believed you needed to know. I normally never leak information like this."

"I know. Thank you for telling me." His handsome face softened into a smile, and he said comfortingly, "You needn't worry. My heart belongs to you."

I wasn't worried... Rock felt an odd sense of relief.

"No matter how beautiful of a dress you make and whoever may wear it, my heart won't be stolen away from you," Ebel cheerfully announced, drawing a smile out of her.

"To be honest with you, your comment offends my skills as a tailor."

"Then are the dresses you make that stunning?"

"You know my skill. I will make it more beautiful than a dream."

Ebel put his finger to his chin as if imagining the dress. His expression melted into a dreamy smile as he said, "In that case, I would love to see you wear it."

"...I am a man, Ebel," she repeated, but it went through one ear and out the other. The golden eyes observing her seemed to already be imagining her in a different outfit.

"Your charms will shine even brighter in a dress." Ebel raptly gave voice to the picture in his head. "A wreath of flowers will crown your wine-colored hair, a necklace of blue gemstones the same shade as your gorgeous eyes will adorn your neck, and a satin weave white silk dress will cascade down your sleek frame. I will take your hand and introduce you to the ladies and gentlemen waiting in the salon. Doesn't that sound like a dreamy moment in time?"

It certainly sounded like a *dream.*

Rock didn't know anything about salons or high society gatherings. Going into a place where snobbish nobles gathered, when she was uneducated in their ways, was more like a nightmare that set her hair on end. She was guaranteed embarrassment.

"You have questionable tastes picturing another man in a dress," she objected again.

He gaped at her. "You think so? You would look good in a dress, though. Of course, I can't get enough of your usual looks either," he whispered, fixing his gaze on Rock across the dinner table.

Rock's usual work attire of white shirt, black vest, and slacks was not particularly attractive or appealing, but Ebel's expression filled with satisfaction over it.

"You are always so clean-cut, it's a home run for me. But since you would look amazing in anything, I want to enjoy you in both styles."

The way he spoke without malice proved his confidence in knowing Rock's true identity. Thinking that arguing with him was a lost cause, she sullenly kept silent.

She'd never imagined herself in a dress. Dresses had always been a garment she made for others. In the three years since she began living dressed as a man, she'd grown accustomed to this male lifestyle and never longed to live as a woman again.

That said, a single treasured memory was buried deep in her heart. One from when her mother still lived. Her mother had been sewing smooth cloth into a dress for one of the village barmaids when she said, "Someday I will sew you a lovely dress too."

Back then, Rock never doubted that "someday" would come.

The sudden revival of that bittersweet memory solicited Rock's yearning for her mother. What kind of dress would Vale Floria have made for her daughter if she were still alive? Rock pondered that answerless question in silence.

Justia arrived at the table where the two sat with completely opposite expressions on their faces. "Oh, what's this I hear about a dress? Is there a girl involved? That's rare for you, Rock," she teased while setting down a plate piled with freshly baked potato bread. "I never hear anything about romance in your life. Did you finally meet someone good?"

"H-Hardly!" Rock denied, her heart nearly bursting out of her chest. She didn't have anyone like that in her life. How could she?

Exasperation overtook Justia's features as she posed with her hands on her hips. "You never change. A tailor should have plenty of opportunities to interact with women. With that attitude, you'll end up single for life."

"I'm not looking for a romantic partner, after all." Rock frowned.

Justia directed a friendly smile at Ebel next. "As you can see, Your Excellency, Rock's a late-bloomer with no prospects. You must have your pick of the litter when it comes to women. Can't you give him some advice?"

That was completely unwanted meddling on her part, but Ebel blandly shook his head. "I hate to dash a lady's hopes, but I don't have much relationship experience with women either."

"Oh my. Now that is surprising. You are such a handsome catch, though!"

"I treasure the few relationships I do have above all else instead."

Those golden eyes casually sent an amorous glance toward Rock. She squirmed in her seat and sat bolt upright.

Never in her wildest dreams would Justia imagine the very man she was asking advice from had been trying to court Rock.

"You can see for yourself what a fine disposition and appearance Rock has. He'll meet someone eventually."

Justia seemed convinced simply by the confidence in Ebel's assertion. "You just got the best endorsement possible, Rock. Treasure the relationships you do form," she advised and left their table in a swoosh of skirts.

Once he confirmed the proprietress was out of sight, Ebel flashed a playful grin at Rock. "You can have the best partner there is as soon as you want."

"I never said I want one," she retorted as she reached for the potato bread. Ebel blissfully watched her chomping on the bread across the table.

"The proprietress called me a handsome catch. What is there to be dissatisfied with?"

"It has nothing to do with being dissatisfied." Rock downed her first slice of bread and glared at him. "Besides, you lied about not having relationship experience."

"That wasn't a lie. You're about my only relationship, Rock."

"What about Lady Michaela?" She asked on the spur of the moment and instantly regretted it. That made it sound as if she was deeply bothered by his relationship with her.

Ebel laughed out loud in front of the internally panicking Rock. "Is it bothering you that much? I told you that my heart belongs to you." Amusement filled his voice as he explained, "I won't deny I was once engaged to Michaela. But our engagement was decided by our parents when we were children. I was a fourteen-year-old boy and Michaela had just turned ten when we were betrothed. It's not the kind of relationship that involved our feelings then or now."

Ebel closed his eyes to revel in the nostalgia. "…If I had to describe our relationship, you could say I viewed her as a younger sister." He picked up a slice of bread and spoke between bites. "My mother left this world young, leaving Father and my best friend Guido as my only pillars of support. Michaela was that best friend's little sister. I wanted to care for her, and I accepted our engagement as the natural course of things."

Though the shape of his feelings was different from romantic love, Michaela was still a person near and dear to Ebel's heart. As was Guido—though in retrospect, his behavior at Rock's shop made his status as Ebel's "pillar of support" a questionable one. In any case, the three of them appeared to have once shared a beautiful relationship. If it was only the werewolf's curse that had altered their relationship from what it once was to what Rock saw today, then perhaps Guido was obsessed with Ebel out of a desire to return to the glory days.

On the other hand, Ebel, who had lost both mother and father, was using the curse that had befallen him as his strength and took on each day with a cheerful outlook. His optimism was so great that it tended to make others perceive his werewolf curse as a light matter. When she thought about it, Rock had never once pitied him. There was no way he didn't experience pain, but Ebel was the kind of man who made others think he didn't.

Rock munched on her bread in silence for several minutes. During that time, she thought about herself. She'd also lost her father right after her mother. Dressing as a man was something she did because she wanted to, not a curse, but she hadn't recovered from her loss yet. Being with Ebel intensely reminded her of that.

What we should be thinking about isn't the beautiful memories of the past, but what will happen in the future. Rock's thought reminded her of the conversation she had with Ebel that morning.

"Oh, right, Ebel, about what you were going to tell me this morning…" Because of the issue with Duke Linus's son, the very thing they had met up to discuss had been completely pushed aside.

Ebel immediately figured out what she wanted. Though he eased the tension from his hardened face, his tone remained serious. "The conversation about Phoebe, right?"

"No, about my father," Rock corrected.

A slight pause filled the air between them before Ebel agreed. "Right. I would like to investigate into that matter more before discussing it with you."

Rock hadn't expected him to say that. Ebel had already obtained a remarkable amount of information on her father, a man who had died several years ago. Would he be able to dig up more details if he tried?

At the same time, she didn't miss the drastic change in his attitude since that morning. Was it just her imagination that he had seemed keen to share information with her earlier, but not now?

"I'm sorry. Won't you please give me some time?" Ebel's request was an earnest one, not intended to dodge the question or mislead her.

As it stood, Ebel was Rock's only lead on her father. She reluctantly agreed. "I don't mind. Please do what you must."

"You can count on me. I'll bring you solid proof next time."

Ebel had no intention of sharing unconfirmed information with her. The desire to hear even rumors about her father coursed through her, but she put a lid on it to respect his wishes.

I just know Ebel will bring me new information on Father. That hope brightened her spirits.

THE pair finished their meal and left, with Justia seeing them off at the door.

"Thank you for the meal. Goodbye…" Rock tried to bid Ebel farewell outside the hash house, but he stopped her with a wry grin.

"Your coldness never ceases to amaze me. Allow me to walk you home."

"It still seems strange to me for two men to have dinner, then walk home together."

"Perhaps. For two men," he said, implying something more before shrugging. "It's late. Getting into a fight with street thugs like the last time isn't a pleasant thing for a man or woman."

At night, the streets in the slums were eerily still except for the few rowdy areas around the pubs. Starlight wasn't bright enough to light every nook and cranny of the labyrinth streets, and Rock would be stuck walking through dark shadows before she arrived at home. Knowing the streets didn't assuage her fears, not after what happened the last time.

"Furthermore, your protector didn't come along tonight."

As he elucidated, there were no traces of someone tailing them. Phoebe seemed to have the wrong impression of their relationship and didn't tag along this time because she thought they were on a real date.

Being completely alone at this hour in the slums was dangerous for a man or woman. Caution meant survival. Rock grudgingly accepted his offer. "Since you insist, please come with me half the way."

"I'll go the whole way to your room with you."

"I sincerely want you to stop halfway."

Bantering, the pair set off into the dark, filthy streets.

ROCK'S room was on the second story of a shady antique shop located one alley over from the main market street. An old woman with more wrinkles than meat on her bones owned the antique shop. She almost never returned Rock's greeting, except for when Rock came to pay rent—then, and only then, the embittered woman turned on the charm. Business didn't seem to be booming for her, but mercenaries occasionally dropped by with questionable artifacts on their way back from exploring the ancient ruins, and Rock had seen some weird objects put out in the sun to dry.

"I live on the second floor of this building. Thank you for escorting me home," Rock informed Ebel, stopping in front of the run-down antique shop.

Tagging along the whole way had done wonders for his mood, as he flashed her a brilliant smile that put the crummy torchlight to shame. "I haven't escorted you all the way home yet. I have to see you to your room."

"No thanks."

"Won't you invite me in for tea as thanks for walking you home?"

"I am grateful to you, but please don't expect such things from me," she huffed, exasperated by this situation, a classic case of a supposed gentleman walking a lady home only to make a pass at her.

She turned on her heel and climbed the outdoor stairs leading to her room, all the while wondering why he didn't tenaciously follow her. He almost always persisted, trying one hand then the next to get his way. In no way did she want him to do that now, but she found it peculiar for him to silently let her go with the last word.

Curious, she looked back and found him still standing in front of the antique shop. Suspicion drew his eyebrows together and his mouth into a frown as he cautiously did a sweep of the area.

"…Is something wrong?" she asked.

"Did you just hear someone calling for me?" he asked in return, confusion lacing his words.

"Other than me? No."

The area around the marketplace was deserted once night fell. She would've heard someone talking to him.

"I thought I heard something…" Ebel's unconvinced expression sent chills racing down her spine.

"P-Please stop it. I won't let you scare me into letting you inside."

"No, that's not my intention," he promptly denied. "I'm certain someone is calling m—" Ebel suddenly dropped to his knees. "AUGHHH…!" A groan ripped from his throat, and he painfully gripped his shoulders.

Rock raced down the stairs and to his side. "Ebel!" She crouched beside him and touched his trembling shoulder. The muscles of his shoulders and arms suddenly swelled beneath his white shirt. "Wh-What is—"

"What in the blazes?! This shouldn't be possi—" Ebel cried out in confusion as he stood in front of the wide-eyed Rock. Before he could finish speaking, his lips split wide open to his ears, and his straight nose jutted out in an uncanny manner. His burnt sienna hair noisily bristled, turning black as if being swallowed by the very darkness around them. Fur sprouted over his face, his fleshy ears vanishing, only for triangular, inhuman ears to pop out of the top of his head. In mere moments, the handsome face Justia always complimented finished transforming into a werewolf's.

His body transformed just as quick. The shirt, vest, and trousers Rock had tailored couldn't withstand his enlarging body and ripped into pieces with a scream-like sound. Beneath the starlight, a burly werewolf covered in black fur appeared.

"Ebel, this is a bad spot for that!" Rock's warning came too late.

The werewolf rose on his haunches, unleashing a guttural howl that shook the empty streets. He blinked his gleaming eyes and took a shaky breath. "I-I don't understand it either. Why am I in this form now...?"

Until now, Ebel had changed into his werewolf form at will. Rock didn't know how it worked for sure, but his transformations always appeared as free and natural as breathing.

Did he just go through that process against his wishes? Obviously, she didn't know why.

"A-At any rate, you mustn't be seen." Rock grabbed hold of the dazed Ebel's oak-tree-like arm. "Let's go in my room for now. Hurry!" She pushed his muscular back up the stairs and shoved him into her room. Then she returned to the street once more to collect his clothes before dashing back inside.

She quickly dragged a match along the striker and set a lantern ablaze with its flame. Warm light illuminated the cramped space, revealing the werewolf hunched over on the floor. It was strange how his presence alone was enough to make her familiar room feel like a supernatural place.

"Are you all right, Ebel?" she asked, holding the lantern over him. He sluggishly brought his head up. She couldn't glean his mental state from the wolf's face.

"Yes... Forgive me for losing my head." His gravelly voice lacked its usual strength and confidence. Nevertheless, he spoke with concern for Rock's well-being. "I accidentally forced you to witness my werewolf transformation. I sincerely hope I didn't frighten you..."

"I'm not frightened. I'm used to it by now." Rock deliberately added a cheerful lilt to her voice and guided Ebel to a chair. The simple wooden chaise with a quilted cushion creaked slightly under the robust werewolf, but it accepted his weight without breaking.

Sitting there with his back curled forward, he let out a small chuckle. "I'm always being saved by you. Thank you." The situation appeared worse than she initially thought as his short laugh gave way to a hopeless sigh. Amid the swaying lantern light, the werewolf's broad shoulders drooped. "I haven't had this much trouble controlling my transformation since the first time."

Rock placed the lantern on the floor and sat beside him. "The first time? You mean when you…"

"Indeed. I told you about it before, no? I'm speaking of the day the curse befell this body."

Rock remembered clearly the story he'd told her after inviting her to Mateus Manor. Included among the late Count Mateus's collection of antiques was a statue entombing the werewolf's curse. A foolish mistake unleashed that curse upon Ebel eight years ago, turning him into a werewolf.

Ebel accepted his fate as a werewolf and showed a familiar ease with the inhuman form, but even he had a "first time."

"I'm capable of transforming at will now, but it wasn't always like that. When I was first cursed, I struggled with how to control this power."

Thinking back, Ebel always transformed when he wanted to in front of her. He switched from person to werewolf and back without much effort.

"Do you think something is causing the same thing as then to happen?" Rock speculated.

Ebel inhaled. "So it appears. To be perfectly honest with you, I have been trying to return to human ever since entering your room."

"You have?! Even when you don't have any clothes?!" Rock sputtered, but clothing was the least of his concerns.

"It's been to no avail. Try as I might, I can't revert back." His pointy ears fell flat against his head and his tail drooped lifelessly. This was clearly a problem he didn't expect to face.

"It's a serious matter if you can't revert back. You are a count."

He shook his head as if to rebuff her remark. "You are mistaken, Rock. It is a serious, trying matter for anyone, regardless of rank, to be stuck as a werewolf."

"I am sure it is, but your title adds another level of difficulty."

On the contrary, however venerable and prestigious the count's family was, the nobles would never permit a werewolf among their ranks. The fearmongering word on the street pinned werewolves as unholy monsters that took on the appearance of men to devour unsuspecting citizens. Status as count didn't have the clout to overthrow the people's wild fears. Not only would the discovery lead to his downfall, but Ebel's very existence would be trampled upon.

"I can hide you here until you revert back," Rock offered, her heart dropping as she considered the worst possible scenario.

Ebel cracked what she assumed was a slight smile but looked more like him baring his fangs. "Thank you. I might have to impose on you if worse comes to pass." He shook his furry head again. "But I would rather come up with the solution to this. Something is clearly the matter with my sudden inability to do something that came to me as naturally as breathing. This is…disturbingly abnormal."

"I agree." Rock was all for helping him, but racking her mind for a solution against an unprincipled curse was an exercise in futility. "Do you have any ideas what caused it?" she asked, speaking as gently as possible to calm him. "If something different from usual occurs, there must be an unusual element at play."

"True…" He groaned, stroking his fluffy chin. One of his ears twitched. "Now that you mention it, I did hear that voice. I heard something calling me from this street."

"You said that right before I went upstairs."

At first, she'd rudely thought it was just a pretense for him to enter her room, but he actually did hear something she hadn't. From on top of the stairs she had confirmed there wasn't a single soul around the alley. Chills crawled along her spine, and she shuddered.

Ebel became lost in thought beside her. "I remember hearing that voice before…" He groaned again, agonized by a memory just out of reach. He raked his claws between his ears, searching his mind for the answer.

Rock watched Ebel's wolf profile in silence. Frustration squeezed at her heart to see him anguished this way. Surprised by how much she sympathized with him in his time of crisis, she frantically put her mind to work.

Not long passed before a certain possibility struck her. "Is there only one cursed statue?" she ventured.

The intentions behind the statue were a mystery to them. But it seemed likely it was made to cast a curse upon unsuspecting people. It was a scary thought, but if someone did create the statue with the purpose of giving birth to more werewolves, then would such a wicked creator stop with just one?

"I don't know. I've always thought it likely that more were out there,"

Ebel answered surprisingly fast, turning his golden eyes on Rock. "But I only know of the one. The statue that cursed me no longer exists either."

"Wasn't it another one of the antiques your father had mercenaries acquire for him?" she asked, looking straight into his gleaming eyes. She felt as if they were on the precipice of grasping the truth. "Let's say there isn't just one in the world. Why don't we consider that another statue is nearby? Think of it this way: another cursed statue's powers are influencing you in a similar way to when you were first cursed."

Rock obviously wasn't an expert on curses, so this was just speculation on her part. But it was more than plausible. If something that hadn't happened since he destroyed the original statue occurred only after he approached her room—

"Nearby…? You mean in your room?"

"No, below it. My room sits on top of an antique shop."

"It does?!" Ebel jumped at that information and grabbed hold of Rock's shoulders with his furry hands.

Fighting back her surprise at the strength and feel of those large, paw-like hands, she nodded. "Y-Yes. My landlady owns it. Sometimes mercenaries bring her artifacts from their ruin explorations."

"I see! Then your theory has merit!" Excited, he leaped from the chaise and whirled toward Rock. "Is it possible to check if the shop has the statue right now, Rock?"

"No, not at this hour… An old lady runs the shop, so…" She was baffled by how fast he took her theory to be truth. "I will check first thing in the morning."

Ebel's massive body trembled with impatience. "Tomorrow morning? I won't be able to do anything until then." The lie of his fur bristled like a windswept meadow and shimmered in the yellow candlelight.

After being momentarily captivated by him, Rock brought up a critical point. "What should I do if that statue is in the shop below? If we theorize you can't return to normal with it around…"

"For now, I want you to take it somewhere far away," Ebel said, then continued along that vein of thought. "After that…I will send an envoy you can entrust it to. Once it's in my hands, I'll take responsibility for destroying it." By the time he finished speaking, his tone had sunk several decibels, the weight of the world bearing down on him. Surprised, Rock lifted her gaze to where the werewolf arched his back, every strand of fur standing on end. He bared his fangs, his ears flicked back, and his nose crumpled. "That thing must be destroyed."

Resolve and anguish echoed in his deep voice, which sounded like someone raking metal over cobblestone.

What took her by surprise was how different from before this image of him was. Hadn't Ebel told her that by becoming a werewolf he had gained a marvelous power? That he didn't resent his father for unleashing this curse on him? Yet the werewolf before her simmered with palpable resentment, outrage, and hatred for the curse.

Keen man that he was, Ebel detected her shock. "Is it strange for me to say such things?" he questioned.

"Yes," she gave him the honest answer he deserved. "You praised the curse as a good thing…"

"For me, it is. I have no regrets as far as that's concerned," he asserted bluntly, not hesitating with what he said next either. "But this curse should end with me. When I think of others being afflicted by it—especially you—I must eradicate the source."

The flame suddenly swayed inside the lantern, and something flashed within those golden eyes. "I believe that is my duty as the bearer of this curse." Not a fragment of hesitation or wavering could be gleaned from his tone.

Overwhelmed, Rock gasped and held her tongue. Thinking it over again, there was nothing magnificent or wonderful about being under a mysterious curse. Ebel took it in stride, but now she didn't know if his cheerfulness was the whole truth.

What she did know was that a curious feeling overcame her when she touched upon his anger and suffering. *I still don't know anything about the man named Ebel Mateus.* That thought clung to her and wouldn't let go.

EBEL "tried" changing back countless times after their conversation with no results. Night advanced into the wee hours, and his werewolf form prevented him from going home. So Rock allowed him to stay at her place.

"To think I would have the opportunity to sleep in your room…"

His tail whipped back and forth at her offer. "Lady Luck is shining down on me. Let's thoroughly enjoy this precious moment."

"There is nothing for you to enjoy. My home is cramped."

Twinkling golden eyes flicked about the room, ignoring Rock's laughter. "Hrm… This is indeed your room. It smells of you."

"Please don't smell my room!" she chided him for getting overexcited as she prepared the sleeping arrangements.

With Phoebe as the only guest she ever had over, Rock owned only one bed. Ebel said he didn't mind sleeping on the floor, but she had mighty reservations about making a count sleep on the floor or chaise.

So she layered several thick quilts on the floor next to her bed and wrapped them in the softest linen. It took some work to create a werewolf-sized bed, but she managed to prepare one just the right size after having Ebel lie down on it several times.

"Would you like a blanket?" she asked, looking down at Ebel resting on her makeshift bed. She thought it was an unnecessary question for a fur-covered wolf, but to her surprise, Ebel, who was curled up on his side, asked for one.

"Yes, please."

"Here you go. Please throw it off if you feel too hot." She shook out the blanket and spread it over the werewolf's body. The large blanket fit snugly around him.

"Thanks, Rock," he said with a tickled laugh. "I always find myself in your care."

"That's not true." She shook her head, then said as gently as possible to assuage his fears, "I hope we can pull everything off smoothly tomorrow so you can return to normal soon."

Ebel stuck his wet nose out from under the blanket and blinked in a human manner. "I don't mind staying this way forever if it means being treated this kindly by you."

"Am I normally not kind to you?" she prompted with a sardonic smile.

He fell momentarily silent before answering in a voice sweeter than any nectar: "Nay. You have been my savior from day one."

Rock stepped away from him without a word, though it wasn't because of his tone or the words he used.

Was it because of the silent night? Or because they were alone together? Every word he said lingered in her ears and wouldn't go away.

ROCK'S room was reasonably small for one person to live there. A large cloth hung from the ceiling to partition the square studio into separate sleeping and living areas. She had used a thin cloth to let through the light from the only window, but it didn't serve as a good partition with guests present.

Lantern in hand, she returned to the living area, and when she looked back at the sleeping area, she saw her bed and the bed she had made directly beside it right through the thin cloth. This threw her into a state of considerable disquiet, as she had planned to change before bed.

"Ebel, would you mind not looking this way while I change?" she asked. The blanket-covered werewolf stirred restlessly.

"Going out of your way to alert me has the adverse effect of rousing my interest."

"Please douse it. I'm putting my trust in you," she said, a threat hanging from her words. Then she placed the lantern at her feet and doffed her clothing.

She stripped off her tailor vest, shirt, and slacks, then unhooked the corset concealing her chest. Sleeping with that uncomfortable thing on would cause too much pain to rest well. Removing her corset around Ebel was the epitome of danger, but he'd be less likely to notice with her being in her pajamas and under the blankets in the dark.

"Phew…" A sigh of relief slipped past her lips once she pulled on her baggy night clothes.

Rock loved the moment at the end of the day when she removed all her clothing and changed into her comfortable pajamas. Everyone feels ultimate bliss in those moments when they are freed from the day's oppressive restraints and only have to fall into peaceful sleep.

Then again, she doubted peaceful sleep was on the agenda tonight.

Finished changing, Rock returned to the sleeping area with the lantern. She slipped through the thin partition and climbed into bed, when Ebel poked his head out from under his blanket.

"You are still awake?"

His pointy ears flicked back and forth at her question. "I couldn't help being distracted by the sound of your clothes."

"Those ears seem like they bring more trouble than they are worth, Ebel."

"You can say that again. On another note, your nightclothes have a whole new appeal of their own." The werewolf looked up at her from his side, his golden eyes perusing her.

"Please don't look." Rock blew out the lantern to escape his keen eyes. Thick darkness fell over the once brightly lit room. "All right, I turned out the lights. Please go to sleep," she instructed, straining her eyes against the dark. Two golden, blinking orbs of light glimmered on the floor. She knew Ebel was there. For whatever bizarre reason, that put her mind at ease.

"Honestly, I doubt I can sleep..."

She couldn't see his face, but she heard clearly the distress in his voice. Rock pulled the blankets close to her chest and asked the pair of golden orbs, "Are you having a hard time keeping calm?"

"Yes. My heart is kicking up such a racket, I can't quiet it."

"I know this must be difficult for you, but try not to think about it too much," Rock said, attempting to be considerate of his feelings. "I will run down to the antique shop as soon as dawn breaks. Please rest until then."

They had no guarantee that would solve anything. They didn't even have any proof that the shop below housed another statue. But Rock wanted to cling to any possibility, no matter how small. She couldn't leave Ebel in this state. All the more so if he was stricken with depression over it.

"...Thank you," Ebel responded with a hint of hesitation before a smile filled his voice. "The biggest cause of my sleeplessness lies in you being beside me in that provocative outfit."

This was what she got in return for showing concern over his situation. Annoyed, she frostily spat out, "I shouldn't have worried about you!" She flipped over on the bed, pointing her back toward him. Then she yanked the blankets up to her head and pretended to go to sleep angry.

She heard Ebel's heartrending voice behind her blanket-covered back. "Did I anger you? I'm sorry. Please face this way again."

Not a single light illuminated the room, making it impossible, under normal circumstances, for anyone to see that Rock had turned her back to him. If they were human, that was. She sat bolt upright in bed and questioned the eyes glowing in the dark. "Can you see me?"

"Wolves have excellent night vision. I can see you clearly even now."

"Your good eyes seem like more trouble than they're worth too. Please refrain from looking at me, then." Rock hugged the blankets to her chest, concealing it. The golden glowing orbs abruptly went out. Either he had shut his eyes or put his head down.

"Does this work?"

Surprisingly, he obeyed without a fuss. Rock lay back down and answered him in a slightly better mood: "Yes."

Silence filled the lightless room for a span of time afterward. Rock shut her eyes in a bid to fall asleep. But her heart thrashed and rollicked, keeping at bay the sleep that should've come long ago. Closing her eyes failed to keep out of her thoughts the knowledge that Ebel was sleeping beside her.

She'd mentioned her theory to him out of a wholehearted desire to cheer him up. This wasn't the first time she'd seen Ebel depressed. Like an honest child, he had openly worn his despondence on his sleeve when Rock had scolded him for ruining his clothes and when he tore his shirt. But what she saw in him tonight was different from the other times—it was closer to utter despair.

Can I lift his spirits and inspire hope in him once more tomorrow? Was her theory even correct? *What happens if I don't find anything close to what he's looking for in the shop?*

The more she thought about it, the deeper into the pits of despair her thoughts plummeted. Unable to take another minute of being haunted by spiraling thoughts, she forewent sleeping for now and opened her eyes. Without much thought, she glanced toward Ebel and found two small golden orbs twinkling near the floor. Moreover, those glowballs suspiciously darted around the room the moment she turned toward him.

"You were still awake?" Rock asked, holding back her laughter at his poor, but funny, attempt at fooling her.

Giving into fate, the glowing eyes stopped restlessly wandering the room. "Um…forgive me. I couldn't resist when I couldn't fall asleep," he apologized, a timorous tone accenting his rumbling voice.

"Me either. Would you like to talk instead?" Rock offered, hoping to escape the downward pull of her emotions. The two golden orbs slowly blinked, followed by a long, tired exhale.

"Rock, may I tell you my story?"

"Sure."

"Thank you." After expressing his gratitude, he broached the topic in a voice softer than the blankets she held to her chest. "Do you remember the night we met?"

"You appeared inside my shop in your current form."

"Indeed. I called you a lad at the time because I didn't know your age. Forgive me."

Others often made that mistake as well. Making people accept a short and wiry "man" with a lyrical, high-pitched voice was harder than picking pockets in the slums.

"It happens all the time. I'm not bothered by it."

Ebel gave a strained laugh at her reply. "You should be. Calling a pretty person like you a lad is the same as any other insult."

Rock didn't respond. Whether he knew her secret or not, she wasn't going to acknowledge it. She felt as though doing so would make her lose something valuable. What that was, she didn't know.

"When I think about it, you and I are very similar," Ebel proceeded, not needing her to answer. "Both of us have obtained a peaceful life by transforming into another version of ourselves. I don't know your circumstances, but I can see the need for you to do it to operate a shop in these parts. I believe you made the correct decision too." He spoke as gently as possible to reach Rock's ears as she maintained her silence. "My feelings are the same as the last time I confided them in you. I don't care if you are a man or woman."

He told her that frequently, and every time, she thought of him as a troublesome fellow.

"Of course, one of those would make me happier than the other. But, whoever you choose to be, these feelings won't change." Ebel paused there, hesitating with what he had to say next. He swallowed audibly before taking the plunge. "How about you? Say I remain a werewolf forever, never to return to being a man again. Would you still lend an ear to my love confession?"

Those words exposed his weakness and fears like never before.

In a sense, he phrased it in a way that was very like him. Whether Rock had been listening to his love confessions until now was up for debate. But on this night, the man who normally whispered his affections with confidence was sharing his heart with unusual reserve. The anxieties hiding inside him became more pronounced.

He might never become human again. That fear chewed away at him more than it did Rock. The man who always took pride in being a werewolf feared being one forever.

Feeling her chest squeeze, Rock sat up in bed. She reached out into the endless darkness and gently stroked the area above those glowing golden orbs. Her hand sunk into the soft, almost bottomless fur and bumped into the malleable ears, letting her know she was touching the top of his head.

"What are...?" Ebel's dubious voice trailed off into a pleased groan.

"Please don't be worried, Ebel," she told him. Comforting words failed to come to mind. But she couldn't just leave him to suffer alone with his fears. "Whether you are man or werewolf, it doesn't change you from being the Ebel I know."

Rock still didn't know a lot about him. The small bits of information she did have made her want to save him from despair. She wanted to set his mind at ease, if only a little. Did that desire stem from his being like her?

"So don't think too deeply about it. Let's get proper rest tonight and tackle the problem in the morning."

Ebel let out a blissful exhale when she rubbed the long fur between his ears. "Yes...let's do that." His fuzzy hand grabbed her slender wrist. "Rock, I have a single request."

"What is it? Waah!"

He pulled Rock off the bed with his brute werewolf strength. Rolling on top of the soft, furry werewolf prevented her from getting hurt, but she raised her voice over his abruptness. "Ebel! You are always so forceful—"

Her objections were swallowed by his arms wrapping tightly around her. "...I know. But I want you at my side tonight." Trembles shook the body that was larger than two men. "You can leave once I fall asleep. Please allow me to cling to your warmth."

His earnest entreaty stumped her. She couldn't spurn him. Not that she didn't realize a piece of him was taking advantage of the situation, but that wasn't enough to neglect him.

Rock ducked her head in his brawny arms. "If I can leave once you fall asleep, then fine."

"Thank you, Rock."

"I'm putting my trust in you. I will pinch off your wet nose if you try anything."

Did he hear her warning? She heard his tail whipping across the makeshift bed.

Ultimately, Rock fell asleep first that night.

After all, she went to sleep in the luxuriously furry arms of a fluffy werewolf. In addition to the ultimate comfort of being surrounded by the softest fur, her wariness easily fell before her accumulating fatigue. It wasn't possible to support her eyelids from rapidly weighing shut.

To top it off, Ebel was gently stroking her hair the whole time. Using his sharp claws in the place of a brush, he combed them smoothly through her hair. Was it the sleepiness pressing down on her that made Rock not only not hate what he was doing, but even enjoy it?

"The first night I became a werewolf, I fell asleep alone on top of the cold floor," he said, beginning to narrate his past in a quiet voice while he played with her hair. "After all, Father had fallen to pieces... He was in such a bad state Ludovicus had to force strong ale down his throat. They quarantined me in fear of me going on a wild rampage, and I spent the night isolated. I returned to being a man the next morning, making that the only night I felt that helpless, but..."

Adrift in partial sleep, Rock listened to his story.

"I couldn't stop myself from remembering the fears that tormented me that night." Joy colored his voice even though he was talking about a painful memory. "I was saved this time by your presence. Thank you..."

Satisfaction filled her at the sound of his voice. She didn't know why. She just wanted Ebel to be happy and optimistic like his usual self.

There was still so much she didn't know about him. Perhaps the real Ebel trembled from old, scarring memories all the time. Even if that were the case, she couldn't stop from wishing that his melancholy woes would be washed clean, leaving only his smile tomorrow.

Until now, she only ever felt that way about her mother and Phoebe.

"I hope you have a good tomorrow," Rock whispered into Ebel's chest on her way to deep sleep.

Although they were not yet lovers, the couple slept on top of the makeshift bed in an affectionate embrace.

🜲 Chapter 5: My Beloved Lady Floria

A soft tickle on Rock's cheek roused her from slumber. Something warm and fluffy surrounded her on all sides. She found herself in the most comfortable bed protecting her from the depressing dawn chill.

"Mnn…" Questioning why she was in a bed that wasn't her own, she slowly opened her eyes. A wolf's face burst into view. Her gaze trailed over the triangular ears, glowing gold eyes, black, wet nose, and large mouth packed with spiky fangs.

The beast's mouth snapped open and spoke to a dazed Rock. "Morning, Rock. Looks like you slept soundly."

Of all the things she could've used for a bed, it had to be a werewolf's enormous body. "G-Good, morning, Ebel." She hurried to her feet. Ebel yawned dynamically, his large mouth opening wider than possible for a human.

"Your sleeping face was most adorable. I would have enjoyed it more if not for this body…"

The memory of what occurred last night replayed vividly in her mind. She'd intended to stay with Ebel until he fell asleep, to comfort him when he was on the brink of utter despair, but she ended up falling asleep before him. Having her sleeping face seen was embarrassing enough, but it paled in comparison to sleeping like a log in the midst of a crisis.

The day broke and morning light shone into Rock's small room, but Ebel's body remained in the same form.

"You still can't change back?" Rock asked straightaway.

Ebel gravely affirmed, "Sadly, yes. Your theory is seeming likelier by the minute."

They had no proof a cursed werewolf statue was stashed in the antique shop downstairs, but they needed to make sure of it.

"Then I will head over to the shop as soon as it opens." Ebel couldn't go anywhere until she solved this problem. Fresh resolve blossomed in her chest.

"Please do. You are my only hope right now," he said, his golden eyes fondly taking in every detail of her morning appearance. He swallowed audibly. "I thought this last night, too, but your nightclothes are truly… tempting."

The werewolf's eyes were keenly riveted on her disheveled nightclothes, particularly her corsetless chest and her shins exposed beneath the hem. Flustered, Rock hid her chest under her crossed arms.

"Ah! I-I will go change!" She bolted to the other side of the thin partition. She whipped around to face the cloth and viciously warned the werewolf resting his muzzle on his paws on the floor, "Don't look this way!"

"I'll use discretion," he answered nonchalantly.

Trying not to think about how far his discretion allowed him to see, Rock doffed her nightclothes, pulled on her corset, and returned to her usual work attire.

Then she set about making breakfast for two. Intelligently perceiving a werewolf couldn't eat properly with his wolf paws, Rock prepared a wheat porridge he could eat with one spoon. Using a large wooden ladle, Ebel ate the sticky porridge filled with pickled white olives.

"I've never eaten such delectable wheat porridge before. Your hands work wonders with food and clothes."

"It's not much, but I am glad it suits your tastes." Genuine relief settled over Rock at his praise. She'd been nervous because this was her first time serving food to someone other than Phoebe.

After sharing an enjoyable breakfast together, Ebel wistfully asked her, "Do you have the clothes I ripped last night?"

"Yes, right here." Rock pointed to the pile of shredded cloth that had once been clothing. His ears drooped against his head, showing his depression in a way only a wolf could.

"I've ruined yet another outfit you made for me…"

"You didn't do it by choice. Don't feel bad."

"I can't do that, but taking care of urgent matters comes first." Ebel fished his unscathed leather wallet from the scrap pile. He handed it over to her without checking the contents. "I want you to use this to retrieve the statue."

The weight of the wallet felt like a ton of bricks. She opened it and looked inside to find it packed with gold coins. "Th-This much? You aren't telling me to use all of it, are you?"

The picture of calm, Ebel watched Rock sputter with her commoner sensibilities. "I don't mind if you use it all. Better that than someone else getting their hands on that abomination."

From Ebel's viewpoint, retrieving the statue at all costs was top priority. But dangling a full wallet in front of an old woman who had been doing business in the slums for decades would only get the sharp-eyed crone to jack up the price.

"I will do my best to retrieve it at the cheapest price," Rock said, stashing the heavy wallet in her pocket.

His eyes rounded. "You're confident you can get it cheap?"

"I do run a business in these parts," she said with a sly grin.

It was time for the trickster tailor to show off her skills.

A business-savvy woman named Selina Trilian owned the antique shop downstairs. Still vigorous past her seventy-something years, she was rumored to be single only because no man was a match for her beauty. Word on the street said foolish mercenaries who tried to get into her good graces by calling her "Madam Trilian" were chased out of the shop by a stream of creative blue language.

As her tenant, Rock had never offended the older woman, but she still received the cold shoulder every day except for when she paid rent.

"Good morning, Lady Trilian," Rock said in greeting upon entering the shop. She referred to the woman, who was not actually a noble, that way because of what Phoebe once told her: "Calling the old crone that pleases her more than anything else."

Lady Trilian didn't lift her face from her open ledger, nor did she return the greeting. Used to it by now, Rock said what she knew would most interest her. "I came as a customer today. May I take a look around?"

"…A customer?" Lady Trilian said, deigning to speak to Rock for the first time. Scowling with her beautiful face of yore concealed beneath layers of wrinkles, she glared at her with sunken eyes. "This is the first you've come as a customer."

Never having been inside before, Rock thoroughly took in every corner of the shop. Curios and antiques collected from who knows where crowded the small shop reeking of mildew. Old relics that collectors supposedly found irresistible—such as cracked agate vases, crystal balls resting on velvet pedestals, hourglasses filled with purple sand behind their cloudy glass, and scales with intricate carvings extending to its weights—filled dusty shelves.

"What are you searching for, laddie?"

Rock strained a smile at her term of address. "Do you have any statues found in the ruins? One the size of your palm." She asked her directly about it. Negotiations couldn't start without finding it first.

Lady Trilian cocked an ashen eyebrow. "I have lots of those. Can you be more specific?"

"It's a statue of a wolf baring its fangs. Supposedly made out of white limestone," Rock said, relaying the information she had received from Ebel beforehand.

The old woman snorted. "News reaches you quick, laddie. Didn't think you'd be after *that* too."

"You have one?"

"Boy, do I have one. But I ain't selling it to a pauper." Her sunken old eyes glinted with her appraisal of Rock. "I heard one of those fetch a hefty price. Aren't you looking for one because you found that out too?"

Others were searching for cursed statues, and it sounded as if there was more than one out there. The person looking was willing to spend a large sum, but it couldn't be Ebel, since he hadn't found more than the one that cursed him. And he didn't allude to having connections to someone who could find them.

Then who else out there wanted one so badly they offered a bounty?

"Who do you plan to sell it to, Lady Trilian?" Rock frankly inquired.

From what she'd heard, it didn't sound like a tasteful statue anyone other than someone with peculiar tastes would willingly collect. Nothing was more dangerous than someone procuring it without knowing about the curse—except maybe, someone who was after it *for* the curse.

"The highest bidder." Lady Trilian's answer was plain and simple.

"It's not just one person after it?"

Her additional question silenced the older woman, who turned suspicious eyes on Rock. "What about you, laddie? Ain't you searching for it because you have a buyer?" she probed.

After a moment of hesitation, Rock answered honestly. "I'm not searching for it because I want to sell it off. I've come representing someone who wants it destroyed."

"They want it destroyed?"

"You didn't know? That statue is cursed." Rock deliberately lowered her voice to an eerie whisper.

The other woman snorted again. "You're wasting your breath trying to scare me, laddie. I ain't selling to you."

"I'm not kidding. It's a curse that turns people into werewolves. You should know the statue looks like a wolf, if you have it." Rock took her intimidation a step further. "Carelessly unleashing the curse will transform you from beautiful human to hairy wolf. Pointy ears will burst from the top of your head, your eyes will turn into glowing slits, your nose will stretch out, and your mouth will split open and fill with gnarly fangs. Your arms and legs will become thicker than oak logs, and fur will sprout all over your hunched-over body."

After all, Rock had seen a werewolf before coming downstairs. Her poignantly delivered description spooked Lady Trilian into wringing her wrinkled hands.

"Did you say werewolf? You say it like you've seen one."

"I'm sure you've heard the rumors about them prowling these parts. I've actually seen a cursed person. Pitiful creature." The landlady had no way of knowing that the werewolf Rock spoke of was currently staying in her room upstairs. "That's why it must be destroyed. Sell it to me, Lady Trilian."

The shrewd landlady gave a dismissive wave of her hand. "You want me to give you a bargain with that tall tale? I didn't think I was renting to an idiot."

"I'm not looking for a bargain. I'll pay you a pretty chunk of coin."

"Try me."

"How's ten gold coins?" Rock started low, and sure enough, Lady Trilian turned away from her and pointed a crooked finger to the door.

"Go home."

Naturally, Rock was only getting started. "How about fifteen?"

"Child's play."

"What about twenty?"

"Not even close."

She showed no signs of agreeing even after increasing the amount.

"But won't you have to find another buyer if I go home now? I doubt you can find someone who wants a cursed statue so soon. Will you be okay in the meanwhile? You won't accidentally get yourself cursed?" Rock tried the intimidation angle again, since it seemed to get her results faster.

Lady Trilian's mouth twitched. "Again with the curse… Werewolves ain't nothing more than street rumors. They don't really exist."

"They do exist." Rock wiped the smile from her face and dropped her voice as low as possible to add extra emphasis. "I was bitten by one. A werewolf lunged at me, knocking me onto the ground, where it took a bite out of me with its gaping wide mouth. Its row of sharp fangs sunk into me from here to here."

She showed off the werewolf's big mouth size by running her fingertip along her shoulder. She never thought she would speak of the time Ebel "kissed" her as a real encounter with a werewolf.

"Werewolves exist. People wouldn't talk about them if they didn't." Rock looked straight into Lady Trilian's eyes and doubled down. "I don't know what the other buyers are after. But, Lady Trilian, you will be in danger if you hold on to this cursed monstrosity."

The much older woman realized the truth in those words and shuddered.

"My job is to deliver that statue to the one who will destroy it. If you sell it to me, you don't have to worry about being cursed and will have a stack of gold coins in your hand right now. How about it?"

Rock's extra push helped Lady Trilian make up her mind. "I did think it was an uncanny statue. I couldn't shake the feeling it was watching me," she muttered as if she sensed the danger in her very bones. Proud woman that she was, she tossed on, "But I'm only selling for thirty gold. Cursed or not, it has that much market value…"

"Sure. I can do thirty," Rock answered, as if it were a done deal.

The old woman brought the statue out from the back of the store and placed it on the counter. Rock pulled thirty gold coins from Ebel's wallet, thoroughly counted them, and handed over the amount.

Lady Trilian screwed up her face when she saw that wallet still bulging with coins. "Couldn't you have paid more, laddie?"

"It's not my money. I can't spend it excessively."

Thus, Rock obtained the cursed wolf statue. Made of white limestone, it was indeed shaped to look like a werewolf baring its fangs. Though the artist had used a simple carving method, the sculpture perfectly captured the werewolf's image. Just as Lady Trilian had said, there was something uncanny about it, and it seemed to be silently staring at Rock now that she held it.

Not wanting to look at its face, she quickly pocketed the palm-sized statue.

Meanwhile, Lady Trilian seemed to regret her decision the moment she let go of the statue. "That curse better be real. I'll chase you out of the building if you made it up."

Rock answered her greedy glare with a wooden smile. "Would you like me to prove it? How about we unleash the curse right here—"

"Don't even joke about it!" The older woman vigorously shook her head, although she still seemed unconvinced. "You're coming to resemble that man even more. The way you smooth talk me right out of my money is exactly the same."

"What man?" she asked, having no idea who she could be referring to.

Lady Trilian frowned. "The man you call Phoebe."

Rock never thought of Phoebe as a man and corrected the other woman with a smile. "You shouldn't refer to her like that."

"As if I care. He used to be the handsomest man around. Wonder what made him lose his mind." An echo of disappointment and attachment clung to her grumbling.

Curiosity sparked, Rock inquired further before she left. "Say, Phoebe used to be a mercenary, right?"

Lady Trilian waved her hands as if shooing out a dog. "Out with you. Before I change my mind."

"Just answer me this. Did Phoebe used to be your valued client?"

"Yeah, he was. He was a much stronger, better man than you," Lady Trilian snapped. Then she sighed. "Train a little and become my kind of man. I'll dote on you."

That made it sound as if she used to dote on Phoebe. Rock instinctively took a step back from the flirtatious glance sent her way by those sunken eyes.

"I-I'm happy the way things are now!" She fled as fast as she could from the antique shop.

The next place she headed was her own store on Market Street. She needed to hide the statue somewhere. Nowhere was safer at the moment than her shop's safe. While she was there, she grabbed a new pair of clothes in case Ebel returned to normal.

AFTER taking care of business at her store, Rock retraced her steps with Ebel's change of clothes. As she neared the staircase, Lady Trilian burst out of the antique shop.

"Hey, what's with all the racket, laddie?!"

"What racket?" Rock stopped, and the older woman marched over to her with a glare that would make pickpockets think twice.

"Coming from your room! Damn noise is ruining my morning!"

Only Ebel should be in her room. She doubted he'd make a ton of noise alone. But Lady Trilian seethed with frustration that had nothing to do with Rock making off with her statue.

"I've just returned from my shop," Rock said truthfully.

"Then that man must've barged in while you were away."

Rock couldn't overlook that possibility. "That man—you mean Phoebe?!"

"What other man is there? I'll triple your rent next month if you're too lo— Hey, laddie! I'm not done talking to you!"

Rock shook off Lady Trilian and dashed up the stairs to her room.

She had forgotten a critical fact. As her guardian, Phoebe helped Rock rent this room and owned a spare key. She usually used that key to drop off food and soap, make meals for Rock when she was busy at work, and come to take care of her when she fell ill. To Rock, Phoebe was her sole relative, whose unannounced visits she always welcomed.

Just not this morning. After all, His Excellency the Werewolf Count was in her room. Retired mercenary or not, there was no way Phoebe could remain calm after discovering a werewolf instead of Rock in her room. Rock couldn't discount her lunging at the werewolf with her stashed dagger.

"Phoebe!" Rock tumbled into her room, where an unexpected scene was unfolding.

First, Phoebe was there. Anger splotched her beautiful face crimson, her chestnut curls were a mess of knots, and she was panting so heavy her teeth were visible in her open mouth. Both of her open hands were flying to grab Ebel, who was sitting on the chaise.

Meanwhile, Ebel appeared as a perfectly handsome young count with burnt sienna hair and a chiseled, furless face. From the looks of it, he'd safely reverted back to being a man and now sat with his naked chest exposed to the cool morning air, a blanket wrapped around his waist to conceal what was below. Distress glimmered in the eyes he looked up at Phoebe with, but his expression relaxed upon noticing Rock first.

"Oh, Rock. You came back at a good time."

Phoebe whipped around with a disconsolate look. "Rock, don't tell me you and this man…!"

Rock didn't have any interest in romantic relationships, but she knew what was being misconstrued right now. Things were different from the situation she had feared, but this was almost as serious.

A basket filled with cheese and apples sat on top of the dining table, and Rock figured Phoebe had come to deliver this to her. Ebel had definitely pretended not to be there when she knocked on the door, which led to her using the spare key to drop off the food. Rock didn't need to use her imagination to guess what chaos ensued.

"I-It's not what you think, Phoebe. There's a reason for this!" She was trying her best to explain through her panic, when Phoebe briskly stomped over to her and seized her slender wrists.

Phoebe peered into her eyes and bluntly scolded, "Why don't you value yourself more?!"

"Wh-What…?"

"A man who lays his hands on a woman before marriage is the scum of the planet!" Furious beyond fury, Phoebe's hands trembled when she placed them on Rock's shoulders.

Feeling pinned down by those flaring blue eyes, Rock timorously argued, "I-I told you that's not what happened. He didn't touch me…"

"Then why is His Excellency here at dawn?!"

"W-We ran into some trouble last night, and I had him stay the night. But nothing happened between us!"

She wasn't lying—for the most part.

Honing in on Rock's hesitation, Phoebe growled, "You say nothing happened when His Excellency is naked from head to toe…?"

"No, well, that is, um…"

It certainly was an unreasonable explanation. He hadn't been naked before Rock left the room—well, to be precise, fur had covered his naked body. Now that the fur had disappeared, Ebel's appearance was an open invitation for misunderstandings.

"I've been trying to explain the same thing since before you arrived, to no avail," Ebel chimed in when Rock was at her wit's end.

Phoebe spun toward him and flayed him with a glare capable of cutting through steel. "SILENCE! Who'd believe the explanation of a man sitting butt naked in another's room?!"

It was Rock, not Ebel, who was overwhelmed by the fury she'd thought Phoebe incapable of. Things were only going to grow markedly worse if left to run their course.

Knowing she had to say something, she weakly asserted, "He has good reason to be naked. See that? His clothes ripped." She pointed to the pile of scraps that had once been Ebel's clothes in the corner.

Phoebe took a cursory glance at it and scowled with mounting suspicion. "What in the blue blazes must be done to turn good clothes into that?"

"Um, I can't…"

I can't tell you that, she finished in her thoughts. After all, Ebel's secret hung in the balance. Not to mention Phoebe was about as likely to believe that story as the truth. Even Rock had thought of werewolves as little more than ghost stories until that night Ebel showed up in her shop and she saw one with her own two eyes.

Ebel couldn't just leave Rock hanging. "…Rock," he started, speaking with a calm that belied his nakedness, "You trust Phoebe, don't you?"

"Y-Yes, I do…," Rock said hesitantly, affirming his abrupt question.

Rock knew Phoebe's anger stemmed from worry and concern for

her. She also knew how much Phoebe cared for her on a daily basis, so her furor made sense. That was exactly why Rock wanted to clear up this misunderstanding, as much for Phoebe as for herself.

"Phoebe is just worried about me. I'm sorry for causing a scene, Ebel."

Phoebe snorted.

Ebel gave an understanding smile. "It's a reasonable misunderstanding. I believe revealing the truth to her is the best way to clear the air. What do you think?"

"You can't be serious, Ebel!" Rock said in panic, but Ebel overflowed with the confidence to do whatever it took to break the deadlock. He didn't have an ounce of hesitation. So Rock faced Phoebe and tried to get her to understand. "P-Phoebe, I want you to listen to me without freaking out…"

Phoebe took that as the opening to a completely different reveal, and the column of her throat moved. "Wh-What is it? Let me be clear: I absolutely won't accept His Excellency until he says he will officially marry you. If you don't get a proper pledge down on paper, he'll run off saying you should be honored he touched you at all—"

"Not that!"

Unconcerned with their argument, Ebel rose slowly from the chaise.

Before the blanket concealing his waist hit the floor, the young count's sinewy limbs were covered with jet-black fur and swelled to increase their mass. His burnt sienna hair and handsome face transformed as if swallowed whole by the wave of rippling fur, and in the second Rock blinked, a puissant werewolf appeared.

"Can I convince you with this appearance, Phoebe?" he asked in a soft, gentle rumbling voice that was hard to believe came from the gaping maw of bladelike incisors and canines.

Phoebe gasped. "What devilry is this?!" she howled, hiding Rock behind her and kicking up the hem of her dress. She drew a dagger from the scabbard in her leather boot and used a defensive forward grip on it. "What are you?"

"I'm a werewolf, Phoebe." Even with the dagger pointed at him, Ebel was imperturbable. His golden eyes, the only part of him that stayed the same between forms, assessed her. "I gained the power to transform into a werewolf from a curse cast on me by one of the

Werewolf Brotherhood statues my father collected."

"Did you say...a werewolf statue...?" Phoebe was noticeably shaken.

"I did." Ebel nodded his canine head and bared his teeth in a slightly wolfish smile. "I met Rock while wandering the streets in this form. Like now, I had torn my clothes and had nothing to wear if I wanted to change back. That was when I discovered the tailor sign and hesitantly went inside." Fondness softened the edges around his golden eyes as he looked over Phoebe at Rock. "Rock was terribly kind to me, selling clothes to a broke monster. I've lost my heart to him ever since that fateful encounter."

For the most part, that matched Rock's memory, though she wasn't confident she was "kind" during her first werewolf encounter.

Still wielding the dagger, Phoebe snarled with distrust. "Lies."

"I swear to God I am not lying. As far as this conversation goes, I have not told a single lie," Ebel declared.

After several hesitant seconds, Phoebe looked over her shoulder. Rock promptly reassured her. "It's true. Ebel's a werewolf, but he's not scary, and he doesn't eat people."

"That's not what I'm worried about."

Phoebe's grimace made Ebel quietly shake his head. "I promise I have not laid my hands on your precious young one."

Phoebe shot him a spiteful glare and sheathed her dagger. Smoothing her skirts over her weapon-filled boots, she heaved a sigh. "I've got the gist of the situation. His Excellency turned into a werewolf and had to stay the night because he had no clothes. That about right?"

"Yes! That's absolutely right, Phoebe!" Relief washed over Rock now that she'd conveyed what she was trying to explain.

Phoebe, on the other hand, was far from relieved as she turned tired eyes on Ebel. "But clearly you can become a werewolf at will if your transformation just now is anything to go by. Care to tell me why you transformed so your clothes ripped off in front of Rock?"

"You're as sharp as I'd expect," Ebel said, complimenting Phoebe before rolling his furry shoulders. He directed his next question to Rock. "Rock, did the shop downstairs have the statue?"

"Yes. I used a chunk of money to safely retrieve it."

"Good job. Thank you."

"I locked the statue in my shop's safe."

"I will send an envoy to pick it up later. I'm sincerely grateful to you." Satisfied by her answers, he returned the conversation to a scowling Phoebe. "I'll fill you in on this as well. It appears the statue that cursed me isn't the only one of its kind."

Phoebe said nothing. Rock craned her neck to get a better view of her grim profile.

"The worst discovery was that I can't control my powers with one nearby. Last night I transformed into the werewolf against my will. All because one of those statues was stored in the antique shop downstairs."

"Lady Trilian's shop. A believable story," Phoebe drawled in a low voice, looking Ebel square in the eyes. He accepted that stony gaze and slowly batted his lashes.

"I believe you have seen that statue before, Phoebe."

That was a shocking declaration. Rock confronted her: "Is that true, Phoebe?"

Phoebe pressed her lips together and hesitated for a short while. During that time, her eyes never left the werewolf, her back protected Rock, and there was a deliberate evenness to each breath she took.

"...It is." After several minutes of tense air, she finally acknowledged it. "After all, that statue—at least, the one brought into Mateus Manor—was discovered by Fredericks Berwick."

Slapped with an even more startling revelation, Rock's eyes bulged. "By Father?"

The statue her mercenary father found during his ruin-scavenging quests had cursed Ebel. She couldn't accept that painful truth right away. *The curse isn't Father's fault.* How she wanted to believe that.

"Rock, it's not your father's fault," Ebel said, sensing her inner turmoil. "It was my father who unleashed the curse. This would have never happened if he hadn't tried it out of curiosity. All the responsibility falls on us. You and your father had nothing to do with it."

So he said, but she didn't think that way. Rather, even her meeting him was starting to feel like the curse's work.

"If Father hadn't found it, you—"

"That's not true." Ebel spoke over her with a shake of his head. "Another mercenary would have found it if he had not."

"You...think so? But..."

The gentlest voice assuaged her doubts. "I hope you can think of this as fate. Believe that you and I met because we were supposed to."

Phoebe stayed silent throughout it all. Watching to see how Ebel handled this, she didn't look away from him for one second.

"You call this fate…?" Rock repeated in a hesitant manner.

She thought it too cruel for Ebel's curse to be predestined. He had lost more than one or two things from being cursed.

But werewolf Ebel tenderly persuaded her. "The curse I suffered that day became the opportunity to fall in love with you. I can finally come to accept it."

"W-We have not fallen in love!" Rock rushed to deny. She couldn't help being embarrassed by that talk in front of Phoebe. Then a sudden thought occurred to her. "You said you were going around talking to mercenaries. Were you searching for the one who found the statue?"

He'd told her he met with several dozen mercenaries and former mercenaries to ask them questions. Along the way, he asked about her father, Fredericks. Perhaps Ebel's goals had been aligned with hers all along.

"I was," Ebel confirmed, as she suspected. "To make sure there were no more statues out there. I was looking for the mercenary to locate the statues, if any others existed, so I could destroy them before the curse was released again." Those golden wolf eyes swung over to the stone-quiet Phoebe. "I've had a hunch there were more for a while now, and today proved that hunch correct."

"I didn't know that…" Rock unconsciously sighed aloud.

The mercenary Ebel was searching for, Rock's father, was no longer of this world. He could've questioned him in-depth about the statue if he were still around. He might've obtained all the information he needed to put an end to the statues.

"If only my father were still alive," she said in a ghost of a whisper, indescribable sorrow breaking her heart. She just thought the same thing she wished so many other times. If only her father were around.

"*If* only. I've longed to meet him all this time too," Ebel agreed, never taking his eyes off Phoebe.

Following his gaze, Rock looked up at Phoebe and urged her for more information. "Say, Phoebe, did you ever hear anything about it? Father must have said something to you if he showed you the statue—"

Up until that moment, Phoebe had had her eyes locked on the

werewolf, her mouth set in a hard line. Rock's comment brought a partial smile to her face, and she plopped her hand on top of Rock's head to stop her from saying any more.

"Phoebe?"

Phoebe glared again at Ebel, leaving Rock to muddle through why she touched her instead of answering. "I only found one statue," she answered fluidly, never easing up on her glower. "That was the only thing of value in that ruin. I heard the Brotherhood used that spot as a secret base. Their headquarters are likely somewhere else."

"…Is that what Sir Fredericks told you?"

Phoebe clicked her tongue and stuck her chin out. "That's right."

"I appreciate your cooperation, Phoebe." The werewolf dropped into a courteous bow.

Annoyed by him in every way, Phoebe roughly ran her hands through her chestnut curls. "So? What are you planning to do, Your Excellency?"

"Continue searching for the statues, of course. I'll destroy them upon discovery. That's it."

"That's it?" she sharply retorted.

The werewolf face didn't shift into any kind of readable expression, but Rock heard the faint exhale. "Aside from that… Oh, yes," he continued with an excited bounce in his voice, "I want your permission to continue seeing Rock after this. I'm content with that for now."

"…Huh?" Rock squeaked dumbly, not following the sudden change in topic.

Phoebe clenched her skirts and flashed her teeth menacingly at him. "For now? You think you have the upper hand now?"

"Please don't misunderstand me, Phoebe." Ebel shook his head, full of composure. "My feelings are sincere. I won't use blackmail."

"Can I trust you?"

"Of course. Anyone who's special to Rock is special to me too."

"…Hmph."

Ebel and Phoebe weren't using complex terminology, but Rock didn't have a clue what they were referring to. What upper hand? Lots of unfriendly words like *blackmail* and *trust* were being thrown around.

"I'll eventually be coming to you to ask for Rock's hand in marriage. I have to look out for you."

Phoebe and Rock jumped at the same time.

"Marriage?!"

"M-Marriage?!"

The werewolf's furry shoulders shook with mirth at their similar surprised reactions. "You were perfectly in sync. You're a lovely pair." Laughing, he joyfully added, "I'm grateful for this fate. I sincerely hope you both feel that way too."

HUMAN Ebel went home after accepting the change of clothes from Rock. Obviously he didn't go home in silence—he secured a promise for another visit and didn't forget to land a kiss on the back of her hand in the interlude.

"I'll send an envoy by the end of today. Keep the statue safe until then."

His parting words were said with such seriousness she couldn't complain about his lips brushing the back of her knuckles.

Once he departed, Rock and Phoebe headed to Floria Clothes Shop.

"Show me that statue," Phoebe importuned before opening for the day, so Rock unlocked the safe and showed her the white limestone statue. After scrutinizing the rough, spooky wolf figure, she gave a pensive affirmation. "It's the same thing all right. So this was a cursed statue... I didn't know."

"Father didn't say anything either?" Rock's question drew a troubled smile from that pretty face.

"Nope. He only knew that the Werewolf Brotherhood had a secret base in those ruins. And also that Count Mateus would buy anything he found there for an exorbitant price."

"Hmm..."

Phoebe seemed to know in-depth details about her father's work too. Ebel had said he didn't meet anyone who knew of her mercenary days, but Lady Trilian did. As Rock always assumed, Phoebe was undeniably intimate with her father on a personal and professional level.

"You see, the Werewolf Brotherhood was supposedly established by those who were oppressed in ancient times," Phoebe said, sharing bits and pieces of information as she remembered it. "They were a group of fanatics who were in love with the werewolves no one believed existed then, either, and they dreamed of someday making that power theirs. But who would've thought they actually obtained the power to become a werewolf?"

"They wanted to become werewolves? Even though it changes them into beasts?" Hard to believe after Rock had seen Ebel.

"It just goes to show the lengths they went to, to stand up to their oppressors," Phoebe chided.

"You still lose a lot in the process."

"Well, it's a fact that they desired the wrong kind of power." Phoebe placed the statue back inside the safe and securely locked it. Once she finished checking and rechecking the lock, she let out a harsh breath. "Fate, huh?"

"It is a strange twist of fate, what with Father being the one who found the statue." Rock gave a mirthless laugh. When she thought of the pain and suffering Ebel went through, she couldn't rejoice over their destiny the way he did.

She knew her father wasn't at fault. Needless to say, it wasn't Ebel's fault, either; nor did he make it sound intentional on his father's part. Rock found the whole thing awfully heartbreaking.

Phoebe, however, was battling another line of thought.

"Rock, I need to confirm one thing with you," she started with a grim expression.

"What is it?"

Phoebe sighed again. With an awfully serious voice, she dropped an unexpected question. "What do you think of His Excellency now?"

"Huh?! Wh-What do I...?" The question alone was enough to fluster Rock beyond help.

Phoebe's brows snapped together, and her lips pursed. "You've gotten awfully bashful about it now."

"I have not! It's not like I've fallen for him or anything like that!" Rock denied it outright, aware of her flushed cheeks. Phoebe's pointed stare cornered her into confiding the truth. "It's not what you think... Sometimes I just feel that His Excellency and I are similar when we're together."

If she had to put a name to the feelings she had for him, it would be empathy.

"His Excellency was cursed because of his father's mistake, but he still deeply loves his father even now."

Though he was oppressed with doubts and anxieties about his cursed body, not once did he utter a word of reproach for his father. Complex feelings on the matter were a given, but that was just another thing that made Ebel and Rock similar.

"I feel the same way. While I have a lot of opinions about Father, I can never hate him."

She loved him for leaving her an inheritance. She took pride in his being a famous mercenary renowned for his swordsmanship. And she wanted to cherish the fact that her mother only ever loved him after they separated.

"I love him even though I've never met him." She felt a tad guilty confessing this to her father's lover. Presumptuous though it was, she thought Phoebe would forgive her for it.

"Rock…" Phoebe looked thunderstruck. Trembling, she stared back into Rock's blue eyes. Mouth set in a hard line, expression stiff, and tears shimmering in her eyes, she looked as if she wanted to say something but couldn't.

"Phoebe…?" Rock gingerly called her name.

Snapping out of it, she screwed up her face into a scowl. "Take my advice. It's too soon for you to marry, Rock!"

"HUH? Wh-Where did that come from?!"

"You're only twenty! Don't be hasty! You have no need to rush!"

"I never even said I was going to marry!"

Who was the one being hasty? Rock quickly denied it, but Phoebe seemed mightily concerned about her future. She was grilled about her marriage intentions for a long time after that.

EBEL'S envoy arrived at Floria Clothes Shop that same evening.

"Kyaa! Master Rock! How I've longed to see you again!" It was Johanna, the blond maid Rock met once at Mateus Manor, who tore into the shop with all the noise and excitement of baby chicks awaiting a meal of worms from their mother.

Not only Rock but even Phoebe was startled by the slightly younger girl's appearance.

"Are you sure you are His Excellency's envoy? Will you be all right?"

"Fret not! Iniel is with me!"

Rock didn't recognize the name, but Johanna pointed to a carriage parked outside the shop window. She recognized the man sitting in the luxury berline carriage drawn by two white Clydesdales. He was the debonair coachman who'd picked Rock and Phoebe up for their visit to Mateus Manor.

"Then, if you please, Master Rock. I shall take custody of the statue." Johanna was frightfully eager about it, so Rock unlocked the safe and handed over the werewolf statue. She carefully wrapped it in a soft, dark cloth and secured it in a cloth bag. "I have received it most assuredly." She curtsied, and when she straightened, her whole adorable face lit up like the morning sun. "Incidentally, His Excellency stayed the night with you last night?" She swooped in close with that question.

"H-He did…" Rock spluttered. She only affirmed the truth, but that was enough to flush Johanna's cheeks with thrilled excitement.

"I knew it! Lovers spending the night under the same roof has such a lovely ring to it!"

"Uh, like I said, His Excellency and I aren't—"

"It's all right! You don't have to spell it out for me!" Johanna decisively cut off Rock's explanation. Dropping her voice to barely a whisper, she asked, "There is but one thing I would like to know. Between you and His Excellency, what role do you take?"

Naturally, Rock didn't understand the meaning behind her question. "What are you talking about?"

Johanna fidgeted as she explained, "When it comes to male love, the number one point of interest is which one takes which position—"

"HOLD IT! What nonsense are you asking my Rock?!" Phoebe intervened.

Johanna drew back in fear. She shot Phoebe a nervous look but didn't want to give up without an answer. "A-Am I not supposed to ask…?"

"You obviously aren't!" Phoebe's roar had instant success.

"Boo… Very well. I will leave it to my imagination for the time being." An oddly dejected Johanna plodded out of the shop with the bag containing the statue.

Once the carriage carrying the maid rolled away, Phoebe's shoulders sagged. "What was His Excellency thinking sending that chatterbox as his envoy…?"

Rock also felt concerned to some degree, but she was more concerned with Johanna's question. "Phoebe, what was Johanna trying to ask me?" she inquired, since she hadn't the faintest idea.

"Don't look for answers to questions you don't understand," Phoebe replied with a sigh. "Ignore her, ignore her."

That answer wasn't very satisfying, but Rock was relieved to have safely handed over the statue.

Even though it had been kept in the safe, she eerily felt its eyes on her back all day long.

PEACE and quiet dominated Rock's life for the next few days.

Ebel didn't visit her shop during that time since he needed to get rid of the statue. A rush order kept Rock holed away in the shop too. Lady Michaela Linus's ball gown needed to be ready in time for her birthday party next month.

She had no other rush orders, only Ebel's cloak, so she concentrated on making the dress. During that time, Phoebe took care of her meals and tending to the shop, arranging more time for Rock to focus on her work.

By the time they entered a new month, Rock had finished the gorgeous ball gown she had always envisioned.

The dress made with the best silk available was a light purple that resembled the receding night before the dawn. Designed with contemporary trends in mind, the dress tied with a dainty ribbon at the back of the neck and had a small tight-fitting waist tailored to Michaela's size.

Rock made the skirt with minimal drapery so that the way it fell accentuated the legs, and she added a bustle to pull the skirt up. The short sleeves were like large bells with open splits allowing for decorative sleeve hemlines, a very popular style with young ladies, and Rock also made use of delicate silk flounces to show off skin while maintaining a ladylike image.

"Nice work. It came out even more elegant than I imagined." Phoebe exhaled with pure satisfaction over the completed dress. "Also, what a stunning hue... The color of the coming dawn is breathtaking."

The dress currently hung on the rattan doll used for display, and Rock suspected it'd look even more perfect on Michaela. Like every job she took on, she put her whole heart into it, and her fears lay more with the embittered older brother's reaction than Michaela's.

"I sure hope Duke Linus's son likes it," she muttered, airing her concerns.

Phoebe's neatly manicured brows snapped together. "Let's shove the money back in his face if he doesn't like it. Then you can tailor it to me."

"You like it that much?" Rock asked, delighted.

"I love it! I could've pulled it off if I had bigger breasts," Phoebe answered, depressed over her big-boned build. Her eyes suddenly shifted to Rock. She assessed her from head to toe. "You might look better in it."

"Me? As if!" She laughed it off, but Phoebe wasn't joking.

"You're in your blooming years. Put in a little effort and you'll shine."

"I don't know about that. I've never worn something like this before."

"Plus, you're close in age and physique with Michaela."

Now that she mentioned it, Michaela was turning the same age as Rock this month. And they were practically the same height. There were a few small differences in their figures, but Phoebe's idea wasn't too far-fetched.

To Rock, though, dresses were merely merchandise, and she couldn't imagine a scenario where she would wear one. Things may have been different if her promise to her mother had come to fruition. Just remembering that twisted her expression, exposing her glum feelings.

"Come now, don't let it get you down, dear. You went through the effort of making it. We'll find a use for it no matter what happens." Phoebe slapped her encouragingly on the back.

Rock shook off the flurry of daunting thoughts and decided to just be happy about finishing the dress. "Thanks, Phoebe. I'm always being saved by your presence."

"Don't thank me for the obvious!" Phoebe bashfully picked lint off her skirt.

👑 👑 👑

FOR the first time in several days, Ebel visited the shop, the very evening Rock put the finishing touches on the gown.

"I finally made some time to see you and give you an update," he said to Rock, looking as if a load had finally been lifted from his shoulders. "I smashed that statue to pieces. As we suspected, being around it increases the werewolf curse's potency, which helped me easily destroy it."

Johanna had successfully delivered the statue to Ebel, then. From his explanation alone, it was hard to imagine what had happened at Mateus Manor after its arrival, but she gleaned from his expression that it took a lot of time and effort. In the end, the statue was destroyed, and peace returned to Ebel's life too.

Ebel also let out an admiring breath over Michaela's displayed gown. "A dress the shade of dawn, huh? This is a marvelous piece of work!"

"Thank you, Ebel."

"Good grief, I can't stop being impressed by your workmanship. Not even the real dawn is as beautiful as this." His compliments flattered Rock and brought her joy.

As for Phoebe, she was giving Ebel the evil eye as she reminded him, "Your Excellency, Lady Michaela will be wearing this."

"I heard. What of it?"

"Lord Guido Linus plans to make his sister wear this in order to seduce you, you know?" Phoebe harshly quipped.

Ebel chuckled cheerfully. "You don't have to worry. My heart already belongs to Rock." He faced Rock and winked. "I believe I already told you that Michaela is like a little sister to me. I will never be seduced by her."

Rock wordlessly lowered her head. She would be lying if she said she didn't care, but she didn't know how best to respond when he put it like that.

Even Ebel had some concerns, though. "Actually, I have been invited to attend Michaela's birthday celebration this month." Unease twisted his handsome face. "As I said, we don't have to worry when it comes to Michaela. But Guido's behavior is unsettling. Including his ordering a dress from you for Michaela."

Rock, too, couldn't understand why Guido not only deliberately visited her shop when he openly despised her, but also ordered a dress from her for his beloved sister. Perhaps, as she feared, he planned to tear apart her work and find fault with the dress.

"I'll keep an eye out as well, but let me know if Guido does anything to offend you," Ebel urged Rock on his way out. "He's my friend, but…I won't forgive him if he hurts you."

Rock quietly noted the resolve on his rarely unsmiling expression.

THE day after she finished the dress, Rock sent a messenger to Linus Manor. A tailor's job didn't end with completed clothes. Dresses, especially, required a fitting prior to delivery in order to make the finer adjustments. The messenger was sent to set a date and time for the fitting as well.

Guido replied that day, sending back a letter stating he wanted the tailor to come alone to the manor on the day of Michaela's birthday party and that he'd be sending a carriage to the slums' entrance to pick her up then.

Reading his pompous request caused Phoebe to scowl. "Little rich boy thinks he's so important!"

"He actually is someone important. He's a duke's eldest son, after all," Rock admonished, but Phoebe's remark came from genuine concern for her.

"Are you going? You're only going to get hurt."

"I'm grateful if I can walk away with a ton of money just by getting my feelings a little hurt."

True, she didn't want to go through with it, but she wouldn't quit a job once she'd accepted it. All she hoped was that the dress she slaved over didn't go to waste.

"Want me to come with you?" Phoebe offered.

Unfortunately, Guido's request specified "only Rock Floria may come." The coachman would just turn her away if she came, and Rock didn't want to put her through this unpleasantness too.

"That's okay. Take care of the shop for me, Phoebe."

"I'll come get you if you're late getting home," Phoebe vowed, sounding even more uneasy after Rock smiled.

"It's in the aristocrat district. You can't walk that distance."

"I'll use whatever I must should the need arise. So, please, rely on me."

Thinking Phoebe was overreacting with her pleading, Rock agreed. "Fine. I'll be counting on you if worse comes to worse, Phoebe."

Guido saw Rock as nothing more than a nuisance. He wouldn't leave such an annoying interloper at his sister's celebration for long. Rock had talked herself into taking the situation too lightly.

ON the day of Michaela's birthday, Rock left before sunset holding a box containing the gown. Seen off by Phoebe, she headed for the gate connecting the slums to the urban areas. A carriage waited where it was supposed to be, and the coachman called to her when she neared.

"Rock Floria, I presume? Get in." Unlike the Mateuses' coachman Iniel, the Linuses' coachman openly showed his disgust for Rock. He jerked his chin toward the carriage with a face that said he'd much rather not have her ride in it, and he didn't open the door for her even though her hands were full. Because of his behavior, she had to do a painful balancing act with the box to get inside.

The carriage raced through the imperial capital's streets, eventually arriving at the aristocratic district around the time the emperor's castle was dyed red by the setting sun.

The beautiful cityscape she thought she would never see after her visit to Mateus Manor was colored by the sunset glow. The unfamiliar district felt awfully uninviting in the red light that swayed like candle flames, making Rock feel out of place and all alone.

Before long, the carriage turned and stopped in the garden of Linus Manor.

More luxurious than Ebel's manor, this expansive residence, imitating a castle with its four spires, loomed on the grounds. The garden was as beautifully landscaped as a corner of the wealthy public square, with a covered gazebo on a cobblestone promenade and even a small fountain. The blue alkanet she had seen at Mateus Manor also blanketed the lawns here, and it swayed cheerlessly in the evening wind.

Rock pushed open the carriage door, hopped down, and headed for the entrance with the dress box.

"Aah, you must be the tailor." Rock didn't need to mention her name to the servant who greeted her outside. "Go through the front and up the first stairs you see and to the reception room at the end of the third floor. Don't enter any other rooms."

"Thank you." Rock bowed to the curt servant and set foot inside the manor, surprised at being directed to the front entrance instead of the servant stairs. Carrying the box in both hands, she carefully ascended the central staircase lit by the dazzlingly beautiful chandelier.

On the way, a man and woman who appeared to be guests passed her on the landing. Dressed up floridly for the evening party, the couple eyed Rock suspiciously when she moved to the wall to let them pass. Rock knew she was out of place here, but she was quickly overawed by the second mansion she had ever been to.

She stopped at the third floor and walked toward the reception room at the end of the corridor. One of the doors suddenly opened beside her.

"Oh, is that you, tailor?" Michaela sounded puzzled.

Rock was struck speechless when she looked her way.

Michaela stood in the doorway already decked out in a gorgeous gown.

At a glance, Rock could tell the violet dress, which perfectly complimented her black hair, was made from the finest satin unavailable on the market. Everything from the high neckline to the pagoda sleeves and crinoline harkened back to the vestal dresses of tradition—and stood in utter contrast to the order Guido placed. Her tightly squeezed waist was decorated by a thin gold chain, and every button was a gorgeously carved gold piece.

Sending waves through her ample satin skirts, Michaela sashayed over to Rock. "What brings you here today?"

"What brings me here? I came to deliver your order."

Michaela marveled at her. "I placed my dress order with another tailor instead. You didn't hear?"

She hadn't heard.

Before the baffled Rock appeared Guido as if he were Michaela's shadow. A wicked sneer curled the lips of the formally attired duke's son upon seeing Rock, but it softened into a smile the moment he saw Michaela as well.

"Michaela. I've arranged it so this tailor will be celebrating you today as well."

Michaela, and obviously Rock, were taken by complete surprise. "Oh my… Why ever so?" she asked, covering her mouth with her hand.

"Because he is also Ebel's *friend*. Inviting him will please Ebel."

"That makes perfect sense. Any friend of Ebel's is a very dear friend to us." Innocently smiling, Michaela cheerfully turned to Rock, who was having trouble swallowing the situation. "I'm delighted you came, tailor. Please enjoy tonight to its fullest."

"What? Pardon me, but what exactly is—" Rock was trying, and failing, to understand the situation.

Not only did they tell her they didn't need the dress they ordered, but they told her she was a guest invited to the party. Needless to say, she hadn't been informed of any of those things and didn't think she had the proper standing to attend.

Something smells fishy. Would a proud man like Guido invite a lowly tailor from the slums to a party out of the goodness of his heart? I don't think so.

"Michaela," Guido said over Rock's question, "You have rounds to make. Go on ahead."

"All right, Brother. See you later, tailor." Michaela happily left in a swish of skirts as her brother watched her go down the corridor.

Once he confirmed his sister had disappeared around the corner, Guido's voice dropped below zero. "Come, tailor. Your room is that way." He flicked his gaze toward the door at the end of the corridor. "Take that box inside with you. Don't dally."

Full of doubt, Rock had little choice but to obey his orders.

It was more of a storage room than a space used to receive guests. By no means did this room—with only one big window and randomly packed with overflowing trunks and old books shoved haphazardly into bookshelves—look like somewhere anyone but the serving staff would use. A flame already flickered inside the sole lantern placed on top of a wooden trunk, pointlessly lighting the dust-covered chamber.

"Put the box there." Guido jerked his chin toward the floor, so Rock slowly lowered the gown box.

Then she voiced her confusion. "May I ask what is going on here?"

Guido snorted and said mockingly, "Nothing much. My little sister just said she didn't want the slutty dress you were making."

"Pardon…?"

"So I placed an order with the best tailor in the imperial capital and had him make a high-quality dress my sister would be happy to wear." Guido exulted in the cruelty he flung at the paralyzed Rock. "No way could a lowly tailor from the slums make a dress keeping in character with the latest fashions. I don't want to make my angelic sister look like a whore in your raunchy dress—if you can even call it a dress."

His words were the greatest insult possible to Rock. First, he offended her by degrading the dress made to his specifications without even looking at it; then he added insult to injury by comparing her with another tailor. Rock was certainly a young tailor with limited experience running a store, but she was confident in her talent.

More than anything else, the gown's design stood as proof of the love and care she put into making it with Michaela in mind. Even a stubborn nob like Guido wouldn't dare call it raunchy or indecorous if he saw it.

But, without ever opening the box, Guido had become drunk on the pleasure he received from tearing her apart. "Any clothes made by the godforsaken devil who seduced Ebel has no place to go but the rubbish bins!"

"How dare you mock another's hard work…!" Rock's frustration raised her voice to a shout.

He leered at her. "You lose your temper as if you matter, insolent scum of the earth."

Rock was several steps beyond losing her temper. If she hadn't been dealing with a duke's son, she would've bashed his smug face in with a right hook. But she maintained enough self-control in her anger to know punching Guido's lights out would only bring about her destruction. She gnashed her teeth and dug her nails into her palms.

"Relax, you guttersnipe. I won't let your work go to waste." Guido's scrutinizing emerald eyes cruised her figure. His rudely insulting gaze traveled from her wine-colored hair to her slender frame, stopping at her feet covered by work boots before returning to her face. "Didn't you hear me? I said you are a party guest tonight." Rock prepared for the worst, but the hit he dealt her was a mental one. "You can have the dress. Appear at the party wearing it."

She thought he had discovered her. Chills rushed through every fiber of her being. Ebel was one thing, but being exposed to this man now spelled doom. It was a given Guido would fly into a rage if he found out the man he was ridiculing for being girlish was actually a woman.

"I-I'm a man. I can't wear a dress." Rock's voice shook, but Guido took that to mean he succeeded in ruffling the younger man's feathers. Pure rapture flashed in his cold eyes.

"And that's why you're going to wear it."

"To what end...?"

"You sunk your claws into Ebel's heart. You shameless heathen. So now you can present yourself before him wearing a woman's gown. Isn't that amusing?" Guido seized Rock's chin in his hand and yanked it up. She grimaced from the icy touch and pain he inflicted by digging his fingers in hard.

"Let go of me!"

"The more I look at you, the more you look like a woman. Good God, there's nothing more disgusting than you." He leaned in till his nose nearly touched hers and inspected her features with the eyes of an interrogator. Rock couldn't jerk her chin free and was stuck with the feel of his breath on her face as he whispered, "I'll show Ebel how different from a woman you are. Then he'll finally come to his senses."

That proved it—Guido still believed Rock was male. He intended to disillusion Ebel by dragging Rock dressed in a woman's gown in front of him. His tastelessly cruel plan had failed before it even started, but Rock had no reason to obediently go along with him either.

"Do you think I am going to obey you? I am going home." She swatted at his hand, but her strength was no match for the death grip of the much larger Guido. He dug his fingers in so hard her jaw popped, wrenching a cry from her lips. "Ow...!"

"Don't you for one second believe you can leave here unscathed. I've summoned a constable unit here under the pretense of guarding the event." Gripping her chin with such force it wouldn't be long before it broke, he threatened her in a low snarl: "They would gladly toss you in the clink if I tell them a street rat from the slums broke in."

To the constables, people residing in the slums were parasites to be gotten rid of. Rock was fully aware Guido wasn't making empty threats.

More than anything else, the eyes looking down the bridge of his nose at her flared with insanity. Some of the vagabonds lurking in the slums had this same look in their eyes. They were the eyes of men and women who had sold their souls to the devil and didn't shy away from murder when push came to shove.

"I'll send you home unharmed as long as you put on that obscene dress," he ordered, finally releasing her. "Get changed now. Time is running out for you," he sneered on his way out of the storage room.

Rock was left alone in the room with the unopened box. Guido's touch still lingered on her aching chin. She couldn't see it, but there were red marks in the shape of his fingers imprinted there. Feeling defiled, she scrubbed at the spot with her sleeve. Then she shouted to vent her anger.

"What the bloody hell is his problem?!"

A vortex of differing emotions swirled inside her. Anger over having the job she put her heart and soul into insulted, irritation over unrewarded work, frustration over her inability to lash out at Guido, and growing contempt on par with the mocking she'd received. And there was a smidgeon of pity for the man.

Just as she previously suspected, it wasn't Ebel's former fiancée who was obsessed with him, but her older brother, Guido. His methods stood no chance of changing Ebel's mind. She could be sure of that now.

"I wonder if Ebel is here yet…" In search of rescue, Rock stumbled over to the window in the back of the storage room. The view overlooked the Linuses' garden, and she saw several dozen parked guest carriages in it.

She strained her eyes in search of the carriage from Mateus Manor, but it was impossible to find in the garden that was already embracing dusk. Unable to spot it after looking for several minutes, she sighed and leaned against the window. "I shouldn't even think about getting help, then."

Of course Ebel would lend her a helping hand if she sought it. But finding him alone without being discovered by the constables on patrol within and without the manor was impractical. With zero understanding of the building's layout, running away by herself looked just as unfeasible.

Plus, this was the third floor. She didn't have the courage to jump from the window. So the only choice left to her was—

Rock glanced at the evening gown box left on the floor. Maybe she would succeed in meeting Ebel if she wore it as Guido wanted. She didn't know what to expect of a nobleman's banquet, but Ebel should find her even in the largest venue full of guests. *Is it okay for me to believe that?*

What caused her to hesitate wasn't outrage toward Guido, but the heart of a woman she hid deep in her chest.

"…Do I have to wear a dress?" she whispered, shoving her hair away from her face.

My hair must be a frizzy mess considering I haven't combed it since morning, and I don't have any makeup with me. Besides, there's not even a mirror in here. Trying to fit a dress I tailored to Michaela's figure will be hard without a mirror. Will a dress even look good on me when I'm easily mistaken for a boy?

"Ugh…." Aggravated, impatient, and hopeless, Rock sighed as she leaned against the window.

All of a sudden, something knocked on the glass behind her. She looked over her shoulder to where someone was hanging down on the opposite side of the window pane. The upside-down face peeping at her was the one she had seen every day for the last three years.

"Phoebe!" she instinctively shouted.

Outside, Phoebe moved her lips. *"Open the window."*

Rock did as asked and threw open the window. Phoebe nimbly swung into the room from the roof.

"Why are you here?"

Phoebe answered her question after closing the window. "I knew the spoiled toff wouldn't send you home without trouble first. So I came to check on you." She put her hands on her hips, which weren't covered in the usual shape-concealing dresses she wore.

A tight-fitting leather jacket and breeches replaced the corset and petticoat and was topped off by a riveted breastplate. Leather boiled in oil was generally used for armor, and Rock knew at a glance that Phoebe was armed for a fight. She affixed a dagger the length of an adult man's arm to her hip and drew her luscious chestnut hair back into a high ponytail. Gallantry and valiance defined her appearance, bringing out a different form of beauty from her usual pretty big-lady looks.

"Your clothes…"

Rock's mention of her clothing brought an awkward look to her face. "Just in case. Infiltrating a building in a dress isn't easy, and I still had my old leather armor laying around."

This was Rock's first time seeing Phoebe dressed in her armor.

Phoebe was the woman who normally brawled barehanded in the streets. Choosing to appear in armor showed just how concerned she was about Rock. Rock's tensed nerves instantly unraveled with relief from Phoebe showing up when she thought help wasn't coming.

"Thank you so much for coming, Phoebe!" Rock threw her arms around her.

Easily holding her up, Phoebe simpered. "Now, this isn't like you, child… What are you doing in a cramped room like this?"

Right! Now's not the time to celebrate. Rock had a pressing problem to diffuse. With little choice, she explained the situation to Phoebe. She included every detail, from Michaela wearing another dress to Guido threatening to sic the constables on her if she didn't wear her gown.

As she listened, Phoebe's expression gradually turned grim, until it exploded with outrage over learning about Guido seizing Rock's chin. "That bastard! How dare he do that to our Rock!" she seethed, with nowhere to take out her wrath. She placed her hands on Rock's shoulders. "Did he do anything else to you? Are you hurt?"

"I'm all right. He did verbally abuse me, though." Rock lifted her shoulders in a half shrug.

Phoebe stomped out her uncontrollable anger. "I can't forgive that either! There's nothing disgusting about you! You're adorable!"

"I-I don't think I am that either…" Rock said bashfully, disagreeing with Guido and Phoebe's assessment.

"He asked for it! We're going to teach him a lesson. Wear the dress, Rock!" Phoebe boldly ordered.

"WHAT?! Are you serious, Phoebe?!"

"You think I would joke about this? Isn't it mortifying to let him get away with making fun of you?"

Of course she was mortified. She couldn't stand Guido stomping all over the time, energy, and emotion she put into tailoring the perfect dress for Michaela. For better or worse, he didn't realize Rock was a woman yet. This was the perfect opportunity to knock him down a peg or two.

Most importantly, if she caught Ebel's eye, he'd turn this bad situation in their favor.

"Will I even look good in a dress?"

Phoebe merrily laughed off Rock's fears. "You sure will. You're Fredericks Berwick's daughter, after all!"

The mention of her father's name slapped sense back into Rock. She remembered how he was said to have been a talented mercenary who slipped into dangerous ruins and returned with the goods with all five limbs intact. He had to have possessed dauntless courage for that.

I can't be a coward when his blood runs through me!

"Leave your appearance to me. I can do your makeup."

Phoebe's encouragement made up Rock's mind. "I'll do it. Will you help me, Phoebe?"

"I wouldn't have it any other way. This is your debut into high society!"

Curious, Rock stared up at her sweetly smiling face framed by her coiffured hair. For some reason, Phoebe had a makeup kit on her even though she was wearing armor.

"Why do you have that with you?" Rock asked, and received a scolding in return.

"Silly question. Carrying makeup on you at all times is the way of the woman."

"It is...?"

"Go on, now. Get changed first."

Given that extra push, Rock started by opening the box.

Finally freed from the dark confines of the box, the silk evening gown shimmered like glass in the lantern's light. Rock was proud of the finished piece, though she never imagined while she was making it that she would be the first to put it on.

Staring at the gown solidified her resolve, and she began unbuttoning her vest and shirt.

"Whoa! Hey! Let me know before you undress!" Phoebe sounded unusually flabbergasted behind her.

"What's the problem? We're both women," Rock said with a laugh, puzzled.

"W-We are, but even women show modesty around each other!"

Rock looked over her shoulder at Phoebe, who'd stubbornly turned her back to her. Phoebe's behavior didn't make sense to Rock, but she went along with it and changed.

The time came for the trickster tailor living a double life to add to her duplicity.

Until today, Rock had handled many types of silk, but this was her first time wearing it. The high-quality silk was slippery soft, and it molded comfortably to her skin. Bedazzled by the heavenly feel of it, she stared down at her body decorated by the gown.

Wearing nothing but pants for the last couple of years made her feel uncomfortable in a skirt. Slight movements gave a beautiful swaying motion to the shimmering semitransparent dawn-colored skirt, which was made from thin cloud-like layers of silk gauze. Since she was a little rounder around the waist than Michaela, she had to tightly tie the sash belt to pull off the same image.

"I'm not sure I can walk well with such a long skirt."

"That's no reason for you to walk with your head down," Phoebe stressed as Rock kept her eyes trained on the floor when she walked. "Hold your head up high."

"I-I know. I'll try." Rock lifted her head and pulled back her shoulders.

As tailored, the trendy gown, which tied in a ribbon behind the neck, exposed Rock's feminine collarbone and smooth shoulders. This wasn't her first time making this style of dress, but she felt a little embarrassed wearing it. The decorative sleeve hemlines swayed whenever she moved her arms, and she was quite taken with that princess-like quality.

"I never thought I would end up wearing this." Whispering those words made her feel embarrassed a little after the fact.

For a long time now, she had dressed as and pretended to be a man. Putting her arms through the sleeves of a dress thrilled her, even though she'd never found discontentment in donning a male lifestyle.

Phoebe took over makeup duty once Rock finished putting her dress in order. "I don't have every tool on me, so this will be a basic job."

Contrary to her words, makeup container after makeup container appeared from her leather pockets. Loose face powder filled a transparent vial, and a soft shade of rouge was housed within a flat wooden container shaped like a button. Two, then three brushes emerged, and Rock, who had never worn makeup, doubted her eyes.

"Do we really need to use all of this?"

"Yes, we do. Now keep your mouth shut for a bit," Phoebe instructed, starting by brushing the loose powder onto Rock's whole face.

As Rock's heart raced impossibly fast from the distinctly sweet smell of the powder, Phoebe picked up another brush and dipped the tip into the rouge. Then she gently, incomparably gentler than the duke's son, grasped Rock's chin and slightly tilted it upward as she placed the brush tip on her lips.

"Th-That tickles..." she said with a laugh when the brush moved over the contour of her lips.

"Quit that. Move again and I'll give you big lips like a monster," Phoebe warned with a wry smile.

Rock snapped her lips shut and swallowed her laughter. The brush vividly colored her mouth. After drawing the contours of her lips, Phoebe used delicate brush strokes to paint the softest parts red. Rock made it through without squirming too much.

Phoebe didn't stop her makeup job there. She used an eyebrow pencil to shape Rock's thin, girlish eyebrows and brushed some color over her eyelids, bringing more definition to her pretty eyes. She finished off with a light splash of blush before spinning Rock around by the shoulders.

"Take a look. You've become a drop-dead gorgeous woman."

Hearing Phoebe's voice at her back, Rock stared in amazement at what was before her eyes in the glass window covered in the black of night. The evening darkness hazily reflected Rock's present appearance back like a mirror. Staring back in surprise was a pretty young lady with glossy lips attired in the light purple gown she put her heart into making.

"Amazing… You do magic with makeup, Phoebe." Rock's rouged lips fell open.

"I've had plenty of experience with it," she boasted. "I'm done with your hair, dear. Face this way."

Rock turned toward Phoebe again and looked up at her first smile that night. Phoebe's expression suddenly darkened as she inspected Rock's dolled-up appearance. Surprise widened her ocean-blue eyes, and she gasped before touching Rock's cheeks with both hands. Tilting her chin up, she intently studied Rock's face as if assessing the authenticity of something nostalgic.

"What's wrong, Phoebe?" Rock asked, finding it strange.

Phoebe quietly exhaled. "I'm shocked… You look perfectly alike."

She didn't say who, but there was only one person she could mean.

Heart prancing at the thought, Rock straight-out asked, "With Father? You think I look like him?"

Phoebe didn't move her eyes from Rock as she answered in a trance, "No. With Vale. You look very much like Vale Floria."

"…What?" It was Rock's turn to gasp. How did her deceased father's lover know what her mother looked like? She'd never heard about them meeting before. "You know my mother?"

Phoebe smiled gently for one whole second before slamming her eyes shut and taking a deep breath to control her feelings. When she opened her eyes, her awe-inspiring expression was enough to take Rock's breath away. "Roxy, you are the child of Fredericks Berwick and Vale Floria."

Phoebe used Rock's real name. The last time she had used it was three long years ago, when they first met. She spoke emphatically to the shaken Rock: "Don't ever falter. Be unabashed, for the you right now has the power to enthrall and win over even the most faultfinding eyes." She softly bumped her forehead against Rock's and vowed, "I will be with you if anything happens. I'll kidnap you if I have to. Charge in there without anything holding you back."

"…Okay." Aware that she was becoming overwhelmed, Rock became flustered. She couldn't shake the feeling the person in front of her wasn't "Phoebe."

👑 👑 👑

"I'LL find a place I can lie low. Rest easy knowing I'll be watching over you," Phoebe reassured Rock before they parted ways in the storage room and Rock set off alone down the corridor.

Had Michaela's birthday celebration already begun? Silence reigned over the empty third-floor corridors. Careful not to tread on her gown's hem, Rock proceeded through the hallway.

Along the way, she took one look back at the closed storage room door. *Who is Phoebe really?* That thought crossed her mind.

She—or rather he—had always been there for Rock. Despite the very thin connection of Rock being her lover's child, Phoebe gallantly looked after Rock, supporting her in every way since the day she began living in the imperial capital.

And now Rock had discovered that Phoebe knew what her mother looked like. Her parents had separated before she was born. It wasn't unfeasible for Phoebe to have known her father since way back then, but something didn't seem right about that. Nor did the part about Ebel not pinning down any information about her mercenary days after interviewing dozens of people. Then there was Lady Trilian describing the younger Phoebe as a good, strong man.

At this point, a single, preposterous hypothesis was forming inside her. Rock broke off that line of thought and purposely stopped looking back. Questions could be saved for later. She had something she must do now. So as not to shame her father's and mother's names, she decided never again to look back.

♛ ♛ ♛

TRAILING her hand down the railing, Rock gracefully descended the central staircase to the first floor where she passed the servant who had met her outside. Taken by her beauty, his eyes widened. He quickly smoothed over his unprofessional reaction with a cordial smile.

"The ballroom is located straight ahead. Please hurry, as the celebration has already begun."

"Thank you." Holding back her laughter at his complete attitude change, Rock curtsied the way her mother taught her all those years ago and set off for the party.

The servant very likely mistook her for a noblewoman. As a tailor,

Rock felt blessed that her dress and a little makeup had this much influence over others.

Thus, the trickster tailor arrived at the duke's ballroom in a beautiful silk evening gown. The six double-leaf doors to the large room were left open, dazzling all who looked in at the effulgent lights of the crystal chandeliers and the lavishly dressed guests who shimmered beneath its glow. Rock was met at the door by the din of laughter exchanged between guests holding silver wineglasses and the soft melody played by the orchestra.

She took a single deep breath.

Holding her head high, she pinched the flat sides of her dress and swept inside the room.

Immediately, every guest near the doors looked at the new arrival. All were enthralled by the young lady in the dawn-colored ball gown, but suspicion immediately overtook them. They knew at a glance that she wasn't someone they had seen at high society events before. The etiquette of a ball required a young lady of her age to be escorted by a male partner or a female chaperone, but she appeared to be unaccompanied.

"I wonder which family she is from."

"She's pretty, but I've never seen her before."

Rock advanced deeper into the room, pretending not to hear their whispers. The space overflowed with nobles enjoying the party how they liked. For some, that meant enjoying a good glass of wine; for others, it meant dining on delicacies with relish, while others were engrossed in good conversation or listening to the orchestra. But even they turned and had their breath taken away when Rock passed by. Countless gazes followed her as she passed, taking in every bit of her beautiful face made more beautiful by the makeup, her exposed shoulders, and dawn-colored gown. Rock kept her head held high as she walked with determination, not letting their whispers or stares trip her up.

Then she spotted Guido and Michaela sitting next to each other at the back of the room. The siblings noticed Rock once she was within visible distance. Guido shot up from his chair and gaped at her. Blinking more frequently than a common snipe, he acted as if he were seeing an illusion. The color leached from his face when he realized she was no phantom.

Beside him, Michaela blinked several times in doubt before eventually covering her mouth with both hands, as though everything had clicked into place for her. A wide surprised yet delighted smile blossomed on her innocently sweet face.

Ignoring his sister's reaction, Guido began bellowing, "Guards! Get that—"

The ballroom stirred so loudly around Rock that it swallowed his angry shout.

Someone was hurrying through the crowd to get to her. Burnt sienna hair swept back, Ebel was clad in elegant clothing fit for a party, and his handsome face was tinged with surprise and impatience. He looked frantic to reach her.

Ultimate relief swept over Rock when she saw him. She expected no less of the werewolf count's keen nose, eyes, and ears. He found her right away, as she had hoped. Slipping through the throng of guests, he hurtled to a stop in front of her.

Gold eyes going rounder than the sun, he breathed out, "I never thought you would appear before me here..." He ran over to her and gazed upon her splendor as if confirming her presence was real. "Or I should say your presence...is like a dream."

Rock bashfully accepted his attention. She couldn't help feeling more ticklish inside than when Phoebe did her makeup, as Ebel's gaze caressed her softly combed hair, rouged lips, and gown. It was all the more flattering because this was the first time she had appeared before him as a woman.

"I have thought you were a gorgeous woman since long ago." Deeply moved, Ebel offered her his hand. The unaccompanied count's single action sent the crowd into a mighty commotion. He paid them no mind. "Please give me your hand. I wish you would grant only me the honor of escorting you this evening."

Raised as a commoner, Rock didn't know the etiquette required in these situations. But she had no reason not to accept the hand Ebel extended to her.

"I believed you would find me, Your Excellency," she told him from the heart, squeezing his hand.

Ebel flashed a swoon-worthy smile and gently squeezed back. "Address me as usual. No matter the place or the company, I want you to call me by name at all times."

"As you wish, Ebel."

Satisfaction glistened in his golden eyes. He seemed about to say her name, but he closed his opened mouth once, thought it over, then inquired of her with a smile, "You know, I still haven't learned your full name."

True enough, Rock had yet to properly introduce herself despite their continual encounters. Now was as good a time as ever to tell him. With that in mind, she spoke the name gifted to her by her parents. "My name is Roxy Floria."

"...A beautiful name for a beautiful lady," Ebel exclaimed, his reaction the complete opposite of when he'd learned of her alias. True joy etched into his handsome features, he gazed into her eyes and whispered in the sweetest voice, "I will treasure every syllable, my beloved Roxy."

People have been staring at my face a lot today. But this is the only moment my cheeks have flushed with such heat. Rock embraced that self-realization.

👑 Chapter 6: Entangled Threads of Fate

AS a tailor, Rock had helped many people dress up, but she never truly appreciated the importance of "dressing up" as much as on this night.

Ladies and gentlemen flocked around her and Ebel as he led her farther into the ballroom by the hand.

"Which family does this beautiful young lady hail from?"

"What an innocent-looking young lass. Is tonight her debut into high society?"

"What a magnificent gown! A distinguished tailor must have designed it."

Inundated with compliments and questions, it took Rock's full concentration to keep her eyes from spinning. The nobles gathered here would've never normally taken an interest in Rock. Rather than be fascinated by her, they would scowl and shoo her away. A beautiful dress seemed to have the magical ability to make even an insignificant little girl look like a noble lady.

"She's the daughter of a distant relative on my mother's side. I am serving as her chaperone, as she is currently in the midst of receiving etiquette lessons." Ebel smoothly made up stories to suit the situation. "As you can see, she is not used to high society events. Please refrain from teasing her."

The ladies and gentlemen laughed as a group, though their curiosity only grew stronger as they bombarded Ebel with questions. He continued to evade each inquiry with a witty response that the guests tittered over.

Thanks to his swift countermeasure, Rock had no need to expose herself to them beyond opening up to their surprise, envy, and compliments. The experience was far from comfortable, as she had no immunity to the resplendence in the air, much less to the high society mannerisms around her. She wanted to at least memorize the guests' outfits for future reference, but the bright light cast by the chandeliers was too blinding to commit anything to memory.

Moreover, she needed to find an opening to inform Ebel about Guido before it was too late. The hostess and her older brother were blocked from view by a wall of noblemen and women.

She had succeeded in catching Guido off guard. But that may only make him fly into a worse rage. Explaining things to Ebel should come sooner rather than later.

She gently tugged on the sleeve of his frock coat between conversations. When he looked over his shoulder at her, she signaled him with her eyes, and he nodded.

"You must be thirsty, Roxy. Allow me to pick out a drink for you." Ebel used that excuse to break free of the chitchat and lead Rock to a corner of the ballroom.

People tired of talking appeased their thirst at the several long tables where an arrangement of alcoholic beverages and finger foods were laid out. Rock never drank a lick of liquor, but the labels attached to the bottles indicated they were some of the finest in the imperial capital. Buttery biscuits, honey-dipped cakes, pomegranates, figs, and an array of luxury foods unavailable to commoners made up the comestibles.

"Do you drink?"

Rock didn't miss the hopeful expectation in his voice, but she shook her head anyway. "I'll refrain, thank you."

"What a shame. Then I will order squeezed grape juice for you instead." He placed the order with the waiter, who poured grape juice into a silver goblet. The juice, which was the same color as her hair, was diluted with water and had just the right balance of sweet and sour to quench her parched throat.

"This is the first time I've downed something this bloody tasty," Rock said, raising her voice in awe and earning a small chuckle from Ebel.

"Perhaps you should use a more ladylike tone in this environment?"

"Ah! This is the first time I have tasted something so exquisitely heavenly?" She tried rewording her statement, but she had a hard time getting used to the polished words she never used.

"You are the center of attention tonight. You never know who could be listening," he said reproachfully, then swept his eyes over her appearance again. "Setting that aside, your beauty is more than I ever imagined..." His golden eyes blazed like torches, as if he were drunk before he had even sipped his drink. "You deserve to be called the dawn goddess right now."

When he whispered in her ear, the heat in his eyes spread to her earlobe. She felt it burning.

"Oh, come on. You exaggerate." Rock bashfully twirled the goblet in her hand.

"I'm not exaggerating. Everyone fawning over you is the greatest evidence." Ebel showered her in romantic lines. "If it pleases you, dear goddess, I wish to gaze upon the real dawn with you."

Because her innocence was the only thing about her that was just as it appeared, Rock was easily bowled over by his advances. She averted her eyes from his formal attire and rushed to change the subject. "W-We have more important things to discuss! Shouldn't you be more concerned about something else?"

"What else deserves my attention more than my radiant goddess?" Ebel asked without a concern.

"A whole bloody lot! I—"

"Language."

"...Something of grave importance does," she rephrased. "I want to tell you why I am even here."

She was reluctant to tell him the whole story. Guido was the bane of her existence, but that wasn't the case for Ebel. The guilt she felt for tattling on him came back in full force.

Before she even began explaining, Ebel frowned as if he had already guessed it. Without waiting for her next words, he whispered, "Guido's doing?"

She slowly nodded. "Yes."

Because he'd arrived at that conclusion by himself, she shared the circumstances surrounding her attendance at this party. She didn't spill her guts about everything as she had with Phoebe, but she covered every detail: coming to drop off the gown only, being ordered to wear the dress she had made for Michaela, and Guido's objective being to change Ebel's mind. She kept to herself the vicious words he'd disparaged her with.

As it was, her story already elicited his outrage.

"...How dare Guido treat you in such a way," he gritted out between his teeth, exhaling a shaky breath as his plucked brows snapped together. "And somewhere out of my sight, of all things. I'm sorry I couldn't protect you."

"Don't apologize. A lot happened, but I'm safe for now." Rock forced a smile for his benefit, and his face contorted with the mental anguish he endured.

"Your strength is my saving rock. At this juncture..." Did his finely chiseled features twist out of grief over being betrayed by a friend? His sorrowful profile, with his eyes closed, was hardened like marble, and it captivated her. The next second, however, his eyes snapped open, and resolve replaced self-torment. "...He is no longer my friend."

What could she say in response to that? The curse inflicted upon him during his sensitive boyhood had robbed him of many things. Now that he was on the verge of losing the old friend he'd shared his pain with, his mental anguish was nearly palpable.

"Ebel..." Words escaping her, Rock said the only thing she could—his name. He turned toward her for comfort.

Waves of commotion rippled through the crowded ballroom just then. They looked behind them to where the throng of people naturally stepped aside to let the hosts—Michaela and Guido—through.

Michaela answered their birthday blessings with a sweet smile as she ran her eyes over the crowds in search of someone. Her innocent face radiated brighter than the morning sun upon spotting Ebel and Rock.

"There they are, Brother!"

Rock didn't hear Guido's response, but she glimpsed his furtive look of disgust. Unaware of her brother's venomous heart, Michaela guided him by the hand straight to them.

Rock had every right to be nervous. Sensing her dismay, Ebel swiftly stepped forward, hiding her behind his reliable back. Though Michaela raised her eyebrows at this peculiar reaction, she was all smiles by the time she arrived before them.

"I knew that was you, tailor," she exclaimed with delight, trying to get a good look around Ebel at Rock. "Ebel has a beautiful lady no one has ever seen before as his partner tonight. Everyone has been busy gossiping over who she might be, but I knew it was you after close inspection." She spoke with the excitement of a child solving a mystery. "I remember saying how you didn't seem like a male tailor during my fitting. So this is why!"

Under normal circumstances, her bubbly personality and cheerfulness may have been pleasant to the ears. But her perkiness felt superficial and imprudent in this moment when Rock was cowering behind Ebel, whose own expression was harder than ice.

"You both kept it quiet to surprise me, didn't you? That's so mean! I was so looking forward to wearing this finished dress before we switched tailors." She looked over her shoulder at her brother, whom she had dragged there. "Can I still have it, Brother?" No sooner did she direct a moue at her brother than her sulking eyes spread wide with surprise.

Guido's stern face seethed with loathing and chagrin. "...Why did you hide it?" he accused, a shaky edge to his voice. His dispassionate, frigid black eyes saw only Ebel. "Why did you deceive me into believing that woman is a man?"

Ebel answered his accusations in a stony voice. "I regretfully only just found out the truth for myself."

Rock nodded behind his back. Anger flushed Guido's face regardless. "Don't lie to me."

"I'm not lying. And when it comes to deceit, Guido, what do you have to say for yourself?" Ebel's tensed back muscles betrayed his desperate attempt to remain levelheaded. Rock rested her hands on his back to give him strength. "I heard of your wicked deeds from her. Want me to expose the whole truth here in front of your beloved Michaela?"

His threat shook Guido, but Michaela was even more rattled by it. "B-Brother...? E-Ebel? Whatever are you talking about?" Suddenly concerned, she looked from her brother to her former fiancé. Neither of them was in a state of mind to coddle her.

"Michaela, go to the other side of the room," Guido snapped, trying to send his sister away.

Her whole countenance changed, and she clung to his arm. "Why? I don't understand any of this—"

"I'll explain later. I must speak with Ebel."

"Is that how you plan to varnish over your shame and mistake? With fabrications?" Ebel criticized, a provoking bite to his tone.

Guido's eyes bulged out of his head. "Shut up!" he barked in a loud voice that echoed through the ballroom.

As a matter of course, that angry shout surprised many people, halted the orchestra's performance, and drew the attention of the guests. Even the gaiety of the party chilled as if everything had been submerged under water.

Ebel stood there unflinching, Rock cringed behind him, and Michaela covered her mouth.

"Brother, stop this fight…!" she demanded, curling her hand into the folds of her skirt.

Guido whipped his head back and forth. "This is for you, too, Michaela. We have to bring Ebel back to his senses."

"But, Brother! Today is my birthday!" The sound of Michaela's sorrowful cry plunged the room into an uproar.

Eyes from every direction stabbed into Rock, making her shift uncomfortably. These were judgmental stares, not curious ones. Of course, the party guests were the uneasy ones, having their festivities soured by an unfriendly argument.

Sensing the mood, Ebel lowered his voice. "Out of respect for Michaela, I'll hold my tongue while the party is going on." He spoke emphatically to make it clear to Guido. "Take my word, though: my friendship with you ends tonight." His serious tone proved this wasn't an empty threat.

Guido, for the first time that night, looked dumbstruck. He stared blankly at Ebel as if he'd never considered that to be possible. "What—"

"I warned you before that I wouldn't tolerate you insulting *her* a second time," Ebel asserted decisively.

That dealt a considerable blow to Guido. The color drained from his hawklike face, turning him whiter than paper. He suddenly spun on his heel, gently removed Michaela's hand from his arm, and staggered away.

"Brother…!" Michaela reached out to grab him, but promptly dropped her arm.

The room still buzzed with conversation. Nobody spoke to Guido as he skulked by, though they turned pitying eyes on him, all wondering about the fate of the party. He swept through the doors, leaving the ballroom and ocean of prying eyes behind.

Neither Rock nor Ebel nor Michaela moved a muscle. It was Ebel's uncomfortable sigh that broke the silence first. "I'm sorry for causing a scene at your important birthday party, Michaela."

A sad smile painted her lips. "Don't be... It wasn't your fault, was it?" Unable to stand there without knowing the truth, she said, "Tell me, Ebel. Did my brother do something horrible? What *did* Brother do?"

"You won't like the answer..." Exposing the truth to the girl he viewed as a little sister wasn't easy for the lionhearted count. He left a long pause before eventually answering her with a steely expression. "I can't discuss the particulars here. But he did something unforgivable."

In that moment, Michaela did not look surprised. Her slender shoulders trembled, as if her bad hunch had been proved true. She hugged herself and slammed her eyes shut. "I am sorry..."

As far as Rock knew, Michaela was always the picture of naiveté next to her brother. And Guido strove to put on a good big-brother image in front of her. Yet had she, as the person closest to him, sensed something off about the brother she looked up to?

Michaela lifted her head and spoke to Rock, who was poking her head out around Ebel's back. "My brother hurt you, didn't he? I apologize on his behalf."

"Um, you don't have to apologize for him..." Rock didn't know the right thing to say. Guido had put her through hell, but Michaela had no part in his crimes.

But for the first time since Rock met her, mature anguish filled the younger girl's cherubic features. "To tell you the truth, Brother has been acting strange recently."

"Strange how?" Ebel asked.

Michaela sifted through her memories as she answered, "He strangely can't ever relax, and occasionally I find him brooding alone in the dark... Guests coming to see him have increased dramatically these days, but he won't let me see them, much less greet them."

It was through those signs that she had vaguely become aware of the change in her brother. Did she say nothing of it until it came to light because her closeness with him blinded her?

"I can't explain it well, but I have had a bad feeling about it for some time." She stopped there before squeezing out her next words, as if she still couldn't make up her mind. "Ebel, I won't ask you to forgive him." Ebel silently arched an eyebrow. She pressed forward with her request. "But please...won't you stop him if he is going down the wrong path? You are the only person who can reach him."

If Guido's attitude before he stormed out of the ballroom was anything to go by, Ebel stood no chance of reaching him now either. Rock was doubtful, but Ebel gave an instant answer anyway.

"I will do whatever is possible."

Relief eased some of the creases in Michaela's brow as she smiled, some traces of regret left in her expression. "Thank you, Ebel. I wanted to be the one to stop him, but alas...I failed." She turned away from them. "I must return to my hostess duties. I need to go make sure that this party will end peacefully," she said with uncharacteristic strength.

Holding back her no-longer-trembling shoulders, Michaela boldly marched into the tumultuous fray of displeased guests.

She managed to ride out the worst of their reactions, repairing the party with all the skill of the lady of the house. The mood couldn't be brought back to its former heights, but the guests were considerate of their young hostess, and the party went on amicably.

Ironically, Michaela becoming the center of attention freed Rock and Ebel from that role. They quenched their thirst and hunger in a corner of the ballroom, quietly seeing out the rest of the evening.

As the party was drawing to a close, the waiter called Ebel over and whispered something in his ear. Ebel's expression darkened, but he didn't tell Rock what was said until later.

"...GUIDO sent word that he wants to speak with me alone." When they stepped into the Linus Manor's garden after the party had finished, Ebel shared the message the waiter had imparted.

Guests could be spotted here and there walking along the night promenade through the grounds on their way home. Rock walked alongside Ebel on the path illuminated by stained-glass garden lamps, both still attired in their formal wear.

"You can take my carriage home. I already informed Iniel to take you," he said, leading her through the garden to where his carriage awaited.

Two reasons prevented Rock from accepting his offer. The first being Phoebe—she hadn't seen her inside the manor since they parted ways in the storage room. Rock had entrusted her with her work clothes and worried about how Phoebe had spent the rest of the evening. Of course, it was needless worry, if she really was a talented mercenary.

The other reason justifiably lay with Ebel and Guido.

"Have you agreed to meet him?" she asked while they walked the cobblestone path to the carriage.

He gave a melancholic reply. "Yes. He said he wants to talk at my manor."

"At yours?"

"He apparently doesn't want to risk Michaela overhearing."

What conversation were they going to have that it required changing locations to Mateus Manor? Even Rock could guess it wouldn't be a conciliatory moment between friends. Quite the contrary.

"Can't I be with you?" The words left her before she knew it. Ebel seemed surprised too. He stopped and blinked at her.

"You want to be with me?"

"Well, I know I won't be of any use to you, but I can't stop worrying... How about I bring Phoebe along?" They stopped walking as Rock made that fervent plea.

He let out a small chuckle, unable to hide his joy. "I never imagined you would worry for me in this way."

"This is nothing to laugh about!" Rock cried out. Ebel's eyes widened, but she continued speaking over his surprise. "I really am worried about you. But that isn't the only thing eating away at me."

The look she saw in Guido's eyes back in the storage room had burned vividly into her mind. The madness blazing in his eyes was several steps beyond insanity. He had committed the unforgivable against Rock, but she had glimpsed a man involved in something much worse.

What that was, she couldn't say just yet. But an unsettling apprehension writhed inside her, for she'd seen her fair share of people with those exact same eyes in the slums and knew where that led them.

"...All you need to know is that it worries me. Please let me join you." Unable to bring herself to bad-mouth Guido in front of Ebel, she appealed to him with a shortened explanation.

The corners of his eyes crinkled as he stared down at her with a surprisingly warmhearted, earnest gaze. These were the eyes of a man who believed everything she said without digging for more information. "Thank you, Roxy. I'm blessed to have met you," he said eventually, quickly adding, "And that is precisely why I can't drag you and Phoebe into this."

"Why not?!"

He cut her short with a pointed look and placed his hand over his heart. He explained his decision with a smile that trembled from the pain he fought to keep inside. "I confided in Guido as soon as I was cursed. I had to tell someone. I couldn't stand keeping the secret by myself. He didn't shun me, but accepted me without fear."

To Rock, it sounded like the story of a friendship more fleeting than a dream. She had only just seen that friendship shatter into pieces. What had changed them so much that they went from having a bond so strong that a werewolf curse did nothing to shake it, to where they were today?

Who had changed? Ebel? Guido? Or both?

"Guido said I was still me. His opinion didn't change even after I showed him that supernatural form. Instead, he cheered me up by saying I had gained the power to protect Michaela. To the bitter end, he was the only one to oppose the annulment..." Ebel shook his head to rid himself of the bittersweet memories. "...So this, too, is my burden to bear as the cursed."

He had steeled his resolve—pestering him wouldn't change his mind now. Her heart drumming to the beat of her bad premonition, Rock was left with praying for his safety as her only option.

"Please tread extra carefully, Ebel."

"I will. I have to, with you worrying after me." A single word of concern from her brought a joyous smile to his tormented face. Seeing that smile only amplified the unease stirring in her chest. Her whole being truly worried about him.

The pair slowly walked through the garden in silence. Cold winds blew on this late night. The colorful garden lamps wavered over the grass, swaying in the dark like ocean waves. Other guests hugged themselves against the chill, speeding up their gait through the promenade. Several groups passed them, and before they knew it, scarcely a person was around.

The blueness of the little alkanet flowers also looked like the color of the grass in the middle of the night. Whereas the promenade was illuminated, the end of the garden was completely swallowed by the dark of night, so Rock couldn't see what was ahead even if she strained her eyes.

So she walked close to Ebel. Saying she wasn't afraid would be a lie, and more than that, a horrible foreboding ate away at her. The silk gown provided no protection against the chilly breeze, and she didn't want to part from the warmth right beside her.

Ebel kept walking at her side, his hand on her back to give her strength the same way she had given him earlier that night.

Eventually, carriages came into view at the garden edge. Ebel stopped there and, with a little more cheer in his voice, pointed out, "Your guardian awaits."

"Oh? Phoebe is waiting?" Rock squinted, but they were too far away to see her or to tell which of the carriages belonged to the Mateuses.

"I can see your guardian waiting from here," Ebel assured her. "I shall take my leave of your company now."

The werewolf count's vision excelled in the dark as usual. Feeling impressed and not wanting to part, Rock took another look at the young man standing beside her.

His swept-back hair accentuated his handsome face, and the expression there was a tender one. His golden eyes, supposedly a mark left by the curse, shined bright like the stars when he returned her gaze.

After Rock had turned her stargazing eyes to him, Ebel's expression faltered. "It's hard for me to leave when you're staring that much…"

"Ah… S-Sorry. Please don't mind me." Self-conscious, she quickly averted her eyes. Though she didn't forget to remind him: "But please be careful." Thinking that wasn't enough, she lengthened her goodbye. "I am going to put my heart into making the cloak you ordered from me, so please be sure to pick it up."

Her second attempt was just as terribly tactless as the first. She ran out of ways to wish for his safety, and she feared showing too much worry might rudely imply that she didn't believe in him. Those were the feelings she managed to squeeze out.

So she didn't mind if he laughed at her, but Ebel didn't laugh.

Instead, he suddenly hugged her to him.

"Ehh! Wah! Ahh!" Coherent words failed to form when he pulled her into his chest and squished her tightly in his arms. She was about to utter another sound as his embrace took away her breath, but his lips covered hers.

In his human form, Ebel's lips were soft.

"...I keep my promises, and I promise to visit you again," he whispered, his breath caressing her before he gently released her. "Now go. And...see you later, Roxy."

Rendered incapable of responding with more than a shaky nod, Rock robotically walked toward the carriages alone.

The night breeze was warm. Her chest hurt. Wearing a gown wasn't the only reason why she was unsteady on her feet. She couldn't bring herself to look back at Ebel watching her go.

With wobbly steps, Rock arrived at the carriages by herself. There she saw Phoebe leaning with her back against one of the many carriages. She recognized that berline and spotted Iniel sitting in the coachman's seat.

Phoebe was wistfully looking up at the starry sky, still in her leather armor and with her hair pulled back. She turned at the sound of Rock's shoes, and relief washed over her face.

"You're late, Rock."

Phoebe's expression was full of life, and she didn't appear hurt anywhere. Confirming her safety relieved Rock too.

"They didn't find you, huh? What a relief..."

"That level of security couldn't find a mouse." Phoebe returned to speaking like her normal self. Though she sheepishly mentioned, "I saw you were the shining star of the evening in your gown."

"Where were you watching from?"

"Obviously from the shadows," she answered vaguely, then puffed out her chest as if boasting about herself. "You were the belle of the ball. I was so proud of you sweeping all those nobs off their feet with your enthralling beauty."

"Only worked because of my beautiful gown."

"And because your cuteness added to it." Phoebe sounded more satisfied than anyone else about the night's success. Rock gasped at her smooth compliment. Phoebe jubilantly grinned away. "You outwitted the duke's twerp too. I'm going to sleep well tonight."

"You saw that part too?"

"Yep. I watched from the beginning up till the point he skulked away after being rejected by His Excellency." For all she boasted about sleeping well later, Phoebe grimaced. She dropped her voice and anxiously said, "But…I don't think things will end at that. Not for that toff."

Rock thought so too. That was why she was so worried about Ebel. He'd said it was his burden to bear. How many more heavy burdens must he take on his cursed shoulders? The curse wasn't even his fault.

"…So? Where is His Excellency? He's not with you?" Phoebe asked after Rock had become lost in thought.

Instantly recalling their parting exchange, Rock answered with flushed cheeks: "N-No. His Excellency told me to take his carriage home because he had to speak with the duke's son."

"I see…" The creases in Phoebe's brow deepened. She quickly shrugged it off and cheerily said, "Well, he's no weakling. He'll beat the crap out of that bastard if he has to."

"Yeah. I'm sure…he will," Rock agreed to convince herself.

She looked back at the garden and didn't see anyone who looked like Ebel there. Lots of light spilled from the windows of Linus Manor, which rose above the vast darkness dimly lit below. Now that the glamor and the lights were far away, the time she had spent in the manor started to feel like a passing dream.

Returning was no longer an option.

Phoebe had rightly pointed out that Ebel wasn't weak. Rock couldn't think of another person aside from Phoebe who could stand their ground against the werewolf count. He was going to be just fine—or so she repeated to herself, placing her hand over her rollicking heart.

"Come now. The wind is getting stronger. Let's make our way home." Phoebe's push forced Rock to tear her eyes away from Linus Manor. Phoebe's smile slipped, and she suddenly inspected Rock's face. Then she commented, "Your lipstick came off."

Rock swayed back on her heels and flew into a flustered panic. "What?! Ah! N-No! It's not that! It's something else!"

"What else could it be?"

"You know, it's because I had a drink inside! That's how it came off!"

Her unnatural panic gave it all away.

"...I'll be the one to beat the snot out of that fancy toff the next time I see him," she growled, voice so deep that cold sweat covered Rock's hands.

It wouldn't be pretty if Phoebe and Ebel fought for real. Rock hoped she wasn't serious, because if she was, she would have to intervene.

"The coachman knows where to take us. Get in." Fuming, Phoebe jerked her finger toward the berline carriage next to her.

Iniel looked over at them, thinking they were talking to him. Seeing Rock's appearance tonight took him by complete surprise. He forgot to greet her as his eyes spread wide, his jaw dropped, and a dumb sound came out.

"Uh... I hope this isn't a rude question, but are you...Master Rock?"

"Yes. I'm sorry for startling you." She shyly apologized and, picking up the sides of her dress, boarded the carriage. Phoebe followed her inside, shutting the door behind them and taking up her spot on the opposite seat.

Inside the moving carriage, Rock studied the person in front of her. Decked out in her formidable armor, Phoebe was still a beauty even without makeup. As long as she didn't open her mouth, she would look like a strong woman who worked out, while also appearing like a good-looking androgynous young man. Since Rock had treated her as a woman all this time, she had never asked her age.

I don't know if we look alike. But if I do share the same blood as this person... then I can understand why so many people showered me with compliments tonight.

"I have something to ask you when we get back," Rock announced, her blue eyes fixing on Phoebe. Accepting Rock's gaze and everything behind it, the eyes that shared the same blue softened with resignation.

"I'm down for that. I just so happen to have a good bottle of wine."

"I don't drink."

"Neither do I. Some occasions call for it, though."

Was she implying she couldn't speak about this sober?

"Besides, you should learn how to hold your drink soon. Before a naughty man makes you drink too much," Phoebe ribbed, making Rock squirm in her seat. She made it sound as if she'd overheard her whole conversation with Ebel too.

Thinking back on it, Rock had dined with Phoebe innumerable times, and not once did she drink in front of her. She just thought

Phoebe wasn't a drinker, but if she wasn't, she wouldn't keep a good wine in reserve. Surely she had put it away to bring out on days when a conversation needed liquor to help it along.

Too much had happened to Rock tonight too. She wanted to thank Phoebe and had many questions to ask. Mayhap alcohol's strength needed to be borrowed on nights like this.

"I'll join you for a glass, then," Rock answered after thinking it through. Phoebe beamed at her.

"Good girl. Come to my room once we get back."

Rock marveled at Phoebe speaking as her usual self even after all they went through today. It was truly a mysterious thing that the person whose shadow she had been chasing all this time had been right next to her all along.

The carriage continued to race through the imperial capital streets submerged in night. During their conversation, the carriage had left the aristocrat district and was currently passing through the shopping district. The streetlights brightly lit the way for the many people still out at this hour in this neighborhood. She saw some of them rushing by from the carriage window.

One of the young men's attire suddenly reminded Rock of her own appearance. "Oh yeah, Phoebe, do you still have my clothes?!"

"Of course, I took them with me. What's wrong?"

"I have to change before we get to the slums. We'll have trouble on our hands if anyone sees me." She accepted the stack of clothes from Phoebe and stressed, "...Can you look the other way?"

"You stripped without a word in front of me earlier," Phoebe pouted, self-consciously turning her face aside.

Rock did that only because she had always thought of Phoebe as a woman. But things were going to be different after what she had learned today, so she didn't want Phoebe watching her change.

ROCK and Phoebe disembarked from the carriage at the entrance to the slums. By then, Rock had removed her makeup and donned her usual disguise as a male tailor.

"I must return to His Excellency now. Please be careful on your way home," Iniel said politely in parting.

They saw him off before heading shoulder to shoulder to Market Street. Phoebe's place was located down a maze of streets that way.

When they neared Market Street, they noticed there was a lot of activity going on for this late at night. On the normally deserted streets, Rock saw groups of people whispering here and there.

"I wonder what all the commotion is about."

"Maybe some drunks got into a bad brawl."

Rock and Phoebe started whispering about the alarming mood too.

"Oh! Rock!" Justia ran over from the other end of the street. She stopped in front of them, her face burning red. "Where did you go?! I've been worried sick about you...!" she panted out between ragged breaths.

"Uhhh—"

"We had a girls' night out. Did something happen?" Phoebe answered, stepping in when Rock didn't have a good excuse.

Justia bent over with her hands on her knees as she caught her breath, and Cargus, who finally caught up to her, rubbed her back. "Burglars broke into Lady Trilian's shop," he answered for her.

"Burglars?!" Rock cried, and Phoebe's brows snapped together.

The slums weren't the safest neighborhood, but few were gutsy enough to attack the shops for fear of bringing street justice down on them.

"When did that happen?"

"Tonight. Several men broke in. The storefront is a wreck."

Finally catching her breath, Justia took over the explanation from her normally taciturn husband. "Don't you live just above that shop? That's why I went to check on you, but then you weren't there or in your shop, and even Phoebe was away from home. We were worried sick about you...!"

Both husband and wife had searched all around the slums out of concern for their young friend.

"Thank you, Justia and Cargus. I'm sorry I made you worry so much." It felt nice to be fretted over, but Rock's own fears lay elsewhere.

Phoebe must've been thinking the same thing, since he (Rock now viewed Phoebe this way after learning the truth) asked first: "By the way, is Lady Trilian safe?"

Justia exchanged looks with Cargus, and then she told them the difficult truth. "No… The burglars hit her. She has a head wound."

Rock and Phoebe exchanged worried looks next.

They hurtled into the alleyway and found a crowd formed outside of Lady Trilian's shop. The constable had only just shown up.

"Scat! This isn't a show!" He was trying to drive away the onlookers with his haughty attitude. The wall of people began scattering, and Phoebe plunged his way through the opening. "You there! Stop! Don't go inside!" The constable ordered them to stop but didn't physically try to stop them, so Rock was able to slip into the shop after Phoebe unimpeded.

Cargus wasn't exaggerating—the antique shop's thick wooden door had been knocked completely off its hinges, and the interior looked like a storm had passed through. Shelves had been flipped over, and broken shards of chinaware, gilded pieces, and other curios littered the damaged floors.

There Lady Trilian sat, dazed, on the floor in the back of the shop. Bright-red blood oozed through the bandage wrapped around her head, her gray hair sticking to it. Rock's heart plummeted at that gruesome red.

"Lady Trilian! Are you all right, dear?!" Phoebe rushed over to her. The older woman jerked her head up.

"You! I told you not to use your bloody feminine wiles around me!"

"Hah?"

"Your manliness stole my heart all those years ago, so why are ya speaking and acting like some woman?! Come back after you've fixed your speech!" Those old sunken eyes sharply speared Phoebe from underneath the bandage.

The tension eased from Phoebe's shoulders. "…Looks like they didn't knock the spunk outta you yet."

Relief settled over Rock as well. Shrewd as Lady Trilian was, Rock still worried how she would fare against the burglars after they wrecked the place this bad. Her wounds weren't pretty, but with her sharp tongue working this well, she would recover.

"How badly did they hurt you? Will you be okay?" Rock asked for confirmation. Lady Trilian's eyes shifted to her, and her expression twisted.

"It ain't too bad. I just went through hell because of that bloody statue."

"What statue…?"

"The wolf statue you plundered from me." She exhaled so deeply Rock feared her soul departed with that breath. "Someone in the same trade brought another one to me. He told me I could have it for free, so I happily accepted, planning to sell it to ya later. But then those thugs came sniffing 'round the place for it the same day."

With her head down to endure the horrible memory, she didn't notice Rock's and Phoebe's frozen expressions and clenched fists. "Those blighters told me to name my price, so I tried to overcharge 'em by a pinch. Then they suddenly slammed their fists into me. The rest is as you can see. They wrecked the place and made off with the statue." She clicked her tongue and spitefully hissed, "That thing really is cursed, isn't it? I hope it curses all those blighters to hell."

If what they stole was another werewolf statue, then its curse was real. Worse yet, not only did they just discover the existence of a third statue, they didn't even know whose hands it had been passed to.

Rock gulped and looked searchingly at Phoebe. Gritting his frustration out between his teeth, he tousled her hair in a display of concern. "…Let's go inform His Excellency," he whispered in her ear. "The sooner the better. As in, right now, Rock."

Lady Trilian was a tough old woman despite her injuries. "I didn't utter a peep 'bout selling ya the other statue." With that declaration, she stood tall and proud. "Don't think I'm just some miserly old woman. I stick to my guns when it counts."

Rock hadn't even considered the possibility until she mentioned it. When she thought of how her room and shop could have been torn apart, too, she realized this wasn't just Lady Trilian's problem.

No, this was my problem the moment that statue became involved.

Just as Ebel had called this fate, she, too, was connected and caught up in the cause and effects of fate. Now was the time for Rock to put an end to the misery caused by the statue her father had brought out of the ancient ruins.

"I wouldn't expect any less of you, Lady Trilian," Rock complimented, her heart and mind set on what she had to do next.

"They could drag me to hell and back and I wouldn't say anything, all to protect the man who captured my heart." All the more vigorous in her old age, Lady Trilian directed a flirtatious glance at Phoebe.

On the receiving end, he gave an exasperated, ladylike smile. "You're forever young, aren't you, dear Trilian?"

"I keep telling ya to stop acting like a woman 'round me!" she shouted and then held her hands over her aching head. She didn't act like a shopkeeper who just had a run-in with burglars.

Not wanting to worsen her injuries, Rock and Phoebe made sure she had everything under control before taking their leave.

They immediately went to check on Rock's room on the second floor. It wasn't that Rock didn't believe Lady Trilian, but there was no telling what the burglars might've done after they wrecked her shop. Fortunately, there were no signs of forced entry, and her room looked just as she had left it that morning. If nothing else, the information about Rock buying one of the statues hadn't been leaked.

"Well, it's not like I have it on my anymore anyway." Rock rolled the tightness out of her shoulders.

But Phoebe's expression grew graver by the moment, and he promptly asked, "Rock, I need you to tell me if you know the answer to this."

"What is it?"

"Does Guido Linus know that His Excellency is a werewolf?"

Rock was astonished that Guido's name was brought up here. Sure, she loathed the cretin, but it never occurred to her that he might be involved in this crime. Without a doubt, he was the closest to Ebel's secret and was one of the very few people privy to that knowledge outside of his father and direct servants.

"He knows. Ebel said he showed him his werewolf form when they were boys," she answered through her hesitation. At the time, Guido had saved Ebel with his kind acceptance.

"...Then we can't discredit the possibility he knows about the statues too." Phoebe, on the other hand, had already narrowed down the culprit to Guido. "One more question. Did His Excellency ever tell you under what circumstances that statue casts its curse?"

"No. I never heard."

Ebel never mentioned it, likely to prevent from dragging Rock in too deep. Someone out there wanted that information bad enough to hurt others. Did the person who hired the burglars know the secret?

"Why do you suspect him, Phoebe?"

Phoebe rubbed his chin. "Didn't he threaten you with the constables he said he had patrolling the manor?"

"He did." Remembering his remark about how easy it was to throw a street rat from the slums into the gallows ticked her off even now.

"Those useless curs were actually there. I spotted them while I was roaming the manor," Phoebe cursed, blue eyes narrowing into slits. "The whole thing is strange when you think about it. I can't believe that toff would bring in the might of the constables just to make your life miserable. On the other hand, that was some heavy-duty security to have around during his precious, precious little sister's birthday."

"You mean he's involved in some other bad business?" Rock interjected.

Phoebe laced his fingers together and nodded. "That's the only logical thing. For instance, he knew some has-been mercenaries were going to drop by, and he wanted the constables around to toss them out if things went south."

"Now that you mention it, Michaela alluded to the same thing. Guido has had an influx of unusual visitors but won't let her see them, much less greet them," Rock said, remembering what Michaela had told her and Ebel at the party. The information strengthened Phoebe's suspicions.

"These are still just marks against him. We don't have enough evidence to draw a line connecting him to it yet." Contrary to these words, Phoebe's blue eyes were already making the circle for Guido's noose. "That said, not many people in this vast capital check both boxes for possessing enough money to motivate those curs into working and for knowing His Excellency's werewolf secret. Of that select few, I'm hedging my bets on His Excellency's ex–best friend."

Phoebe had plenty of reason to suspect Guido. As one who had glimpsed his insanity up close and personal, Rock feared he was liable to do anything at this point. Deep down, she secretly wished it was just paranoia on her part. After all, Ebel would be heartbroken if he knew Guido wanted that statue so bad he nearly had a woman killed for it.

"Let's say it is Guido. Why would he want the statue?" Rock muttered aloud as they hurried through the dark streets after leaving her room.

Still decked out in full armor, Phoebe's face turned grim as he answered, "Your guess is as good as mine. Whatever the reason, it will become something he can threaten His Excellency with."

"I want to believe...he wouldn't go that far," Rock lamented.

Phoebe shook his head reproachfully. "You're a real softy if you can say something like that after what that nob did to you."

"Don't get me wrong. I trust the pickpockets on the streets more than Guido." She wanted to believe in him for Ebel's sake. Rock didn't want to see Ebel hurt again. She also had no intention of averting her eyes from reality either. Pressing her lips into a flat line, Rock tossed another doubt at Phoebe. "By the way, we aren't going to walk our way to the count's, are we?"

They were racing through the shadowy streets at a fast pace, but their legs would give out before they made it by foot to the aristocrat district. Dawn would break before they arrived even if they ran through the night.

Phoebe grinned. "Leave our ride to me. I'm a master at these things."

"...And what *things* would that be?"

Instead of answering Rock's third question, Phoebe sped up with a spirited bounce to his step.

They eventually arrived at the stables located on the outskirts of the slums.

The imperial capital was built around the emperor's castle as its center, and the slums, as the farthest district from that center, was an impoverished residential area that had sprung up along the walls protecting the capital. Located at the edge of the slums, these stables lent and sold horses to people traveling outside the capital's walls. These stables also boarded and took in horses belonging to people traveling to the capital.

By the time Phoebe and Rock ran into the stables, it was so late at night the date was about to change. Several of the horses tied up outside looked as if they were asleep on their feet. The stable master greeted them reeking of alcohol, already having knocked back a drink or two.

"You're back again, Phoebe?"

"Yes. You really helped me out earlier," Phoebe said in relaxed reply. He whispered behind his hand to Rock, "I had him introduce me to a good wagon to follow you."

So that was how Phoebe got to Linus Manor. Rock really respected Phoebe's quick thinking and his ability to take action at the drop of the hat.

Are we going to catch another ride on a wagon, then? Rock wondered.

"I want to borrow a horse this time." Phoebe held out several gold coins. The stable master was suspicious, though he accepted it.

"Where are you goin' at this hour, she-man?"

"To the aristocrat district again. We're going to pass through a number of districts, so give me a strong horse with fast legs."

"Screw you. I'm not gonna lend out one of my horses for that!" the stable master yelled hysterically.

Rock was shocked as well. The imperial capital was divided into different districts, such as the aristocrat district, the holy church district, and the shopping district, and each one was connected by a large guarded gate. Citizens were free to come and go from any district, but only if they possessed citizenship. As a resident of the slums, citizenship was a pipe dream for Rock, and that was why she had never visited the aristocrat district until Ebel invited her there.

And to the constables charged with protecting each gate, residents of the slums were worse than plague-bearing rats. They were free to choose if they wanted to ignore them, chase them away, or arrest them and interrogate them on a whim.

Phoebe claimed he was going to take a single horse through not one but several of those heavily guarded gates.

"Relax. I'll bring back your charge without so much as a tuft of hair missing. You know my talents."

The stable master carefully studied Phoebe's confident face. It was then that he noticed the man who always showed up in dresses was armed to the teeth. "Why the hurry? Don't tell me you're gonna launch a night attack on some unsuspecting fool?" he queried, presuming they were out for blood.

Phoebe didn't even bat an eyelash. "A good friend is in dire need. Of course I'd hurry," he asserted without an ounce of hesitation. Rock could tell from his tone that it wasn't just an excuse to get through the moment—the truth lay in those words.

A good friend in dire need—Ebel held a different position in Rock's heart than Phoebe's, but either way, she couldn't say nothing, so she got up close to the master and appealed to his better half.

"A friend who is very near and dear to us is in need! They may be in grave danger if we don't warn them soon… Please, won't you lend us a horse?!"

"S-Sure. If that's what you need it for…" The stable master, overwhelmed by her plea, stared at Rock's beseeching face. He returned his gaze to Phoebe and whispered loud enough to be heard, "You've got an awfully cute lady with you for a she-man. Is she your woman?"

"She's *my* precious girl. I'll beat you to death if you give her a dirty look." Phoebe's voice was oozing with barbs, but it rung sweetly in Rock's ears.

She didn't have to confirm what he meant by those words yet. Just having Phoebe come to Ebel's aid with her was enough. She depended on him.

The stable master lent them a large black horse, claiming he was the best horse in the stable, with his stellar night vision and the ability to swiftly carry two adults on his back.

"I forgot to ask: Do you have horseback-riding experience?" Phoebe asked belatedly.

Rock answered with an unconvincing grin. "At a trot. I took a few rides when I lived in the village."

"So practically zero experience. How about riding with someone else?"

"Never tried."

"All you have to do is sit still, so it's easier than riding alone." Phoebe checked the condition of the saddle and stirrups before pulling a hood over Rock's head. "Okay, I'm lifting you up. Stay still for me."

"Wh-Whoa!"

He easily lifted her onto the front of the saddle. Then he hopped onto the back and reached under her arms to take hold of the reins.

"Sorry your first time riding with a man had to be taken by me." Phoebe sounded awfully happy for someone who was apologizing. His voice lilted with excitement. "You can lean against me. Once you are holding on tight, you can relax from there."

Rock timidly leaned against him. A trotting horse's back wasn't the most stable of seats, even with a saddle. Unused to horseback riding, Rock was a bundle of nerves until Phoebe secured her between his arms. For a whole second, she was filled with peace of mind. The warm body holding her upright felt nostalgic, and she trusted the person behind it with all her heart.

But that peace of mind lasted only until the horse broke into a gallop.

"Here we go. Hold on tight, because this is going to be a fast ride!"

"Okay… By the way, how fast is fast?"

"Keep your mouth shut. You'll bite your tongue." Phoebe kicked his boots into the horse's sides.

The stable master's best horse broke into a gallop and raced through the imperial capital's streets at the speed of an arrow. Even with two adults on his back, he ran with such strength his hooves scraped the cobblestones. Carried at the speed of a rushing river, Rock, whose consciousness couldn't keep up with her body, would have fallen off if not for Phoebe's arms holding her in place.

Caving into her fear, she belted out what seemed like a never-ending scream: "WAAAAAAAAAAAAAAHHHHH!"

The horse galloped regardless of his riders' fears. Rock's hood violently shook and slapped against her cheeks. They made a mad dash through the imperial capital submerged in night, breaking through the headwinds that dried out her open eyes.

They passed through several gates along the way. At one of those gates, a bored constable on night duty tried to stop their passage.

"Halt! Where are you going at this hour?"

Phoebe neither panicked nor caused a scene with his straightforward reply. "We have an urgent message for Count Ebel Mateus. Please let us through!"

"No! Get off the horse!" The constable obviously didn't believe them.

"We're in a hurry, I said! Coming through!" Phoebe bellowed, spurring the horse back into a gallop. The constable's barked orders and angry shouts whipped behind them and out of earshot with the wind.

Rock didn't know what shortcuts Phoebe took or how he skillfully maneuvered the horse, but he succeeded in shaking the constables off at every gate. By the time they arrived at Mateus Manor, everything was so still aside from the sound of the horse's hooves beating the ground.

"You held up well." Phoebe stopped the horse and helped a wobbly Rock to the ground. He stroked the horse's mane to thank him for his hard work.

Rock sank to the ground after that whirlwind of a ride and couldn't stand back up. Even from the ground, she could glimpse the state of the manor before her. Lights shone in several of the windows—especially the ones on the second floor. She recognized one bay window as the one she had looked out of from Ebel's study. For a second, she thought she glimpsed someone's back through the window.

"Master Rock?!" The manor's front door swung open, and Johanna fell out. Paler than the moonlight, she dashed over to Rock and dug her hands into her vest. "Aaah! It's an answer to our prayers that you're here! His Excellency—His Excellency is in trouble!" Tears spilled down her drawn cheeks, alarming Rock and Phoebe.

"His Excellency is? What happened?!"

"Lord Linus barged in right after His Excellency came home." Convulsing with sobs, Johanna's knuckles turned white as she clenched the fireplace poker still gripped in her hand. Did she intend to use it as a weapon? "I showed him into His Excellency's study because His Excellency asked me to, but then Lord Linus suddenly started raving like a lunatic, and then His Excellency transformed into a werewolf against his will—"

Rock burst into action before hearing the rest. She rose on her formerly wobbly legs and stormed into the manor. She remembered that his study was located on the second floor at the end of the corridor straight back from the stairs. Though she had run off before anyone else, Phoebe outran her on the way, but Rock still managed to arrive just after he kicked in the door, and she tumbled inside the study behind him.

"Ebel!" Rock cried, the scene inside unfolding before her a second later.

Guido Linus was thrusting something into the face of the werewolf cowering on the floor. Gripped in his hand was none other than a cursed werewolf statue.

Werewolf Ebel slowly raised his muzzle. Once those golden orbs locked on the doorway, a strangled moan ripped passed his fangs. "Roxy...!"

Rock's heart heaved at the sound of relief, surprise, and grief fluctuating in that single utterance. She had no way of knowing what had gone down before she showed up. But Johanna's retelling was right about one thing—Ebel had been forced to transform against his will.

The ripped shreds of clothes scattered around him were proof of that. From the rich texture of the shredded fabric, Rock instantly knew it was the formal wear he'd been wearing at the party, and she sunk her teeth into her bottom lip.

Just how much did Guido have to ruin about this night before he was satisfied?

Guido turned toward the doorway too. The look in his eyes grew venomous when he saw Rock, and he viciously snarled, "You again, street tailor? What did you come for?"

"I could ask you the same question!" Rock snapped back. "Do you know what that statue is?!"

It didn't take a detective to piece together that he held the very statue pilfered from Lady Trilian's shop. The white statue carved out of limestone depicted a werewolf baring its fangs. Rock shuddered as the sensation of touching that smooth surface once before revived in her hands.

Guido's lips curled up in mockery of her foolish question. "Of course I do. The power of the werewolf is hidden within this." His eyes narrowed to slits as he fastened them on the statue he had thrust in Ebel's face. "I'd heard there were more than two out there, but it was backbreaking work getting my hands on one."

"Backbreaking work? Don't you mean the work of bludgeoning heads?" Phoebe snarled.

Guido had the nerve to cock an eyebrow at him. "I just paid for the goods. I don't know how it was obtained."

Rock sharply inhaled at his heartless remark. His money had driven criminals to beat up Lady Trilian and wreck her shop.

"Keep your mouths shut, outsiders. I have business with Ebel." Guido looked down his nose at Ebel hunched over on the floor. "Start talking already. Tell me how to become a werewolf."

So he didn't know how to unleash the statue's curse either. What was he going to do once he found out?

"I can't do that," Ebel answered in pain.

Guido huffed like an upset child. "Why not? It's not fair for you to keep it all to yourself."

"I'm not trying to keep it to myself. I can't tell you because I don't want you to bear the weight of knowing."

"Those who want the power of the werewolf should have it. Am I wrong, Ebel?" Guido began spewing words Rock never expected to hear from him. "I'm repeating myself here, but I want your powers." Madness gleamed bewitchingly in his human eyes. "Ever since I first laid eyes upon that form, I found beauty in its unworldliness. The power to become a werewolf is miraculous! It hides infinite possibilities beyond human knowledge. What's so wrong with wanting that?"

Full of passion, those delusional eyes were riveted on the completely changed appearance of his friend—not on the young man with burnt sienna hair, forest-green eyes, and the handsome face depicted in the portrait downstairs, but on the Ebel whose face was a wolf's.

"As long as I'm in possession of such power, I can protect Michaela where you've abandoned her," Guido said, drawing false conclusions. "I'll protect her. I need the werewolf's power to do that." His voice carried the hopes of a man crazed with delusional ambitions.

"Don't be a fool!" Ebel's sorrowful cry carried the complete opposite emotion.

Guido's desires made no sense to Rock. How could he yearn for the same curse after seeing his best friend tormented by it? Phoebe once said that these statues harbored the power desired by an oppressed people to fight back against their oppressors in ancient times. But what they lost in return was just as great. Rock felt disgusted by that story and questioned their motives. Even more so after hearing about the suffering Ebel went through.

Yet Guido still wanted that power.

"Are you insane?!" she interjected.

Guido's face twisted with annoyance. "I told you to keep your mouth shut, outsider. This has nothing to do with you."

"No, it does have something to do with me. I know how much Ebel suffers!"

That night Ebel stayed with her, she heard the feelings he kept buried inside. He told her of the previous Count Mateus's mental breakdown and Ebel's solitary night sleeping on the cold floor that first day he was cursed. That was but the tip of the iceberg for the disasters to follow as Ebel lost a great many things since. His grief-stricken father, his adorable fiancée, and now, the best friend he had trusted with all his heart.

The man who should've known that more than any other, the one who should've seen Ebel's suffering up close, desired the very same fate for himself. Could that be anything other than insanity?

"You should know it well too! Don't you understand just what burdens Ebel's been carrying all this time?" Rock sharply accused.

Guido scoffed as if he were beyond reproach. "And what do you know of Ebel?" Before she could answer, he mocked her for her ignorance. "Ebel's a strong man. He wasn't crushed by the curse inflicted upon him, and he has taken on each day with positivity. Not only did he not succumb to the werewolf's power, but he learned to control it!"

Guido certainly spoke of one side of Ebel. Unashamed and unbroken by being a werewolf, Ebel always acted cheerfully around Rock too. He continually used that power to rid the world of similar tragedies and to clear his father of the regrets that followed him to the deathbed. Those were facts.

But just as everyone masters different masks for different occasions in life, optimism didn't define Ebel in his entirety. After all this time, Guido still didn't know what was hidden beneath the masks he wore.

"You stand at his side pretending to be his sweetheart, and you don't even know that much?" Guido sneered.

Rock took his contemptuous glare head-on. "Say whatever you like about me. But I can't forgive anyone who hurts Ebel."

Unleashing the curse for a second time would most assuredly be a knife to Ebel's chest. And for Michaela as well. Rock had to do whatever it took to stop him before that happened.

"Roxy, stand back—it's getting dangerous." Phoebe stepped forward to protect Rock. He whipped the dagger out of his boot and pointed it at Guido. "This is what comes next when talk fails. Drop the statue if you don't want to die."

"Wha—?" Even Guido's stubborn face twisted with fear in the face of Phoebe's sharp blade.

"Don't, Phoebe!" Ebel yelled in an attempt to stay his hand. Phoebe's eyes bulged.

"Hah? Why—" He glanced once in Ebel's direction, unnaturally stopping midsentence before sheathing his dagger. Grinding his frustration between his teeth, he slipped into a martial arts stance.

Rock watched them, not quite sure how to interpret that exchange. Why did Ebel stop Phoebe? And why did Phoebe listen without a fight?

She raked her eyes over the room and suddenly realized they weren't alone in the study that had changed since her last visit. Ludovicus, the butler, stayed pressed up against the relief wall, and Iniel, the coachman, hid crouched in the shadow of the knocked-over mahogany desk. They appeared to be watching the course of events with caution, as if they were reluctantly remaining as passive onlookers when they wanted to take action.

Rock noticed Johanna had caught up to them and was standing behind her. Trembling, with her face whiter than paper, she, too, stood there unmoving with the fireplace poker clutched in her hands. Or maybe she couldn't move.

Why? There must be a reason why they can't go after Guido, Rock deduced.

Guido didn't miss Ebel's telling reaction either. "Why did you stop him, Ebel?" Guido stared down at him, a flash of insight crossing his face, ready to drive Ebel into the corner. "You have a reason not to let harm come to me. No?"

Ebel's triangular ears trembled as he shook his head hard. "Guido! Stop this nonsense already!"

"Is it the dagger? Do you need a knife to unlock the werewolf curse?"

That sounded like the right answer. Ebel didn't answer him, but Rock heard Johanna swallow her cry behind her. Instead of replying, Ebel loudly gnashed his fangs.

"I'm begging you, Guido—don't do this. I don't want you drawn into the misery of this curse!"

"I'm not being drawn into it by you. I'm going to obtain this power because I want it for myself!"

"Michaela will be heartbroken if she loses you to the curse as well!"

At the mention of his younger sister's name, the blood rushed to Guido's head, and a vein popped in his neck. "Ha! My sister will be overjoyed to have me protecting her! Especially now that you can't be trusted!"

"What sister would rejoice over her brother being cursed?!" Ebel cried out, trying desperately to make him understand, but his words no longer reached Guido.

Guido slowly exhaled with an expression of mounting elation and disappointment. "You abandoned Michaela! Don't speak as if you know her better than me…!"

In a sense, Guido was another victim whose life was thrown off course by the werewolf curse. As the man who rejoiced over his best friend and sister's engagement, he believed Ebel would use his newfound powers for Michaela too. Maybe he just couldn't get over them breaking off the engagement, but did it make sense for him to choose becoming cursed because of it?

Or was that another effect cast by the curse's power?

What if it wasn't all just coincidental that Phoebe obtained the statue, the previous Count Mateus unleashed its curse, the cursed Ebel confided that secret in Guido, and Guido, a future duke, became infatuated with its power?

Each was a separate dot on the paper, but Rock strongly believed everything was connected and entangled.

Rock shuddered as Guido drew a small dagger from his jacket. The beautifully ornate, jewel-encrusted dagger looked as if it had little value outside of being a decorative letter opener, but in this moment, it glinted with a bewitching light. Guido pressed the tip of the blade into one of the fingertips holding the statue and dragged his hawkish gaze over Ebel's face.

"Is it blood?"

As he expected, Ebel didn't answer. His golden eyes stayed riveted on Guido as he wrenched out a final appeal to his friend: "Guido, don't do this. Don't believe for one moment that being cursed is a blessing."

"Save your bullshit for another sucker. Answer my question."

"There's nothing good about becoming a werewolf!" He spat out his true feelings as if it were poison on his tongue. These were the feelings he never spoke of to Rock and likely never uttered aloud before.

Guido's eyes were too blinded by a lust for power to see it. "Fine. If you won't answer me, I'll just try it!" He twisted the blade into his finger.

"STOP!"

"You bastard!"

Ebel and Phoebe shouted and charged him at the same time.

Rock wasn't sure if her eyes caught everything that happened next. It ended faster than it started. Ebel and Phoebe lunged at Guido and knocked the ornate dagger from his hand. It fell on top of the fancy study rug, and Ludovicus dove from the wall and snatched it up.

Guido was slammed against the floor with his right arm twisted behind his back by Ebel and the left by Phoebe. Phoebe wrenched the statue from his fingers and tossed it to Rock.

"Take it somewhere far away!"

"Okay!" Rock caught the statue and propelled herself forward to run from the room. But the next second, she experienced a shock so great she felt as if time had stopped forever.

The statue started crumbling in her hands. In a blink of an eye, it lost its shape and spilled through her fingers, forming a pile of white dust on the rug.

"N-No way…," she gasped, then inspected the dust mound. There she spotted a few specks of blood in the white dust, and she spun around.

Rock saw Guido's body swelling under his clothes as Johanna, Iniel, Phoebe, and Ebel tried to hold him down. His clothes exploded as if breaking him out of his shell, and a body covered in black fur appeared from the shreds. The mouth that was trying to yell something jutted out and split open, the teeth inside transformed into impossibly sharp fangs, and the black fur on his head parted for inhuman ears to sprout. His eyes flew open, revealing glowing golden orbs like Ebel's, but his screamed death and hatred.

The second werewolf rose on his haunches.

Howling, wilder than from any healthy beast, echoed through the room as he brought his menacing head back. Saliva dripped from his large, yellowing incisors. He swung his meaty arms, sending the humans on top of him flying. Johanna and Iniel slammed against the floor, and even Phoebe, who clung on with all his strength, was thrown against the wall.

"No!" Rock screamed.

In front of her, werewolf Guido slammed his fist hard into Ebel.

With less sanity than a wolf infected with rabies, he pounded his clawed fists into the other werewolf with enough strength to break his own shoulder.

"GUAH!" Ebel just managed to hold his ground despite a right hook to the side of his muzzle. The impact brought him to his knees.

Guido raised his bladelike claws up and was about to bring them down on Ebel's face.

"EBEL!" Rock lunged at Guido's back.

A weak woman was no threat to a blood-crazed werewolf. His hammer-like arm snapped out to meet her as if he were swatting a fly, and Rock arced through the air, until her back collided with something hard.

A dull pain that knocked the air out of her lungs coursed through her body and stole her consciousness.

Chapter 7: Kiss Me If We Make It to Dawn

ROCK was dreaming. It was a dream that brought up nostalgic memories, like reading an old diary.

The dream took her back to the small cabin she had called home when she used to live in the farming village with her mother. While her mother, Vale, got dinner ready, Rock mended clothes in the kitchen beside her. Her mother had taught her how to sew at ten, and this was a memory from the time she was finally getting used to using a needle and thread. She enjoyed making accessories with her needlework, she rejoiced when she succeeded in mending a tear, and she practiced on any piece of ripped clothing she found.

"Lookie look! I did it, Mom!"

Hearing her daughter's voice, Vale stopped in the middle of cooking and checked her finished work. "You've gotten good, Roxy." She would praise her and pat her on the head whenever she did a good job.

Always kind, her mother was a very beautiful woman on the inside and out. Rock had inherited her wine-colored hair from her. She taught Rock everything she needed to know about the art of making clothes, from how to make a stitch to threading a needle. There weren't many tailoring jobs in a poor rural village, and it wasn't an easy life by any means, but there was always peace in their home.

"I'm going to be a tailor, too, when I get bigger!"

Her mother always beamed at her whenever she said that. "Want to open a shop with me when you get bigger, then?"

"I do!"

"What kind of tailor do you want to be, Roxy?"

The young Rock pondered her mother's question. She wanted to be a tailor, but she never thought about what kind.

She tilted her head to the side and tapped her finger against her chin. "A tailor who makes lots of money!"

Vale burst out laughing at her adult answer. "Your eye for money is just like a certain someone's."

"Who's that? Who's that?"

"No one... Making money is important, too, Roxy," she agreed first, before softly telling her, "You see, I became a tailor because I wanted to make my customers happy."

"Happy?"

"Yes, happy. There's not a person in this world who doesn't wear clothes, right?"

On normal days, on special days, on nights, and on weekends, everyone wears clothes.

The clothes Rock used to wear back then were all made by Vale. Everything from the everyday clothes she wore to work the fields, her work clothes for tending the shop, her nice dresses for attending church, her pajamas, and even her undergarments were made by Vale. Each piece of clothing her mother made fit comfortably and perfectly to Rock's body.

"Clothes give a subtle, untainted happiness when someone puts them on and feels more comfortable or when they stand in front of the mirror and like themselves more today than they did yesterday." Vale hugged her small daughter and kissed her gently on the cheek. "A tailor, you see, is a profession that offers modest happiness to people."

It was a heartwarming, bittersweet, and very sad memory. Tears trickled down from Rock's closed eyes, informing her that she was dreaming.

"Roxy! Roxy!" Ebel was calling for her somewhere close.

Snapping awake, she opened her eyes, and a big, black furball filled her tear-blurred vision. Sharp pain shot through her shoulder when she lifted her arm to wipe her eyes. "Agh!"

"Try not to move it. You hit your shoulder pretty hard," Ebel said, exhaling a deep sigh of relief. "But thank goodness... I didn't know what to do if you never woke up."

Rock blinked away the tears in her eyes, and Ebel's face peering into hers became clearer. His pointy ears were flat against his head with worry, and his golden eyes wavered with his inner turmoil. She saw an unfamiliar stone ceiling past his broad, furry shoulders.

"Ebel, where are we…?" She tasted blood when she spoke, but her pain wasn't bad enough to prevent her from talking. Her back ached when she breathed in, but it didn't feel like anything was broken.

"Inside the secret passage I brought you to before," Ebel answered in a subdued voice. "The one connected to my study's closet. Don't remember?"

That was enough to bring the events before she passed out flooding back into her mind. Guido had unleashed the curse hidden within the statue, transforming into a full werewolf and going mad enough that he flung Iniel, Johanna, and Phoebe into the air.

"Wh-Where is everyone? What happened after I blacked out?" Rock tried to sit up, but the werewolf's big paw stopped her.

"I don't know. I focused all my efforts on picking you up and escaping in here." Ebel weakly shook his head, a bloody gash marring his left ear from the time Guido was pounding him. Wet blood oozed from the wound, indicating not much time had passed since then.

"Then we have to make sure they are all—"

"I'll go, so stay here for me," Ebel said over her, quietly pointing out, "You hit your back and shoulder. You shouldn't move."

Just because she sustained injuries didn't mean she could sit still and do nothing. She clung to his furry hand and pulled herself up, enduring the shockwaves of pain. She wasn't bleeding anywhere visible, and while her joints ached, she was capable of standing.

"I'm coming with you," she insisted. "I want to make sure everyone is safe, and I'm worried about that man too."

"I'll handle Guido," Ebel asserted, speaking strongly for the first time. "He still isn't in his right mind. It's my duty to stop him."

"The more people the better. I'm joining you."

"You can't. It's too dangerous."

Rock gleaned the urgency in his obstinate refusal. He didn't want her coming with him no matter what.

"That's how it is the first time. You lose your mind and self-awareness. Father stopped my rampage long enough for me to regain control and hold myself back, but…" His agonized sigh echoed in the narrow space. "It has to be me…who stops Guido this time."

"You blame yourself too much if you feel responsible for his choices, Ebel," Rock argued, drawing a pained half smile from him.

"Your kindness knows no bounds. But this is still my responsibility."

"How?! The curse is at fault, not you!"

"Even so. As one who has been cursed, I shouldn't have allowed another to experience that misery." As Rock feared, Ebel blamed himself for what happened with Guido. "I should've noticed sooner that Guido was infatuated with the werewolf. I have to be the one to put him in his place before he harms anyone else." Balling his inhuman hand into a fist, he wrenched out in a shaky voice, "I'll stop him, even if it means we both go down."

His grim determination struck Rock in the heart. What he had said before Guido unleashed the curse upon himself rang in her ears: *"There's nothing good about becoming a werewolf!"*

She didn't question that was how he truly felt deep down, but at the same time, it gutted her. Those were the feelings behind the man who was always optimistic and cheerful in front of her. Beneath his sunny smile and level composure was a man who lamented his fate.

Rock was a tailor. Before her mother died, she called it a profession that offers modest happiness to others. Even Rock should have the power to make the person suffering in front of her, the man she cared about, happy.

"Don't think about going down with him!" Rock seized Ebel's shoulders and brought her face to his wet, black nose. She stared into those cursed and glowing, yet still beautiful, eyes. "You have me, don't you?!" She emphatically appealed to those wide-open eyes. "I only know the part of your life that I have been around for. But the you who smiled and had fun with me wasn't fake. There will be even more fun and happy things to come! I will make you happy! I won't be happy if you don't continue to be with me from now on!"

They made a promise. She promised to put her heart and soul into the cloak he ordered, and he promised to come for it.

If her mother was right, and being a tailor meant giving others happiness, Ebel should experience happiness from putting on that cloak. The joy over donning new clothes and having them fit like a glove, and the blissful comfort of it, would surely bring him happiness.

Maybe, just maybe, Rock was capable of bringing him even more happiness than what her work alone was able to do.

"Please do me this favor and let me come with you," Rock beseeched. Ebel stared dumbly back at her, so she took the honesty approach: "Even if you tell me no, I'll follow you against all odds!"

Ebel wasn't her only concern—her heart ached to know how Phoebe and the others were faring. She even worried for Guido.

"Mother used to say that tailoring is a profession that offers happiness to others."

Various customers, good and bad, made use of her services. Rock wished happiness for them, regardless of who they were.

"I don't wish misfortune upon anyone. Not even on Guido Linus... That man will surely suffer when he regains himself. Hurting many people and being cursed will be burdens he will forever carry. And that's exactly why we must stop him before his mistakes become unbearable."

Just as Ebel had regained his humanity, Guido wasn't stuck inside the body of a werewolf forever. He should revert back to human with time. They had no way of telling what his thoughts would be like then. Perhaps he would taste suffering over being cursed as Ebel had. Even regret what he had done.

Stopping Guido from rampaging wasn't the end, but only the beginning.

"It's your turn to step in when he regrets what he has done, Ebel." Rock moved her hands from his shoulders to cup his cheeks. The werewolf's muzzle was soft to the touch, fluffy, and a little warm. Though his appearance was completely different, blood pumped through the veins beneath all that fur, and so did the same spark of life. "You are the only one capable of showing Guido Linus that while there is pain and suffering in being a werewolf, there is also joy and happiness."

Rock closed her eyes and slowly tilted her head toward his. She planted an awkward kiss on top of his werewolf nose. "...I will make you happy." She had confidence that she was capable of doing that. "So you both have to live."

For a long moment, Ebel stared at her as if his breath had been taken away. His golden eyes opened as wide as they could go, his triangular ears perked up, and he zoned out as if captivated by her.

After what felt like eternity, he blinked and croaked, "…Why the nose?"

"Is that really your first question?" Rock frowned to hide her embarrassment. "I didn't know where to kiss your big mouth." The werewolf's black lips opened sideways, and she couldn't figure out how to kiss them. Plus, it was strange for her first kiss to taste of blood. "But my lips would be buried in fur if I kissed you on the cheek or forehead."

She pinched the black fur under her hands, and Ebel chuckled. "Then I want another one when I'm human again."

"I'll do it as often as you want if that is what makes you happy."

"It will make me happier than I've ever been at any other point in my life." He put his hands on her back and helped her stand as gently as he could. After sharing another look with her, he gallantly proclaimed, "I'm going to leave this passage, find Guido, and stop him if need be. I'm going to beat into him how to live as a werewolf. You're coming with me, aren't you, Roxy?"

"Absolutely, Ebel," she agreed without a moment's delay. Ebel's change of heart made her happier than anything else could.

THEY raced through the narrow passages winding throughout the manor. Along the way, they heard through the walls and floor beneath them howls, erratic footsteps, and the crash of things breaking. With every sound, Rock worried about Phoebe and the others.

After taking several corners, Ebel moved the wall at the end of the passage, revealing a familiar reception room for them to jump inside. The room Rock had waited in during her last visit was empty. Darkness still reigned outside the windows, and straining her eyes with the assistance of the starlight, she saw it hadn't been wrecked yet.

"Looks like they haven't come this way."

Ebel's ears flicked back and forth. "I hear people running. Likely Guido and…someone else." The werewolf count's amplified hearing easily picked up on who was moving through the manor. Though that didn't guarantee the person fleeing was going to stay safe.

Rock and Ebel bolted into the corridor.

The erratic footsteps grew louder as they advanced through the corridors and neared the staircase leading upstairs. Rock warily peeked around the corner just as someone tall dropped onto the carpeted landing lit by the crystal chandelier. The person who was tossed on the landing, rather than willingly jumping down, rolled to their feet and cursed.

"Stubborn bastard!" Groaning with blood dribbling down his lips, Phoebe glared at the top of the stairs with his dagger out.

"Phoebe!" Rock cried out against her better judgment.

She knew he would be safe, but confirming it with her own eyes brought the first sense of relief she felt that night. His chestnut curls had been pulled loose from his ponytail, and his damaged leather armor was dangling off his muscular frame. For all that, he stood in one piece, which couldn't be said for the rest of the manor.

Phoebe shifted only his eyes her way, and momentary relief swept over his brave face. His relief dispersed as he locked eyes on the monster closing in on him from above, and he bit down on his lower lip.

"Roxy, run! He's coming!"

A deranged howl pierced the air, adding urgency to Phoebe's warning. The inhuman roar steadily drew closer with the thundering beat of four limbs pounding the floor above.

"This way, Phoebe!" Ebel shouted. He threw open one of the doors downstairs and urged Rock and Phoebe to follow him in.

Rock looked over her shoulder at Phoebe, but Phoebe was already moving. He scooped her under his arm and plunged into the room after Ebel.

It appeared to be the dining room. The center of the room was taken up by a rectangular dark marble dining table, surrounded on all sides by upholstered chairs. Unlit candlesticks sat in ornate silver holders on either end of the table. A fire wasn't burning in the fireplace when Ebel twisted his enormous body inside and quickly disappeared above. From the looks of it, another hidden door leading upstairs was built within the fireplace.

Rock and Phoebe peeked inside and saw golden eyes glowing within the dark, narrow passage snaking upstairs.

"Come in here for now." Ebel reached down his furry hand and grabbed Rock first. He easily lifted her up with one hand and did the same for Phoebe next.

Right after they climbed inside the passage, they heard clawed feet scraping around the wooden corridors in front of the dining room. Did he lack the intelligence to realize the dining room door was open? The deranged werewolf's howl and thundering steps passed right by and disappeared down the corridor.

Three sighs echoed within the small crawlspace above the fireplace.

Rock inventoried her surroundings. Ebel had pulled her into a small stone room similar to what lay beyond the secret passage connected to his study. The warm light of a lantern burned here too, hinting at someone's frequent use of its confined space. The hidden passage continued beyond the room, but she couldn't tell at a glance where it led around all the bends.

"What is this place?"

Ebel's pointed ears turned toward Phoebe's logical question. "This is a secret passage for emergency escapes. It's mostly used to hide my true form."

"Heh…" Phoebe drawled out that single syllable.

"Irony is, I never thought I'd need it to ward off another werewolf." Gloom hung over Ebel's voice, but his secret passage had saved their lives.

"Anyway, you saved my butt out there." Phoebe flopped back on the stone floor and exhaled an exhausted breath.

"Are you all right? Hurt anywhere?" Rock scooted over to him, earning an indescribably bitter smile.

"I made it out alive by the skin of my teeth. I'm more or less in one piece, though the blighter clawed me more than once." He made light of it, but Rock knew what he went through was anything but. If he hadn't been wearing armor, he would've been torn to shreds. "Look at you, girl. You're covered in cuts and bruises." He rested his palm on her cheek.

Intense pain accompanied his warm and gentle touch. Stinging pain from the cuts on her lip turned her smile into a wince. "I haven't looked in the mirror yet. But it's not as bad as it looks."

"I hope it doesn't leave a scar… How could this happen to you before marriage?" Phoebe lamented.

Ebel quickly chimed in, "You don't have to worry about her marriage prospects. I'll take responsibility and marry her."

"Nobody asked you to," Phoebe quipped, while Rock hid her blush beside him. Ebel just dropped a crazy proposal in the middle of all the chaos. However, the idyllic mood ended there.

Ebel suddenly took a deep breath and asked Phoebe, "How are... Ludovicus and the others?" The werewolf's facial expression didn't change much, but fear audibly laced his words.

Phoebe shifted into a serious demeanor to answer him. "The butler is fine. The coachman and maid...were breathing the last I checked."

"...They were?" Ebel clenched his jaw.

Wiping the bloody sweat from his brow, Phoebe ranted, "I couldn't see to them with that wolf bastard bearing down on us. They wouldn't have survived another attack, so I left them to the butler and lured Lord Wolf away. It was the start of a fun game of tag, where being caught means a nice blade to the throat." His eyes drifted to Rock, and his tone softened by several degrees. "I wanted to check on you, but you weren't in the study. Believing you were safe with His Excellency, I ran that mangy mutt in circles around the house."

"It took everything I had just to get her out of there." Ebel looked at Rock with sadness in his eyes.

Phoebe gave a slow nod. "That was the best choice. I would've done the same."

Rock suddenly wondered what she would have done in their position. What if she could save only one person in that room? Bravery had her jumping on Guido's back without thinking about herself, and still she knew she wouldn't have been able to make the decision Ebel had. Chances were that she would've been rooted to the floor without choosing anyone at all.

What did she have to do if she wanted to save them all—not just one? Her next choices mattered if she wanted to make that happen.

Face set in a hard mask, Phoebe asked the most important question. "So? What do we prioritize next? How do you want to handle him, Your Excellency?"

After speaking with Rock, Ebel had his answer ready. "I won't let Guido die. We're going to save him and everyone else."

"Are you sane...?" Phoebe swore. He knew how difficult that was going to be to pull off. With a bitter edge to his voice, he questioned, "Or rather, is there even a way to bring back his sanity?"

Ebel blinked his golden eyes. "A strong will can control the werewolf's power. Though that's beyond Guido in his current state."

"How about we knock him out?" Rock interjected, drawing on her memory of what Ebel told her about his first night as a werewolf. He'd spent that night in solitude, sleeping on top of the cold stone floor. "You went to sleep and woke up back to normal after your first transformation, right? Won't the same apply to Guido?"

"I hope it will, but the problem is how we get him to sleep." Ebel stroked his furry chin, the lantern light reflecting off his thick claws. "If we're lucky, we can exhaust him until he falls asleep, but it's unlikely our stamina will last longer than his. We're stuck with either finding a way to knock him out or punching him until he comes to his senses."

"That's a sketchy strategy. You want to capture him alive, I take it?" Phoebe assumed, exasperated.

"Sorry, but that's the only option on the table." Ebel didn't want to consider the alternative.

"You think you and I can take him in a fair fight? Lord Wolf's not to be underestimated, Your Excellency."

"We have the upper hand here. Launching a surprise attack increases our chances of success."

More than being a rough strategy without much thought, it was a strategy that clung to a faint hope. Neither Ebel nor Phoebe knew if what they were plotting was possible. Rock understood they didn't have many options if they wanted to take him alive. Guido was no different from a wild beast incapable of understanding words. Even so, they had to capture him alive and bring back the man from within the beast.

"How about we lay a trap for him?" Rock suggested. Ebel and Phoebe turned toward her. She explained her plan to them with urgency. "I'll make a bag you can capture Guido alive with. Whether it be sheets, blankets, or curtains, I'll use whatever big fabrics we can get our hands on to sew a sturdy bag you can use to stop his movement." She wanted to increase their faint hope of success to something with more certainty. "Our opponent is a werewolf. A bag won't keep him tripped up for long, but if we can rob him of his sight and movement for a short time, our chances of success will double."

"Good idea. We can turn the tides in our favor if we pull it off," Phoebe said, approving the idea on the spot, and Ebel consented right after.

"Agreed. It's a decent plan." He scratched the spot between his pointy ears and hesitantly asked, "I know it's rude to ask this, but…can you pull off such a quick sew job?"

"I am a tailor. You can rest assured I will have it done," Rock answered with pride. This job was going to require more speed and accuracy from her than any other in her career.

The three of them crawled through the narrow confines of the passage leading from the small room and exited into a room on the third floor.

"This is my room," Ebel explained. A bed fit for a king took up the back wall. The room, much larger than Rock's entire flat, was decorated with étagère, decorative wall tapestries, and scenic oil paintings. Unlike the splendor of the reception room, only practical wooden furnishings filled his bedroom. "You can use anything you find."

With the owner's permission, Rock stripped the blankets and sheets from the bed. She had a sewing kit on her at all times. She pulled a needle and thread from the kit hanging from her belt and immediately got to work.

Just as she began sewing the blanket to the sheet, Ebel, ears twitching, alerted them of their target's proximity: "…He's come."

Rock's ears didn't pick up on anything yet, but she felt a slight vibration through the floor she sat on. No one could guess what drove Guido now that he'd lost control, but he seemed to be searching high and low for someone to satiate his desire to rampage more.

"I'll go play with him," Phoebe proposed.

Startled, Rock's eyes followed him when he stood up. "W-Will you be okay? Isn't it dangerous?"

He laughed off her concerns. "Don't worry. I'm just going to continue our game of tag."

"But—"

"You don't want him barging in here before you're ready, right? We have to lure him away," Phoebe said, trying to persuade Rock before she persisted in arguing, then he glanced over at Ebel.

Ebel nodded without any words passing between them. "I'll protect Roxy. We'll catch up to you as soon as she's finished sewing the bag."

"Let me know when you're armed and ready. I'll bring him to you,"

Phoebe said, explaining the plan to Ebel. Then, seeing that Rock was still worried, he told her, "Work hard at your role in this."

"…I will," she squeezed out.

Phoebe flashed her a winning smile and winked. "Let's pop open that bottle of wine when we get home. I love ya, Roxy." He quietly opened the door, stepped into the corridor, and silently shut the door behind him. The sound of his running echoed through the halls until it, too, became out of earshot.

Threaded needle in hand, Rock's gaze lingered on the closed door. She was dumbstruck by the words her father left her with. She had said the same thing to Phoebe when she thought he was someone else, none the wiser that she had directly told her father that she loved him.

"…Love, eh?" Ebel repeated in a deep growl, sending Rock into a panic.

"Um, he's…well, he's my father. Probably. I'm pretty positive," she explained as best she could.

Ebel let out a short chuckle, not all too surprised. "For a while now, I thought that might be the case."

Maybe her eyes were blinded to the truth because of how close they had been.

"I've got to say you're a lot like your parents," Ebel murmured, convinced they were father and daughter while Rock was still reeling in shock.

She hoped that was true. She wanted to be brave like her father, kind like her mother, and a tailor who did quick work.

Rock put her heart and soul into every stitch for her father and everyone else whose safety rode on this plan succeeding.

She finally finished sewing a large bag out of the blanket and sheets. Using bedding as the base material created a big bag she could fit completely inside. It was large enough to rob the werewolf of its sight and movement.

Rock and Ebel left his bedroom carrying the finished bag. They were on the third floor, while Guido and Phoebe were carrying out their game of tag on the floor below. Impatience coursed through Rock as she heard the howls of the werewolf who showed no signs of slowing down.

Tamping down her feelings, she prepared the trap with calm

mindfulness. "I would lay a snare trap if we were trying to catch a small animal." Growing up in a farming village gave her some experience with trapping.

"What's a snare trap?" Ebel asked.

"It's a hunting method that ensnares the limbs of the animal that stepped on the snare, or noose, and suspends it in the air. But it's not great for something of werewolf size…" The biggest thing she caught in the village was a wild boar. Against a werewolf, the best it could manage was restraining his arms and legs, but suspension was unlikely with their tools. "The only methods available to us right now are to either drop the bag on him from above or to knock him down and pull the bag over his head and pull the straps tight."

"Knocking him over sounds like it has a higher chance of success," Ebel surmised while his ears twitched. "Launching an attack on a nine-foot-tall werewolf from above poses too many complications. Just dropping the bag on him from up high won't cover a rampaging werewolf."

"None of the options will be easy," Rock concluded, preparing herself for what was to come.

"But we can do it," Ebel cheerfully exclaimed to set her mind at ease. "God will show us the way."

Rock didn't believe in God. But if her prayers would reach Him starting now, she would gladly become His follower. "May your god protect you," she said without sarcasm.

Ebel's golden eyes flashed and captured her in their sights. "I also have the goddess of victory on my side. Everything will go well."

"…Yes, yes it will." She even wanted to believe in the sayings that set her teeth on edge. Setting aside her fear, she gave a steely nod and set about enacting their plan.

Mateus Manor's third-floor corridor extended to the left and right of the grand staircase. Over ten rooms lined the corridor, and aside from Ebel's bedroom, almost all of them were used for guests.

Rock and Ebel opened two guest room doors facing each other in the corridor and moved the beds in each room close to the doors. In the place of rope, they corded thin pieces of cloth they tore off the curtains and tightly tied the ends to the bed legs in each room. By pulling the cord taut across the corridor with each heavy bed as an anchor, they were setting a trap to trip the werewolf.

Guido was supposed to trip over the cord long enough for them to pull the bag over his head, pull the straps closed, and punch him until he settled down—that was the plan.

"I'm going to lure Guido over. Hide," Ebel said before he ran for the stairs.

Rock darted into another guest room with the bag and left the door open a crack to keep an eye on the corridor.

Before long, heavy footfalls approached from the staircase.

"Up the stairs to the left!" Ebel shouted and appeared at the top of the stairs first. He was in the same werewolf form as Guido, but they ran completely different. Ebel ran with his shoulders back, his arms swinging, and his head held high—just like a person.

Phoebe followed right behind him. He had enough leeway for a quick glance over his shoulder at the werewolf charging him. Unlike Ebel, this werewolf's back was hunched, and he tore across the floor on all fours like a savage beast. Pieces of the floor cracked beneath his claws and flew behind him.

"Phoebe, watch the ground!"

"Got it!" Phoebe responded to Rock's warning.

Ebel, then Phoebe, jumped over the trap and hurtled into the guest room with Rock. Ebel took the bag and went right back into the corridor, while Rock and Phoebe watched over him from the doorway.

Rock's warning to Phoebe didn't register in Guido's dish-like ears, nor did he notice the trip trap stretched across the corridor. His forelegs caught on the taut cord as he ran after them without slowing down. The cord pulled tight, slamming the beds loudly against the door frame. Werewolf Guido pitched forward, the cord not breaking under his weight, and his whole body lifted off the ground for a second before he dove muzzle first into the floor.

The impact shook the mansion and sent tingling shockwaves through Rock.

"Now!" Ebel sprung forward and pulled the bag over the downed Guido just as he was rising on his haunches, but the bag robbed him of sight, and he began violently struggling. He thrashed his legs and arms, howled louder than a stormy night, and shook his bulky frame like an enraged bull trying to throw off a rider. "GUH!"

Despite being a werewolf himself, Ebel was weaker for being in control, and Guido nearly threw him off, so he hopped on his back to better restrain him.

"Is he a bottomless pit of energy or what?!" Phoebe flew out of the room and pinned down the arm about to throw Ebel off.

Guido truly seemed to have endless energy as a werewolf. A night of rampaging did nothing to drain him of stamina or rage. He continued thrashing about so violently, he nearly peeled Ebel and Phoebe off him.

The longer this dragged out, the more likely they were going to lose.

"Guido, cut it out already!" Ebel snarled, baring his fangs as he restrained Guido's arms.

Casting off Ebel's calls to sanity, Guido gave his body one big shake, sending Ebel and Phoebe flying off his back like a dog shaking water off his fur. Ebel's back collided with the corridor wall, and Phoebe rolled head over feet into Rock's guest room.

"No!" Rock cried, bolting out of the guest room past Phoebe.

With no one to hold Guido down, he'd rip the bag off in no time. She had to stop that at all costs. No one had pulled the cord to tighten the bag around him yet. That was something she could do!

"Roxy, don't be reckless!" Phoebe yelled, but Rock lunged for Guido anyway.

Strangely enough, she wasn't scared. *I'll become the real goddess of victory,* she thought. *I'm Fredericks Berwick and Vale Floria's daughter. I have nothing to fear, and everything to save. I want to always be proud of my father's strength and my mother's kindness that course through me!*

"You bloody wolf...stay still, would ya?!" She wrapped her arms around what was likely the thick neck of the werewolf wrestling with the bag, and squeezed with all the strength in her body. Her strength was nothing to write home about, but Guido howled like a wolf with a thorn stuck in its paw, and he twisted and bucked to knock her off. "I can't pull it tight if you struggle, dumb wolf!"

Clinging on to the werewolf's neck for dear life made it impossible to pull the string in her hand unless she wanted to be flung off her unwieldy mount. Then she spotted Ebel staggering to his feet at the end of the corridor.

"EBEL!" she shouted. What words suited a goddess of victory? She didn't have the time to think about it, so she screamed the first thing that came to mind at the top of her lungs: "PUNCH HIS LIGHTSSSSSSS OUUUUUUUUT!"

"You got it!" Ebel launched off the floor like a wolf springing on its prey. The werewolf approached faster than her eyes could follow and swung back his fist without a moment's hesitation.

Alas, Rock's remaining strength gave out there. Guido flung her to the floor with ease, and she kept only her eyes locked on him as Phoebe caught her.

Ebel's fist had already rammed through the bag into Guido. The bag made it impossible to tell where his fist landed a hit. A loud crack echoed down the corridor, and Guido rolled back on his arches, collapsing on the floor with a thwack.

"Come back to us, Guido!" Ebel slammed his left claw down on Guido's shoulder, holding him down, and drew back his right fist for a second punch. His fist made contact with what he knew was his face this time, and the cloth bag turned red with blood.

"Urgh…" came a moan that clearly didn't belong to a deranged beast.

Rock wasn't the only one who caught that telling sound. After a second's hesitation, Ebel ripped the bag off Guido, who was still in his werewolf form underneath. Blood dribbled from his big muzzle, but he cracked opened his eyes and faltered, "Ebel…why did you hit me?"

"You've regained…your mind?" Ebel gasped.

Guido blinked his golden eyes. "What are you— No, what did I… What have I…?" He looked at his hands, and a ragged breath was ripped from his throat at the inhuman claws there. "Why did I want to become this thing…this werewolf? I wanted this? How? I'd never…"

"Didn't you become a werewolf because you wanted to?" Phoebe clipped, his arms protectively around Rock.

Werewolf Guido visibly trembled before them. "I-I don't know. I definitely wanted that statue, but…!"

"I hate to be the bearer of bad news, but you've been cursed now," Ebel informed him in an even voice that hid his emotions. "You have no choice but to live with it. Prepare yourself."

"You're lying, Ebel! Tell me it's a bad joke!" Distraught, Guido pushed himself off the ground and started shaking Ebel by the shoulder. That did nothing to change his answer.

"This is no lie or joke. You brought it upon yourself," Ebel stated definitively, anguish in his voice.

Guido sat there in shock for a few moments before wailing like a man and an injured beast.

👑 👑 👑

GUIDO Linus was in terrible shock. Too haggard to walk by himself, Ebel and Phoebe assisted him to one of the undamaged guest rooms.

Shoved into one of the king-sized beds, Guido buried his wolf face into his paws. "I remember it all... From threatening you to forcing you to teach me how to become a werewolf." While he spoke of it, he sounded as if he couldn't believe his own actions. "Why did I want to become cursed...? How could I want this...?"

"Mayhap this is an extension of the curse's power," Ebel speculated in a whisper, not completely convinced himself. "I've heard the statue's call before. Some other power aside from the werewolf's curse may be locked within those statues."

Unfathomable fear caused Rock to shudder as she listened beside them. She had come to the same conclusion a while back. What if everything was conducted by the curse? Their encounter Ebel called fate, the way the statues were collected into this one area as if inviting them to find them, and Guido becoming a werewolf—what if all of it was intentional?

"What will Michaela say if she sees me like this?" Guido was grief-stricken. "If she learns her brother was cursed to be a monster, she'll—"

"Michaela loves you," Ebel declared over his cry. "She will continue to protect you as she always has."

Guido dropped his hands from his face, his eyes bulging. "Protect? Michaela will protect...me?"

"You won't survive in the imperial capital without human allies. Just as I couldn't have."

Did Ebel's advice reach Guido this time? For a long while, he wordlessly stared up at Ebel's werewolf face, eerily similar to his own.

Peace had finally come to Mateus Manor after everything that had happened.

"Roxy, I'm sorry, but would you mind bringing a bottle of liquor from my room?" Ebel whispered in her ear after Guido fell silent. "He's not going to fall asleep after what has transpired. Guido needs alcohol."

"Sure."

Rock left the guest room with Phoebe. She swept her eyes around the corridor and saw the sorry state they had left the manor in. Doors were bashed in, the plush rug was torn up, the floor was covered in scratch marks, and blood was splattered on the floor and walls. Flipped-over beds blocked the doors to the two rooms they anchored their trap to. Thinking about the cleanup made her head spin.

Even Ebel's bedroom had been wrecked by ripping the curtains off the windows and stripping the bed of its sheets and blanket. She had a perfect view out the curtainless windows of the dawning sky.

"Another day is dawning, Phoebe," Rock commented, drawing a sigh from Phoebe, who was rummaging through the antique liquor cabinet.

"Bloody hell, that was one miserable night. I didn't get a wink of sleep."

"You'd have some talent if you did," Rock said, bursting out laughing, the exhaustion finally hitting her now that the adrenaline was running out. Sleep was the first thing she wanted to do after they helped Guido settle down. "I didn't sleep either, but I dreamed while I was unconscious."

"What kind of dream?"

"A dream of the time I lived with Mother in the village."

Phoebe's hand froze around a bottle.

"From the time I still dressed and acted like a girl. We were talking about Father too...I think."

Did she feel a little self-conscious because she was talking about her early childhood? Or was it because the father in her mother's stories was standing right in front of her?

Face in a hard mask, Phoebe glared at the bottle's label. It was difficult to tell if those blue eyes were actually reading the letters on the label. After what felt like forever, he turned toward her with a gentle smile. "Sounds like a good dream, Roxy."

"...It was." Rock nodded.

Phoebe's eyes thoughtfully wandered away from her face. Then, after a pause, he asked, "By the way, what did Vale say about—"

"YOUR EXCELLENCY! MASTER ROCK!" A shrieking voice

bounced off the walls, erasing Phoebe's question. "This is Johanna! Where are you?! Are you all right?!"

They heard her running up the stairs with all the commotion of a parade. At least they knew Johanna was safe now.

"Here comes the loud one." Despite his grimace, relief washed over Phoebe.

Rock was also relieved from the bottom of her heart. A noisy but peaceful dawn was breaking over Mateus Manor.

JOHANNA appeared before Rock and Phoebe in much higher spirits than they expected. Bandages were wrapped around her ankles beneath her skirt and purple bruises swelled under her eyes and on her chin, but a smile burst onto her face when she saw Rock.

"Oh, Master Rock! I am so very relieved to see you safe!" She ran up the stairs, and when Rock met her in the third-floor corridor, she jumped into her arms. Rock staggered back but caught her. Johanna's openly expressed emotions had a way of making Rock feel shy.

"Th-Thank you. Did you get out all right?"

Johanna lifted her face from Rock's chest and answered her with mock seriousness. "I wasn't the least bit all right! I don't want to go through such a horrible experience too many times! The whole night felt like a scene right out of a play!"

"...Why does it sound like you enjoyed yourself?" Phoebe muttered behind Rock.

Either not hearing Phoebe or simply ignoring him, Johanna stared worriedly into Rock's eyes. "Oh, Master Rock, your beautiful face has been injured too... What a shame!!"

Ludovicus and Iniel trudged up the stairs after her with several bruises and lacerations on their faces also. Everyone was going to see the morning injured, but in one piece.

"It's just a few bruises. I will be fine. His Excellency is doing fine as well."

"Where is His Excellency?"

"The room down the corridor." Rock pointed at the closed guest room door. "Lord Linus has finally calmed down, so he is sitting with him right now."

The butler and coachman ran down the corridor and into the room. Hearing their master was okay wasn't the same as confirming it with their own eyes.

Only Johanna remained clinging to Rock. She trembled as large teardrops filled her eyes.

"Johanna? Are you sure you feel all right?" Worried, Rock looked the younger girl over again.

Johanna sniffled and whimpered, "I-I am all right... K-Knowing everyone is safe for real...suddenly brought the tears..." Unable to keep it in any longer, she broke down crying.

Johanna had bravely swung around the fireplace poker last night, but she looked quite a bit younger than Rock. Rock didn't know how she had ended up working for the Mateuses, but it seemed unlikely she went through traumatizing events like last night often. It must've been a terrifying and crazy night for her too. Rock fully sympathized with the desire to cry after being surrounded by a peaceful morning at the end of a nightmarish night.

So Rock stayed with her through the tears, rubbing soothing circles into her back. Left out of the girlie moment, Phoebe uncomfortably shifted but didn't interfere. Rock saw the corners of his eyes crease when he averted them from the hugging girls.

"I'm fine now. Thank you." After crying her eyes out, Johanna took a step back from Rock and finally smiled. It was a bashful, girlish smile. "I can never apologize to His Excellency enough for monopolizing his Master Rock."

"Rock doesn't belong to His Excellency yet," Phoebe groused again.

Johanna completely ignored him as a sparkle danced in her teary eyes. "You two have just overcome a daunting obstacle together! Now is the time to thoroughly express and test your love for one another! Please do it right here and right now! Preferably in front of me!"

Though Rock was relieved Johanna had stopped crying, she was overwhelmed by her confusing statements yet again. "Uh...what are you talking about?"

Ebel happened to appear at the other end of the corridor just as she was stuck for an answer. He strode quickly over to them in his werewolf form and asked, "Roxy, did you find the liquor cabinet?"

"Oh, I'm sorry." Reuniting with Johanna and the others made it completely slip her mind. Fortunately, Phoebe had chosen a bottle and brought it with him.

Ebel accepted it from him, and his sharp wolf features softened when he noticed Johanna. "I'm glad to see you aren't seriously injured either, Johanna."

"Thank you, Your Excellency...," she absently answered. Her prior excitement vanished as she curiously studied Ebel's face. Since she was a maid in his service, Ebel's werewolf form shouldn't have been too surprising for her, but she seemed to be in shock.

"Is something the matter?" Ebel promptly questioned, finding her behavior strange as well.

She looked from Ebel to Rock and mechanically moved her lips. "Your Excellency...did you...just call Master Rock 'Roxy'?"

"...Ah," Ebel uttered as if he'd just screwed up monstrously.

Rock quickly caught on too. Johanna had no way of learning about Rock's true identity last night. She couldn't fault the girl for being baffled by hearing Ebel call her by a woman's name.

Ebel and Iniel had already found out. She had little reason to hide the truth now.

"Right, about that, Johanna, I've actually—"

Ebel and Phoebe spoke over her at the same time.

"Save it for later, Rock."

"I wouldn't say anything 'bout it right now."

They quickly tried to stop her, but they were too late, for Rock said the rest.

"—been pretending to be a man all this time. I'm sorry for keeping it a secret from you."

Johanna stopped blinking. "Y-You are a woman?" she asked breathlessly.

"Yes."

"In other words, you were cross-dressing as a man?"

"That would be correct."

Phoebe's and Ebel's eyes rolled skyward at her courteous reply.

All the muscles in Johanna's face froze. "Ah...!" she cried and fell backward.

"Ack! Johanna! You were that shocked?!" Rock quickly caught her as

Johanna fainted in her arms.

"This is serious. Let's carry her to a bed." Ebel was alarmed, and Phoebe exhaled a worn-out breath.

"That's why I told you not to say anything!"

Ebel assisted Rock in carrying Johanna into a different room from Guido, and they laid her on the bed. According to her employer, Ebel, Johanna had a *slight* tendency to become histrionic.

"Apparently she saw a thrilling play in town a while back. It was a forbidden love story between two men set during Ancient Empire times…"

Influenced by that story, Johanna entertained a great interest and personal attachment to Ebel and Rock's romance. The excitement of being able to see the same situation as her favorite play unfold before her very eyes overstimulated her.

"I think I have the general idea now…," Rock vaguely replied, then followed it up with her honest thoughts: "She must've been disappointed to find out I'm a woman."

Ebel rolled his broad, furry shoulders. "This is just my guess, but…I think once she has a little time to calm down, she will exclaim, 'Cross-dressing is just like something out of a play too!'" he said, mimicking Johanna's excited voice.

"Whatever her reaction, it won't be a quiet one," Phoebe opined with a scowl.

Guido was able to fall asleep after a bottle of strong liquor, but it was too soon to leave him unguarded. So the men, including Phoebe, decided to take turns on watch duty. Everyone needed sleep and time to rest.

Meanwhile, Rock, who wasn't strong enough to deal with Guido should he rampage again, watched over Johanna instead.

"You must be exhausted too. Use any room you like to get some rest, should you need it," Ebel recommended, but Rock felt partially responsible for the unconscious maid. She didn't have anything better to do at the moment, so she wanted to stay by Johanna's side as long as her fatigued body allowed.

But Rock hadn't slept a wink in over twenty-four hours either. Exhaustion pressed in on her as she sat alone on the chair during her first moment of true rest after a long, painful night. She shut the curtains against the bright morning light blazing into the room, bringing about a comfortable darkness.

She slumped back into the chair and began dozing off before she knew it.

HOW much time had passed since she nodded off? During her shallow sleep, she felt someone lift her off the chair and carry her somewhere. Her eyelids were too heavy to open, but she felt someone's arms around her.

Rock experienced a floating sensation while she was still partially asleep. She heard soft footfalls and a door creak open, and she sensed her body being gently lowered inside a dimly lit room. Cool sheets and a soft pillow welcomed her into their embrace.

Someone's smooth hands gently stroked her hair.

"Mn…" She wrenched open her heavy eyes because she wanted to see who that hand belonged to. Beyond her blurry vision sat a handsome young man with burnt sienna hair and glowing golden eyes. He perched on the edge of the bed and was leaning across the space between them to look down at her face.

"Did I accidentally wake you?" Surprise flashed in his golden eyes.

Rock blinked repeatedly as her eyes traced every curve of his human face. When she finally noticed she was lying on a bed, she quickly pushed herself upright. "Shoot… I accidentally fell asleep!"

"Don't feel bad. You should sleep longer," Ebel softly persuaded as he looked fondly down at her. "Don't worry about Johanna. She's sleeping very comfortably."

"She is…?"

Johanna had fainted from a night's worth of fatigue and stress. The shocking truth she learned about Rock just added the final brick that knocked her out.

"I see you are back to normal too, Ebel." Rock pointed out his change since she'd fallen asleep.

Ebel threaded a hand through his hair as he gave a crooked smile. "I can't be running around the house naked all day long, after all. I wanted to put on some clothes."

He had pulled on a new white shirt and dark trousers. His three-piece suit had ripped right from his back during all the chaos last night, leaving him covered in fur, but naked, ever since.

When he had been a covered werewolf all that time, she hadn't been conscious of his nakedness, but now her cheeks flushed. "Now that you put it like that, you make a good point…"

Ebel roared with laughter at the look on her face. "I can't have you getting embarrassed on me. I'll have a hard time transforming around you."

Uncomfortable, she drew her knees up to her chest and wrapped her arms around them.

His laughter quickly died off, and his gaze dropped to the blankets. "I'm sending word to Michaela once the sun rises." Imagining her reaction stiffened his face and tightened his voice. "I plan to invite her here to see Guido. Would you mind being there for it?"

"Sure, I don't mind," she readily agreed, having come too far to turn back now. It was probably her fate to see this through to the end too. She had only just promised Ebel that she would be there for him.

"Thank you. I need someone there giving me emotional support too," he admitted, relief easing the tightness from his voice. He caressed Rock's cheek with his soft human hand. Her heart tripped a beat from his gentle, warm touch. She covered his hand with her own, bringing a blissful smile to his lips. "You truly are my goddess."

"You exaggerate."

"I'm not exaggerating. I, this manor, and everyone in it were saved by you."

Abashed by his high opinion of her, she buried her head in her knees. Not even she understood why she'd taken action when it counted. She never knew so much courage and bravery slept within her. If asked whether she could do the same thing again, she'd have to think about it.

In the end, everything worked out. There was so much left to think about and do, but for now, she earned a few moments of rest. Sleep rapidly closed in on her when she knew she could relax.

Ebel chuckled at her stifling a yawn. "Get some sleep. Ask if you need anything. I can have a bath and food prepared for you whenever you like."

"Please let me sleep for a bit, then."

Exhaustion was the only thing she felt right now. This was normally the time she woke up feeling hungry, but her body vehemently hungered for sleep over food.

"Of course." Ebel's hand left her cheek as she rubbed her eyes. His fingertips brushed over her lips next. "Won't you make me the happiest man alive with your lips before you sleep?" Rock gaped at him, not following what he was implying. He flashed a roguish smile, unwilling to back down. "You promised to do it as often as I want, no?"

"Ah! I-I did, didn't I?" She turned even redder with the memory.

"I want you to keep your promise from then," he coaxed with a joyous expression.

"R-Right now?"

"Right now. Promises should be fulfilled sooner rather than later."

Ebel looked determined to leave with a kiss, so she steeled herself to do it. "In that case, I-I will…" She awkwardly bobbed her head.

"Please do." Ebel quietly closed his eyes.

Kissing a werewolf was different from kissing a man.

The count's handsome face, capable of stopping people dead in their tracks, was right before her eyes. His long closed eyelashes framed his beautiful features, which were seemingly molded from granite and took Rock's breath away. The man's lips were easier to find than the wolf's, and she shouldn't have needed a special technique to press her lips against his, but she felt daunted as she leaned her face closer. Growing more embarrassed the nearer she drew, Rock shut her eyes as their noses were within touching distance.

Then she leaned in a little closer. She was positive her lips were lined up with his before she closed her eyes, but they missed their mark and pressed against the corner of his lips.

"That's not right...," she said aloud unthinkingly, and she knew Ebel was holding back his laughter. Flustered, she gave it another go. Drawing back her lips, she went straight in for another kiss. Except this time their noses collided before their lips did, and Rock groaned from the pain. "Ouch! ...S-Sorry."

"Don't worry about it."

She opened her eyes and saw Ebel holding his aching nose as well. He must've been hurting from their collision. "I'm not a very good kisser," she admitted with a dry laugh, but Ebel didn't laugh at her.

"I prefer it this way," he said, pulling her into his arms and stealing her lips.

She couldn't breathe through her roughly sealed lips. He greedily devoured her mouth, though his touch was soft. He sweetly nibbled on the tender side of her bottom lip and twined his fingers in her hair. In no time, she lost all bearing.

"Ah! Ebel! Wai—," Rock feebly cried out between ragged breaths when he pushed her down on the soft bed.

All of a sudden, his lips left hers, and he drew away from her. She timidly opened her eyes and saw his lips curved in a seductive smile. Gazing down in satisfaction at her chest rising and falling with the breath he stole from her, he said, "Good night, Roxy." And then he sauntered out of the room with a hop in his step, leaving her in a daze on the bed.

After the door quietly closed behind him, Rock stared at the stucco ceiling and muttered, "I'm wide-awake now, though..." She meant that as a complaint against him, but curiously enough, her lips spread in a big smile, and her voice didn't sound at all dissatisfied.

Dissatisfied or not, he'd still made her unable to sleep. Half an hour later, she was still tossing and turning on top of the bed where he'd left her.

ROCK thought she would never fall asleep, but her fatigue won the battle. The bed inside the count's guest room was more comfortable than clouds, and she slept like a log.

When she woke up, sunlight the color of candle flames filtered into the room. Confused momentarily by the unfamiliar stucco ceiling with a cherub relief, she stirred in bed and felt all her bones and muscles twinge with a dull ache. With the pain came a slow reminder that this wasn't her bedroom. She was sleeping inside Mateus Manor, located in the aristocrat district.

"You're up?"

Beside her, she heard a voice she could never mistake. Rock shifted her eyes to the left where Phoebe was peering into her face. He had dragged a chair over to the bed and had been sitting with his legs crossed.

"Have I been asleep long…?" she asked, though her parched throat told her the answer first. With how dried out she felt, she must've been asleep for a long time.

"It's evening now." Phoebe jerked his chin toward the window across from the bed.

The glowing sun painted the imperial capital's sky in deep shades of orange and red like a fire burning in the sky and spreading to the white clouds. The fiery orange sunset alerting the capital of the day's end pierced through the room's windows.

Blinded by its brightness, Rock returned her gaze to Phoebe. She realized he'd let down his chestnut tresses. He'd cast off his shredded leathers in exchange for a white button-up shirt and beige suspender trousers she didn't recognize.

"Ah, this?" he said, tugging on the suspenders under her assessing gaze. "His Excellency lent them to me. I said I wanted a dress, but he said they didn't have any my size."

"I'd think not."

The only lady residing in Mateus Manor was Johanna. Her wardrobe wouldn't contain any dresses that'd fit the full-head-taller Phoebe.

The shirt wouldn't button all the way up for him, so he left the first three buttons undone. The twining cords of muscle in his calves peeked out under the trousers, and he looked very uncomfortable inside the tight clothes. The clothes themselves were tailored from fine materials, which meant they likely belonged to Ebel.

Thinking about him filled her chest with an unscratchable itch. Rock sat up in bed and tossed a question to Phoebe to distract from her thoughts. "Anything happen while I was asleep?"

A line appeared between Phoebe's brows. "Guido Linus returned to normal."

"To normal? You mean back to being a man?"

"Yeah. He just came to, and His Excellency is with him now."

His form returned to normal, but that didn't mean the werewolf curse had lifted. Rock's frown pulled a torn expression from Phoebe too.

"Also, Lady Michaela will be arriving late tonight."

What kind of conversation would these close siblings have when they saw each other? What would Michaela say to her cursed brother, and how would Ebel feel watching them from the sidelines? Rock's heart ached for them.

I promised Ebel I would be there for him.

"Then I better get a move on it." Rock stretched on the bed, shifting her thoughts to what she could control. Her bruised back and throttled bones ached like a knife in her side, but lots of sleep washed away her fatigue. With her sleepiness gone, she felt her hunger, and she bashfully stated, "I want to have something light to eat before Lady Michaela arrives."

"I thought you'd say that, so I brought the goods." Phoebe cracked a devious grin and picked up a dark amber glass bottle from the round rosewood table next to the bed. It looked like an expensive bottle of liquor. "His Excellency said we could have it. It's a pricey bottle of wine."

He apparently wanted to have that promised drink now.

"Is it better than the one you've stashed all these years, Phoebe?"

He grinned at her. "Good question. We'll have to drink that one later to be sure." He raked a hand through his silky locks to hide his sheepishness. "You have questions for me, right? I have some stuff I want to tell you too."

"...Yeah." Rock gave her head a big nod.

The guest rooms on the third floor all had large bay windows. Phoebe opened the bay window, carried the round table over to the windowsill, and laid the bottle, wine glasses, and several snacks on top of it.

"The maid's still zonked out."

Which meant all the food he could get them was premade or raw. He put out a platter of hard bread, goat cheese, salted nuts, and apples. To the starving Rock, it looked like a feast.

They leaned against the windowsill and held up their wine-filled glasses. Phoebe brought it to his lips without hesitation, but Rock sniffed it first. The liquor her hair shared its color with had a fruity smell that wasn't quite grape.

She took a small sip, and a shifting kaleidoscope of flavors different from grape juice spread across her tongue with tingling vibrancy. The full-bodied, mellow spices of the wine left a talcum-like trail on the tongue and inner cheeks.

"Tastes better than I thought it would," Rock admitted, giving her honest opinion, and Phoebe laughed.

"That's because it's a good wine. Though it doesn't hold a candle to the one I've got at home." He looked affectionately at Rock as she tipped back the glass. "Maybe we should save that one to celebrate a bigger occasion."

"What would be a big occasion?"

"Won't there be all sorts coming in the future?" Phoebe answered ambiguously, the night breeze gently tousling his hair.

From the window, they had a perfect view of the manor's garden and the darkening cityscape. Under the sky where the stars began to twinkle, the aristocrat district and the emperor's castle looked stunning in the lingering sunlight. Now Rock gazed out, with curious attachment, on the scenery she had thought otherworldly during her first visit. She took in the nightscape as she savored each drop of her first glass of wine.

"I wonder if I'll get drunk from a single glass," she joked, expressing her fears, but Phoebe answered her seriously.

"You won't. Whoever you take after, you'll have a strong resistance to alcohol."

"Neat."

"Vale, especially, could hold her liquor."

"No way!" Rock's voice cracked. That was an unexpected side of her mother she never knew. Thinking back, she couldn't remember seeing her mother drink once.

Did she drink a lot with Father? Having a hard time believing it, Rock looked questioningly up at Phoebe.

He tipped back his glass again and faintly smiled. "Where should I start? What do you want to know?"

Rock wanted to know so much. But what she wanted to know most had to be—

"How you met Mother!"

"…It's not an exciting story." Embarrassed, Phoebe uncomfortably pushed his hair off his face. He didn't speak until he took another long sip of wine. "I met Vale during one of my mercenary missions."

That was what she'd thought. Rock nodded along as she munched on a loaf of bread, when Phoebe suddenly asked an unexpected question.

"Did you ever learn her real name?"

"Her real name? It's not Vale Floria?" Rock always believed that was the name her mother was given at birth.

"Floria was her mother's maiden name. Her real name is Valencia Alexis. She was the daughter of a lower-ranking imperial nobleman."

Phoebe blurted information so absurd that it nearly knocked the piece of bread out of Rock's half-open mouth. She scarfed the rest of it down and swallowed so she could cough out, "You're joking, right?"

"You think I would joke at a time like this?" Phoebe chided her with a dry smile. "As it stands now, a lot went down, and she fled her father's home, so she's no longer considered Alexis's daughter anymore. You won't get roped into anything complicated because of it."

Either way, it was still a shocking truth. She'd never fathomed that her mother was born and raised in the imperial capital, much less as a nobleman's daughter. She had a hard time believing such noble blood coursed through her.

"Did you guys elope or something?" Rock asked, thinking it was the obvious answer when he said she fled home.

Phoebe gave his head a big shake. "That'd be asking for a death sentence. I didn't think she'd chase after me either."

"Mother left her family on her own?" Catching his slip of tongue, she pressed in further: "Because she fell in love with you, right?"

Phoebe averted his eyes, struggling to answer. "Well…you could put it that way."

"Hmm."

"Stop grinning, Roxy." His large, bony hand ruffled her wine-colored hair until it was a mess. Rock giggled from the tickling. He smiled a little too. "But you know, things weren't so clear-cut for me."

Phoebe fell silent for a while after that.

With his hair down and his mouth shut, he possessed impeccable beauty that would have him mistaken for a gorgeous woman. Under the gradually fading afterglow, Rock studied every facet of his profile. She wanted to know how her mother had felt when she looked at him.

Once the evening breeze shifted into a night breeze, Phoebe solemnly cut to the topic he had the hardest time expressing. "...You see, I..." He picked up an apple and cleanly split it in two to distract himself. "From the day I became self-aware, I never knew if I was a man or woman."

Rock accepted his confession with one half of the apple. "You didn't?"

"Yeah. I wanted to grow out my hair and wear dresses. I hated hanging around crass men, but I also hated being all clingy with women. I left my hometown because I wanted to live free of those restrictions."

Phoebe's past wasn't full of pleasant memories. Plenty of people mocked him in the imperial capital—and this city was a hot pot of races and cultures. There was no telling what horrible treatment he had received for being different in a smaller city or town.

He devoured his half of the apple in three bites and inclined his head, his curls cascading over his shoulder. "That's why I didn't think anything was possible between Vale and I when we met. She was practically the most ladylike woman I ever met. I was like, 'I'll never fall for her.'"

"But you fell for her," Rock supplied, relentless in getting the story out of him as she bit into her apple. Phoebe shot her a vengeful glare.

"How could I not? She chased after me and wouldn't go away when I told her to, insisting she was happy with a feminine man like me."

"She wore you down."

"Pretty much."

Rock wished she could have seen how her parents interacted back then. Her thoughts traveled back to something Phoebe had said before. "But wait, aren't you the one who said, 'A man who lays his hands on a woman before marriage is the scum of the planet'?" That was what he'd said when he found Ebel naked in her room. "You aren't a hypocrite, are you?"

She asked it only as a leading question, but it had an immediate effect, as Phoebe playfully ground his knuckles into her cheek with the look of someone who was caught with their pants down. She let out a tiny yelp, and he laughed as he gently stroked her face.

"...I was scum," he admitted under his breath. "I wasn't with her in the end. That makes me the scummiest."

That was the part Rock was most bothered by too. She always thought her father abandoned her and her mother. But he actually loved his wife and daughter. And her mother loved her father until her dying breath.

Why did two people who loved each other have to be apart?

"Why didn't you live with her?"

Phoebe downed the rest of his glass when she hit on the heart of the matter. He deeply inhaled before answering. "Simply put, I was dumped."

"WHAT?!"

"Vale wasn't suited for living in the slums." Another sigh. "She left her family and her riches and opened a tailor shop in the imperial slums. I helped her with her work while we lived together. But Vale was a little too softhearted to do business in such a rough area."

Rock understood what he meant by her mother not being suited to the slums. Living there for just a few years had turned a country-girl like Rock into a cheapskate. She couldn't see someone as gentle and kindhearted as her mother adapting to that rough and gruff environment.

"That's why I planned to buy our citizenship." Pain edged into Phoebe's voice. "We could've opened a shop in the fancy business district as citizens. But you need a small fortune to buy one. So I returned to my mercenary work and tried to earn gold fast."

Rock could guess the reason for her parents' separation after hearing that. "Mother hated you doing that."

"Yeah. She thought I'd never come back one day."

"I'm sure she must have been scared. Worried sick about something happening to you." Rock could understand how she felt after yesterday. But Phoebe might not have at the time.

"I always planned to come home alive, though," he said in a lonely whisper and stared at the stars hanging in the distant sky outside the window. "Vale seemed to have finally made up her mind once you were born. She thought she had to leave the imperial capital to make me quit being a mercenary. She shot me down when I told her I was coming with her. She said she wanted me to live free…and then she left."

As long as he had a family to look after, Phoebe would continue taking on high-risk, high-reward mercenary jobs. Vale knew that and left him, hoping that would stop him.

"You never thought to chase after us?"

Phoebe hesitated before answering, "I did… Or rather, I visited you guys many times."

"No way! You came to that rural village?"

"Yeah. I snuck in without anyone noticing." His sigh had a melancholy ring to it. "Whenever she found out I was around, she would always smile for me, but she magically saw right through the fact that I hadn't quit being a mercenary. She worried about me every time we met. I really am scum." He filled his empty glass with another round of wine and derided himself. "But I couldn't quit. I planned to go get her as soon as I saved up enough to buy our citizenship. Problem was that there weren't any big wars these past few years for me to earn real money off of."

Rock assumed that was around the time the previous Count Mateus hired him to go ruin hunting and the money he had saved up was the "inheritance" he had given over to her when she showed up.

The more she learned about the truth, the more she found herself a captive of irritation and heartbreak.

"You should have just stayed together if you loved each other," Rock griped, blurting out her frank opinion. "All you get is loneliness if you separate after falling in love."

Saying that now wouldn't change the past. On the contrary, her frankness may only hurt her father. Even so, she had to raise her objections after overcoming the craziness running amok in her life lately.

But Phoebe only quietly smiled. After downing his second glass of wine, he looked down at Rock and reasoned with her. "That's a sound argument, but it's easier said than done. What would you do if someone forced you to pick between the man you loved and your shop? You'd hesitate to choose, right?"

Rock pondered it, but this wasn't a decision she could put on a scale.

She established her shop with the money her father risked his life to earn—she would never let it go to waste. As for the person she loved—he wasn't someone she could talk about in theory yet. She simply wanted to be with him and wanted to support him. That was it.

So as not to lose to her father, Rock downed the rest of her wine in one gulp too. Taking charge of that boldness, she flat-out declared, "I'd choose both. I don't want to lose either."

Phoebe's eyes opened wide, as if to take in something amusing. "Heh." He cracked a smile while he refilled her glass. "That's an ambitious choice. Must be nice to be young."

"You make it sound like you aren't young anymore!"

"Don't be stupid. I'm already past forty. I ain't young." Before Rock could argue further, he leveled with her: "There are some things love can't solve. Both Vale and I had things we couldn't give up on. That's why we couldn't stay together. That's all there was to it."

Rock couldn't accept that that was all there was to it. Was it really that difficult to obtain everything that mattered to you and hold on to it?

"I never thought someone like me could have a real family." Surrender seeped into that admittance. "I had it made just having that joy for a couple of years. I was happy." Tipping back his glass, he lovingly looked at his daughter. "Especially now that I have such an adorable daughter with me. There's nothing more I could want."

Rock wordlessly stared down at her full glass. She didn't know what kind of life Phoebe had lived before he met her mother. But from the way he'd declared that his marriage of only a few years was the happiest time of his life, what led up to it had to have been miserable. Short-lived and full of strife as it was, he was undeniably happy during those days.

Yet now the woman who brought him that happiness was gone forever. Rock was all he had left in the world.

"What were Vale's last days like?" Phoebe asked the painful question this time.

Speaking about those days wasn't easy for Rock. But Phoebe looked at his daughter, determined to learn what happened to the woman he loved. He had every right to know, so she told him.

"Her fever was so high, she was moaning and thrashing through it. She kept deliriously repeating…Father's name." The memory of looking after her mother in her final moments haunted Rock to this day.

"...I see." Phoebe sunk his teeth into his bottom lip. She heard his throat work as he tried to swallow back the emotions surging through him.

Thus, the two people who continued to love each other never had a chance to live together again. Not only Phoebe, but her mother, Vale, regretted that in the end. How she must have regretted not being there for the man she loved and for leaving her daughter alone in the world.

In those final moments, Vale told Rock, *"Your father lives in the imperial capital. Find Fredericks Berwick. I know he will help you."*

Her words became reality. Since she'd found him, Phoebe was always at Rock's side. He encouraged her when she was down and did whatever it took to help her when she was in trouble. Just last night, he came to her rescue, and it was only because of him she was able to march in a dress into the fancy foray.

"Mother told me to go find my father." Rock needed her father to know that. "She believed from the bottom of her heart that you would help me."

"Well, yeah. I'd do that much at least." He shrugged as if it wasn't a big deal. Unfazed by his third glass of wine, he calmly nodded. "Like I told you earlier, I'm a person who doesn't even know if I'm a man or a woman. It's as much of a mystery at this age as it was when I was a kid, and I might never figure it out." The wind swept back his beautiful long hair. "But that doesn't change the fact that I'm your father."

The final vestiges of sunlight disappeared below the horizon, and the stars illuminated his pretty face. Not an ounce of doubt or loss was reflected there.

"You're the one steady family I've gained after all this time. As long as I have this relationship, as long as I have you, I don't have any reason to doubt who or what I am."

"...Father," Rock called in a shaky voice.

Am I getting tipsy? A mess of emotions that made her want to both jump for joy and break into sobs fought for supremacy inside her. She felt the same way as her father. She had lost so much and gone through so many painful experiences, but at long last, she had found the person she was always looking for. And it was someone she'd thought was out of her reach forever.

"I always wanted to meet you. I constantly imagined what kind of person my father was."

"Then you must've been disappointed with this." He waved a hand over himself.

"I'm not disappointed!" she firmly denied. "My father turned out to be even nicer, stronger, and cooler than I ever imagined!"

Phoebe choked on his sip of wine, her admiration too much for his ears. "...I planned to take the secret to my grave," he admitted after he cleared his throat. "Wouldn't most kids be appalled to find out their da's a cross-dresser?"

Rock told him the truth. "I was in real shock at first."

Following her mother's last wishes, she'd visited the last known whereabouts of her father and found his beautiful lover, who turned out to be a man, there instead. Anyone would be surprised by that.

"It didn't help to be told that my father was dead and Phoebe was the only one there. I was shocked and sad." She had thought she really was all alone in the world now. "But 'Phoebe' became like family and stuck around with me. As time passed, I started to see how my father could fall in love with Phoebe. Because Phoebe was such an amazing person."

It never occurred to Rock that Phoebe was her father, but now that she knew, everything made sense. Especially the reason why he always saved her, even at risk to himself. Devotion to another even in the face of danger came from love.

"Thank you for being with me all this time."

As if to slowly digest his daughter's gratitude, Phoebe closed his eyes. "I'll always be there for you. At least until you get married."

"Then you'll be stuck with me for a while," Rock asserted without batting an eye.

Phoebe half-jokingly and half-searchingly asked, "You mean it? You don't have plans to marry already, do you?"

"Wh-Why would I?!"

Rock and Ebel had confirmed their feelings for each other, but they hadn't discussed the future yet. He was a count. Taking a wife probably wouldn't be as easy as a romantic fling. Problems would surely arise when that time came—though she had a feeling Ebel already knew how to solve every problem that came their way. After all, he was the very same man who proclaimed he didn't mind courting another man.

So Rock didn't let it get her down. She wanted to enjoy the love she had only just awakened to.

"I've decided to work even harder at being a tailor." Remembering her dream, Rock cheerfully continued, "Mother used to say that being a tailor is a profession that brings people happiness. So I want to make lots of people happy with the clothes I create."

"I see. That's a great dream," Phoebe responded, as if he wasn't included in that dream, so she rushed to make it clear to him.

"You're included in that too, Father!"

"Me? I'm more than happy enough just having you—"

"Not good enough! I've decided to be a good daughter who's devoted to her father!" After all they had been through, their wish to be father and daughter had finally come true. She wanted to repay him for all he had done for her and bring him the happiness her mother couldn't. "I'm going to make you happier than ever before, Father!" She looked him square in the eyes and vowed, "You'd better look forward to it!"

Phoebe smiled fondly at his daughter with a softness she had never seen before. Those deep blue pools of his eyes glistened and rippled. "You grew up into a fine woman, Roxy."

Rock was tickled pink by his moving compliment. "I'm so happy to hear you say that."

"Yeah. For the first time in a long time…I'm truly happy. I feel like this is the dawn of a long night." He hid his broad smile behind another sip of wine.

Watching him ignited Rock's mischievous side. She placed her right hand on his shoulder and stretched up on her tippy toes. And, just like her mother used to do to her, she gently pressed her lips against his cheek. An affectionate kiss given to a precious family member.

Yuruka Morisaki

"Oh…" Even Phoebe didn't know how to react to that one. After Rock pulled away, he couldn't wipe the giddy grin off his face. "Don't tell me you're drunk, Roxy?"

"I'm not drunk. Family members show affection this way," she instructed, taking his challenge head-on, knowing it was his way of hiding his shyness. "Mother often kissed me on the cheek. So it shouldn't be a problem for me to kiss you on the cheek, Father."

"I never said it was wrong." Phoebe desperately fought to keep his face straight, but it was a losing battle. In the end, he let his bliss show through when he said, "But you shouldn't be handing these out left and right. You should save it for the man you'll love someday."

No problem there.

Rock held her glass up as she replied, "I already did, so I'm good."

Phoebe's head jerked toward her. His dopey grin slipped and he blandly asked, "…What did you just say?"

"Hm? About what?" Rock played dumbed, but her father wasn't going to accept that response.

"You did it?! With who? His Excellency?" he asked with torrential speed.

Rock laughed at his panic. "Father, I'm already twenty. You don't have to worry about me like I'm a child."

"Didn't you just say you aren't going to get married yet?!"

"And I'm not saying I'm getting married now either."

"It's even worse if you did it with someone you aren't getting married to!" Phoebe went into a fit, blind to his own past.

He really is my father, Rock felt anew.

"Thank you for worrying about me, Father," she said in gratitude and planted another kiss on his cheek. Every human emotion flashed across his face.

"D-Don't distract me! When did you learn to use these womanly wiles?!"

"It's not womanly wiles. I mean everything I said."

Rock had lots of people she cared about in her life now.

Maybe she was getting a little tipsy. But she was on cloud nine. She had so many people in reach that she wanted to make happy. She couldn't pick just one person after all, but she didn't have to—she would make them all happy.

Having the leisure to think that way brought her untellable bliss.

♛ Chapter 8: The Trickster Tailor Is Back in Business

MICHAELA arrived at Mateus Manor around nightfall. Already informed about what had happened, she followed Ludovicus to Guido's room with her face set in a hard mask. Ebel and Rock trailed behind her. Rock sobered right up when she saw Michaela. Gloom took the place of her slight intoxication as they proceeded down the wrecked corridors.

Guido was sitting up on the guest room bed in human form. He wore nice, tailor-made clothing, likely Ebel's, and waited in the room with his head hung like a prisoner awaiting his sentence.

His head shot up when Michaela swept into the room. "Michaela…!" he called hoarsely, blanching.

"Brother!" Michaela cried and ran to his side. She fell to her knees at his feet and firmly held his shaking hands. She impatiently questioned, "I heard what happened from Ebel. Oh, Brother, why did you…?"

"I'm sorry, Michaela," he rasped, gravely shaking his head. "I can't erase what I've done with an apology. That is how great a crime I've committed. I brought the werewolf curse upon myself and hurt many people."

Michaela saw the damage he'd left behind on her way to this room: the butler greeting her at the door covered in red bandages, shattered doors, claw marks on the walls and floors, ripped rugs, shredded paintings, and broken vases strewn about the corridors and halls. Time was necessary before Mateus Manor regained its former splendor.

Unfortunately, even after everyone recovered from their injuries and the manor was repaired, Guido's curse would remain. He stared at his sister with different-colored eyes—eyes the same luminous gold as Ebel's.

"I had been concerned for the longest time over your strange behavior." Michaela's emerald eyes wavered like a sad wind through a dark-green forest. Until last night, Guido's eyes shared that same color. "But it never crossed my mind that you were trying to become a werewolf... You were the most grief-stricken of us all when you learned of Ebel's curse! How could you want that sad fate for yourself?!"

Rock silently cast down her eyes at Michaela's anguished cry. At one point, Guido had sympathized with Ebel's suffering. So what changed him?

"Michaela, we believe Guido was manipulated by the curse," Ebel interjected, placing a hand on her quivering shoulder. "His intentions weren't the only thing at play in all of this. Understand that—"

"Enough. Don't protect me, Ebel," Guido cut in, bringing his free hand to his face. "The burning desire I had was real. You were beautiful as a werewolf and had enough willpower to control that mighty power. When I brooded over who would protect my unmarried sister after you broke off the engagement—the thought definitely crossed my mind that I could do it if I had the same power as you."

He spoke in a flat voice devoid of emotion up until a moan wrenched free of his throat. "But...I don't understand it either. At a certain point, my desire became like an insatiable thirst. I needed that statue—I needed it so bad I didn't care how much money it cost or who I had to sacrifice to obtain it. I couldn't resist the call." It had become a dreadful memory for Guido. Involuntary shakes racked his body. "Now I'm not even sure if that rapacious desire was my own. And that's nothing compared with the confusion hanging over me about wanting to become a werewolf... Did I truly want this? Me?"

"I sensed someone else's will coming from that cursed statue," Ebel said, continuing that line of thought. "Didn't I mention I heard it calling to me before?" he asked Rock. She nodded. "It's no ordinary statue, and I don't just mean because it's cursed. It may very well...have a will of its own."

"A will?" Rock repeated.

Ebel silently nodded, threading a hand through his hair. "Yes. Guido wasn't searching for the statue—the statue was calling to him."

"How can that be?!" Guido choked, letting out a stifled moan. A single night of the supernatural had aged him and made him haggard.

Rock had drawn the same spooky conclusion before. The werewolf statue in Lady Trilian's shop had definitely called to Ebel. And hearing its voice rendered him incapable of controlling the werewolf inside.

In the same way, that statue might've detected the thirst for power lurking in Guido's heart and steered everything in the direction that would grant him power. But to what end? What were these statues after by cursing nobleman after nobleman? Fear of the unknown was the greatest fear of all.

"I'm going to continue searching out those statues," Ebel asserted, his expression bleak. "And I am going to destroy every last source of the curse that exists in this world. That is my calling."

His words didn't harbor the same sorrowful twinge as before. That empowered Rock to continue after him. "I'll help you with that, Ebel."

He turned toward her, some of the harshness slipping from his face. "Thank you, Roxy. You are my rock in this."

So far they had discovered three statues. Phoebe had uncovered the first, and the last two were brought into Lady Trilian's shop by mercenaries. In which case, their best bet was to search for more in the slums crawling with improvident mercenaries who took on any job to eat their next meal.

If their fates were really entwined with these statues, then they would surely come across them again.

"…Where do I go from here?" Guido let out a harsh breath as if he were collapsing under the pressure. "Do I have to live with this body?! Live cursed as some beast that's neither human nor animal?!"

Michaela pulled his trembling shoulders into a tight embrace. "Brother, get a grip on yourself! Ebel has lived through the same suffering!"

"I have, Guido." Ebel's golden eyes coolly lingered on Guido. "I have lived these past eight years with a cursed body. Anything I can do, you can do too."

It wasn't as easy as he made it sound.

Rock watched as Ebel didn't reveal any of the suffering he went through. That was his show of kindness to an old friend. No matter what was said, troubles came hand in hand with life. All the more so for someone who lived with a curse.

Cursed as he was, he was not alone in his suffering.

"He's absolutely right, Brother. You have me." Michaela hugged him and squeezed her eyes shut in prayer. "From here on out, I shall protect you and the Linus family. Let's walk this road together."

"Michaela…" Guido called his sister's name with the complacent look of a man who had just been exorcized of a malicious demon.

From his expression, Rock finally felt as if the curtain had closed on this trying incident.

ONCE the siblings finished their touching reunion, Michaela changed rooms, saying she wished to speak with the others. She invited Ebel and Rock to talk, much to Rock's surprise. A plaintive expression overtook Michaela when she faced them in the relatively undamaged reception room.

"I know what my brother has done cannot be swept under the rug with an apology." Her clasped hands trembled as she forced her pallid lips to move. "However…in order to protect my brother who has become a werewolf and the Linus name, I do not want his crimes brought before the public."

Rock didn't know how the Empire's laws applied to nobility. But even a duke's family wouldn't walk away unscathed from a direct heir committing a crime against another noble. Michaela wouldn't be able to protect Guido if he were expelled from their ranks or if their family was publicly ruined.

"I fully realize I am making a selfish request of you." The pleading Michaela no longer looked her twenty years of age. "Can we please settle this matter through reparations? I assure you we will pay any price you name. Payment may not be immediate, but I give you my word we will make amends," she swore, flattening her blue lips into a firm line and fixing her steely gaze upon Ebel.

Ebel, on the other hand, appeared to have known what she was going to say. He replied immediately. "I can agree to that. I'd only be placing myself in danger as another werewolf if judgment is passed on

Guido."

Michaela stopped shaking and heaved a long sigh. "Ebel...thank you." Tears shimmered in her relieved eyes as if she had expected the worst to come from him.

After that, Michaela and Ebel came to an agreement over the reparations to be paid. Ebel wrote up the contract with practiced ease and Michaela nervously signed it. Little conversation passed between them, nor was there room for their former joking relationship; they only solemnly determined the terms of the contract.

Even Rock, with her love of money, felt uncomfortable with this mood. The amount recorded on the contract was eye-popping, and she had a hard time believing that sum was real. She didn't understand why she was even called to be a part of this settlement between the Linuses and Mateuses.

Her doubts were cleared by Michaela after she finished signing.

"Miss Roxy Floria," Michaela addressed her as such.

"Y-Yes?" Being formally addressed caused her to fix her posture.

Michaela spoke to her with the same solemnness she had used with Ebel. "We have caused you a great deal of trouble too. If there is anything I can do to compensate you—"

"No! You don't have to compensate me for anything!" Rock spluttered.

Guido certainly had picked on her, and that inconvenience caused her shop to stay closed for a day and a half, so she had sustained losses. But not only had she been paid for that luxurious dress, but she was allowed to keep it. While she had been injured and feared for her life, she didn't feel right accepting reparations.

"I cannot accept your money. The gesture is enough for me."

"But..." Michaela naturally couldn't accept that.

So Rock thought of someone who had suffered greater losses.

"Rather than me, there is a woman, Selina Trilian, who runs an antique shop under her name in the slums," Rock said, speaking on behalf of the other woman. "Burglars after that statue broke into her shop, wrecked the place, and beat her up. I would like you to ask after her instead."

"...That is another foul deed my brother committed, isn't it?" Michaela buried her face in her hands. But she promptly dropped her hands, set her mouth in a hard line, and made peace with what she had to do. "Thank you for informing me. I promise to make amends to her as well."

Deep down, she probably wanted to break down crying. But Michaela wrapped up the reparation talks without becoming emotional, fulfilling her role as the Linus's representative.

Brave as she was, an expression befitting of her age flickered across her youthful face before she left. "...Miss Roxy...how I wish we could have met under different circumstances." Her lashes fluttered shut. "I longed to have a nice long chat with you when we met last night."

Rock couldn't stay quiet when she heard the regret coloring those words. Bearing such hardship at her age would surely fill Michaela with sadness and anxiety. Rock sincerely hoped that some of her anguish would be healed and that peace would return to the Linuses by the next time they met.

"I would be happy to chat with you any time you like. Please call on me once things have settled down," Rock offered, earning wide-eyed stares from both Michaela and Ebel.

Ebel quickly replaced his surprise with a gentle smile. "Michaela, Roxy means what she says."

For the first time this night, Michaela tearfully smiled. "Thank you, Miss Roxy. Someday for sure, then..." She wiped away her tears, and some of the anxiety left her tensed face. "You are so kind. I wouldn't expect any less of the woman Ebel chose as his sweetheart."

"Wha—? Um, well..."

"Right? Isn't she a marvelous woman on the inside and out?" Ebel proudly boasted over Rock's hesitation.

Neither of them denied their relationship.

ONCE they finished their discussion, Michaela left Mateus Manor with Guido in tow. Guido was still a husk of his former self, but Michaela stoutheartedly supported him. No one doubted that they would continue to walk through life supporting each other like that.

"Ever since we were kids, Guido was Michaela's whole world," Ebel murmured after the Linus siblings left. "Guido was always her number one. That's one thing that has never changed."

Phoebe picked up on his nostalgic tone and decided to tease him about it. "Heh. Sounds like you had your heart broken by the fair lady, Your Excellency."

"I didn't. Michaela has always been like a little sister to me." Ebel laughed it off and anxiously added, "There's nothing between us, Roxy. So you don't have anything to worry about."

Rock wasn't worried about anything in that department. She was mostly brimming with curiosity over how Ebel spent time with his friends as a boy. She planned to ask Michaela all about it when they finally sat down for that chat.

As for worries, Phoebe's lay elsewhere as well. "Was it smart not to accept compensation, Roxy?" He hadn't been around for the negotiations, but that was the first thing he said after hearing about it afterward.

"I couldn't accept her money." Rock quickly shook her head, whipping her short hair into her cheeks.

"They're responsible for you shutting down your shop for a whole day and a half," Ebel said in unusual agreement with Phoebe. "You have every right to be compensated for your time."

"Logically, sure…"

Not wanting to take money from Michaela was one reason, but she also didn't know how much of a loss she had sustained from being closed for a day and a half. Without being there, she had no way of knowing if she would've made a killing because lots of customers came by or if business would've been slow.

Besides, a shrewd businesswoman shouldn't be blinded by a one-time compensation.

"It'll all work out. I turned Lady Michaela into a repeat customer, after all."

"How did you do that?"

Phoebe and Ebel both raised their eyebrows at her.

As a matter of fact, Rock had secretly sold Michaela on becoming a customer before she left. *"His Excellency often makes use of my services to tailor clothes for when he transforms into a werewolf. Please stop by if you would like to place a similar order for your brother,"* she had told her.

Michaela happily jumped on the opportunity. In due time, the

Linuses were very likely to become golden customers as well.

Guido's reaction was anyone's guess, but as long as he was going to live with the werewolf curse, the day he needed Rock's assistance would surely come.

"Your shrewd business practices never cease to amaze me," Ebel said in awe of her. "I'll also stop by once things settle down. I need to pick up my cloak and place an order for a new set of formal wear."

"Please do. I will happily await your visit!" Rock naturally answered him with a full smile.

Phoebe looked as if he had something to say, but he kept it under wraps behind his smile for now—either because he knew lots of money was involved or perhaps because of something else altogether.

ROCK and Phoebe returned to the slums early the next morning. They mounted the horse they borrowed from the stables and trotted back at a much slower pace than they had come. Thanks to Ebel sending word ahead to the constables, they were able to pass through the gates unhindered, leading to a most peaceful ride indeed.

But people understandably worried when a shopkeeper was gone for more than a day in the slums.

"Where in the world did you go?! Goodness gracious, you're going to make me go gray with worry…!" Justia broke down crying when Rock dropped by the hash house before opening shop for the day.

Cargus rushed over from the stove, relief coloring his sleepless face. "I'm glad to see you're safe and sound."

"I'm sorry for worrying you. Phoebe and I are both fine."

Justia calmed down when she heard Rock's earnest apology. She sniffled as she said, "Word on the street says that you and Phoebe took off to beat some sense into the burglars who hit Lady Trilian's place."

They were pretty close with that rumor. She was coming home from having just knocked some sense into the man who hired the burglars. After debating whether she should tell them that, Rock went with a vague answer instead.

"Lady Trilian should be getting some good news soon."

"For crying out loud, child… Phoebe is one thing, but you don't have to go be a hero too." Justia pinched Rock's upper arm. "Don't do dangerous stuff when I've made pudding tougher than you. If you want to go thrill-seeking, do it after you bulk up."

Rock cracked a dry smile and glanced down at her arms. They were too slender and unreliable for a man. But there was so much these arms and hands were capable of. Gender had nothing to do with her worth. What she needed to do next wasn't bulk up to better pose as a man. She needed to polish her skills as a tailor.

"I'm going to shelve the dangerous adventures for a while and concentrate on the things a tailor should be doing," she insisted, to put the couple's mind at ease.

And then she thoroughly reveled in the joys of having people in her life who cared about her and in the freshly baked potato bread they gave her.

LADY Trilian received her good news several days later.

The constable who brought the news informed her that they had apprehended the burglars, who then confessed to breaking in, so reparations for damages and losses sustained by her shop would be paid out of their savings. Rock knew that wasn't the true story, but Lady Trilian didn't care about the truth.

"It's not half bad receiving a huge chunk of coin just for being broken into," she crowed, despite the scar left on her head. "I might welcome them the second time if this is what I get in return."

Since she was that happy about it, Michaela had to have paid her very well. It was wise of her not to inform the older woman that the money came from the Linus family. Lady Trilian definitely would've squeezed every last gold coin out of her.

At any rate, Lady Trilian was in remarkably good spirits over the small fortune that had come her way.

"I gave you a scare, didn't I, laddie?" She spoke to Rock first, and rare as that was, something even rarer happened—a broad smile etched into her thick wrinkles. "I'll reduce your rent to half price next month. A good businesswoman knows when to give a discount."

How very like Lady Trilian not to just make the next month rent-free.

"Thank you, Lady Trilian." Rock thanked her despite the complex emotions swirling through her.

Those emotions had nothing to do with Lady Trilian's healthy obstinacy. She hadn't said anything about it yet, but she actually planned on moving out soon. Her current room was conveniently close to her shop on Market Street, but it was a little too small for father and daughter to live in together. Phoebe also resided in a small house, so the father-daughter duo had been discussing finding a place where they could live together.

Would she find a new place to live first? Or would she pay next month's rent first? Wherever the dice may fall, Rock would be content with it.

As for Rock, she continued living her double life as a trickster tailor.

She decided to because Phoebe was still stressing, "You're safer running your shop in the slums as a man."

Rock was of the same opinion. It wasn't easy getting by in the slums as a woman. She intended to continue her act as a cross-dressing tailor as long as she lived and worked in the slums to avoid burdening herself with extra troubles. Sure, everyone would continue to mock her for being weak and a lightweight, but she had no plans to bulk up this late in the game.

As for Phoebe, he, too, showed up at the shop with perfect makeup and amazing hair and in beautiful dresses.

"I've been helping out while wearing this look all along. I'm gonna go with it as long as I'm at work," he said in a throaty purr. Wearing the dress Rock tailored, with his golden tresses down, he looked like any other big-boned, beautiful woman out there. Though he seemed to be at odds with himself over it. "I'm this old and I still don't know how I want to live," he told her with a wistful smile. "Since there's nothing holding me back, I'm just going to do everything I want to. I'll wear dresses at the shop and do fatherly things when we get home. I've finally found something to live for."

He patted Rock on the head with his large, angular hand. His hand was completely different from her mother's, but it brought the same warmth and joy.

Rock wanted Phoebe to live in whatever way made him happy. She had a dream she wanted to make come true on top of that.

"How do you feel about saving up and buying our citizenship?" That was the dream Phoebe had never reached. "Once we're bona fide citizens, we'll open a shop in the business district. Doesn't that sound like a great plan?"

The slums were good enough for etching out a living, but they were far from safe. In the business district, Rock could run her business as Roxy Floria without fears of repercussions.

"It's good to have big dreams, but you need to prepare yourself for it mentally," Phoebe advised. "Citizenship is something you can't buy just because you have the money—you need to curry favor with the nobles."

"We can just have His Excellency speak for us," Rock said, completely set on relying on him.

It'd be a waste not to make use of the connections she had gained. Furthermore, opening a shop in the business district would make it easier for Ebel to stop by. The slums were too far of a distance from the aristocrat district for the werewolf count to constantly walk to see her. Was it a tad calculating on her part that she wanted to make it so easy for him to visit that he would even drop by for window-shopping?

"We'd better think up a name for our shop, then."

Rock tilted her head and put her finger to her chin. "How about 'Floria-Berwick Clothes Shop?'"

Phoebe buckled over laughing at the first thing that came to her mind. "Why don't you put a little more thought into it?"

"I'm bad at brainstorming. Do you have any ideas?" she asked in return.

He answered without a second thought. "'Roxy' works for me."

"This is supposed to be a shop's name." Rock was baffled by the name he suggested.

Phoebe's rouged lips curled into a boastful smile. "Isn't it a good name? Your father here came up with it."

Rock gaped at him and blinked several times. She'd never thought about who might've come up with her name. She vaguely assumed it was her mother because she never even knew what her father looked like.

"I think it's an amazing name. I love it too," Rock agreed with a broad smile. "Thank you for such a lovely gift, Father."

Phoebe bashfully poked Rock's cheek. "I told you to call me Phoebe at work."

"You're the one who called yourself father."

"Did I?"

Amused by Phoebe's feigned ignorance, Rock burst out laughing too.

Knowing that it was the first thing her father gave her made Rock fall all the more in love with her name. It was a little embarrassing naming her shop after herself, but she could get used to others saying that name. She had a feeling Ebel would love it too.

"How about 'Clothing Shop Roxy'?"

"'Tailor Roxy' sounds good too."

"Oh, I like that. We'd better work hard to buy our citizenship, then!"

Rock's goal was set. She was going to achieve the dream her parents had come just short of and own an even bigger shop. Then, as a tailor, she was going to bring happiness to a great many people.

That was Rock's true dream.

Meanwhile, Phoebe seemed to have some concerns about her goal. "I get the feeling His Excellency is going to say you don't have to buy your citizenship when you tell him…"

"Oh? You think so? Why?"

"Obviously he'll say there's a faster way to get it. Listen to me well— do *not*, by any means, ever consult him about it until you have the money saved up," Phoebe stressed.

Rock was trying to figure out why when the bell above the door jangled, informing her of a welcome visitor. In the doorway stood a handsome young man with burnt sienna hair and golden eyes. A fond smile reached those golden eyes when they met Rock's.

"Hello. Is business flourishing, shopkeeper?"

"Welcome, Ebel." Happy to see him, Rock ran over to the door and lifted her gaze to the face she was starting to miss.

Ten days had passed since that daunting night. During that time, Ebel had been busy tending to his manor's repairs. He was dying to see Rock but had held off until things settled down.

The face she finally got to see after all this time looked a little more worn down than in her memory.

"Did you lose some weight?" she asked, worried about him.

"A bit, yes," he reluctantly admitted. "I was just too busy to eat much." He promptly followed that with a cheerful note. "Thanks to all that hard work, my home is perfectly back in order. Come over any time you want, Roxy."

"Call her Rock at work, Your Excellency," Phoebe corrected.

Ebel's eyes rounded. "Oh, right." After taking in her appearance, he understood Phoebe's request.

Today she wore her usual male tailor attire of a shirt, vest, and slacks. Nothing should've changed from before, but Ebel's gaze lingered as if he were impressed by how she pulled it off.

"I can only ever see you as a woman. You've become even more beautiful than before." These were the words of the werewolf count with keen senses. He was probably telling the truth, but it made her shy away from him.

"I can't have that. I'm a trickster tailor, after all."

What was the point of being a trickster if she couldn't trick people? But there would always be someone out in the wider world capable of seeing through the trick to the truth. Strange as it was, Rock felt blessed to have met that person.

After they exchanged greetings, Rock led Ebel to the fitting room. She needed to measure him for a new three-piece suit to replace the one he ripped on the night of the party. Phoebe hovered behind her, but Rock wanted to be the one to measure Ebel. Measuring tape pinched between her fingers, she carefully measured around his neck, shoulders, chest, and waist.

"…I was right. You have lost weight," she worriedly noted after writing down his numbers.

Ebel chuckled to wipe away her worry. "I'll get right back on track if you dine with me."

"In that case, I would be happy to join you anytime," Rock consented, expressing a thousand feelings in that one acceptance.

She felt as if her routine had finally returned to normal since everything that happened that night. Of course, it couldn't be called peaceful, knowing more of those statues were out there and with Ebel having unfinished business left to resolve. It was for those reasons that Rock strove to brighten Ebel's day-to-day life and add a flourish of joy to it.

"How would you like me to tailor your new formal wear?"

"The one thing I know for sure is that I want it to pair well with your dress," he cheerfully answered.

"My dress...?"

"Your evening gown that looks like it captured the dawn within its folds. I want to gaze upon you dressed in it once more."

Rock still had the silk dress she made for Michaela in her possession. She couldn't hand over an article of clothing she had worn herself, not to mention one that Guido rejected. She had carefully stowed it away, thinking another opportunity to wear it would never arise.

Would she have another reason to put her arms through the gown's lacy sleeves?

"I want you to make me a suit that will go with your gown when I stand next to you," Ebel said, taking hold of Rock's hand that was gripping the measuring tape. He planted a soft kiss on her fingers.

Heat rushing to her cheeks, Rock answered, "You will look perfect next to me no matter what you wear, Ebel."

"Then I want something that will make me look even better. I want you to make it in such a way that you will fall in love with me all over again."

How was she supposed to answer that when she was the tailor and the lover?

But Rock wanted to meet her customer's demands as a tailor. Plus, she had only just learned the joys of dressing up for someone else. Nothing could be happier than allowing the person she loved to enjoy the same experience.

👑 Afterword

HELLO, I'm Yuruka Morisaki.

Thank you very much for picking up a copy of *The Werewolf Count and the Trickster Tailor*.

This is a story about the cast of characters living out double lives. The heroine Rock pretends to be a man in order to protect herself, while Ebel must hide his identity as a werewolf to keep up appearances as count. Phoebe chose to live as a woman after deciding to live true to herself. Each character has endured strife because of their double lives, but they have made it through every day optimistically and enjoyed themselves in the process.

I wrote this series as a story about people who overcome hardship, sorrow, and despair. Rock and Ebel have to confront the class difference between them, and the werewolf curse afflicting Ebel and the others will continue to be a source of grief, but I know they will be able to positively overcome any trial and have fun doing it. Guido has a lot of hardship to go through from here on out as well, but with his kind younger sister at his side, he, too, will find happiness.

I hope you, my dear readers, also had your day made better by reading their story. I would be even more delighted if you enjoyed it!

Until we meet again in volume 2!

Werewolf Count AND THE Trickster Tailor

LITTLE PRINCESS IN FAIRY FOREST
STORY BY: TSUBAKI TOKINO
ILLUSTRATION BY: TAKASHI KONNO
STANDALONE | OUT NOW

Join Princess Lala and Sir Gideon as they flee for their lives from the traitor who killed the royal family and wants to wed Lala! Gideon is willing to do anything to protect his princess, even if it means engaging the mighty dragons in combat! Tsubaki Tokino's fairy tale inspired Little Princess in Fairy Forest!

ANOTHER WORLD'S ZOMBIE APOCALYPSE IS NOT MY PROBLEM!
STORY BY: HARU YAYARI
ILLUSTRATION BY: FUYUKI
STANDALONE | OUT NOW

Just when I thought navigating high school was bad enough, I woke up to a rotting, post-apocalyptic world!

THE ECCENTRIC MASTER AND THE FAKE LOVER!
STORY BY: ROKA SAYUKI
ILLUSTRATION BY: ITARU
VOL. 1 OUT NOW

Yanked into another world full of dangerous magic and parasitic plants, Nichika does the one thing she can to survive: become the apprentice to an eccentric witch!

THE CHAMPIONS OF JUSTICE AND THE SUPREME RULER OF EVIL
STORY BY: KAEDE KIKYOU
ILLUSTRATION BY: TOBARI
STANDALONE | OUT NOW

Mia's a supervillain bent on world domination who lacks tact in enacting her evil schemes! Will the lazy superheroes be able to stop her?

BEAST † BLOOD
STORY BY: TSUKASA YAMAZAKI
ILLUSTRATION BY: KIYU KANAE
VOL. 1 OUT NOW

Biotech Scientist Euphemia's world suddenly gets flipped upside down when her sister hires a sexy alien mercenary to be her bodyguard!

THE CURSED PRINCESS AND THE LUCKY KNIGHT
STORY BY: UTA NARUSAWA
ILLUSTRATION BY: TAKASHI KIRIYA
STANDALONE | OUT NOW

Orphan Sonia leaves the abbey only to be haunted by her own castle! Is an arranged marriage to a knight her only salvation from the family curse?

Made in the USA
Coppell, TX
13 September 2023

21545186R00162